SECRET

OF THE

SEVENS

LYNN LINDQUIST

D1166820

Woodbury, Minnesota

First Edition
First Printing, 2015

Book design by Bob Gaul
Cover design by Lisa Novak
Cover images: iStockphoto.com/11874622/©MarcusLindstrom
iStockphoto.com/55411964/©ThomasShanahan

Flux, an imprint of Llewellyn Worldwide Ltd.

This is a work of fiction. Names, characters, places, and incidents are either the product of the author's imagination or are used fictitiously, and any resemblance to actual persons living or dead, business establishments, events, or locales is entirely coincidental. Cover model used for illustrative purposes only and may not endorse or represent the book's subject.

Library of Congress Cataloging-in-Publication Data
Lindquist, Lynn.
  Secret of the Sevens/Lynn Lindquist.—First edition.
      pages cm
  Summary: When eighteen-year-old Talan Michaels accepts an invitation to join a mysterious secret society at his boarding school, he becomes involved in a conspiracy involving secret passages, cryptic riddles, and a decades-old murder mystery that he must solve to save the school—and, perhaps, lives.
  ISBN 978-0-7387-4404-9
  [1. Secret societies—Fiction. 2. Boarding schools—Fiction. 3. Schools—Fiction. 4. Murder—Fiction. 5. Orphans—Fiction. 6. Mystery and detective stories.] I. Title.
  PZ7.1.L557Sec 2015
  [Fic]—dc23

                                                        2015002569

                              Flux
                    Llewellyn Worldwide Ltd.
                      2143 Wooddale Drive
                    Woodbury, MN 55125-2989
                        www.fluxnow.com

            Printed in the United States of America

To the Author of all things, from your storyteller.

ONE

I can be such an ass. I know this, and yet I can't seem to stop myself.

The closer we get to the graveyard, the tighter Emily squeezes my arm. "So this is it." I lower my voice. "The site of the infamous Singer School murders."

The air, chilly from a rain shower earlier tonight, smells like moss and damp dirt. With a full moon casting shadows across the crumbling tombstones, this location looks straight out of a horror movie. *Perfect.*

"If there ever was such a thing as a haunted place"—I say it softly so she leans closer—"this would be a sure bet."

Okay, so maybe it's not the nicest place to bring a newbie, but visiting the Singer graveyard is practically a rite of passage at our school. Hell, most of my script comes from Marcus' annual hazing of the freshman football team. And Jake used the same tour when he dragged half the JV baseball roster through here last Halloween. I can't help it if I prefer the company of women.

I tow Emily through the gate.

"This cemetery's most famous residents are William and Mary Singer." I keep my voice fluid and monotone. Marcus says it gives the words a more ominous feel. "I'm sure you learned all about them when you enrolled. They founded our school. "

Emily stares up at me with Muppet eyes, but doesn't answer. My arm snakes around her waist. Her heart races through her thin T-shirt, and I almost feel sorry for her. *Almost*. When she's pressed against me, it's hard to feel anything but those curves.

"William Singer owned Singer Enterprises. He was a wealthy oil tycoon who grew up in foster care. When he and his wife couldn't have children, they decided to start a philanthropic boarding school for kids from troubled homes." I'm rolling through my speech, smoother than a tour guide on a Disneyland ride.

We're twenty feet into the tombstones when I point out a small building in the distance. "The story goes that Mary died exactly where her mausoleum stands today, when her skull was crushed after she was thrown from her horse."

My face dips toward Emily's like I'm sharing a secret. "William was heartbroken. He spent the next five years mourning her and expanding the school that was so important to her. They say he lost his mind when he lost his heart." I love that line. Came up with it myself.

When Emily cranes her neck to look at the mausoleum,

I brush my lips against her ear. "At exactly 8:00 p.m. every night," I whisper, "Mr. Singer would leave his estate home and walk down Rucker Road, on that same gravel path that stretches between the chapel and Mary's tomb. For five years, he visited her vault every evening to say good night to his sweetheart."

Emily slowly twists her head back toward me. I can see a wad of chewing gum in the side of her open mouth. She grips the front of my T-shirt with trembling hands.

And the award for outstanding actor in a dramatic role goes to … me.

"Until that fateful night when William entered Mary's tomb to kiss the nameplate outside her crypt, never realizing it would be his last night … on this side of the wall." Now all that's missing is organ music and a far-off howling.

Emily swallows hard. "Talan?" She grabs my bicep like it's a life preserver. "I think I want to go back now."

Oh come on, I haven't even started my grand finale …

"Of course." I run my fingertips down her arms and feel goose bumps. "I just have one more spot to show you, and then we'll leave."

My hand presses on her lower back to veer her toward the remains of the burned-out chapel, but the girl isn't budging. Sometimes I'm too talented for my own good. I push her a little, but her feet are set firmer than the headstones in the ground. I give up. I'm manipulative, but I'm no bully. I can improvise.

I nod to the ruins. "See there?" She blinks sidelong at the chapel remnants. "William Singer was murdered in that chapel. It's been almost two decades and it's still a mystery. Legend says that Mr. Singer handpicked seven students to form a mysterious society. They wore hooded cloaks and no one knew their identities or purpose. He trusted them with all kinds of secrets and treasures, but they ended up murdering him for his money. On a warm March night, they ambushed him and bashed his head with a heavy stone. Maybe the very headstone you're standing on."

Emily jumps off the grave marker for *Eliza Becker 1850–1860.*

Sensitive guy that I am, I gather her into a hug. "The students got trapped in a fire they lit to hide the evidence. They ended up dying right along with William Singer … right where those ruins stand today."

With a blank expression, Emily turns and stares at the skeleton of the chapel. I can't see her face, but I'm betting it's as white as the moon about now. I coil my arms around her waist and rest my chin on her shoulder. Despite my attempts at cuddling, she's rigor-mortis stiff.

I whisper in her ear, "The weird thing is—"

I stop and wait for her to turn around. Slowly, she twists inside my embrace and stares up, hungry for me to finish. Her bottom lip quivers in anticipation.

Here we go. Grand Finale:

"—there were only five bodies discovered with Mr. Singer's. Which means two members of the secret society were never found." I'm about to bring it all home when Emily takes off running.

Damn. Didn't see that coming. Usually they beg to get out of there and hang on me the whole trek back.

I bolt after her. It's almost curfew and the cemetery is off-limits to students. Not to mention that the headmaster's house is just down the road from here. If Emily gets lost or caught, it's an infraction for both of us. I already have a curfew violation, and I just got off probation for my grades.

The two of us reach campus at the same time. "Whoa, Emily. Slow down. It's just a story, relax."

She steps toward me, huffing and coughing. "Sorry," she says, all breathy, "but you scared the crap out of me." Emily giggles in a pitch that would bother dogs, and my shoulders creep towards my ears. "I started thinking maybe you were one of the missing students," she says.

My face crumples. She obviously wasn't listening very carefully to my lines. "It happened almost twenty years ago. That would make me, like, thirty-eight years old."

"Oh yeah." She giggles again. When she snorts as an encore, her curves lose some of their appeal.

The clock tower bongs eleven times, warning me it's now past curfew. *Damn.* Is a quick hookup worth a month's detention? Probably.

But another detention means I'd be benched for the first football game of the season. No way I want to be riding the pine for the Oakland game. I love playing linebacker. But I also love women. Talk about a moral dilemma.

Emily takes a step closer and bats her eyes at me, running a purple fingernail up my arm. I'm about to surrender when her finger lands on the scar on my bicep. She traces the bumpy T with her finger. "Is the T for Talan?" she asks. "The gangs in my old neighborhood did that too."

I backpedal a few steps. "Well, it's already a couple minutes past curfew."

Her head tilts and her eyebrows scrunch together like I'm throwing away a winning lottery ticket. I take another step backward and nod my head in the direction of my student home. "I should probably get back before I'm busted."

When she snaps her gum, it hits me like a starting gun. I spin around and take off running. Ignoring her calls, I race past the library and over the soccer fields. Weaving through the park, dodging playground equipment and hurdling bushes, I'm making record time when I finally reach my yard.

Light forces itself through the back door, but no one's inside the kitchen. I jiggle the knob quietly. It's already locked. *Dang.* Mom Shanahan must already be starting room checks. If only I left my window open.

I race around the side yard to Marcus' room and see Mom Shanahan in the doorway talking to him. There's no way I'm going to sneak into any of the rooms on this side of the house. She'll catch me for sure. I creep around the south wall instead, ducking under the window where Mr. Shanahan sits filling out paperwork in his office. No way I'll get in here, either. I'm left with only one option.

There's a single bedroom on the opposite side of the house. If I can climb in that window, it'd be fairly easy to slip out of the room and into the basement. I could pretend I was in the bathroom down there the whole time. It's perfect. It's also the last place Mom Shanahan would suspect me of sneaking in. I race around the backyard and peek through the glass.

Delaney is already sleeping. *Of course.*

Her bed is right beneath the window. She's stretched out under a white sheet with her back to me, all smooth and curved like a snowdrift.

I tap on the glass. "Delaney. Open up the window. It's Talan."

Laney rolls over, half asleep. She glances at the window and jumps up, clutching the sheet to her chest. When she recognizes me, angry lines gather between her big brown eyes. Lifting one arm, she yanks the drapes closed on my face.

"Very funny." My voice rises above a whisper. "C'mon. Please, Laney. Let me in before I get caught."

I peek through a break in her curtains. She lies back down, pulling the covers over her head.

"I'm not leaving until you let me in. Please … you're my last chance."

Delaney sits up slowly, unclenches her fists, and swings the drapes open again. Her slitted eyes tell me my last chance isn't looking too good.

"Please?" I plead with folded hands. "If you help me out, I'll owe you. I'll do whatever you want. You won't be sorry."

I give her my best pouty look and she rolls her eyes. Still, she reaches over, unlocks the window, and scoots back to make room for me. I climb over the sill and slither onto her bed.

"Hurry and shut the window," she whispers. "It's freezing in here now, thanks to you."

I can't help myself. I glide my hand over her sheets. "I know how we can warm it up."

"Please tell me it's by setting you on fire." Laney pushes my legs off the side of her bed. "Move. Now. You're getting mud all over my clean comforter."

Her voice is irritated. If she tells on me now, I'll lose my starting position for sure. Time to work the charm. I bump my shoulder into hers and flash my trademark dimples. "Why are you in such a hurry to get rid of me? You should enjoy me while you can. When you get chosen for the Pillars tomorrow, you'll hardly get to see me anymore."

"*If* I get chosen." She climbs around me to the end of her bed. "Don't jinx me."

I slide over and sidle up to her again. "You'll get picked. And then you'll move to Winchester House with the other pampered pledges and forget all about your beloved housebrothers."

She chews on her thumbnail, the way she always does when she's nervous. "There's no guarantee I'll be chosen."

"Gimme a break," I say. "All that volunteering and studying and leadership crap? You're a sure thing. They'll probably retire your halo in the Singer School Trophy Case."

Her lips compress to a faded hyphen. "Get outta my room, you jackash."

"Jackash," I snicker. "I love that. I'm going to miss that dorkiness. The way you won't curse. The way you blush whenever Marcus talks about sex. No drinking, no weed, God forbid you miss curfew. You couldn't break a rule if your life depended on it, could you?" I shake my head.

"Just once, before you leave, I want to hear you swear. C'mon, do it for me—tell me to fuck off."

"I say it to you all the time in my head, trust me."

"Say it out loud."

"You're ridiculous. I'm not going to swear for you."

"You can't do it, can you?"

She shoves me in the arm. "I definitely won't miss you picking on me, you pain in the asp."

I bust out laughing and have to muffle myself.

Laney goes to whack me, but I cuff her wrist. Her other hand rises to attack and I grab that one too. "Settle, Laney. This is probably my last chance to tease you." I hold her arms apart. "Don't deprive a poor orphan of one of the few pleasures in his life."

Laney's eyes soften. That always gets her. Laney is the proverbial tenderhearted-do-gooder. She must get it from her mom and dad. The Shanahans have worked as houseparents at Singer School for almost twenty-five years, fostering teenage boys no one else wants for a salary no one else would put up with.

"You won't tell your parents, will you, Lane? Cut me a break one last time before you go. I can't miss the season opener. It's my last chance to kick some Oakland ass." I let her wrists go and they drop to her sides.

"You should have thought of that before you went nightcrawling."

"So will you help me?"

Her shoulders rise and fall in a heaping sigh. "Oh, whatever." She's frowning. I'm not sure if it's at me or herself.

"So, who was the lucky flavor of the day this time?" She stands up. "Vanessa? Taylor? Ashley?"

Laney moves in front of me with her hands on her hips, leaving me face-to-face with her chest. Delaney Shanahan is a brainiac, goody-goody pain-in-the-ass, but she has a hell of a body housing all that nerdiness. It takes me a second to remember the answer to her question. "Emily Dombrose," I spit out.

"The new girl?" She crosses her arms, blocking my view. "So you ran out of desperate women and you're preying on the newbies now?"

"You know, Laney, you sound like you might be jealous."

Her mouth opens but it takes a second for the words to come out. "I have a boyfriend. Remember?"

"Oh yeah, Colon Le Douche."

She leans forward, jutting her jaw centimeters from mine. "Kollin LeBeau. And he's awesome." I fight the urge to look down her shirt. "You're the one who sounds jealous, if you ask me."

The skin between her eyes crinkles, but she doesn't move away. We're so close, I can feel her breath on my lips. We're caught in a staring contest and a game of chicken to see who backs away first. I try not to get distracted by her wide eyes and heart-shaped lips. I've seen the destruction girls like Laney can do to guys who don't know any better.

I go on offense, moving a centimeter closer. "Is that zit cream on your face?"

Her hand flies to her nose, and she draws back a couple inches.

I love to mess with this girl.

"You probably floss before bed too, don't you? Right after you memorize a page in the dictionary and recite your prayers. Such a waste of a perfectly good vagina."

She clenches her jaw so tight that her collar bones bulge. *I win.*

"That's it." Laney jerks around and points to the door. "Get outta my room, you perv. I'm telling."

So much for winning. "No. Don't!"

She storms for the door and I leap up to block her way. "Why shouldn't I?"

"Because you'd never hurt anyone, not even me. Not to mention that you love Singer School. You wouldn't want to hurt our chances to beat Oakland, would you?"

"Dang you!" She throws her hands in the air. "Fine. But you owe me. And it has to be something big. Did you ever once consider what would happen to me if someone caught you sneaking out of my room?"

"Your reputation would improve?"

She pinches my arm.

"Ow!" I lower my voice and grab her wrist again. "You wouldn't get in any trouble. You're the poster child for Singer School. You could tell them we were studying when our clothes accidentally fell off and they'd believe you. Plus, our houseparents are your *parents*. What do you think they'd do, kick you out? I'm the one that'd get tossed like Tuesday's trash."

She shoves me toward the door. "That's not what I

mean, and you know it." Her eyes lock on mine. "I could lose the Pillars."

We reach for the doorknob at the same time and my hand lands over hers. I'm running out of time here. I've got to get downstairs ASAP, and I need to know for sure that she'll cover for me. "Okay, okay. Whatever you want. I swear. You decide. Just let me go now before I get caught."

She hesitates, then opens the door a sliver and peeks out. She tiptoes to the end of the hall and peers around the corner, waving to me when it's okay for me to leave. I creep along the wall to the basement door.

As I brush past her, she whispers a reminder. "You owe me now."

TWO

The next morning I sprint the whole way, but I'm still late. As usual. I yank the auditorium door open and hesitate. Everyone is shoulder to shoulder, not a single empty seat in sight.

I hear a rowdy laugh and spot Marcus in the center of his minions. He nods to me. Yeah, thanks for saving a seat, bro.

Jake calls my name from four rows down. Before I take two steps, Alyssa Hernandez waltzes up, tossing her long hair over her shoulder. She says something to Jake and his head nods like a bobblehead. She slips into the seat and Jake gives me an apologetic look before he goes back to grinning like an idiot.

To my right, Jessica Kingston waves frantically and points to the seat next to her. I pretend not to see her; I'm not setting myself up to let that crazy chick think I'm into her.

Professor Haney comes up behind me and scoots me down the aisle toward the front seats.

I spot Delaney in the first row, next to Kollin. Of course. He probably wanted to sit close so he wouldn't have to walk very far when they called his name. Other than Delaney, Kollin is most likely to be one of the six students chosen as a Pillar, the biggest honor given to Singer students. He's going to be insufferable when he gets it.

There's an open spot in the row behind them, a seat over from Laney. I slide down the row and poke her shoulder. I might as well be nice since she saved my butt last night. "Good luck, Shanahan."

"Late again, huh?" She gives me a nervous smile and shakes her head. "That'll teach you. Now you're stuck sitting up front with us nerds."

Kollin snaps at her, "Speak for yourself." He twists around to glare at me. "In one hour, every student at Singer will wish they were us."

I'd tell him to fuck off, but he's right. Singer's not your typical boarding school, after all; it's a private school for underprivileged kids from troubled homes. To most students here, being selected as a Pillar is par to winning the lottery. Pillars get privileges and perks that no one else gets. Things like extended curfews, cell phones, Skybox tickets, and even passes to leave campus whenever they want. They get full-ride scholarships, generous allowances, and private suites in Winchester House, the nicest student home on campus.

Behind me, a group of Laney's friends yell to wish her luck. She blushes and mouths *thank you*, then clasps her trembling hands in her lap.

Headmaster Boyle stands sentinel on the far right side

on the stage, his eyes trained on me. He glowers and nods to let me know he sees me. School doesn't officially start for three more days, and he's already on my case. Boyle must suspect something's up for me to be sitting apart from my usual crowd. The guy's had a permanent radar on me ever since I blew up his pencil sharpener in fourth grade.

When Boyle retreats to the podium and recites the same speech he gives every year at orientation, I get distracted by the soft brown waves in Delaney's hair. My eyes trace a sun-streaked path to the curled ends. She usually wears a ponytail, but she went all out today with makeup and a new dress.

A crackle from the microphone diverts my attention back to Boyle's speech. "Our honorable founders William and Mary Singer believed that a child's life should be molded by his character and aspirations rather than his limitations. They dedicated their lives and fortune to Singer School, so that everyone in this room could have the resources and opportunities to achieve great things in the world."

Yep. Same speech.

My eyes return to Laney's tanned shoulders and the yellow straps that hold her sundress up. It takes me back to the first time I ever saw her.

My grandma motions to the end seats in the back row of the auditorium. "Let's sit here, Tally." She hobbles into the aisle, struggling to keep her balance on the sloped floor.

I shimmy into the row and plead with her again. "Mom said she's going to get better and come get me. She says you'll both get better and I can come home then. She promised."

Gram points to the second chair over, and I sit. "You're going to be happy here, Talan. This is a wonderful place or I wouldn't put you here."

"But mom said—"

She lowers herself into her seat and pats my hand. "Your mom is sick. She needs help."

"I know what it is. It's drugs."

Gram brushes my shaggy bangs out of my eyes. "You know too much for a seven-year-old." She lifts my chin with her finger. "You're better off here. They'll take care of you and give you everything we can't. Nice clothes, your own room, toys—"

"I don't care." As the principal begins his speech, I lean closer to Gram. "Please don't leave me here."

"I have to, honey. I can't take care of you anymore, and your mom is in trouble. This is a safe place for you. Remember how scared you were when the police came?"

I nod.

"You'll be happy here. Give it a chance."

The principal is saying big words I don't understand. Gram is breathy and gray next to me, and I don't want to argue and upset her. It's hard enough for her to be away from her oxygen tank.

I sigh and turn my head toward the stage. A girl in the row in front of us is staring at me. She must have been listening.

She's wearing a bright yellow sundress, and her hair is pulled tight into a ponytail. She looks cleaner than the girls I go to Emerson Elementary with. I can smell the soap on her skin from where I'm sitting.

I glare at her, but she waves and gives me a nervous smile.

When I give her the finger, she rolls her eyes and giggles at me. She's pretty and perfect and happy.

I never hated anyone so much in my life.

The sound of clapping snaps me out of it.

"Before we announce this year's Pillar nominees," Headmaster Boyle says, "allow me to introduce the new Chairman of the Board of Singer Enterprises—Stephen Kane."

A slick, polished guy wearing a sharp black suit and perfectly coiffed hair strides onstage, waving like a game show host. Everything about the guy is shiny: his shoes, his hair, his thick gold watch, even the pocket square poking out of his breast pocket. He's smoother than hundred-year-old Scotch.

A redheaded woman follows him onstage, fingering her diamond necklace and scanning the audience before sitting in a folding chair near the backdrop. She claps twice and checks the time on her watch like she's late for a spa appointment.

For a man who insists that students greet adults with strong handshakes, Headmaster Boyle shakes Mr. Kane's hand like there's poison ivy on it. He trudges back to his seat next to the redhead, taking his stiff scowl with him.

Kane rests one arm on the lectern and flashes a smile so white I can see it when I close my eyes. "Thank you, Matthew. It's an honor to be here today." His chest puffs out as if he's accepting an Academy Award. "When I took over as Chairman of the Board at Singer Enterprises last spring, I took the task of selecting this year's Pillar pledges very seriously. You see, I'm not just an alumnus of Singer School. I was also the first Pillar ever selected, after the heartbreaking scandal that rocked this fine institution."

Did he just say that? Although everyone at our school knows about the murder of William Singer, adults avoid the subject like a scar you pretend you don't notice on someone's face. It seems strange to bring it up on a day when we're supposed to be welcoming new students. No matter how you word it, it's pretty creepy that our school's founder was murdered by some students in a secret society.

Kane rambles on. "It was difficult to choose from so many exceptionally qualified candidates, but I'm satisfied I've selected six students that will serve us very well indeed. In honor of the new Pillars and recent changes at Singer Enterprises, I've taken it upon myself to update the school's motto to reflect more modern ideals."

He strolls to the side of the stage and tugs on a long rope hanging from the ceiling. An enormous banner flops down, echoing through the auditorium as it bangs the floor. "Success through excellence!" he announces with a self-satisfied smile. Several people clap weakly and I wonder if he pulled this lame motto off a coffee mug.

Kane gazes around the crowd and strides back to the podium. "This new motto reminds us all to strive for those qualities which define Pillar excellence." Kane reads the words listed on the banner: "Pride, Passion, Achievement, Strength, Glory, and Leadership."

He snatches the microphone out of its stand and struts across the front of the stage like a rock star. "I'm here to promise you, you can expect a new era of success for Singer Enterprises *and* for Singer School. We've got the energy and the talent to lead the next wave of movers and shakers.

And you—every one of you—now has the potential and backing to create the kind of life you deserve. Excellence will be richly rewarded here."

His dark, intense eyes sweep over the auditorium, while the reflection of his smile bounces off Professor Solomon's bald head and burns a hole in my retinas.

The guy's got charisma, I'll give him that.

"For instance," he says, "this year we're expanding the Pillar program to include additional opportunities such as trips to Aspen over Christmas and Dubai over the summer, college internships at the Singer Enterprises headquarters, and networking with famous celebrities and successful business leaders.

A buzz rises in the audience, and Kane holds up one hand.

"So without further ado"—Kane pulls an index card from his pocket—"it's now my great pleasure to announce the names of the newest Pillars."

Laney's back straightens and the muscles in her jaw lock in a tight smile. She takes slow breaths as Kane reads the first three names: "Congratulations to ... Kayla Kaminski, Iman Kabal, and Zack Hunter. Would the first three nominees please rise and accept your certificates?"

A surprised chatter rolls through the crowd. With the exception of Zack, these are not exceptional students. And even Zack doesn't make sense as a Pillar. He's full of something, all right, but it isn't excellence.

Laney takes a sharp breath and holds it. Her face grows pale. To her left, Kollin mumbles, "What the ... "

"Next," Kane reads, "I have chosen … Samantha Mann and Nick Robinson."

If I had a drink in my mouth, this is where I'd spit it out. Mann and Robinson are notorious scumbags. When Samantha's houseparents found a stolen purse in her room last year, she lied and blamed it on her roommate. They couldn't prove which girl took it, so they both lost privileges for a month.

Nick Robinson is even slimier than Samantha. He got caught selling weed on campus, then offered a deal to the administration to narc out everyone who bought from him to save himself from being expelled. Any community service he listed on his Pillar application would have been required by court order.

As the first of the Pillars step onstage to shake Kane's hand and receive their awards, there's chaos in the crowd. I look around the room, half-expecting it to be some kind of joke. Everyone reflects the same shocked expression. Everyone but the new Pillars, who gather onstage passing smug smiles and high-fiving one another.

Laney and Kollin stare at each other, bug-eyed and open mouthed. In the surreal blur of announcements, I realize there's only one Pillar left to be named. Which means at least one of them won't make it.

Kane returns to the microphone. "Your final Pillar for this school year is—"

Laney pleads with her eyes.

"—Cameron Moore!"

A collective gasp rises at the same time Delaney's shoulders sink like a drop on a roller coaster. Cameron Moore is so shady, even the teachers are shaking their heads.

Laney's eyes fill fast, and she tries to blink away the tears. Her bottom lip quivers as it forms a plastic smile. She swallows hard, holds her head high, and claps for the newest Pillars.

"That's bullshit!"

The voice comes out of nowhere. It's angry. And defiant. *And mine.*

I'm on my feet now, shaking with an anger I can't explain. Laney's wide, glassy eyes bounce between me and the front stage. Kane ignores my outburst and greets Cameron Moore when he walks to the podium.

"Bullshit!" I yell louder.

Headmaster Boyle zeroes his eyes on mine until we're locked in some kind of face-off. The corners of his mouth curl into a strange smile and a chill skips along my spine. I sneer at him, waiting for some sort of explanation from the man who constantly drills us about being fair and honorable.

I'm about to shout again when a wrinkled hand squeezes the top of my shoulder. "That's enough, Mr. Michaels!" Professor Solomon grabs my collar and yanks me backward. "You're coming to the office with me."

THREE

I don't get home from detention until after six. Most of my housebrothers have finished eating and are doing their chores in the kitchen. Only Marcus and Mr. and Mrs. Shanahan are left at the dining room table, finishing their lasagna.

"Well hello, Talan," Marcus snickers. "Where you been all day?"

I look at my houseparents and say nothing. Mom Shanahan hates when her boys get in trouble. Both she and Dad Shanahan keep eating without acknowledging me.

Marcus grins and pulls out my chair. "Have a seat and tell us about your day, dear."

I glance at the table. Mom Shanahan knows her lasagna is my favorite food. I move closer to the Shanahans. "I'm ... I'm sure you've already heard." I pull a blue slip from my pocket and unfold it. "I spent the day in detention." I read from the slip: "'For a profane outburst during an assembly.'"

I walk around the chair and try to hand the slip to Mom, but she doesn't take it. I fidget with the paper. Now what do I do?

"Marcus, could you please finish your dinner in the kitchen?" Dad Shanahan growls. "And close the door behind you."

Marcus carries his plate into the next room. The door clicks shut but the Shanahans still don't say anything. I can't remember it ever being this quiet in here. My eyes dart around the room. Mom slowly sips her tea as Dad takes another bite of garlic bread.

The skin on the back of my neck grows clammy. I rock back and forth, shifting my weight from foot to foot, waiting for the Shanahans to make the next move. It's like being locked in solitary confinement with your executioners.

I clear my throat and mumble, "Headmaster Boyle couldn't suspend me since classes haven't technically started, but I lost privileges until school begins next Monday."

Nothing. Not even a nod.

My heart speeds up. "I'm sorry," I blurt out. "But it sucked the way they screwed your daughter. Laney deserved to be a Pillar more than anyone." I slide the detention slip onto the table next to Mom Shanahan's plate. "I'll make myself a sandwich and take it to my room."

I try to circle past her, but she pulls out Laney's empty chair to block my path. When she stands up, I cower at what's coming. Mom Shanahan can give a real earful. But she doesn't. She puts her hand on my shoulder, presses me into Laney's seat, and cuts me a massive piece of lasagna.

"What Principal Boyle doesn't know won't hurt him," she whispers.

I blink a few times. When I finally look over at Dad, he breaks out into this huge grin and winks at me. My shoulders relax and I let out a breath.

It's then I realize I'm eating off of Delaney's clean plate. "So where is Laney? Didn't she eat?"

Mom nods toward the doorway. "She hasn't left her room since she got home this afternoon. Maybe you could talk to her when you're done with chores."

I practically choke on my mouthful. "Man, she must be pretty bad off if you're sending me to her room. You're such a Nazi about boys in there. You're going to disengage all the booby-traps, aren't you?"

Dad Shanahan smiles. "We can turn off the electric fence for one night."

———

After dinner and chores, I wash up and knock on Laney's door.

No answer.

I knock again.

A shaky voice says, "I told you, I'm not hungry."

"It's Talan. Open up."

The door creaks open and two bloodshot eyes appear. "I don't feel like seeing anybody right now."

I put my hand on the doorframe and lean in. "Your mom and dad sent me to check on you."

Shock waves appear above her eyebrows. "Without a chaperone?" She peeks into the hall and looks around. "No guard dog? Not even pepper spray? They must really be worried about me. Tell them to call off the suicide watch. I'm fine."

"I know. But let me in anyway." I squeeze past her and wander around. "I want to see what your room looks like with the lights on."

I lift an empty pint of cookie-dough ice cream off her desk. "I thought you weren't hungry."

She forces a half-smile. "That was medicinal."

"Well anyhow, I'm sorry about the Pillars." I sit on her bed. "That whole thing was bullshit."

"So I heard." Her half-smile blooms to a full one. "The whole school heard, actually." She slides next to me on the mattress. "What was that about anyway? Were you defending me or something?"

"No! I . . . I just hate Cameron Moore." I rub my neck. "That whole Pillar thing is stupid to begin with. Why does someone deserve all those perks just because they get better grades and suck-up to the teachers? Why should a kid like me be penalized because I have a learning disability?"

"How can you say that, Talan? It's not just about grades. You know how hard I work organizing activities and volunteering all the time."

"So? Anyone can volunteer."

Her face pinches. "Oh? Then why don't you? At least my time is spent helping other kids. You get more attention for running around in a red football jersey a few hours every weekend. The jocks get plenty of perks here, and you know it."

"Geez, okay already." I sigh. "I'm sorry I said anything. I'm just crabby I had to waste one of the last days of summer stuck inside with Headmaster Boyle."

"Yeah, well, you're lucky he didn't suspend you."

"He almost did. Mr. Kane wanted him to, but all Boyle could do was take privileges and give me detention. Oh, and Professor Solomon convinced him to put me in his Ethics and Virtues class, too."

"Oh Shitsu," she says, gnawing the corner of her bottom lip.

"What?"

"Well, I have some good news and some bad news." Laney scratches her forehead. "Which do you want first?"

The expression on her face guarantees my day is about to get worse. "The good, I guess."

"Kollin and I are signed up for that class, so we'll have it together."

"Having a class with Kollin is the good news? I can hardly wait to hear the bad news."

"All the Pillars will be in there too. It's part of the requirements when you apply."

"Damn!" I pound my fist into her pillow. "I should have known Headmaster Boyle would burn me. His eyes practically lit up when Solomon suggested it. I swear the guy hates my guts. He always has."

"Well, *I'm* glad you'll be there. I can use an ally. It's gonna suck listening to Cameron Moore and the Pillars bragging about all the cool stuff they're getting."

I squeeze a stuffed dolphin sitting on her bed, gripping it like a football. "What the heck happened today, anyhow?" I pull my arm back, aiming for an imaginary receiver. "These Pillars aren't anything like the ones they usually choose."

Before I can nail the door with Flipper, Laney snatches the thing from my hand and sets it carefully on her shelf. "That's because Mr. Rathbone was always the Chairman of the Board. My dad said he always relied on the teachers' suggestions when he selected the Pillars. But Stephen Kane took over when Rathbone died, and he insisted on choosing the Pillars himself."

I scoot back, snuggling into the mound of pillows lined neatly against her headboard. "It doesn't make sense. We get a lecture from this Kane guy on how excellent Pillars are, and then he chooses the biggest group of losers at our school. Who is this Kane idiot, anyhow?"

Laney stands up and wanders slowly toward her desk. "Mom said Stephen Kane was a hero when he went here. He was the boy who discovered the fire that killed William Singer and those students. Kane tried to rescue them, but it was too late. The Board was so impressed that they rewarded him by putting him in charge of reinventing Mr. Singer's secret society. He helped come up with the Pillars as the replacement. That's why he was the first Pillar."

"Reinvent the secret society? Why would they want to do that?" I shake my head. "After the murder, you'd think they'd want to forget it ever existed."

Laney slides into her desk chair. "They had to, for legal reasons. Mr. Singer's will left all of his assets, including Singer Enterprises, in a trust to Singer School. That way, the school could go on even after he was gone. The board of directors was to continue running the business, but the will stated that there was a group of students at the school who had the authority to veto any board decisions they felt would hurt the school. The will referred to them as the Society of Seven. The Sevens were set up to protect the school, but five died in the fire and the other two never came forward."

"Because they'd get arrested for murder."

"That's the theory. Anyhow, the Board needed to create something right away that filled that description in the will, so they worked with Kane to come up with the Pillars. To avoid any more trouble, they decided there'd be six seniors selected every year, with the Chairman of the Board acting as the seventh member and advisor so that they wouldn't be secret anymore."

"So why do you think Singer started it as a secret society? There had to be something gross or illegal going on."

Laney doesn't answer. She's deep in thought, tapping her knuckles on the desktop.

"So how do you know all this, anyway?" I add. "About Singer's will and all that?"

She swivels in her chair, turning her back to me. "I did some research once."

"For a paper or something?"

Her head lifts toward a photo of her family on her bulletin board. "Something like that." She's quiet again.

When I hear her sniffling, I swing my legs over the side of her bed. "I know you wanted to be a Pillar, Lane, but it'll be okay. I'm sure you're already guaranteed a scholarship with all your A's and compulsive community service."

She straightens up quick and wipes her face with her palms. Her desk chair turns a few degrees in my direction.

"C'mon. Who needs Winchester House when you have us?" I lean back on my elbows. "Admit it, you'd totally miss us. Think about all our great times together. No more of Jake's laundry-day headlocks, where he forces you to whiff his reeking socks? Or the way everyone farts and blames it on you? You don't get that kind of attention just anywhere. Remember when Marcus and me stole your underwear from the dryer and wrapped them up for Headmaster Boyle as a birthday present?"

"Is this supposed to be making me feel better?" she whimpers. But when she swivels the rest of the way to face me, there is a smile, if just a little one. "You know, I *would* have missed this place. I probably would have been here all the time anyhow."

"Then why mope about it? You're already gonna graduate with a pile of awards."

"I never cared about that. That's not why I wanted it."

"Then why? So you could spend more time with Kollin?"

"It doesn't matter." She glances at her bulletin board and pulls her hair back. "I'm fine now. Really."

Just then, the door swings open and Dad Shanahan's head pops through. His wrinkled brow relaxes when he sees Laney and me on opposite sides of the room. "You feeling better, sweetie?"

Laney nods and Mr. Shanahan says, "Why don't you come out and have some dinner, then? C'mon ... make your mom and dad happy and eat something."

When Laney stands up, I read something in her expression that catches me off guard.

Disgust.

FOUR

The Pillars are gathered in the front of the classroom when I walk in. Perched on the teacher's desk, Cameron Moore glares as I trudge past him to the back of the room.

I plop down in an open desk next to Emily. "Hey."

She looks up at me from her magazine and then back down to the quiz she's filling out. "Hey."

She must be pissed about our cemetery date. Whatever. I wasn't looking for a girlfriend anyhow.

Laney and Kollin stroll in a minute later. Laney frowns at the Pillars before glancing around the room. Her eyes skip from me to Emily and back to me again. She gives me a half-smile. I nod and slouch in my seat until a voice jolts me to attention.

"Mr. Moore!" Professor Solomon bellows from the doorway.

Cameron hops down as our teacher shuffles in.

Stooped at the waist, Solomon hobbles turtle-slow toward his desk. Wisps of fine white hair cling to his head like a spiderweb. Brown age spots speckle his face and hands. He leans on his cane, surveying Cameron Moore through wire-rimmed glasses that teeter on the tip of his nose.

This is my first course with Solomon, and that's no accident. Senile Solomon is well-known for failing more kids than anyone at Singer. Your chance of getting an A in his class is the statistical equivalent of Haley's comet flying over Wrigley Field at the exact moment the Cubs clinch the World Series. Not that it matters much to me, but they call him the GPA Killer.

Solomon's sunken eyes narrow on Cameron. The room is quieter than the inside of a casket until the old guy slams his cane on the desktop. "If you ever use my desk as your chair again, I'll use your report card as an invitation to summer school. Are we clear?"

"Of course, sir." Cameron nods manically. "I apologize." He rushes for the first open chair.

Solomon's eyes scan the dead-silent room.

"Excuse me." Zack Hunter's hand creeps up. "Sir?"

Solomon glares at him over the top of his glasses.

"As you're probably aware, sir, this year the Pillars are supposed to meet every Monday in the Board Room in lieu of this class. We have our first meeting this afternoon, in five minutes. We're eager to get going, if that's okay."

Laney's eyes and mouth drop simultaneously, like they're attached to the same anchor.

"I'm aware," Solomon sniffs, then turns to the rest of

us. "Apparently, Mr. Kane feels the Pillars can learn more from meeting with him than they would in my class." His mouth tightens. "I've also been advised that the Pillars are to be excused for numerous field trips and quarterly board meetings."

Zack high-fives Cameron, and Professor Solomon points his cane at them. "Just so there's no misunderstanding, Pillars will be expected to make up everything they miss in class. For instance, you will be expected to read the first two chapters in your textbook tonight and write five pages summarizing the main ideas." Solomon grumbles something under his breath and waves his hand at the door. "Pillars, you're excused."

The six students grab their backpacks and stroll out, leaving only five of us. Solomon slams the door and growls, "The rest of you, move to the front desks."

I follow Emily and park myself in an open seat next to Jose Aguilar, an angry ex-gangbanger. I've always wanted to check out his tattoos, but then he glares at me and I end up inspecting my nails instead.

Solomon rests against the dry-erase board and waits for us to get settled. "This is a class on *character* and *virtue*," he pronounces. The way he spits it out, you'd think it was a class on terror and intimidation.

Laney pulls out her textbook and flips to the first page.

"You may close that, Ms. Shanahan," he says. "You won't find today's lecture in your texts. I've decided that if Stephen Kane can veer from the curriculum every Monday, then I can as well."

Kollin lifts his hand.

"I know what you're going to ask, Mr. LeBeau. And no. The non-Pillar students will have no homework tonight. Consider that a bonus assignment I gave the Pillars—for being such *excellent* students. Now, if we may begin."

He points his cane at the Pillar banner hanging next to him. "Mr. Aguilar, what are the six attributes of excellence as defined by Singer's new Chairman of the Board?"

Jose reads the list: "Leadership, Pride, Passion, Achievement, Strength, and Glory."

Under my breath, I mumble, "Bullshit."

Solomon's head swivels 180 degrees. Just my luck; the guy's entire body is rotting, but his ears are sharper than a satellite dish. He wobbles to his desk and tears a slip of paper off a pad. "Profanity is not allowed in my classroom." He scribbles something on the form and hands it to me. "Apparently you haven't learned your lesson, Mr. Michaels. Or perhaps you're just eager for a little more of Principal Boyle's attention?"

Crap. Afternoon detention.

The professor returns to the board. "Our new Chairman of the Board has an interesting interpretation of the purpose of this school," he says. "Fortunately for us, our founder defined personal excellence differently. My dear friend William Singer devoted his life and wealth so that students could mold productive lives according to values that enrich the world. His motto for this school will always be *virtus sola nobilitas*—virtue alone is noble. From the ceiling in Founders Hall to the scroll above our gates, the seven virtues remain our beacon."

He grabs a blue marker and scribbles six of them on the board:

1. Courage
2. Compassion
3. Justice
4. Faith
5. Sacrifice
6. Wisdom

"Now let's consider Mr. Kane's definition of success." Solomon limps over to the banner. "*Leadership* is authority over another," he mutters, "and *pride* is a high opinion of oneself. *Passion* is any strong emotion—love or hate or even sex or anger."

He pauses to catch his breath. "*Achievement* indicates an accomplishment of personal goals, *strength* is an individual's power in relation to someone else, and *glory* is recognition for personal achievements."

Solomon points a shaky finger at Kollin. "Mr. LeBeau. Who would you say benefits most from these qualities?"

Kollin squirms ten different ways before guessing. "The person who possesses them?"

"Precisely. These qualities benefit one's self." Solomon shakes his ghoulish head. "One could argue that Hitler possessed all six of those qualities, and his legacy is anything but excellent."

Our attention hones in on Solomon's every twitch. Suddenly this is getting interesting. "Now consider our founder's interpretation of personal excellence," he continues. "Courage, compassion, justice, faith, sacrifice, and wisdom." He peers down at Laney. "Ms. Shanahan. Can you tell me how the qualities on *this* list differ from the Pillar list?"

She looks from the banner to the board and squeaks out, "They serve others rather than oneself?"

Solomon roars, "Exactly!" and scribbles one last virtue on the list on the board:

7. Service

Then he pulls out his chair and eases himself into it, his eyes slowly panning each of our faces. There's a fury in his voice that doesn't fit his feeble body. "Virtue requires the sacrifice of self in *service* of others. That's why *it* will always be more excellent than some"—he looks directly at me—"*bullshit* definition of success."

I'm so stunned, I drop my pencil.

The old guy seems pretty pleased with himself. "The Singer School motto will always be *virtus sola nobilitas*—virtue alone is noble. No matter what our new chairman of the board says."

FIVE

The great thing about Adderall is it totally helps me focus. The bad thing is, I'm not always focusing on the right thing. While my math teacher is introducing herself and the fascinating world of Senior Calculus, I'm still cracking up over Senile Solomon calling the Pillars *bullshit*.

Professor Anderson answers a knock on the door and steps outside. She returns a second later, waving a yellow pass. "Mr. Michaels, you're wanted in the Hadley building."

Great. What did I do this time? I scoop up my things and pluck the slip from her hand.

It reads: *Talan Michaels. Appointment: 2:30. Room 07, Hadley Hall.*

I cut across the quad toward the oldest building on campus. Why would they want to see me here? Except for the thing at assembly, I can't think of anything I've done wrong recently. That they know of, anyhow.

I open the front door and flash my pass at the security guard. He reads the note over a couple times as I sign in. "Room 07? I don't see a lot of passes for rooms in the basement." He hands it back and points to a doorway. "Take that stairwell there."

The muscles in my shoulders stiffen as I ramble down the rickety steps into a dark corridor. The air is humid and musty. There's a single dim bulb hanging from the ceiling in the center of the long hallway.

Unnerved, I squint to read the faded numbers on the old wood doors. The darkness in the narrow hall is starting to trigger my claustrophobia. When my shoes squeak like a bad speaker, I twist around, thinking someone's behind me. What am I freaking out about? There's no one else here. I'm alone.

Alone.

In a strange building.

For a meeting I knew nothing about.

In an empty hallway...in a dimly lit basement...that no one ever uses.

The hairs on my arm stand up. My eyes shift around, searching the walls for anything familiar.

"Hello?"

No answer.

All the classroom lights are off except for one at the very end of the hall. A strip of light glows from under the door. I drift toward it like an insect to a bug zapper.

The door to room 07 creaks as I open it and wander inside. The room is empty, except for a chalkboard on one wall with a message:

Yes. Talan. The letter is for you. And it's real.

My breath catches in my throat. What letter? What's going on? I look around the room and then peer out into the hallway, but there's still no one around.

Scanning the room again, I spot a black velvet envelope with a red wax seal sitting on the ledge of the chalkboard. I go over and grab it, just as a cold sweat starts to collect under my shirt.

Inside is a card printed with fancy writing:

Master Talan Michaels,

You have been chosen for membership in the resurrected Society of Seven. Participation in The Society requires absolute loyalty, a lifelong oath of silence, and a commitment of sacrificial service to the true purposes of our brotherhood. In return, the secrets of The Society are bestowed upon the pledges, including access to fraternal wealth and wisdom. Upon final initiation into The Society, each member is assigned the Great Responsibility and awarded the Great Reward: the use of Society resources to fulfill your greatest desire.

Choose or refuse, you will have until midnight tonight to decide. If refusing, destroy this card and speak of it never, lest ye choose to invite misery upon yourself. Be warned: Do not take this vow lightly.

If accepting, return this invitation by way of the

mausoleum of Mary Harper Singer, behind the chapel ruins in the cemetery off Rucker Road. Slide this card under the palm of the weeping angel that watches over our beloved matriarch.

Noblesse Oblige: "To whom much is given, much is expected."

I shove the card back inside the envelope. "Funny," I yell. "If you're listening, you wasted a lot of time and energy trying to punk me."

It's completely quiet, except for the sound of my heart hammering in my ears. I jam the envelope in my pocket and dash into the hall, hoping to catch the prankster outside. The corridor is empty. As I walk down the hall, the darkness makes me jumpy. My steps get quicker until I'm jogging up the stairs two at a time. By the time I fling open the door at the top and reach the security guard, I'm soaked with sweat.

"No one showed up for your meeting?" he asks.

"No. How'd you know that?"

"I would have seen if someone went downstairs. This is the only door to the basement."

I swipe perspiration from my forehead. "Did you notice who went down there earlier today?"

"No one. It's been dead since I opened the building at seven. I'd have seen it if someone came in."

"Someone must have come by. The lights were on in room 07."

"Couldn't have been."

"Well, they were."

"You probably flicked them on and forgot. No one's been down there for months. I'm sure of it."

I look back at the door, and a shiver grips my spine.

"Son?" The guard taps me on the shoulder. "You need to get back to class."

———————

The whole walk back to Calculus, I try to figure it out. Who would prank me? I don't have any enemies except for Kollin, and he wouldn't waste his precious time on something that could get him suspended. I suppose Marcus or Jake might have done it, but neither of them have access to Hadley Hall, or to passes for that matter. Only administrators could have pulled this off, and they wouldn't do it. After what happened to Mr. Singer, secret societies are more than prohibited at Singer—they're taboo.

The weirdness of everything starts to obsess me, and I can't stop thinking about it all the way through detention with Headmaster Boyle. It'd take more than one person to pull this off. Who had the resources or a burning need to play me for an idiot?

Rinsing out the last garbage can that Boyle made me scrub as punishment, I look up just as Cameron Moore strolls by the cafeteria window in a tailored blue blazer, playing with his new cell phone.

The Pillars.

I charge out the side door and grab his arm. "Moore!"

He stares at my hand like I'm some grubby peasant who just got grime on his opera jacket.

"I know what you're up to," I say.

His head jerks back, his face crumpling like a used napkin. "Dude. Back off. I have no idea what you're talking about." He shakes my arm off and walks away, his focus returning to his new phone.

I almost believe him. But two steps later, he stops cold. His back straightens and he slowly spins around. His eyebrows pull to the center and his squinty gaze looks me up and down. Suddenly, I'm worthy of his attention.

He walks toward me, his head tilting slightly. "Wait. What exactly are you saying?" he whispers.

"You know damn well what I mean. The Sevens are back? You might have screwed people with that Pillar thing, but this time you fucked with the wrong person." I walk away and leave him standing there.

Back in the cafeteria, I put the last garbage can away and glance out the window. Moore stands frozen in the same spot where I left him, texting like mad. It's a new look for his cocky face—a mix of confusion and fear.

SIX

I should have known the goodwill would run dry. When I get home from detention, Mom Shanahan is pissed. "A detention on the first day of school? And right after regaining privileges? This is certainly not the way to start your senior year, Talan."

I try to look innocent. "I swear I was whispering. I don't know how Solomon could have heard me."

She raises her eyebrows and brushes past me. "Finish your dinner and chores and get to your homework."

I scarf down my enchiladas and scrub the kitchen counters in a hurry. I need to talk to Laney. She's the smartest person I know. She can help me figure out what the Pillars are up to.

I catch her just as she bolts out her bedroom door. "Hold up. I need to talk to you."

She grabs her backpack off the hook by the door and shoves something inside. "Later, Talan. I've got to be somewhere before it gets dark."

Mom Shanahan strolls up behind her. "You going somewhere, Lane?"

"I have to get to the library for an assignment. For my Ethics and Virtues class."

When Mom leaves, I shake my head at Laney. "Solomon said only the Pillars had homework. Remember?"

"Oh. Right. Well, I have tons of other homework I need to do." She swings her backpack over her shoulder.

"On the first day of school?"

"Listen, I can't talk right now. I've gotta hurry."

Laney spins around and I notice something poking out of the top of her bag—a black envelope. It takes me a minute to place it, but when I do, it hits me like a slap.

She got an invitation to join the Sevens too.

"Wait, Laney. Hang on—"

She waves off my outstretched hand and calls goodbye to her mom.

"Laney, hold up!" I yell, but the back door slams in my face.

Mom Shanahan pops her head around the corner.

"I—I'm going with her." I point to the back door. "To the library. We have Solomon's class together." I toss my dishrag in the sink and charge for the door.

"You don't even have your backpack."

"We're using Laney's book. I gotta go."

I jog down the driveway, but Laney's nowhere in sight. I remember the envelope in my back pocket. The mausoleum. She must be headed for the graveyard.

Damn it, Laney, don't fall for it! They're trying to make fools of us.

I run through the yards, past the playground and ball fields until I spot her in the distance. "Laney, wait!"

Thinking she can ditch me, she dashes through the woods. I race after her, but the best I can do is keep her in sight. I'm out of breath when I finally catch up. "Laney," I gasp. "Stop already."

"You can't be here. Go away."

"The invitation isn't real. It's a joke."

Her legs fossilize, then she slowly turns. "How do you know about that?"

I pull the envelope from my back pocket and wave it at her. "I got one too." I take a deep breath. "Do you think I'd get chosen for something like that? I think the Pillars are playing a joke on us. Don't fall for it."

Her face turns to stone. "It's not the Pillars, Talan. This is for real."

"Don't be so gullible. They're trying to play us."

"Don't be so cynical. I'm telling you, this is *real*. They know something about me that the Pillars wouldn't." She stands directly in front of me, her brown eyes penetrating my skeptical stare. "The Sevens are real," she says quietly. "I'm sure of it. They're back. And they want *us*."

It never even crossed my mind that this could be legit. A secret society that's willing to grant my greatest desire like a fairy godmother? No way.

"Laney, think about it. Why would they want me?"

"Oh geez, Talan, a million reasons that I don't have

time to give you. Are you coming?" She nods toward the mausoleum. "We need to do this before Security makes its rounds. Are you in or not?"

"I don't … I don't … We need to think about this."

She puts her hands on her waist. "Please. Since when do you take time and think things through, Mr. ADD?"

I shift my weight from one foot to the other, struggling for words to convince her. "It doesn't make any sense. The Sevens have been dead for almost twenty years."

Laney shakes her head and moves closer. "Only five students died in that fire. Remember? Two were never found. They kept the secrets. They know what happened. They know a lot of things."

"Come on, Laney, we could get hurt. Even if someone is resurrecting the Sevens, it can't be good. They were murderers! They stole William Singer's money and then they killed him."

"I told you before, that was just a theory. There was a large amount of money missing, so the detectives considered it a possible motive. They never had any proof the Sevens took it."

I grab her arm and tug her toward the road. "It's a joke, Laney. C'mon. Let's go home."

"No. It's real! I'm positive about this." She pushes off me, stepping backward. "You don't have to believe or go through with this, but I do. Go home if you want. But please, don't tell. You owe me one, remember?"

Before I can say another word, she turns and sprints to the mausoleum behind the chapel ruins. Light seeps from a small stained-glass window at the top of the tomb. God, what's she thinking? Someone could be waiting in there to hurt her. I take off after her, weaving between the headstones.

Circling the outside of the mausoleum, I check the graveyard for anyone who might be lurking, but there's no one in sight. When I get back to the front steps, Laney's already gone in.

My heart pounds a drum solo as I jerk the door open and stumble inside.

Laney stands facing the rear wall, inspecting seven candles on a marble shelf there.

The flickering flames illuminate two brass plates on the wall to my left: *William Singer. Mary Singer.* I look down at the smooth marble drawers below them with the morbid realization that they contain the corpses of our school's murdered founder and his wife. Suddenly I picture William, standing where I am now, kissing that same nameplate every night for five years. My body chills like I plunged into an icy lake.

The candles throw Laney's shadow around the room as she spins to take it all in. I glance around too, alert for signs of danger, although I have no idea what I'm looking for.

Laney gravitates to the center of the room, hypnotized by a life-size marble sculpture of an angel bending over a coffin. It's an eerie monument, especially at night. The angel rests her grief-stricken face on the lid. Her body collapses over the top of an intricately carved casket with her arms stretched in despair. The candlelight flickers and all I can think is how we need to get out of here.

Laney's fingers skim the wings and glide down the

angel's arm to her hand. "It's beautiful, don't you think?" she whispers.

"It's creepy. Come on, Lane. Can we please go before we get in trouble?"

She reads over the invitation. "It says to slide this card under the palm of the weeping angel. I don't get it." She moves closer. "Her hand is lying flat on the coffin."

The two of us crouch together and examine the hand close up.

"Wait," she says, "look at the fingertips. They're raised slightly off the surface." She slips the card beneath the pads of the angel's fingers. Suddenly, the card is sucked into the marble coffin and disappears.

Laney jumps back. "Oh my God. It's gone!"

Startled by her voice, a bird squawks and flies across the rafters. Laney shrieks and presses her hand to her chest. "Okay. We need to get out of here. Now!" She grabs my wrist and jerks me toward the door.

My heart's still racing as I shake her hand off mine. I yank the card from my back pocket and slide it under the angel's fingertips.

"If you're going for it, then I am too."

SEVEN

Laney slinks out the mausoleum door and starts running. I rush out and sprint alongside her like we're in some kind of race.

When we finally reach the woods, I check over my shoulder and feel a rush of relief that no one is following us. "Okay, Laney, slow down. We can talk now."

My brain is buzzing from everything that's happened, whirling with images of secret handshakes, crazy dares, and wild parties. What'd that invite say again? Something about money?

Suddenly, I'm smiling.

Laney stops and says, "What do you think happens next? What do you suppose they want from us?"

Yeah, right. She's asking me? I shrug. "While this sounds cool, we can't be certain it's real. I mean, it could still be a prank. Right?"

Her gaze traps mine. "Trust me on this, it isn't. For one thing, it's too involved. Who would go to the trouble of getting invitations and wax seals? How would they know about the slit under the angel's fingers? And how does a kid get the school secretary to authorize a pass and open the science labs on the first day of class?"

"Is that where you got your invitation? Mine was in Hadley Hall."

"Whatever. The point is, a normal student couldn't pull this off."

"Yeah, but one of the Pillars—"

"None of the Pillars are smart enough." Her fingers thrum the strap of her backpack. "Plus, they'd never risk everything they have now on a joke. Remember what happened when Headmaster Boyle overheard those lacrosse players talking about starting a secret society? They got suspended for a week, and they didn't even do anything."

"I know." I study the little vertical lines between her eyes. "Which is why I'm shocked you're going along with this. You're usually such a rule-follower."

"Yeah? Well look where that got me." There's an anger in her eyes I haven't seen since I put her training bra on the statue of George Washington in the quad.

"Is that why you're doing this? 'Cause you're pissed about the Pillar thing?"

"There's a lot of reasons. You know, maybe I'm sick of being a goody-goody. Maybe I want a little adventure."

"Delaney Shanahan, a badass? I don't buy it." I laugh and her spine stiffens. "You're too much of a good girl."

"Good girls can be badasp, too."

"Oh please. You can't make a move without checking in the Perfect Handbook."

"What's that supposed to mean?"

"You play everything so safe. Perfect daughter, perfect student, perfect grades, perfect behavior. Even your boyfriend is perfect. Perfectly boring, too."

She crosses her arms. "So I'm playing it safe with a 'perfectly boring' boyfriend, huh? Look who's talking. What's so brave about bouncing from girl to girl? It's disgusting how you use them. I think *you're* scared—you can't handle getting serious."

"I've never used a girl in my life. I *never* lie and I *never* lead them on. I always tell them the truth up front: I'm not interested in a relationship. Unlike you and that yawn you call a boyfriend."

"I'm done." Laney whips around and stomps away. "Just because we joined the Sevens together doesn't mean I have to put up with your crap."

"No, wait." I tug her back. "I'm sorry. Really. This whole thing happened so fast, I'm still trying to process everything. Please? I need to ask you something."

She turns slowly, her fists clenched against her hips.

"What did the invitation say about a 'great reward' again? Something about using the Society's resources to fulfill our greatest desire?"

She looks like she drank lemon juice. "It figures that's all you care about. Always looking out for number one."

"If I don't, who will?"

Laney rolls her eyes. "I'm tired, and I don't want to talk about this anymore. I'm going home."

I hold her still. "Just answer me. Do you think they *could* mean money? I know that Singer shared his fortune and secrets with the Sevens, at least until they got greedy and killed him. And you said yourself that the police thought the Sevens stole the missing money."

Laney shoves me aside. "I told you that was just a theory," she snaps. "Nothing was ever proven."

She storms off, and I jog to catch up. "So why are *you* doing this, then? Why would you risk getting expelled? You think it'll make you rich and famous or something?"

"God Talan, we've been housemates half our lives and that's how little you know me? Right... rich and famous, that's me. I'm all into the superficial."

"Then what is it?"

She hurries on, avoiding my eyes. "Let's just say I'm curious." The minute I open my mouth, she interrupts. "So why are *you* doing it, Tal? You owe someone a lot of money or something? I thought you were convinced this was some kind of joke."

I rub the back of my neck. "I have no idea what this is about. But I have a feeling it's gonna be trouble."

"Then why'd you return your invitation?"

"I don't mind trouble. And I definitely wouldn't mind a little cash."

Delaney sulks and walks on. She gets so quiet I can hear the twigs crunching beneath our steps.

"So... have you told Kollin?" I ask.

She glances sideways at me. "Of course not. I'm sworn to secrecy."

"You told *me*." I give her a crooked smile.

"I didn't tell you. *You* told *me*. I ran away from you."

"Oh yeah."

She sighs, stops, and turns to me. "But I'm glad you did," she confesses. "I've been a wreck since I got that invitation. I feel better going through this with someone." There's a glint in her eyes when she adds, "Even if it's you."

She drops her chin, chews her thumbnail for a few seconds, then lifts her wide eyes to mine. "What do you suppose they want from us, Talan?"

"Nothing much," I tease. "Just our souls."

EIGHT

A few weeks pass and we don't hear anything. The intensity of it all begins to fade and I'm starting to wonder if it was some sort of weird prank after all. Maybe that's a good thing. It's not like I don't have enough problems in my life already without a secret society with all-campus access stalking me.

It's five minutes before curfew on Wednesday night when Laney storms into the family room. Juan, Marcus, Jake, and I are huddled around the TV in the middle of a heated game of *Cyber Combat Zone*.

"Talan," she calls from the doorway. When I don't answer, she yells louder. "Talan!"

My eyes stay focused on the TV. "What?"

"You need to go to the computer room now."

"Talan, look out," Marcus says. "Jake's on the roof. Oooooooh. Nice shot."

"Talan," she shouts, "the computer room!"

"What?"

"You need to go on the computer. Now. So you can check your email."

My eyes are riveted to the screen. "I don't need to check my email," I say. There's a guy on the stairwell about to blow Marcus apart. My hand jerks the control. "Look out, look out!"

"Yes, you do!" Laney insists. "For that project we're working on together. For Solomon's class. He emailed our assignments."

"I have no idea what you're talking about, but I'm in the middle of tenth level. Can this wait?"

Laney bolts over, shoving Jake aside to completely block the screen. Marcus moans, and I flip my controller to the ground. "What the heck, Shanahan? You screwed up our capture."

I finally notice her bug-eyed glare. "We're in the same group, remember?" She picks up the controller and whips it in my direction. "There are seven assignments. *Seven.* Remember? Now get in there and print your email, you dumbash."

Oh, right...something's happened. I hand my controller to Jake and jump up to follow her into the computer room.

Behind me, Marcus mumbles, "Remind me never to take a class with Senile Solomon."

Laney checks the hall before closing the door. She nudges me toward a computer. "I was googling articles on the Society of Seven tonight. Nothing came up except some lame '80s pop band, which I guess makes sense since it's a secret society."

"Is that it? I'd like to finish this game before lights-out."

She eyes me with disdain. "No, that's not 'it.' I got an email from the Sevens. See if you got one too."

A cold current zips down my spine. She pulls a chair out for me and watches out the door as I log in.

A single message appears:

To: tmichaels56@Singer.edu
From: Number 7

Dear Pledge:

You will be given seven tests to prove your worth and loyalty prior to your initiation into the Society of Seven.

Commit the following poem to memory. Your first test depends on it.

When darkness fills you up with fright,
Tread straight, straight, straight into the night.
Left, right, left—the soldier's pace—
Until it leads right to a place
Where everything you thought you knew,
Will turn around. And you will, too.
Left to sort what's wrong from right,
And why you're going to have to fight,
to take what's left
and make it right.

My fingers twitch on the keyboard as my heart pounds. It takes a minute to unscramble my thoughts.

Laney moves from her post and reads the email over my

shoulder. "Yep, that's the same one I got." She heads back to the door and says, "Print the poem and then delete the email."

"So you think this is real?"

"Talan, how can you even question it at this point? Yes, it's real, and maybe once in your life you can be serious and step up. I know you're smart, but sometimes you really don't act like it."

I'd have no problem stepping up if I knew what I was stepping up to.

I'm pulling my copy from the printer when Laney turns suddenly, waving her arms like a traffic cop. "Mom's coming." She rushes to a desk at the opposite end of the room and fakes zipping her backpack closed.

Mom calls through the door, "Time for bed."

I bury the paper deep in my pocket like I'm hiding heroin. It makes me think of my mother.

NINE

The next morning, I corner Laney by her locker before school. "Did you memorize the poem?"

She enters her combination. "Yep. Did you?"

"Yeah, but I'm still not sure about this, Laney. We do have friends who know both our email addresses."

She cuts me off with a loud squeak and slams her locker closed again. "Talan, there's a black envelope inside my locker."

My pulse racing, I scan the crowded hallway. "No one's looking. Open it."

"Here?"

"No. In the women's bathroom. I'll follow you inside and we can read it together in a stall. I'm sure no one will notice us there." I roll my eyes. "Yes, here. I'll be your lookout. Just open it."

With her hands inside her locker, she slides a handwritten note out of the envelope. "If this is a prank, it's a great one. How'd they get this in here? The slots are too narrow for it to fit through."

I shrug and check the hall for prying eyes. "What's it say?" She reads softly:

First Test—Courage:
"Courage is found in unlikely places."—J.R.R. Tolkien

Time: This Evening, 7:00 P.M.
Place: Rear Elevator, First Floor, Jefferson Library.
1. Close with 2
2. Seven times the LL
3. Seven times the Help

She stares at it, then stuffs the paper inside her math book. "What the heck does that even mean?" The hallway's getting busier, so she leans close and whispers, "You should check if you got one. Maybe yours has different clues."

Her lips graze my cheek, and I get the strangest rush. Out of nowhere, I imagine being kissed by those lips. And liking it.

"O-okay," I mutter. "You wait here."

My head is still buzzing as I walk down to my locker. Inside, I find my own black envelope with the exact message as hers. I nod at her and mouth *same*.

Suddenly, Kollin creeps up behind her and covers her eyes. She screams, and everyone turns and looks. *Nice timing, idiot.*

Standing side by side, Laney and Kollin look like two

mannequin models of preppy perfection. He smiles down at her, and I almost forget the envelope in my hand. I slide it into my pocket.

They walk past me on their way to class. "Listen," Kollin is saying, "do you want to go into town this weekend? Maybe do the movie thing again?"

Now the buzz feels more like a hangover. Laney loves movies. I wouldn't mind going sometime, but Singer School is pretty strict about leaving campus. You have to have straight A's for two consecutive semesters, with perfect behavior and full privileges, in order to go into town. That cuts out about 99 percent of the student body, including me.

Laney gnaws on her fingernail. "Maybe." She glances back as she passes me and says, "I need to check what's going on at home first."

She winks and I swear to God, my heart races. What the hell is wrong with me? If Vanessa Jackson was around, I'd drag her into the janitor's closet until I was sure whatever this is was out of my system.

A second later, Kollin turns around and gives me a dirty look that has the same effect.

———

By the time I get home from football practice, Laney's already gone. Dad Shanahan catches me in the kitchen. "Your counselor emailed that you never showed for your appointment yesterday," he says. "Ms. Bennett claims that's the second one you've missed with her. She's eager to get going on your college planning."

"I'm on it," I say, but honestly, it seems like a waste of time.

I rush through dinner and chores and head for my room. I'm running late and still haven't showered, plus I'm stressing about what we're going to find at seven o'clock.

I grab my towel and a change of clothes and duck into the bathroom.

While the water warms up in the shower, I lean against the wall and picture Laney this morning, chewing her thumbnail like a chipmunk on crack. It was already red.

My stomach knots.

I step inside and try to clear my head. The stream from the shower drenches me. As I lather up, my fingers brush across the scar on my chest and trigger a memory. All at once, I'm eight years old again.

The rain comes down so hard it hurts, and I'm scared. What if I can't find Chicago? What if an animal runs out of the woods and attacks me? What if this car coming down the road doesn't see me in the darkness and hits me?

I leave the shoulder and veer toward a gate in the fence, trudging through the soaking grass. Suddenly, lightning flashes and lights up a yard full of statues and tombstones to my right. The different shapes and outlines look like a mob of shadowed ghosts—squatting, standing, and hunched over, all of them just waiting to get me.

My voice is trapped in my throat. My feet won't move. A

burst of lightning close behind me sends me flying forward into the swampy soil. The air is still crackling when I push myself up on shaky arms and see the most terrifying sight of all. An enormous winged statue towers above me, pointing at a grave. Is she saying it's for me? I spin around and sprint as fast I can, slipping and sliding all the way out the gate and onto the road again. Between the wind and thunder and fear, I don't notice that the car has pulled onto the shoulder behind me.

"Where you going, little man?" a voice calls between thunder claps.

I twist around to see Mr. Shanahan. Delaney must have snitched. I told her to leave me alone, but she never does. She watches me all the time. I'll get her for tattling.

The rain is pouring down so hard, by the time Mr. Shanahan comes around the car and reaches me, he's drenched too. Between the storm and the cemetery and not knowing where I'm even going, I'm not sure what to do.

Mr. Shanahan reaches for me, blinking rain out of his eyes. "What's going on, Talan?"

It's not that he's a bad guy, but I need to go home. "I…I'm running away."

"Why?" He bends over. "Did someone hurt you?"

I shake my head.

Mr. Shanahan squats down in front of me and brushes my sopping bangs from my eyes. "Buddy," he says over the storm, "I want to help you, but I can't if you don't talk to me. Will you get in the car, and we can talk at the house?"

I shake my head. "I don't want to go there. I want to see my mom. She said I could come home after a while."

His shoulders slump and he sighs so loud I hear it over thunder in the distance. He kneels in front of me and gently grips my shoulders. "Talan, your mom has an addiction. She hasn't gotten the help she needs yet."

"I want to go home!" I yell.

His hands squeeze my shoulders. "Your mom's not there anymore. We can talk about it at the house if you'll come back with us."

With us?

I notice Delaney for the first time. She's watching me from the back seat with her palms and face pressed against the window.

"We'll take good care of you for as long as you need," he finishes.

"My mom needs me," I yell.

"She isn't there!" Although the wind and rain are pelting his face, he locks his eyes on mine, swallows hard, and says, "Your mom is in jail, buddy. She's going to be there for a long time."

"No!"

"I'm sorry. Maybe we can take a trip and visit her in a few months if the school can arrange it. Or maybe we can call her."

I'm done and I know it. Gram in a nursing home and mom in jail. No home to go to. No family. A cemetery of monsters behind me and a storm everywhere I look. Except straight ahead. Mr. Shanahan kneels in front of me, his jeans soaking in the puddle beneath him, his hands stretched out to help me.

I crumple into his chest. Big, wet arms coil around me. "Let's go home, buddy."

We trudge back to the car and Delaney opens the door for me to get in. I shiver and shake in the back seat as Mr.

Shanahan pulls a wide U-turn back to the student home. Delaney scoots close and puts her arm around me. She squeezes my arm, right where a scar is.

I shove her hard. "I hate you, you stupid girl."

"Laney," Mr. Shanahan says softly. "Let Talan have a little space. Okay?"

I stare out the blurry window to hide my tears. I don't even move when Laney takes her coat off and wraps it around my shoulders.

I snap out of it and realize how late I must be. Laney is probably already waiting for me at the library. Alone.

As I throw my clothes on, the same thought I've had for the last ten years pops into my head: *Delaney Shanahan is an annoying do-gooder.* But there's also a second thought I can't ignore anymore. One that's always there, too, lurking like a shadow in the background: *Delaney Shanahan is the best person I've ever known.*

I don't care if it's the Pillars or the Sevens. If someone hurts her, I'll fucking kill them.

TEN

My hair is still damp from the shower and I'm wheezing when I reach the library. It's two minutes to 7:00. Where the heck is she?

The note from the Sevens said something about the rear elevator. I dart for the back of the building, dodging bookcases and pissed librarians. I turn the corner and see Laney in the distance, pushing the *up* button. She steps inside the elevator and disappears.

I shout, "Hold the door," but it's already closing. Frantic, I shove my hand inside the narrow opening and the doors bang my elbow.

"Owwww." The elevator slowly opens and I collapse against the edge, clutching my sore arm and panting. "You were ... gonna leave ... without me?"

Laney yanks me inside. "Talan, you scared me to death. Can't you ever be on time?"

I massage my elbow. "So ... what do we do now?"

Laney pulls her copy of the note from her pocket. "I've been thinking about this all day and I think I figured it out." She moves in close to me. "See how it says: 'Close with two. Seven times the LL. Seven times the HELP'?" Her eyes lift to mine. "I think 'close with two' means we push the elevator button for the second floor."

She leans over and presses the *2* button on the panel before glancing back at the note. "'Seven times the LL' must mean we hit the button marked LL seven times." She bends over and counts out loud as she punches the button for the lower level seven times.

She checks the paper again while I put my hands on my knees to catch my breath.

"The next instruction is 'Seven times the help.' That's got to be the button with the bell. It looks like the word 'help' used to be on it but it's worn off a little."

She's right. When I lean close, I can make out the letters.

Laney pushes the help button seven times. The elevator lurches hard. The light reads that we're bound for floor 2, but the elevator's actually dropping. It rattles and clangs before stopping abruptly. We reach out for each other to steady ourselves. A moment later, the lights dim.

Now my heart is pounding harder than it did on the sprint over here.

There's a tremble in Laney's voice that doesn't help. "Oh no. I hope we didn't break it."

"*We?*" I smack at the open-door button, but it doesn't move. "I knew this was a joke." I press the help button next, but nothing happens so I pound on the door.

All of a sudden, there's a loud creak behind us. We spin around and watch the back panel of the elevator disappear. It slides completely off to the left, revealing a small, shadowy room behind it.

Holy. Shit.

We latch onto each other like magnets. I can feel her heartbeat racing mine as we stare into the darkness.

After a minute, we unclench and awkwardly back away from each other.

"Still think it's a joke?" she mutters.

She squeezes my wrist and creeps out the back of the elevator, slowly dragging me with her. The elevator casts enough light to show crumbling, red-brick walls around us. The dank, musty room is suffocating and I'm seriously ready to call this whole thing off. My chest lifts and falls with heavy breaths. We take a few more steps and my foot knocks something over on the concrete floor. Two high-beam flashlights roll at our feet.

"What the hell?" I mutter.

As we bend over to pick them up, the elevator doors whip closed and it starts to ascend. We fumble to get the flashlights turned on and the minute we do, the dark space is shattered with beams like we're announcing the grand opening of a new morgue.

"Hello?" Laney calls out.

Silence. This is creepy. Like a horror film, and I'm one of those idiots who's gone down into the haunted basement to see what the noise is instead of running like hell. The flashlight's decently heavy, but a little pepper spray or some brass knuckles would be nice about now. Hell, I'd take holy water in a spray bottle at this point.

Delaney's beam settles on the farthest wall. "There's a tunnel there. Do you see it? Everything else is solid brick." Her face tightens. "God Talan, what should we do?"

Fear creeps into my voice. "What do you mean, what should we do? You're the brainiac." I flick my flashlight at the empty elevator shaft. "I hate to say it, but it looks like our ride left without us."

"Let me think for a minute." Laney concentrates on the note, her face as grim as the room around us.

The muscles in my back and neck grow tense. "The darkness is really freaking me out," I confess. "I think I should tell you—"

Her head jerks up. "That's it—the darkness! The poem!"

"Huh?"

"The poem we had to memorize: 'When darkness fills you up with fright, tread straight, straight, straight into the night.' We're supposed to go straight into the tunnel."

"Are you insane? What if it's a furnace or something?"

"It's not a furnace, it's a utility tunnel. I gave parent tours for student council last year, and we talked about how this was a small college before William Singer bought the property. A lot of older colleges used underground tunnels to deliver coal and stuff between the buildings."

"Okay, fine, so it's a utility tunnel. Where does it go?"

"There's only one way to find out."

She takes my arm and tows me forward, but I yank it free. "Wait! I need to tell you something. I, uh … I'm claustrophobic. I don't know if I can do this."

She gives me her *shut up Talan* look and reaches for my hand, but I jerk it away.

Her jaw drops. "Oh. I'm sorry. I thought you were joking. Wait—we've lived half our lives together and I never knew that? How come you never mentioned it before?"

I rub my hands together so she doesn't see them shake. "Why would I tell anyone that?"

"Well, how come you were fine in the elevator?"

"Elevators are bright and the ride is short. I hate dark, closed spaces. They freak me out." The muscles in my back and neck feel like rocks.

"I'm sorry." She stares up the shaft where the elevator abandoned us. "I don't know what else we can do, though. That tunnel is our only way out now." She walks over to the passageway and shines her light down it. "The hallway is a decent size, if that helps. It's just dark." She looks back at me, pity in her eyes.

My stomach rumbles like the washing machine when I stuff too much in there.

"Are you going to be okay?" Her eyes scan the walls again, looking for anything she might have missed. When they land back on mine, they're full of concern. "Do you want to wait here? I can go alone and try to find a way out."

"No, I'm okay." *Except for my exploding heart and the radioactive nausea building in my gut.* "We'll go together."

She comes alongside me and hooks her arm around mine, squeezing it tight. "I'll help you the whole time, don't worry."

I want to pretend I'm fine, but it's no use. One step in and the tunnel feels tighter than a noose. I take deep breaths and shuffle down the passage.

Our beams of light bounce around an arched passage-way lined with disintegrating bricks. It's humid and stuffy, like a clammy summer night by a dirty river. The deeper we go, the more the air reeks of mildew and decay, a cross between vomit and rotting fish. I swallow to keep from gagging, but it's no use. My stomach is already upset. I pull my arm away, spin around, and puke all over the wall.

Laney rubs my back, but I nudge her hand away. Between gags, I warn her, "If you tell anyone about this I swear I'll kill you, Shanahan."

She strokes my shoulder. "Of course I wouldn't tell anyone."

I'm humiliated and pissed and I swear the minute I figure out who's behind this, I'm going to pummel them until they're throwing up too. I wipe my mouth with my sleeve and steady myself against the wall. I figure Laney will gag at the sight and smell. Instead, she wedges herself under my arm and helps me up.

"C'mon." She squeezes my hand. "You can do this. I'm here for you."

"Do you have any toothpaste?" I give her a weak smile. I'm clammy and shaky, but I don't want her to let go. Her voice and touch soothe me.

As we continue down the hall, my stomach settles a little. After a while, we stumble on an intersection.

"Should we turn or keep going forward?" she asks.

I think for a minute. "Don't turn. The poem said straight, remember? 'Straight, straight, straight into the night.'"

"Oh, that's right. Nice catch, Talan."

I breathe through my nose and walk on, trying to concentrate on anything but the walls trapping me in this underground prison. I think about the way Laney's soft hair tickles my neck as she leans into me, and how good she always smells, even in this sewer hole. Like lavender.

I'm not even sure what a lavender is; I just remember reading the word on a bottle of her lotion once. Laney was sitting at a chair in the kitchen, slowly rubbing the cream on her bare legs, and I was watching her, thinking… well… never mind.

We pass another tunnel to the left, and then another. A few more feet and Laney steps right into a nasty web. She karate chops the air and wiggles around until she's sure she's shaken every bit of it off her. I lean against the wall and laugh weakly until a humongous roach races across my shoe. To say I scream like a little girl is an insult to little girls. I yelp like a Chihuahua, kicking and shaking my foot like I'm putting out a fire.

Whatever tough guy reputation I once had is now trashed. But it's Laney, right? What do I care what Shanahan thinks? Still, my face burns when she laughs and says, "I didn't know you could River Dance."

"Yeah? Well, I didn't know you were an epileptic ninja." I imitate her martial arts moves.

She laughs even harder, and it feels like some kind of prize. Slowly, she catches her breath, smiling and staring at me with a weird expression. She rubs the back of her neck, clears her throat, and steps toward me, gently slipping her arm around mine again. "Let's go."

We march ahead, a little faster now. I don't say it out loud, but all my fears rush back about this secret society thing. What were we thinking? The last group of Sevens were murderers. For all we know, we could be the next victims instead of the next pledges. No one even knows we're here. Who would find us if we just made the biggest mistake of our lives and climbed into our own underground graves? I'd turn and run but I know Laney wouldn't follow, and I can't leave her here.

We come up to a wall and Laney swivels her flashlight from side to side. "It's a T-intersection. Which way now?"

"The next line of the poem is 'Left, right, left—the soldier's pace.' I think that means our next turns are left, right and left."

With our arms linked together, we veer left, armed with only our flashlights.

I squeeze Laney's arm tight, and her voice reassures me. "There's our next turn up ahead."

We swing down a passageway to our right and plod on a few more minutes more before another tunnel comes up. "We take this left," I remind her.

We creep another hundred yards before Laney blurts out, "The quiet is spooking me. Let's talk about something, okay? So ... so what's with the claustrophobia? Since when have you had claustrophobia?"

"Since I was little. My mother locked me in a closet once and forgot about me."

Why did I tell her that? I've never told anyone that.

Suddenly, Laney's not so chatty. She stares up at me, waiting for me to elaborate.

"The day DCFS removed me from our home, the social worker guessed that I'd been there almost two days. Mom thought I'd be okay while she went to score drugs. She hadn't planned on getting arrested."

Laney squeezes my arm tighter. I gotta admit, I don't really mind right now. Still, I'm eager to change the subject. "So can I ask you a question, Laney? Since I'm risking my life, following dicey instructions given to us by a secret society that murdered for profit, do you think you can at least explain to me why this is so important to you?"

"I'll tell you if you tell me why you need the money so bad."

When I don't answer, she says, "Okay then, let me guess. Gambling debt? Child support payments? No, I know. To pay for rehab for your cereal addiction."

I try to come up with one of my typical, smart-ass answers, but I'm too fixated on the darkness to be clever. "The money is for me."

She slips her hand out from my arm. "Of course." Her voice carries an edge now. "I should have guessed. Money you'll probably blow on vodka and girls."

"Vodka? Money I'll *probably* blow on rent and ramen."

Her squinty eyes travel up and down me. "What do you mean?"

"Not everyone has a mommy and daddy to take care of them, Laney. You know the deal. Once you graduate, you're done at Singer. My free ride is over the second they hand me my diploma. I have no family to go back to and I'm not going to college. I'll be homeless again. Did you ever think of that? Because I think about it every day."

"Oh…"

I turn and walk ahead so I don't have to face her pity eyes.

"Mom and Dad would help," she blurts out, behind me. "Or maybe the school could—"

"No." I spin around. "The school will forget about me. And you and your parents will forget about me. Just like my father, whoever the hell he was, forgot about me. Just like Gram, who dumped me at Singer and my mother, who forgot me in the closet. I can take care of myself."

My chest tightens so much it hurts. I don't want to talk about this anymore.

I walk away, but she catches up and touches my sleeve. "We'll figure something out."

"There's nothing to figure out," I say. "You asked what I wanted the money for and I told you—I need to set myself up somewhere until I can find a decent job. Unlike you, when I graduate I don't have a family or a future waiting for me."

Laney acts like I spit on her. "What do you mean you don't have any family? You have a family. We're your family."

"What don't you get about this? It's not the same for me as it is for you. I was abandoned by my mom, Laney. Your parents may have raised me, but they aren't my real mom and dad."

"That's *exactly* the same as me," she snaps.

"What are you talking about?"

"I'm adopted. My real mother abandoned me too."

The words are slow to sink in.

"You're adopted? Why didn't I know that?"

Her face tightens. "Nobody knows. My parents hide it

from everyone. They never even told *me*." She stares up at the ceiling and blows out a slow breath. "Do you remember the community service project I spearheaded sophomore year?"

"Which one? You do more volunteering than United Way."

"The blood drive."

"Yeah?"

"Well, my parents came. Of course. To make a long story short, they both donated type O blood." She rubs the back of her neck and mumbles. "I'm type A."

I shrug my shoulders.

"Geez, you took biology. Don't you remember anything from the genetics unit? Two type O parents wouldn't have a type A child. It's impossible. That's how I figured it out. They lied to me all those years."

"You're kidding? ... Well, what'd they say when you confronted them?"

"They got all flustered and denied it. Said I was 'mistaken.' When I gave them proof, they refused to talk about it. The next day, they came to me and finally admitted it was true, but insisted I let it go. They said they loved me and I had to trust them for now. They told me that someday I'd know everything."

"But why would they lie about it?"

Her voice quivers. "Because they're hiding something bad."

"No way. Not Mom and Dad. How could you even say that?"

"Think about it. They're all about taking in foster kids. Me being adopted isn't something they'd be ashamed of or uncomfortable sharing. Plus, they're fanatics about honesty."

"But what would they be hiding?"

"I have no idea because they refuse to talk about it. I've imagined all kinds of dark secrets, like they stole me or my real mother was some horrible monster."

"It doesn't make sense."

"Exactly. That's why I joined the Sevens. That's what I want for my greatest desire—I want to know who my mother was and what happened to her." She crosses her arms. "I'm counting on you not to tell anyone, Talan."

I nod, and she slowly turns and walks away. I trail behind her in stunned silence until her flashlight reveals another passageway.

"There's our next intersection," she says softly. "Where are we in the poem?"

"Okay, it goes: 'Until it leads right to a place, where everything you thought you knew, will turn around. And you will, too.'"

Laney says, "We turn right, then," and swings down the dark passage. "Look! There's a light ahead."

Up high, and in the distance, light streams from a shaft in the ceiling. I'm so happy to see it until I realize that we have no idea where it's coming from. The tunnel dead-ends below it, but metal rungs protrude from the wall there. We lower our beams as we near it.

Laney opens her mouth to say something, but she's silenced by voices in the distance. We stare at each other and then up the chute. The voices are too muffled to make out. I climb the lowest rungs until my head barely rises above the hatch.

The space around me is empty—a shadowy room that's the size of a large closet. I wave for Laney to follow me up.

We climb out, turn off our flashlights, and look in different directions. Laney points to a long horizontal vent that rides high along one wall near the ceiling. She cups her hand over my ear. "We must be in a hidden room or utility closet or something. Listen," she whispers. "The voices are coming through the cold air return up there."

Light sneaks through the slanted slats in the metal register, illuminating the room with stolen light. Standing against the back wall, I see a brilliant crystal chandelier through the grates. Laughter passes through the slits, too. Laney holds a finger to her lips and nods toward a ladder that was conveniently left in the corner, right below the vent.

A familiar voice on the other side of the wall calls out, "Is everyone having a good time?"

Younger voices laugh and cheer. They sound kind of drunk.

"This is what being a Pillar is all about. Success through excellence!"

A familiar voice answers, "We're all really grateful for your generosity, Mr. Kane."

It takes me a moment to recognize Cameron Moore's suck-up tone. Laney's eyes grow wide, signaling me she recognizes it too. I climb the ladder, leaning against the wall so that my face is in the shadows, and reach to help her up.

The scene we spy when we gaze down through the narrow slats looks like Christmas at the Playboy Mansion, minus the skin. A long elegant table stretches across the center of a dark, wood-paneled room. The tabletop is crowded with plates of half-eaten lobster and steak, with ornate side dishes that look like art projects. There's a tower of what looks like little bonbons and some lattice-work thing with pieces of chocolate-dipped fruit stuck to it. Open bottles of champagne are everywhere, along with crumpled wrapping paper and empty boxes.

I can see Stephen Kane standing with Cameron in front of a wall-to-wall cabinet at the opposite end of the room, pouring himself a glass of brandy. The other Pillars relax around the table, dressed in tailored suits and shimmering dresses. Samantha Mann pulls back her hair while Kayla Kaminski fastens a sparkly necklace at the nape of Samantha's neck. They both scream and make a toast when it's on her properly, glinting in the light.

Not to be outdone, Kayla fingers her own necklace to show off the diamond pendant that hangs low in the plunging neckline of her gown. Across from them, Zack Hunter, Iman Kabal, and Nick Robinson are deeply engrossed in comparing new laptops.

Stephen Kane takes a sip from his glass. "To business relationships!" He raises his goblet. "You all know I was able to achieve great things after my time at Singer. The least I can do is pay it forward, guys. Here's to the Pillars."

"The Pillars!" they all cheer.

"We certainly appreciate it," Cameron says. *God, the guy just can't stop.*

Kane lays his hand on Cam's shoulder like a proud father. "And I appreciate your support at the board meeting." He addresses the other Pillars. "Consider this a lesson in orchestrating a mutually rewarding business arrangement. When you approve my plan to sell the school along with Singer Enterprises, we'll all prosper exponentially."

Six heads nod their support.

Kane lifts his glass again. "To teamwork!"

The church bell rings with eight deafening *bongs* that sound like they're coming from just outside the wall. Which means we're in the north end of the Executive Building, right next to Providence Church. I've never been inside this building. It's off-limits to students and only used by Singer executives.

"My driver is waiting to take you back to Winchester House," Kane tells them. "Which reminds me, I've been talking to an acquaintance who owns a Lexus dealership." He flashes his shiny smile. "There may be some cars in your future."

Zack fist-bumps Nick as Kane walks them out the door. Kayla stops to scoop up some glasses from the floor, but Kane waves his hand at her. "No, Ms. Kaminski. We hire people for that."

As the last Pillar staggers out, I rub my face and try to process what I've just seen. Laney is already climbing down the ladder in a stupor. She pulls out her flashlight and I follow her back down the chute. My head is swimming and I'm starting to feel sick again. I can't process anything in the dark confines of this creepy tube.

I step off the last rung and she whispers, "I can't believe

what we just heard! Listen, we need to hurry to get back in time. Do you remember the way?"

I normally have a killer memory, but the darkness has me freaking again. Suddenly, it occurs to me. "It's the second half of the poem. We left off at the place that said 'everything you thought you knew, will turn around, and you will, too.' The next part said, 'Left to sort what's wrong from right, and why you're going to have to fight—"

Laney finishes, "To take what's left and make it right."

"So we take the first left." I start jogging to get the hell out of here, fumbling with my flashlight.

Laney flicks hers on and catches up. "Well at least we know now that this is real." She stares up at me. "And we know what the Sevens want from us."

"We do?" I only slow when we make the first turn.

"Of course. They want us to stop Stephen Kane and the Pillars from selling the school." She's talking faster and faster, like she's the one with ADHD. "It's sickening. An old man hanging around teenagers, plying them with drinks and expensive gifts. Buying them off to get their support to sell our school."

I focus on our next turn ahead. If only it weren't so suffocating down here.

"I can't believe the Pillars would betray their friends like that," Laney rattles on. "I mean, what happens to the students here? A lot of them have nowhere else to go."

"It doesn't matter to us. We're graduating."

She inhales sharply. "*Talan*, I can't believe you said that. What about our friends who aren't? What about our housebrothers? What happens to them if Singer closes?"

I hadn't considered that. Still, I want out of this claustrophobic maze so bad I can hardly think straight. "I don't know; I'm sure they'll figure something out."

The truth is, I thought this secret society would be about parties, pranks, and perks. I don't have a lot of other options for money, but this Sevens thing isn't exactly what I expected. My mind jumps back and forth from everything we've seen so far to the dark tunnel that wraps around me like a straitjacket.

"What about my parents?" Laney says. "They've devoted their whole lives to Singer School. Where will they go? What'll they do?"

I love the Shanahans, but right now, the only ass I'm worried about saving is my own. "They'll still need house-parents. Maybe nothing will change."

I'm getting used to the smell down here, but it still makes me woozy. *Focus. One more left and a right. But then what?*

Laney's wound up and won't stop talking. "See, I told you the Sevens were real! They aren't the bad guys. They never were. There's more to them than that scandal, and we'll figure it out."

I stop to catch my breath. "Kane is up to something, I'll give you that. He wants to sell the school. I don't think we can assume anything else. Aren't you kind of making a stretch about the Sevens? Why do you want to believe so badly that the Sevens were innocent? Because the Pillars rejected you and the Sevens want us?"

She flinches at my words. "Are you kidding me? The Pillars are disgusting. I'm glad they didn't choose me. They're up to something all right. And they're going down."

As I look at her standing there with her hands on her hips, her messed-up hair falling over intense brown eyes, I suddenly realize that she's not the same Delaney. "What's gotten into you, Shanahan?"

She avoids my stare and brushes past me so I have to race to keep up. "Nothing. I just hate the thought of these Pillars getting all those perks and awards they don't deserve. There's a waiting list a mile long for kids who need to get into Singer, and Kane is wasting tuition money on a car for Kayla Kaminski? The Pillars are supposed to be model students looking out for the school, not selling out to Stephen Kane. The Sevens must want to save our school. *That's* the group I want to be in."

"I don't know. I'm thinking the Pillars' secret club looks a hell of a lot funner than ours."

Her hand flies up to smack me, and I duck. "I'm kidding!"

Our flashlights are jumping like two headlights rolling down a bumpy road. When we reach the last long corridor, there's a light at the far end. We get closer, and I can tell the elevator is waiting for us with its back panel slid open. I want to cry with relief.

Inside, Laney stabs the button for the first floor and the back wall slithers into place again, making the elevator look like every other I've ever been in.

Except for the black envelope taped to the center of the rear wall.

My hand is still shaking when I pull it down. The note inside reads:

"A prudent question is one-half of wisdom."—Francis Bacon

ELEVEN

On Saturday morning, I wake up to the smell of burnt toast wafting down the hallway. Chris and Mike must be cooking again. They both want to be star chefs someday, but it's taken them two years to master the hot dog. They're sophomores, twin brothers from Michigan. Their mom is bipolar and their dad is in jail. Where will they go if Singer closes?

I drag my butt into the kitchen and Chris sings, a little too brightly, his typical, "Taaaaaa-lan."

I wrinkle my nose. "What'd you scorch today?"

"First batch, yes. But check these out." Chris pulls a tray of gooey, ad-perfect cinnamon buns out of the oven and waves the pan in front of my face. "If at first you don't succeed—"

Mike and I join in, "Try, try again."

It's one of the sayings Singer drills into your head from childhood.

"Dorky," Chris says, "but true."

I reach for the tray and he slaps my hand. "Manners, boy." He scoops me out a piece and watches me devour it.

"Mmmm. Ecstasy," I moan. He beams like I'm Gordon Ramsey. I finish and wipe my fingers on my T-shirt. "That was almost worth getting up for."

"We know." They high five each other.

Marcus, Jake, and Joshua stagger into the kitchen. "Hey, where were you last night?" Marcus asks me. "Did you forget about our workout?"

"Oh man, I'm sorry. I was . . . at the library."

"No. Really." He laughs. "Where were you?"

"The library. Really."

Jake grabs a gallon of milk from the refrigerator and starts guzzling.

"The library? You?" Marcus says. "Why? Is the new *Sports Illustrated* swimsuit edition in? No, can't be. It's fall."

"Ha ha. I was studying."

Jake spits his mouthful across the counter. He starts wiping it up with his sleeve and peers at me. "Okay, spill. Where were you?"

"You were hooking up with someone, weren't you?" Marcus says. "It has to be bad, or you'd tell us. It was Large Marge, wasn't it?"

"No—"

"I bet it was Professor Gaytan," Joshua says. "She's a PILF."

"Shut up, losers." I grab a glass and fill it with water from the sink. "Hey, do you guys know if Laney's up yet?"

Marcus takes the milk jug from Jake. "She's in the family room watching TV." He downs the rest of it and puts the empty container back in the fridge, adding, "Le Douche just came over." He wipes his mouth on his shirt and wiggles his eyebrows at Jake and me. "Maybe they need a chaperone?"

Jake slams the refrigerator door. "Definitely."

The two take off for the family room and I'm right behind them. Picking on LeBeau is sort of a hobby for us.

Jake immediately dives onto the couch between Kollin and Delaney. He shimmies them apart and wraps his arms around their shoulders. "Can I cuddle too?"

Marcus nabs the remote from the armrest before Laney can grab it away. "Give it back!" she snaps.

He tosses it to me, and I switch the channels. The local cable station is replaying one of our football games from last season. "Now *this* is worth watching," I tell them. "This was a great game, and you two blew it off to watch a stupid movie. I had twelve tackles."

"We didn't blow it off. We left during the second half." Kollin sneers. "It was too embarrassing to watch once you were down by thirty."

If I clench my teeth any harder, they'll crack. "What's embarrassing is that shirt." My eyes wander over Kollin's chest. "Did Lady Gaga pick that out for you?"

"Ohhhh, nice one," Jake says.

Kollin looks me up and down. "I'm supposed to take fashion advice from you? The only thing missing from your wardrobe is an empty moonshine bottle."

Laney jumps up and stands between us. "Can you two stop fighting for once and try to—"

I talk over her. "If you're such an expert on looking good, LeBeau, how come I'm the one who's hooked up with every hot girl at this school?"

Kollin's nostrils flare, but he keeps his voice steady. "Because I don't want to hook up with every hot girl."

"Because you can't get a hot girl."

"Because I have the one I want, idiot."

Dang. He's got me there. I start to say something, but Kollin lunges for the remote in my hand. I twist away in time but lose my balance and stumble backward. My feet fly forward and knock Kollin down on top of me. Before I know it, we're rolling on the floor, wrestling and punching each other.

Delaney wedges herself between us, trying to push us apart. "Knock it off!"

Of course, we don't. We roll from side to side, arms flailing and testosterone steaming from our pores. "Stop it!" she screams. "You're gonna hurt each other." She pushes with all her might to separate us, but we outweigh her by two hundred pounds.

She shouts up at Marcus and Jake, "Help me before they get in trouble!"

I get a good blow in before Laney lodges herself between us again. Jake and Marcus only intervene when Kollin's stray punch skims Delaney's cheek.

A second later, a voice booms, "What's going on in here?" Dad Shanahan charges in from the doorway. "Well?" He looks at each of us. When none of us answer, he goes to the one person he knows will always tell the truth. "Delaney, what's this about?"

She doesn't say anything.

"Nothing," I answer, out of breath. "We were goofing around and I fell into the table." I reach down and pick up the remote and a magazine that fell to the floor.

Laney snatches the remote from my hand and flips the channel back to her movie. "Kollin and I were watching TV, that's all. They came in to bug us. They were about to leave. Right, Talan?"

I look from Laney to Kollin to Dad Shanahan. "Right."

"Well, go then," Dad says. "And keep the ruckus down. I have a pile of paperwork and I can't keep running in here to babysit you kids."

"C'mon, guys." Marcus and Jake follow me toward the door. As I pass Kollin, he collapses on the couch, his arms folded across his chest.

———

I'm playing basketball out front later with Mike when I hear Laney and Kollin yelling from the back of the house. He chases her through the side yard and they turn the corner, laughing and wheezing. She stops in her tracks when she sees Mike and me shooting hoops in the driveway.

"Hey, Lane. Hey, Kollin," Mike says. He attempts a failed layup, which he rebounds under the net.

"Hi, Mike," they say in sync. They stare at me with poison eyes, but say nothing.

I grab the ball from Mike's hands and pivot around him. It's so obvious we're ignoring each other that it's awkward. Mike's eyes bounce between Laney and me.

Kollin glides his hand down to Laney's waist. "Well, I'm gonna go."

Laney turns to him. "Okay."

He kisses her forehead and glares at me over her shoulder. Then he ambles off, but stops about ten feet away and glances back. "Hey, Lane?"

"Yeah?"

He smirks at me before telling Laney, "You're hot."

Laney smiles wide until she turns around and catches me rolling my eyes. When my next shot bounces off the rim and lands in the grass next to her, she kicks the ball so hard it ends up in the retention pond across the street. She grins and walks inside.

I rescue the ball and hand it to Mike. "Play without me for a while. I need to talk to Laney."

––––––––––

She's eating ice cream alone in the kitchen when I come in. I'm not about to apologize when her lame boyfriend started the whole fight, but I'll take the high road. We're in this Sevens thing together and there's no time for this now.

I pour a bowl of Cocoa Puffs and pull out the chair next to her. "So what's our next move, you know, with the ... situation. Have you heard anything?"

She shakes her head, avoiding my eyes.

"I've been thinking a lot about it." I shovel a mouthful and swallow it down. "Like, for one thing, if someone really is resurrecting the Sevens, why are we the only ones invited? Shouldn't there be seven of us?"

She doesn't answer.

"And why would they chose me? I mean, you're a brainiac, but why would they want me?"

She crumples her napkin, smushes it into the bowl with her unfinished ice cream, and scoots her chair back.

"I mean, it's not like I—"

Before I finish, Laney leans over and interrupts me. "You're right, Talan." She circles around me to the sink. "I have no idea why anyone in their right mind would want you."

She tosses her bowl and spoon into the dishwasher while I pick my jaw up from the floor. It's the meanest thing I've ever heard her say, and she walks out without a second glance.

Suddenly, I'm not so hungry. I dump my cereal in the sink and wonder why it feels like I'm wearing a concrete shirt. What do I care what the Proud Prude thinks? Only... I do. There's a soreness in my throat and lungs that I can't shake.

"Talan? You okay?" Mike's voice is right next to me, but Laney's is still louder in my head. "Talan?"

"Huh?" I wipe my suddenly sweaty hands on my jeans. "Sorry. I was spacing out."

"You okay?"

"Yeah, I'm just tired. I think I'll lie down."

I show up to dinner dreading Laney's presence.

"Pass the meatloaf," she grumbles to me as I sit down.

I ignore her and start to eat.

"Are you deaf? I asked you to pass me the—"

As she talks, I turn my back on her and ask Marcus, "Hey, do you want to hang with Shannon and Taylor later?"

"Oh, for Pete's sake," Laney snaps. "Whatever."

She reaches around me for the meatloaf at the same time I turn back. My arm bumps the plate, and hot gravy dumps all over my sleeve.

"Ow, that burns!" I jump up, whipping my fork at the table. When it lands, a mound of mashed potatoes splatters all over her. "Dang it, Laney." I try to wipe the gravy off my sleeve with a napkin, but it only makes it worse. "Great. I was going to wear this tonight."

She flicks a glob of potatoes off her face and gives me a look that could sear through me. "Me? What did I do? You bumped into *me*. And then you pummeled me with potatoes." She shoves me hard in the arm. "If you'd handed it to me when I asked … "

Dad Shanahan slams his fist down and we all jump. "What is going on with you two?" he roars.

Laney and I glare at each other and wipe food off ourselves.

"You both knock it off this instant," Mom orders. "If you can't eat civilly, you don't belong at our table."

Heat burns my cheeks. "I'm not good enough to belong anywhere, according to your daughter."

Laney gets up in my face, gritting her teeth like a snarling bulldog. "What are you talking about? You're the one that thinks you're so great. Big party guy—Mister Player. Wow, I'm so impressed by your awesome resume of banging girls and failing classes."

The room gets so quiet, I can hear the blood rushing in my ears. My brain scrambles for words to defend myself, but there aren't any. Maybe because she's right.

Mom's voice hits that octave where you better duck or run. "Delaney Shanahan! That's enough! Get to your room. Now!"

"Fine!" Laney stands up and slams her chair into the table. "I lost my appetite the second he sat down anyhow."

"I don't know what's gotten into you, young lady, but you're now grounded for the evening."

She bolts out the door. "Good! At least I won't have to see him or his big ego!"

I don't have to look up to know everyone is staring at me. I stab at my meatloaf, wishing it was Laney. That's not true. What I wish is that she'd explain why she's treating me like crap. We were getting along so good with all this Sevens stuff. Not sure why that would change now. She's used to Kollin and me fighting. I don't know why this time is anything different.

Why should I care what she thinks anyway? It's not like I want a relationship with Laney, or with any girl. And I never said I was valedictorian material. She's the one who always said I was smart. She said I used my learning disorder as an excuse to play dumb, but I wasn't.

Well, I guess she knows better now.

TWELVE

For the next week, Laney and I do our best to ignore each other. But one Sunday a month, the Shanahans plan an off-campus outing for our "family." Waterparks, mini-golf, that kind of thing. Today, Laney's mom is taking her to look for a dress for the Homecoming dance, so her dad got tickets for the rest of us to catch a baseball game.

We pile into the van around noon to head to the city. As usual, I'm the last one in. When I sit next to Laney in my regular seat, she gets up and moves to the bench behind me.

"What's your problem anyway?" I ask her. "Got your period or something?" She totally hates when I say stuff like that. I face forward and smile even more when I feel her kick the back of my seat.

Hanging with my brothers at the game is a riot, as usual. Even though the Cubs get slaughtered, as usual. My gut twists when I realize that this is my last year for this. It'll be their last year, too, if Singer closes.

After the game, we wait for Mom and Laney outside Macy's. As Laney climbs into the van, her smile dissolves. She ignores me the whole ride home.

Her loss. It's late and I have more important stuff to think about. I have a hundred pages to read in *To Kill a Mockingbird*, which means a good twenty minutes online, skimming over the SparkNotes.

In my room, I flick the lights on and throw my hoodie on my desk, sending a large black envelope flying to the floor. Oh shit.

The Sevens were here.

There's a letter inside, along with something plasticy. It's a report cover—the kind you turn your term papers in or use for a fancy presentation. The clear surface is marked with black dots and dashes. I set it on my bed and read the note:

Second Test—Service:
"The best way to find yourself is to lose yourself
in the service of others."—Mahatma Gandhi

This challenge comes in several parts.
A puzzle in pieces for you.
Each designed to teach as it tests.
The first should be simple to do:
A message in code
Can't be decoded
If you only have half a clue.

It sounds like we're supposed to track down the rest of the clue. My first reaction is to get Laney, but then I remember. Laney doesn't think I'm smart enough to be chosen by the Sevens? Well, screw that. I'll figure it out before she does.

I shove both pieces into my backpack and carry it to the computer room.

The clear sheet covered with dots and dashes… is that Morse code? I google *Morse code* and try to match the shapes with letters, but it doesn't spell anything. In fact, on closer inspection, the marks on the sheet aren't just dashes and dots. They're sloppy squares and scribbles drawn in permanent marker. And now I really don't have any idea what to do.

As I'm thinking about Laney, almost magically she strolls in. She's already changed into her pajamas, her hair pulled back in a ponytail and her face scrubbed clean. She smells like soap and toothpaste.

She hesitates when she sees me, then parks herself at the computer farthest from mine. I decide to be the bigger person. "So," I ask, "did you get the—"

As I'm talking, Juan walks in and plunks his history book on the desk across from us. I slide the sheet into my backpack.

"Huh?" he says.

"I was talking to Laney." I look sidelong at her and carefully ask, "Did you get the… second test?"

Her nose crinkles and she nods slightly.

I choose my words carefully with Juan sitting so close. "I'm putting the puzzle pieces together now. You know. Working out the message."

Her back stiffens. She looks from Juan to me.

"It's pretty tricky. You need any help?" I ask her.

"From you? No."

Something in her tone grates on my last nerve. "I was just being nice. In case you needed help."

"You help me? No thanks, I can do it myself." She signs onto her computer. "You know what they said. Anyone with more than 'half a clue' should be able to get it."

My cheeks and neck flush hot. I clench my fists under the table. I can't believe she's being such a bitch right now.

Juan lifts his eyes at our rising voices. "Are you guys gonna keep talking? 'Cause I have a paper I have to finish."

"No," I say. "I'm done here."

I scoop up my things, stomp back to my room, and fling my backpack on my bed.

So I don't have a clue, huh princess? We'll see who figures it out first.

I pin the plastic cover on my bulletin board and back away, hoping that from a distance, the markings will merge into writing or a symbol. I get nothing. I pull it down and hold the sheet up to the light, looking for something to pop out. I study it from different sides and angles. From the right side, it kinds looks like Scooby Doo. With bunny ears. And no mouth. Great. The Sevens are testing our wisdom and all I have to offer is a mute rabbit-dog detective.

I plop down on the corner of my bed and run my fingers through my hair. After a while, I give up. I need Laney if I'm going to figure this out. The realization makes me furious and depressed.

Mom and Dad are talking to Marcus' mom on speakerphone in their office when I sneak past and down the hallway. I knock on Laney's door.

Inside, I hear a muffled, "What now, Mom?"

"It's me, Lane." When she doesn't answer, I add, "Can we talk?"

She takes her time coming to the door. When she finally cracks it open, I slip in.

"Bold move considering it's past curfew," she says. "What do you want, Talan?"

"You know what I want. I want to know what your deal is. We were getting along great, and now you're being a class-A bitch."

She crosses her arms over her chest. "You're such a jerk."

"What? *What* is your problem?"

"You are. You think you're so much better than me. You ... you just suck." She walks around me and crumples on her bed, her head down.

"I don't think I'm better than you. *You* think you're better than *me*. Like that little comment you made about not knowing why anyone would want me. What was that about?"

"Yeah. You're one to talk." When she lifts her eyes to mine, they're wet. She imitates me: "Hey Kollin, too bad you can't get a hot girl."

I shake my head. "What are you talking about?"

"That one day ... that day you fought with Kollin? You said that. You said to Kollin that you got all the hot girls and he couldn't get any."

My voice goes flat. "Christ, Laney. I wasn't talking about

you." I comb my hand through my hair. "You know you're pretty."

"Pretty unhot, apparently."

"No. Like … cute."

"Oh, shut up. I don't need your approval. Or any guy's. I grew up with a house full of you males. Trust me, you're nothing special. You're always checking out your muscles in the mirror. You fart for entertainment, and you touch yourselves every five minutes to make sure your package is still there. I don't give a care what you think."

I want to laugh about how she can't curse, but I stop myself. "Apparently you do, or you wouldn't be so pissed."

Her mouth forms different vowel shapes, but no words come out. "What I think," she finally stammers, "is I'm sick of you picking on me."

"Oh bull. I don't pick on you."

"Really? You nicknamed me Brainy Laney in middle school. Freshman year, all I heard was how I'd never been kissed. Sophomore year you called me the Proud Prude until Mom made you stop. And how about last year? Constantly riding me about Kollin? Kollin's a great guy, and all you do is rip on him. It's like I'm living with a bully."

"I'm just teasing you."

"And you know what I hate the most?" Her lower lip quivers. "The way you're always calling me nerdling and brainiac, like it's an insult to be smart." Laney's jaw tightens. "Guess what, Michaels? It isn't. I love being smart. You should try it sometime."

"I never knew you felt like this. Hell, you dish out worse all the time."

"Only when you start it. And I'd never say anything if I thought it would really hurt you."

"Neither would I." I lay my hand on her shoulder and she shakes it off. She opens the door and nudges me out. "Go away. Now."

I turn to say something, but she closes the door on me.

Forget it. I tried. I'm done. This is exactly why I don't get involved with girls. I know better than to care.

THIRTEEN

I toss and turn all night, replaying Laney's words in my head. I think of the way her voice broke when she accused me of bullying her, and my skin crawls. I kick the covers off and rearrange my pillow.

She's crazy. I hate bullies. I'm no bully.

By morning, I'm annoyed *and* overtired. I've got to talk to Laney before school or I'll never be able to concentrate. Everyone's at the refrigerator in the kitchen grabbing their lunches but her. Her sack is already gone, and her backpack isn't on her hook.

I look for her at lunch, but she's not sitting with her friends. Kollin is there, but her usual seat next to him is vacant. Marcus is alone at our table when I sit down next to him.

Why am I letting this get to me? It's Laney's fault for overreacting about a stupid remark. It's Laney's fault for making me lose sleep over this. It's Laney's fault for getting worked up over some innocent teasing. It's Laney's fault for...

Damn. Why am I such an ass?

"What's with you?" Marcus asks, crunching on his chips.

"Huh?"

"You're sitting there all pissed, staring at LeBeau like he just screwed your girlfriend."

I snap without thinking, "Laney's *not* my girlfriend!"

Marcus jerks his head back. "No duh." His eyebrows bunch together. "It's an expression. You were staring over at his table like you wanted to kick some ass."

How do I explain this without explaining it? "I just hate the guy, that's all."

"Whatever. Are you gonna eat your chips?" Marcus points at my lunch, sitting untouched on my brown paper bag.

"No. Take 'em."

Dang you, Laney. I stand up and grab my backpack off the floor.

"Where you going, dude?"

"I need to talk to someone." I slide my lunch in front of him. "Here. It's all yours."

"What's with you lately, bro?"

I ignore him and walk out the cafeteria.

———

Delaney is exactly where I guessed she'd be—sitting in Solomon's room a half hour before class starts. She doesn't notice when I walk in. She's staring into a textbook with her eyes frozen on one spot, her mouth drooping at the corners. One finger is unconsciously picking at the corner of the page.

I want to tell her I'm sorry. I want to explain that I'm not the smooth talker everyone thinks I am. I want to admit that I wish I was smart and serious and innocent, like her. That I'd be those things in a heartbeat if I could. But I can't.

I want to say all those things, but what comes out is, "I thought I'd find you here. Are you brushing up on your Ethics and Virtue?"

The second she notices me, her mouth shrinks to a tight line. "Yes. I thought it'd probably be a good idea," she says, "considering I spent half my morning thinking of ways to torture you."

"You spent half your morning thinking about me?"

She grunts and returns to her book.

I park myself in the chair in front of her, straddling it backward.

"What do you want, Talan?"

"I want to talk to you."

She doesn't look up. "Let me guess. You're here to brag that you've solved the puzzle?"

"No." I take a deep breath. "To apologize."

She stops picking at the page and slowly closes the cover of her book.

A knot twists in my gut. "Laney, why didn't you ever tell me you felt that way? About the teasing?"

The edge in her voice disappears. "I have to tell you I don't like being made fun of?"

I lean my face in front of hers until she looks at me. "Yeah, you do. I can't read your mind. You always went along before and dished it right back. I thought, well, I thought it was kind of funny. I figured you did too."

She shakes her head slowly.

"I never meant it mean. I was teasing…like flirting. I do that to all the girls."

"If that's flirting, you suck at it."

"I'm sorry then. But you know I didn't mean to hurt you. God Laney, I hate bullies. You don't know the shit I went through with bullies as a kid. Always calling me retarded because I couldn't read and knocking me around. They made my old school hell for me."

Her tone changes instantly. "I'm sorry."

I hate her pitying me, yet my body warms when her voice goes all tender like that. "Don't be," I joke. "Look how incredibly cool and popular I turned out."

She laughs a little, and it thaws the chill between us.

"Anyhow, things got better once I got to Singer," I say. "From my first night. In fact, I still remember this one kid. He carried my garbage bag of stuff to your mom and dad's house for me. He was huge, like a grown-up. He must have been a junior or senior. He looked down at me at one point and said, 'Don't worry, little man, you'll like it here. Your past doesn't have to dictate your future.' I had no clue what *dictate* meant, but he gave me some of his M&M's, so I figured it was a good thing."

God, I sound like a pussy.

"Of course, I still fantasize about going back and kicking the shit out of those bullies." I wink at her. "But don't tell your parents that. I'd hate for them to think all those child psychology classes were wasted on me."

Laney makes one of those smiles that shows in her eyes. It takes me hostage for a second.

"I'm sorry if I hurt you...forgive me?" I smirk and add, "You know I have to work on my social skills."

It's a joke in our family. When I first came to Singer, I got a ton of counseling for abandonment issues. The Shanahans were constantly working with me on my social skills, until one day I said, "I think my social skills would be better if I could punch some people."

The minute she gives me her lopsided smile, I know we're okay.

"All right, but no more teasing," she says.

"I promise."

She gets quiet again, and her finger returns to flicking the corner of her textbook. "So...have you figured out the message?"

"No. You were right," I say. "I'm not as smart as you."

Wiggly lines appear across her forehead. "I never said that."

"You said you liked being smart and I should try it some time. You also told me you didn't know why anyone would want me."

Her face scrunches. "Geez, you know I only said those things because I was hurt. I've always said you were smart."

"I take ADD meds and get C's."

"You also never open a book. You could pull good grades if you tried."

"I hate reading."

"'Cause it's harder for you. That doesn't mean you're

dumb. I hear how you talk. Your vocabulary is better than most kids in my AP English. There are different kinds of smart, Talan. You have an amazing memory, you're witty, and you think quick under pressure. Me? I'm academic. Give me textbooks and formulas and I can figure out things. Well, some things. I spent hours on that stupid message and couldn't solve it either."

"We should be working together." I move my chair closer and lock eyes with her. "We make a good team."

Her mouth curls into a smile. "Yeah…"

The first bell rings and I move to my regular seat behind her. Jose Aguilar, Kollin, and Emily trickle in first, followed by the Pillars. Assholes. I can barely stand to look at them after witnessing that party.

Professor Solomon shuffles in last, and our classroom becomes a silent movie. We sit perfectly still as he sets his briefcase on the desk and pulls out a notepad.

"Before the Pillars leave for their meeting, I'd like to assign your group projects. While they're due at the end of the term, I'd suggest you begin as early as possible, as they'll account for 70 percent of your grade. Each group is responsible for researching a famous public figure. You will write a ten-page paper, applying the concepts from class to illustrate the impact your subject has had on today's culture and on your lives in particular."

Solomon orders us to move our desks together in a U-shape. Laney slides her chair to my left, and Kollin glides his to her opposite side.

Then Solomon scoots his bifocals down and walks

around the half circle, pairing us and writing our groups in his notebook. "Ms. Mann and Mr. Moore, you will be presenting together. Ms. Kaminski, you'll be with Mr. Kabal. Mr. Hunter and Mr. Robinson..."

When Solomon reaches me, Kollin's face gets tight. It's obvious what's coming. Solomon points to Laney and me. "Ms. Shanahan and Mr. Michaels—you'll be working together. And since we have an odd number of students, you last three"—he points to Kollin, Emily, and Jose—"can collaborate."

Kollin glances to his left. *Weird.* Did he just wink at Emily?

Professor Solomon dismisses the Pillars. A minute later, he starts a lecture on morality. Like Pavlov's dog, I'm instantly dozing.

The classroom phone buzzes me awake.

Solomon listens, nods, and then hangs up and glares at me. "You're wanted for a meeting in the Executive Building, Mr. Michaels." He fills out a pass and shuffles over with it. "You'll be out for the whole period."

Decent.

I hop up and head for the door.

"You might want to pick up some coffee on your way," Solomon mutters.

As I trek across campus, I realize that I've never known of any students except the Pillars being called to the Executive Building. Is this another Sevens thing? But then Laney would've been called too. My arms and legs tingle with nervous energy.

The Executive Building is one of the oldest buildings on campus, all red brick and ivy outside. I'm surprised when the lobby inside is completely different. It's 100 percent modern, with touch-screens and abstract sculptures scattered around what I'm guessing are incredibly uncomfortable sofas. An uptight guy in a blue suit mans the reception desk, which stretches in front of the door like a *do not enter* sign. He's busy typing something into a computer and ignoring me.

I knock on the countertop. "Excuse me. I'm here for a meeting? My name is Talan Michaels."

He gives me the once-over and mutters something to himself. Then he taps something on his keyboard and perks up. His eyebrows lift and he straightens in his padded seat. "My apologies, sir," he mumbles. "He's expecting you. Right this way."

I follow him past a waterfall and glass elevator to a huge wooden door. He opens it for me like I'm the friggin' president. Am I supposed to tip him or something? He rushes away and I slip in and look around.

A fancy wood desk sits at one end of the room with two empty seats in front of it. It's all modern and glassy in here, too, except for a huge leather chair on the opposite side of the desk, which is turned away to face out the window. My heartbeat accelerates as it slowly swivels around.

"Mr. Michaels. So nice of you to join me."

What? Stephen Kane? This can't be Sevens business. What's Kane doing here? Shouldn't he be off partying with the Pillars or something?

Kane stands and thrusts out his hand for me to shake.

I shove my fists in my pockets and do my best to hide the confusion that's lobbing around inside my head.

"Why am I here?" I ask.

He points to the chair next to me and waves me to sit. "I believe we may have gotten off on the wrong foot. I'm hoping we can rectify that."

I sit, leaning forward on the edge of my seat. I don't plan on staying long. "I have no idea what you're talking about."

Kane glides into his seat and regards me with eyes that say *don't mess with me*. "You don't like me much, do you, Mr. Michaels?"

"I don't even know you, Mr. Kane. But I would like to know why you called me out of class to come here."

He leans back in his chair and steeples his fingers. "Did you know that I considered you for the Pillars?"

My stomach lurches. Is that supposed to be a compliment? "I'm hardly Pillar material."

"Oh, I think you are. In fact, I remember reading your student records and thinking how much we had in common. Did you know I was abandoned like you? My father deserted me, just like yours. And my mom? She makes yours look like Mother of the Year." His eyes zero in on mine. "She was a simple woman. It didn't take much to make her happy. Belts, sticks..." He shows me the scars on his hands. "Scalding water."

Kane rests his arms on his desk. "My uncle removed me from my home and brought me to Singer. You see, we're similar creatures, you and I. We were both abandoned and dumped here. And we both learned to look out for ourselves. I wonder if you don't agree?"

The comment bothers me more than I can explain.

"What I'm wondering," I say, "is how you got access to my personal files when I didn't apply to be a Pillar. I'm sure that's against some privacy rule or something."

"I've learned to get around the rules. Another thing we have in common, I think."

"Is there a point to this autobiography?"

"Just that we're alike, you and I." Kane flashes that confident grin. "See, I'm not so bad, Mr. Michaels. I survived a painful childhood, just like you. I worked hard and turned out very successful. Like you, I learned to take care of myself. Does that sound familiar?"

It sickens me how familiar it sounds, but there's no way I'm admitting that. "No, not really. I need to get back to class. Can you can tell me what you want so we can get this over with?"

He leans forward, lacing his fingers together. "I can be blunt too, Talan. I believe you have information I might need."

I play dumb, which isn't hard because I have no freaking clue what he's talking about. "What information?"

He stares deep in my eyes. "Let's just say that I was told you have information that can be used against me."

"You were told wrong. I have no idea what you're talking about." I stand up and push my chair back.

"If you're lying, I can make your life very hard."

It makes me laugh. "Yeah, well, my life has always been hard, as you know from reading my file."

"I can also make your life very easy."

"Like I said, I have no idea what information you're talking about. So I guess I'll be taking care of myself."

As I head to the door, Kane raises his voice behind me. "But can you take care of your friends, Talan? Because if you cross me, I assure you that I can make their lives harder too."

I push the door open without looking back. There's no way I'm turning around. No way. Because if I turn around, Kane will see that he actually scared me with that last threat.

FOURTEEN

After football practice, I find Laney tapping away at a keyboard in the computer room.

"Good, you're here. I need to talk to you." I quietly close the door. "Remember how I got called out of Solomon's class today?"

She nods, but her eyes remain on the screen.

"Stephen Kane called me into his office for a meeting."

Her head jerks up. "Oh my God. What did he want?"

I park myself sideways in the chair next to her. "He said he heard I had some info that could be used against him." There's no way I'm telling her the part where he said I was Pillar material.

"What info?" Her head tilts. "You mean all that stuff we heard at their party?"

"I don't think so. That's probably going to be common knowledge eventually."

"About bribing the Pillars?"

"They'd just deny it. They're all liars, like him."

Laney's eyebrows lift. "Do you think he knows about the Sevens?"

"I'm not sure. I told him I didn't know what he was taking about. Then he threatened me and I left."

"What?" Her voice cracks. "He threatened you?"

"Well, kind of. He said he could make my life hard or make trouble for my friends if I crossed him."

Laney leans back in her chair. Her eyes look huge against her pale face.

"Don't worry, Kane's all talk," I say. "I just wanted you to know."

She gnaws her thumbnail as her eyes drift back to her computer.

I lean around her to see what she's staring at. "What are you doing?"

"Working on the clue. I've tried every method on the Internet to decode it: ciphers; substitution methods; even frequency analysis. I still can't make sense of it."

"Translate to English please."

She points at the screen. "I'm keying the first row of characters into Google to see if anything comes up."

"Still lost. What are you talking about?"

"The clue from the Sevens. I swear, you have the attention span of a drunk ferret. I'm typing in the first row of characters exactly as it's written on the paper. I know it's a long shot, but I've tried everything else."

I scrunch my eyes and read the screen over her shoulder.

A piece of paper lies next to the keyboard covered with some kind of gibberish. On the screen, the same kind of random letters, numbers, and symbols stretch across the search field.

I shake my head. "My message from the Sevens didn't have letters and numbers like that."

Laney's head twists around. "You didn't get a poem about a challenge coming in parts like puzzle pieces?"

"Yeah, I got that. But it didn't have rows of letters and numbers on it."

She sits back in her chair and lifts the paper next to the keyboard. "The second page did."

"I didn't get a second page. I got a plastic thing with black marks on it."

"So our clues were different?" she says. "Were we supposed to put them together?"

A light bulb goes on in my head. "A message in code, that can't be decoded..."

Laney finishes my sentence: "If you only have half a clue."

"Duh! I'll be right back with *my* half clue." I hop up and bolt for the door.

I charge down the hall, but Mom Shanahan waylays me before I make it to my room. "It's suppertime. Can you call everyone for me?"

I lap the house, knocking on doors and giving the two-minute dinner warning.

On my way back around, Chris stops me outside the computer room. "Did you hear about the statue?"

"What statue?"

"The statue of William Singer outside the school gate. Someone smashed it in the middle of the night."

"Smashed it? What do you mean?"

"Like, took a sledgehammer or something and smashed the head off. Then they spray-painted sevens around the base."

"What?" My legs grow wobbly.

"You know. Sevens. Like the number '7.' They wrote it on all four sides of the base. I heard Boyle was pissed. He has Security all over it. He said it's an automatic expulsion when he finds out who did it."

"But who would do that? Who would have anything against William Singer?" I ask.

"And sign it with sevens," Chris says. "Is that supposed to be funny? What's that about?"

"Talan!" Mom yells from the kitchen. "Did you call everyone for dinner?"

Chris veers around me as I answer her: "I'll be right there! I still need to get Laney."

I duck into the computer room, but Laney is already on her way out. "I just heard. About the statue and dinner. We'll have to finish this later—how's Founders Hall at seven?"

I nod. "Ready for another mystery, Dr. Watson?"

"Sure," she says. "Except I think I should be Sherlock and you should be Watson."

"I want to be Sherlock."

"We'll talk about it later, Watson."

"Whatever, Watson."

FIFTEEN

The wind picks up a handful of leaves and whips them into the corners of the quad. They fly around like ghosts chasing each other. Maybe it's the gloomy October sky or the way the quad is empty tonight, but something feels creepy.

I'm all alone, but I hear footsteps echo mine. I stop to throw my Barbecue Ruffles bag out and they stop. I rush past Headmaster Boyle's office window and they speed up. But when I look around, all I see are the shadows of the buildings stretching across the walkways.

It happens again when I reach the Visitors Center. I spin around fast enough to see a figure dart behind the maintenance building. He's dressed completely in black, from the hoodie pulled up around his face to his dress shoes. *Dress shoes?*

If someone is following me, I need to lose them before I meet Laney. I duck inside the Visitors Center and hide in a stall in the restroom.

My heart thrashes against my ribs when the bathroom door creaks open. I watch through the crack in the stall door, holding my breath. Whoever it is lingers by the sinks. Underneath the side wall, I see black penny loafers shining in the fluorescent lighting.

A gloved hand dips down, slides an object into my stall, and disappears. I jump away, banging into the other wall.

Heart racing, I fumble with the lock and sprint out just as the restroom door closes. I tear into the lobby, but black-hoodie-and-penny-loafer guy has vanished. I take a few steps toward the door and—

Damn. I left my backpack in the bathroom. My backpack with the clues from the Sevens in it. I race inside, and it's still right where I left it.

When I lift it, something rolls at my feet—the object that penny-loafer guy slipped under the wall. My heart hammers in my ears as I bend down to pick it up.

A crinkled piece of paper is Scotch-taped around a softball-sized object. Loose pieces rattle inside the package. There's writing on the paper, so I carefully peel off the tape. Inside it are large, cream-colored fragments of a broken shell or something. I start to assemble them together until it becomes obvious what they are. *A human skull.*

My hands shake so hard I set the pieces down before I drop them. Someone's written my name on the outside of the paper. I flip it over and read:

THE SEVENS ARE DEAD AND BURIED.
KEEP YOUR MOUTH SHUT OR YOU WILL BE, TOO.

SIXTEEN

Laney glares at me from a bench outside Founders Hall, tapping her foot as I approach. "Late as usual. I've been—"

I ignore her and rush inside, ducking down the first hallway.

She appears a moment later. "What the heck?"

I peer out into the atrium to make sure we're alone. "Laney, I was followed coming here."

"What?"

"I tried to lose them. I ducked into a john at the Visitors Center. Whoever it was slid this"—I dig into the backpack and fish out the skull—"under the door."

"Gross!" She jumps back at first. Then she creeps forward and pokes it. "Is that real?"

"I think so. And this was taped around it." I hold out the note.

She reads the paper and flips it over. Her lip trembles when she says, "Do you think it's from Kane?"

"It was someone a lot skinnier than Kane. From the clothes, I'd say it was a student, but I couldn't see his face under his hoodie. He was wearing a black jeans, and get this—black penny loafers. All shiny and stiff like they were new. "

"It was a Pillar."

"How do you know?"

"I heard Zack bragging today. They all got new clothes and shoes over the weekend. Kane apparently took them on a shopping spree. Who else would have new dress shoes around here?"

My brain is buzzing. "Yeah, but how would the Pillars know about the Sevens?"

"I'm not sure," she says. "Maybe we were careless with a clue or missed something. Did we leave a note or invitation somewhere they'd see it?"

"I don't know. We've been pretty careful. Unless. Maybe—"

"Maybe what?"

"Ah, crap!"

"What?"

"When I first got the invitation to join the Sevens, I thought it was a prank. Remember? I told you I thought the Pillars were trying to make fools of us?"

"So?"

"Well…" My voice lowers. "I might have said something to Cameron Moore."

Her face goes slack. "You might have or you did?"

I lean my back against the wall. "I did."

"Oh my God, Tal! What were you thinking?" She

drops to the floor and runs her hands through her hair. "What did you tell him?"

"Give me a second to think here." I slide down the wall to the ground next to her. "I remember telling him he fucked with the wrong person. I blurted something out about the Sevens and him messing with me. Then I stormed back inside so Boyle wouldn't catch me out of detention."

"Dang it! Dangitdangitdangdangit! We're screwed!"

Five *dang its* and a *screwed*. The girl is worked up.

"Don't panic. I couldn't have said anything important, I didn't know anything about the Sevens then, much less you being part of it. They're probably feeling me out, just in case. In fact"—I grab the letter to show her—"your name isn't even on here. It's only addressed to me, so they probably don't know about 'us' at all."

"This is getting complicated. First the vandalism to Mr. Singer's monument, and now this? Maybe you should lay low for a while." Laney fingers the crushed skull in my hand. "We're dealing with some seriously messed-up people."

"We knew that going in. The Sevens warned us in the invitation."

"Still," she says. "If they don't suspect me and they're watching you, maybe I should take it from here."

"No way. You think I'm letting Kane and the Pillars bully me? Screw that. We'll be more careful, that's all. We'll just double-check if we're being watched, avoid each other in public, hide our clues—"

"The clue!" she cuts me off. "Come on, we still have to share half-clues." She stands up and peeks around the corner before sliding the envelope out of her backpack. She pulls out the same cover letter I have, along with the other paper with the random letters and symbols. I dig out my marked-up report cover and slide her page inside it.

Words instantly appear through the plastic sheet as blocks of characters are hidden under the black marks. The uncovered letters pop out, forming phrases and sentences.

"Success!"

"Finally! What a relief. Okay, how about if I read the words and you jot them down?" She pulls out a spiral notebook and pen and hands them to me.

For the next twenty minutes, I transcribe as Laney reads the words that emerge from the unshadowed letters. We fiddle with the spacing and punctuation for a while. When we're done, we've got another poem:

AT FOUNDERS HALL, LET THE HUNT BEGIN,
YOUR LESSON STARTS THE MOMENT YOU'RE IN.
LOOK FOR A TRUTH HIDDEN INSIDE A LIE,
IT'S A WARNING YOU OUGHT TO KNOW—
EIGHT LETTERS SPELL IT OUT
      IF YOU
CHECK THE COLUMN ALONG WITH THE ROW.
    —OH—
& LAST BUT NOT LEAST,
FOR LATER...A CLUE:
SEVENS ARE BRED TO BE LOYAL AND TRUE.
YOUR FOUNDER WAS WISE...INDEED.
ARE YOU?

"Man, there's a warning in here, too." I sigh.

"I know. Let's check it out."

The two of us tiptoe into the atrium, quietly peeking down the vacant hallways that extend from it. When I'm convinced no one is lurking anywhere, I let out a breath that could fill a balloon.

We spin around like synchronized swimmers, mesmerized by architecture and artwork I hardly ever noticed before. We occasionally have meetings and assemblies at Founders Hall, but this late in the evening it looks totally different. A cloudy night blackens the atrium windows, coloring the place with gray shadows. The lights in the adjacent corridors and meeting rooms are turned off. Darkness reaches out from every doorway I pass.

There are secrets here, I'm sure of it. Laney stares at every wall as if a hidden passageway is about to pop out at us.

As I circle back to the front door, my eyes are drawn up to the dome ceiling. Laney walks over and stands next to me. She lifts the sheet and reads the first clue. "It says, 'Your lesson starts the moment you're in.'"

My eyes dart around, searching for an envelope or message somewhere obvious.

"Keep reading," I tell her.

She holds the notebook close and whispers, "Look for a truth hidden inside a lie, it's a warning you ought to know—eight letters spell it out if you check the column along with the row."

Decorative columns stand at the entrance of each hallway, but there's nothing written on or near them.

Our eyes catch on the ceiling above us. The seven virtues that Solomon taught us are painted around the top of the atrium, circling the base of the dome.

"Is that it?" I ask. "Are they saying the virtues are a lie?"

"There's a lot more than eight letters up there, and there isn't anything written on the columns. Let's keep looking. We need to check everything with letters and words. And we should split up," Laney adds. "I'll take the art on the walls. You search the architecture."

She looks over each painting, print, and photograph, including the brass plates that name the piece and artist. At the same time, I'm inspecting every column, wall, and sculpture for anything with writing.

After a while, my brain surrenders. "There's nothing that makes sense with that clue."

"Keep looking," she says, studying a painting nearby. "It's here. We just have to find it."

Frustrated, I trudge back to the main door to start fresh. A plaque by the entrance dedicates the building to Mary Singer. I skim over the words and letters again.

"Laney!"

She races over before I even lift my head.

"*The lesson starts from the moment you're in.* Here it is. Just like the clue said."

I point out the plaque and she reads the inscription:

THE SINGER BOARD OF DIRECTORS, WITH RESPECT AND AFFECTION,
HEREBY DEDICATE FOUNDERS HALL TO MARY HARPER SINGER.
ERECTED TO HONOR HER LIFETIME OF SERVICE TO UNDERPRIVILEGED
YOUTH. SHE REMAINS AN INSPIRATION FOR HER UNYIELDING DEDICATION,
LOVING DEVOTION, AND UNSELFISH EFFORTS FOR OUR STUDENTS.
IN MEMORY OF OUR COFOUNDER, MARY HARPER SINGER, WHO REMAINS
EVER IN OUR HEARTS.
DEDICATED ON THIS DATE, THE 7TH OF JULY, 1995.

She shrugs. "I don't get it. What am I missing?"

"Put it together with the other clue. It said: *eight letters spell it out if you check the column along with the row.* You have to read the column of letters going down." I point to the first letter in each row on the dedication.

"T-H-E-Y-L-I-E-D," she says. Then she gasps. "Oh my God!"

She stares at the plaque for a minute before turning back to me, wide-eyed. "*They lied.* Wow ... He must have been really angry at them to write that here."

"Now *I* don't get it," I say. "Who put that message on the plaque?"

"William Singer, of course. Founders Hall was Mr. Singer's pet project after his wife died. They taught us all about it when I gave those parent tours for Student Council last year. After his wife died, he devoted himself to Founders Hall and expanding the school in her honor. Some say he was totally obsessed with the project."

I shrug. "Okay, so Singer worded the plaque and hid the message. But who was he saying lied?"

"Well, if you read it 'along with the rows,' then it refers to the Board of Directors."

"What'd they lie about?"

Her shoulders lift. "I think he's calling them hypocrites, but I'm not sure why. That wasn't exactly in the script for the parent tours."

"What are you two doing here?" The voice makes both of us jump.

When we spin around, Kollin is standing five feet behind us.

Laney stutters, "We were, we were … "

"We were researching our Ethics project," I tell him. "We decided to write about William Singer. This place is loaded with history on him."

His voice lightens. "Oh."

"What are you doing here?" Laney asks.

Emily comes in the front door right then and stops in her tracks. She stares at Kollin and then marches past like she didn't notice any of us. Kollin follows her with his eyes. She crosses the atrium and walks straight out the back door.

Kollin's face is red as a rash when he turns back to Laney.

"That was weird," I say.

Laney shakes her head and shrugs. "So anyway," she says, "what are *you* doing here?"

Kollin rubs the back of his neck. "I … the same thing as you. I'm here to get ideas for my presentation. Maybe we'll do Mary Singer."

The three of us stand there saying nothing. It's more awkward than a sixth grade dance.

"Well, I guess we're done then," I tell them. "I'll leave you two alone."

"No, I gotta go too." Kollin glances toward the back exit. "I'll see you tomorrow, Lane." He kisses her quick and jogs across the rotunda.

When the back door clacks shut, I move alongside Laney. "That was strange. He just got here and he's leaving? And did you see how he and Emily looked at each other? What was that about?"

Laney brushes past me toward the front door. "You don't know what you're talking about."

I follow her outside. "They looked like they—"

She turns and says through gritted teeth, "I know what you're implying. Kollin wouldn't cheat on me with Emily Dombrose."

Laney's pissed. Again. Time for another dose of damage control. "Of course not."

She ignores me and walks faster, her hands balled into fists at her sides.

I tag along beside her. "Only the dumbest guy in the world would risk losing you."

The creases in her brow evaporate. "You're such a BS-er."

"No I'm not."

"Really?" Her head cocks to one side as she imitates my voice. "We're here because we're working on our Ethics project for Solomon's class. We're doing it on William Singer."

"Well, that was different. That was to save my ass."

"Same reason you're BS-ing me now." She dismisses me with a wave of her hand and continues walking. "Just drop it."

My brain scrambles to think of a way to keep her talking.

I nudge her with my elbow. "Hey, did I ever tell you how I got this last envelope from the Sevens?" She avoids my eyes, focusing on the windows of the buildings we pass. "It was in my room when we got back from the city."

She stops cold and turns slowly to face me. "What?"

"The envelope was in my bedroom after we got home Sunday."

"How'd it get in your room? Do you think one of the guys put it there?" Her jaw drops. "Oh crap. Maybe you were right all along. Maybe this is some elaborate prank." Her eyes skip around to check if we're being watched.

"No way. I stopped believing that a long time ago. I don't know a single person that'd know enough to mastermind all this."

We start to walk again. Her eyes are locked on the sidewalk, but the way she's chomping her bottom lip tells me she's worried.

"In fact, it's *definitely* not someone in our house," I reassure her. "I was the last one out to the van and the first one back to my room when we got home. It couldn't have been left by someone in our house. It has to be someone outside our family."

She lifts her eyes and says in a low voice, "Then how'd they get into your room?"

I wouldn't admit this to her, but I spent last night with one eye open, wondering the same thing. "I don't know. My window was locked, but maybe someone left another one open. Or maybe your parents forgot to lock the back door."

"I guess." She nibbles her nail. "My envelope was in the

student council mailbox. It was locked up in the office when I went to pick up the tickets for the homecoming dance."

The look on her face makes me wonder if she just got the same chill I did.

"Whoever is behind this has access to a lot of places, and they know a lot of secrets about our school." She twists her shaking hands together into a knot of fingers.

I joke to lighten her mood. "Maybe it's the ghost of William Singer trying to resurrect the Sevens. Maybe he haunts the tunnels trying to punish the Sevens for murdering him."

"For crying out loud," Laney snaps at me, "the Sevens didn't murder William Singer! When are you going to get that through your head?"

"Relax, Laney. I was kidding. But you know, until we know for sure what's going on, we have to be cautious. I know you've convinced yourself that the Sevens were innocent, but there was a police investigation that declared them murderers."

"No, it didn't. That's just part of the urban legend. No charges were ever filed."

"Because the killers were dead."

"It was never more than a theory. Trust me, I've read every article ever written on it. Money was missing, and there was circumstantial evidence and anonymous tips that blamed the Sevens. It doesn't mean anything. The Sevens were set up. The police were mistaken." Her nose wrinkles. "Or to quote our founder, maybe 'they lied.'"

Laney trudges on, her gaze stretching a mile away. "Do you think Professor Solomon could be behind this?"

"Solomon? Why Solomon?"

"I realized something when I was reading the atrium ceiling. The Society of Seven is testing us on the virtues that Solomon drilled us on that first day. Like with our first test, where we uncovered the truth about Kane? That test was titled *Courage*. This test was labeled *Service*. It's also pretty obvious that Solomon doesn't like them or Kane."

"Solomon doesn't like anyone."

"Think about it. Solomon's been around a long time, and he said Singer was a good friend of his. He's also got access to passes, and he's probably one of the few people smart enough to pull this off."

"Maybe. It was Solomon who suggested Boyle put me in his Ethics and Virtues class. Maybe he wanted to teach us this stuff together. Or keep an eye on us or something. But if it is Solomon, why wouldn't he just take us aside and tell us what he knows and what he wants from us?"

"Isn't it obvious? He needs to know he can trust us first. He could get fired for this. Everyone already wonders why he hasn't retired yet; Singer School is probably all he has."

I consider it for a second. "Do you think we should ask him if he's behind this? Maybe we should tell him we figured it out."

"No way!" she says, cutting through the yard to the back of our house. "If we're wrong, we'd screw ourselves. And even if we were sure, we couldn't say anything to him. You remember what the invitation said. We committed to a vow of secrecy. We can't break that, no matter what. He has to reveal himself to us."

We reach our back door and Laney peeks through the window. "It's clear."

"Damn, I just thought of something," I say.

Her hand freezes on the door knob. "What?"

"Now I'm going to have to pay attention in class."

SEVENTEEN

Thursday night, I'm scrounging through the kitchen for a snack. I start a bag of popcorn in the microwave and think back to the message hidden on the plaque in Founder's Hall. What was old man Singer trying to tell us?

The microwave buzzes and Joshua yells from the next room, "Talan?"

"In here." I pull out the bag and tear it open. "What do you want?"

"Phone call."

I carry my snack and backpack to the private phone booth and take the phone from Josh. I tuck the receiver between my ear and neck and step inside the small space, closing the door while juggling everything. "Hello?"

"Look. Under. The. Doormat."

I freeze. The caller sounds like Darth Vader with a stutter. "Uh, excuse me?"

When the voice repeats, "Under. The. Doormat," I realize that the caller is speaking through a voice changer, like you see in the movies and TV shows.

The phone shakes in my hand. "Who is this?"

"Number Seven," he answers, and hangs up.

I almost drop my popcorn. For a couple seconds, I forget how to breathe. Getting notes is one thing—it's impersonal and distant. But hearing a live voice gives me the willies. It didn't sound like Solomon either, even with a voice changer. Who would even have access to a voice changer? I know there's probably a cell phone app for that, but students aren't allowed cell phones at Singer. *Except for the Pillars.* Is this another clue from the Sevens, or another threat from Kane and his little tribe of scumbags?

Laney strolls past the window in the door of the phone booth, and I swing it open to catch her.

"Careful!" She swerves around me. "You almost nailed me."

"Laney!"

She must recognize the fear on my face because she hightails it back toward me.

I show her the phone in my shaking hand. "He called."

"Who?"

I stare at the receiver in my hand. "He called himself Number Seven—the same name that was on the email."

Her eyebrows shoot up. She takes the phone from me and hangs it up. Then she grabs my wrist and tows me down the empty hall. "What did he say?" she whispers. "What did he want?"

"Umm." I close my eyes to focus. "He said, 'Look under the doormat.'"

I open my eyes in time to see Laney jogging to the front foyer. "Wait," I tell her. "We can't be sure this isn't a trick from Kane or the Pillars. Just to be careful, I better get it."

She hesitates, then nods.

I peer down the empty halls that connect to the entryway, then grab a black envelope from under the doormat on the porch and start to bolt to my room.

"Wait," she says, "I want to see too. We're a team, remember?"

"Fine. Let's find a private place."

I follow Laney around the house looking for somewhere we can be alone. Mom Shanahan is in the kitchen now, and of course she's sitting in a chair that has a perfect view of Laney's bedroom. Dad is in his office, two doors down from my room, and Jake's using the computer room. Chris and Marcus are playing video games in the family room. Mike is folding clothes in the laundry room, and Juan and Joshua are playing pool in the basement. After canvassing the entire house, we're back where we started, standing in the hall outside the bathroom.

I like my family, but there's never any privacy. The only place you're ever alone is the shower. I look at Laney and consider it for a second. My thoughts drift and I feel myself flush.

Laney throws her hands in the air. "I give up. Where are we supposed to read this?"

I nod my head toward the bathroom door.

"What?"

I nod at the door a couple more times.

"The bathroom?"

I lift an eyebrow. "Got a better idea?"

Laney sighs and looks around. She glances down at the envelope hanging out my hoodie pocket and slowly tiptoes into the bathroom. I lock the door behind us.

This is the main bathroom all us guys share. It's basically a locker room with rows of sinks and stalls, a bench, and a huge mirror on one wall.

Laney looks around and whispers, "I've always wondered what it looks like in here."

I wiggle my eyebrows. "Want me to show you how the showers work?"

Laney rolls her eyes and yanks the letter from my pocket. She spends a minute going over it. "It's another clue from the Sevens."

I look over her shoulder. "How can you be sure?"

"The writing is the same. Plus, they've all come in the same black envelope."

She holds the note between us and leans into me so we can read it together. I get distracted when a lock of her soft hair brushes against my cheek. I can smell her lavender lotion again. Her body is snuggled against me, and I keep thinking how the showers are only a few feet away. I can't help but stare at her mouth as she reads to herself. Her lips are full and red and her breath smells like peppermint.

She glances up and startles me. "What do you think?"

I haven't read a single word of it. I open my mouth but I can't think of an answer to BS my way out of this one.

She waits for a response, but all I can do is stare back. Our bodies are pressed together. Our mouths are just inches apart. If I dip my face forward just slightly, I could taste that peppermint myself. I've done this move a hundred times before, but right now I'm frozen with fear.

The next few seconds pass in slow motion. She blinks her dark lashes at me and I watch the corners of her mouth curl up. With any other girl, I'd read that as an invitation. But Laney isn't any other girl. One stupid move screws up everything. Still, the peppermint draws me an inch closer.

Laney doesn't flinch. She's staring up with her big doe eyes when I finally decide it's now or never. But the moment I tilt my head down toward hers, she turns back to the letter. My nose grazes her hair and I jerk my head away, twisting it around like I was stretching my neck.

"Looks like we'll be back at Founders Hall tomorrow," she says.

Unable to form words, I nod.

"You've got the homecoming game at night. Should we meet after school?"

More nodding.

She hands me the paper and unlocks the door with a loud click that echoes in the bathroom and my brain. My shaking hands fold the note and stuff it in my pocket. Laney opens the door and steps into the hall.

Just when I'm thinking my life can't get any more complicated, I rush out behind her...and run smack into Mom Shanahan.

EIGHTEEN

It's the mother of all gasps.

Mom jumps back, her expression contorting into all kinds of shock and worry. She stares open-mouthed at me, wearing the second-most-horrified face since the existence of mankind.

I'm pretty sure I've snagged the prize for first.

"Oh-oh-oh-oh," Mom stutters, her voice getting louder with each *oh*. She waves her pointer finger between Laney and me.

"What?" Laney says.

Mom's eyes draw tight, probably to hold in all the steam coming from her ears. "Don't you 'What?' me, Delaney Shanahan," she says through locked teeth. "What were you doing in the boy's bathroom with Talan?"

In a BS answer that makes me look like an amateur, Laney says, "I thought I heard someone crying in there when I walked by. I knocked on the door but no one answered, so I went in to check."

Mom's eyes travel back and forth between us like they're collecting data for some lie-detector program in her brain. "What would Talan be crying about?"

My eyes roam the ceiling looking for an excuse. Fortunately, Laney's got this.

"He just got dumped, Mom. It's private. Geez, Mrs. Nosy. Do you mind?"

Mom studies my face with slitted eyes. "It doesn't look like he was crying to me."

"Don't be ridiculous. What other reason would I have to be in the bathroom with Talan?"

"You're two teenagers with normal hormones?"

"Mom, gross! He's like my brother." She fake gags and casually walks away.

Mom stands in the middle of the hall shaking her head, her arms folded across her chest. Laney sounded pretty convincing, but there's no reason to stand here and give Mom more reasons to doubt us. Playing heartbroken, I bow my head and shuffle into my room.

The minute the door shuts, I crash on my bed and cover my face with my pillow. Thank God I didn't kiss her. Her words sting my brain: "Gross! He's like my brother."

It plays over and over like a recurring nightmare. According to Laney, we're trapped inside the black hole of just-friends.

I bend the pillow behind my neck and pull out the Sevens note to take my mind off it.

Third Test—Compassion:

"Be kind, for everyone you meet is
fighting a hard battle."—Plato

> *More secrets abound*
> *Where the last one was found.*
> *Be wise. Memorize*
> *all you learn in this game.*
> *For riddles and half-clues*
> *Will come up again.*
>
> *A pediment proverb*
> *is your next clue.*
> *Your founder was wise...indeed.*
> *Are you?*

Laney's right. The first two lines of the poem send us right back to Founders Hall. And it's the same two closing lines from the riddle we just solved. Outside of that, I got nothing.

————

I'm buttering toast in the kitchen the next morning when Laney walks up. She stands next to me and pops in two slices for herself. She whispers, "Were you impressed with my quick thinking yesterday? Mom totally bought it." She smirks at me. "I could have a career as a double agent."

I actually still feel kind of crappy about the whole thing. "Oh yeah, you're a real badass."

Her face pinches. "What are you all pouty about?"

"Nothing." I bite off a chunk of toast and swallow it down hard.

"Tell me. We're partners, remember? We shouldn't have secrets."

"No." I take another mouthful and turn my back to her.

She grabs my arm and spins me around. "What is it? Did I do something? Share, Michaels."

I lean back against the counter and cross my arms. "I'm a guy. Guys don't share."

"Guys don't share, huh?" Her sigh sounds like a groan. "Listen, I don't want another fight. We need each other. If you're upset about something, just say it."

I stretch my arm to the counter next to her. "You want me to say it? Fine. I didn't like how you called me *gross* to your mom yesterday. There, I said it. You happy now? I'm growing ovaries."

Laney throws her hands in the air. "It was a fib—so she wouldn't think we were going at it in the bathroom. Of course I don't think you're gross." Her arms fall to her sides. "I can't believe you'd be so sensitive about that, considering how conceited you are."

What an insult. She just called me sensitive.

"I'm sorry, but I can't have you risking my reputation with slurs like that." I toss my backpack over my shoulder and swagger out the door to school.

Behind me, Laney mumbles, "Like I said…"

———

The rest of my day drags like it's trapped behind a crossing gate, waiting for a mile-long train full of *boring* to pass. Everything moves slower than Solomon's lecture on purity until 3:00 p.m., when I can finally meet Laney at Founders Hall. She's waiting near the door when I get there.

Laney's jaw drops.

"What?" I check my fly.

"You're on time." She snickers. "Were we supposed to meet at noon or something?"

"Funny." I walk past her, hiding my smile, and push open the double doors.

"Did you bring the clue?" she asks.

"Of course. Do you think I'm an idiot?" I dig inside my backpack, praying I remembered to pack it. *Score.* I yank it out and hand it to her.

She does some visual reconnaissance before she unfolds the note and begins reading: "More secrets abound where the last one was found."

We're standing by the plaque in the atrium, exactly where we found the message yesterday. We pivot around, scanning the space for envelopes or anything obvious. *Nothing.*

Laney lifts the sheet and continues reading, "Be wise. Memorize all you learn in this game. For riddles and half-clues will come up again...A pediment proverb is your next clue."

The space between her eyes crinkles. "Do you know what a pediment is?"

"It's the triangular space above a window or entrance," I say, all casual. "It's usually part of the gable of the roof. A lot of times, it's decorated and stuff."

"Oh." She seems impressed. I'm totally glad I memorized all that until she tilts her head and asks, "Did you look that up?"

"Umm, well, yeah."

"It's a good thing, because I thought a pediment was some kind of stone."

The atrium is a dome, but the ceiling above the entrance slopes down. We quickly locate the pediment above us, directly over the front doors. The mural painted inside the triangular space depicts different Singer School landmarks. A sentence stretches across the bottom: *THE SECRET TO LIVING A WORTHWHILE LIFE IS REVEALED BY MAKING A POSITIVE DIFFERENCE IN THE LIVES OF OTHERS.*

"That must be our pediment proverb," I say.

"Talan, I think I know this one!" Laney squints while she thinks. "I remember reading those same words somewhere recently—*living a worthwhile life.*"

Her eyes flash open. "Last night. When we were in here looking for letters to go with that second clue." She bites her thumbnail and slowly spins around, surveying the atrium walls. Then she drops her hand and charges to the opposite end of the room.

When I catch up, she's bent over slightly, examining an engraved plate underneath a painting on the wall. She points out the painting's title to me—*Living a Worthwhile Life*. I take a step back to study the picture.

It's a scene with Mary Singer lifting a small girl onto a horse. They're both in riding clothes, and Mrs. Singer has three prize ribbons attached to the lapels of her jacket. A large trophy sits on the ground by her feet.

"What's with the ribbons and trophy?" I say.

"Mary Singer was a champion equestrian."

"I know, but what would she need those for when she's teaching a kid to ride a horse?"

Laney scratches her forehead and stares at the trophy. "Aside from her husband, Mary Singer's two passions were horses and children. Maybe Mr. Singer was trying to show that. The nameplate underneath says he commissioned the picture after her death."

I look over my shoulder and read the pediment proverb out loud again. "The secret to living a worthwhile life is revealed by making a positive difference in the lives of others." I turn back and see Laney running her fingertips over the portrait.

"So there's a secret in here, huh, Mr. Singer?" she says. She leans close, tracing her fingers over every detail on the canvas. Her eyes scour every color and brushstroke. I stand back to see if I notice anything from a distance.

"Here it is! I got it!" Laney jumps up and pulls me toward the lower right corner. She points at the artist's signature in the corner:

Maryalways Woreahelmet

She inhales sharply. "Mary always wore a helmet."

Damn, it's not a name at all. I lift my eyes and there it is—a helmet on Mary and one on the little girl. "Why would it say that?"

"I don't know," she answers, "but the nameplate says

the artist was Tomas Vasquez. That's definitely not the autograph for Tomas Vasquez."

"But what would that have to do with the pediment proverb? Read the clue again."

She lifts the paper and recites, "Be wise. Memorize all you learn from this game. For riddles and half-clues will come up again."

I rub the stubble on my chin. "Maybe this picture is only half a clue. We sort of learned our lesson on that when we had to combine our separate envelopes to figure out the last message. Maybe the Sevens are telling us that these clues will be coming in pairs, too."

"You know, I think you're right. That's brilliant, Tal." Laney drifts toward the center of the room. "The letter said 'more secrets abound where the last one was found,' so the other half-clue must be around here somewhere." Her eyes skim the walls as she turns in a circle. "Maybe it has something to do with a column again."

"What did you say?" I shake my head and hit my ear like I didn't hear her.

She moves closer and repeats, "I said there's gotta be a half-clue in here, somewhere. Maybe in another column of writing or something."

"No, not that." I cup my hand behind my ear. "I missed what you said about me being brilliant."

Her lips purse in a way that tells me I'm getting to her. "Brilliant," she says, with a glint in her eyes, "and yet idiotic at the same time. I guess you're multitalented, Michaels."

"First you call me brilliant, and now I'm multitalented? I'm blushing from all your flattery."

Laney rolls her eyes and walks away. She follows the wall around the atrium, her gaze traveling up and down and back to the paper in her hand. I head in the opposite direction to cover more ground.

A few feet away from the painting of Mary Singer is a large, framed photo of the Singer Board of Directors. Their clothes and hairstyles make it look like it's the 1980s. I gaze at the grumpy faces of the board members and wonder what Mr. Singer meant by *they lied*.

The mat around the photograph has a rectangular cutout centered at the bottom. I crouch down to read the writing:

MAKING A POSITIVE DIFFERENCE IN THE LIVES OF OTHERS.

The Singer Enterprises Mission Statement:
Our purpose is to create value and superior energy products to benefit our customers, employees, and investors, while giving back to the community by investing in schools, individuals, and organizations that improve our world.

"Hey Laney, come here!" I wave her over. "It's time for me to show off more of my genius."

She comes over to where I'm half-kneeling on the floor. "Finally figure out how to tie your shoe?"

"You're just jealous because I found this first." I press my finger on the glass over the phrase *MAKING A POSITIVE DIFFERENCE IN THE LIVES OF OTHERS.* "It's the exact same phrase as in the pediment proverb."

Her face lights up when she reads it. "Oh, wow. The wording is identical." She lays her hand on the glass and stares into the photograph like she's spying on the board members through a one-way mirror. "The secret to a worthwhile life is revealed by making a positive difference in the lives of others," she recites. "That's got to mean that the secret to *that* painting is hidden in *this* picture."

Together, we inspect every inch of the photograph.

"Wait. What's this?" I point to tiny gold letters that angle up slightly in the bottom right corner. "It's the same gold color as in *Maryalways Woreahelmet,* but the letters are small and faded. It says … Numbers 35:17."

"I don't get it. What's Numbers 35:17 supposed to mean?"

"No idea," I answer. "Unless … don't artists sometimes number their pictures?"

"In fine art," she says. "Like when you're printing limited editions of stuff. But not for a photo like this. But I'm sure it means something—that's the same gold ink."

I waver between the two pictures and think out loud. "The secret of *Mary always wore a helmet*"—I turn my attention to the photograph of the Board—"is revealed by *Numbers 35:17.*"

"Is there anything in or near these pictures with the numbers 35 or 17?" Laney asks.

We search around a bit, but there aren't any numbers anywhere. I glance at the clock. "Lane, we're out of time. I need to eat and get ready for my game."

"Keep thinking about it," she says. "We'll brainstorm tomorrow, before the dance. Singer definitely hid messages, and someone wants us to find them."

NINETEEN

The next afternoon, Coach lets us out late from films and I dash home to talk to Delaney. I walk into the kitchen and Juan says, "Good game last night."

"Thanks." I pour a bowl of Frosted Flakes and poke my head into the family room. *Empty.* "Have you seen Laney?"

"Kollin is treating her to a mini-makeover for the homecoming dance. The cosmetology students are doing a fundraiser for the Vocational Department."

Kollin. Laney may think LeBeau's so great, but the Sevens chose *me.* That feels almost as good as the look on her face when I showed her the clue in the Board of Directors photograph.

The whole time I'm showering and shaving, I'm focusing on the clues, trying to come up with something else I can impress her with. Unfortunately, all the Adderall in the world can't help me translate *Numbers 35:17* by myself.

I plunk down in a chair in the study, sign onto a computer, and google *Numbers 35:17.*

And gentlemen, we have a winner. All ten results on the first page point to the same thing—a verse from the Bible:

Numbers 35:17 If anyone is holding a stone and strikes someone a fatal blow with it, that person is a murderer; murderers should be put to death.

Holy shit.

Let me think. William Singer died in a fire following a blow to the head. But that can't be it, because the half-clues were left by Mr. Singer before he was murdered. Also, the half-clue from the pediment proverb linked this verse to the phrase *Mary always wore a helmet.*

When it finally dawns on me, I jump up so fast that I nail my leg on the underside of the desk. I bend over, groaning and limping around in agony and ecstasy at the same time, because I now understand what Mr. Singer so desperately wanted someone to know. Pain burns my thigh and knee, but I don't even care. I can't wait to tell Laney.

I hobble through the halls and knock on her door to see if she's back yet. Adrenaline and excitement have my heart racing.

She answers, "Just a sec."

I'm totally pumped to tell her what I figured out when she opens her door and...

Laney stands there in a short, clingy red dress. Her brown hair hangs in soft curls over her bare shoulders and her doe eyes are widened even more by whatever makeover magic they performed on her. I can't remember how to talk when she says, "What's up?"

I can't even remember what I came for because, well... hello... tight red dress.

I don't want them to... I tell them not to... I practically scream *don't you dare*... but my eyes refuse to listen to my brain. They trace a path from her spiky heels up her ridiculously long legs, over every curve and inch of thin material covering her, up, up, up, slowly riding the waves of her body with my eyes until they finally stall at the deep red lipstick on her mouth. My legs get wobbly and my body grows warm.

"What's the matter with you? You're as red as a tomato. Have you been drinking, Talan?"

She knows she looks good. I can tell by the smile crinkles at the corners of her lips and eyes. She gently sways her hips forward and back so the bottom of her dress wraps around her thighs, revealing even more leg. She plays with a lock of her hair and asks, "Do I look all right? Brandy Compton did my makeup."

When she brushes something off the top of her dress, I don't dare look. I might never speak again. I stare at her plump cherry lips instead and imagine us kissing. Getting red lipstick on my mouth and collar and neck and—

Laney interrupts my fantasy. "Mom hates it, of course," she says. "She thinks it's way too much makeup for me." She leans over to fix a strap on her heels and my eyes wander. They bungee back into their sockets the moment she straightens up again. "I thought they did a good job. Kollin said I looked beautiful."

Kollin. Damn. That's right. Laney is Kollin's girl. Those are Kollin's lips to kiss, and Kollin's lipstick to fantasize about.

Suddenly, I hate how amazing she looks.

She raises her eyebrows and smiles. "Well come on, what do you think?"

My words slip out thoughtless and stupid. "You're … you're wearing too much makeup."

Her smile flatlines and her eyes go from flirty to moist. She slowly lifts her hand and touches her mouth with her fingers. She stares at me like I just fed her stuffed dolphin to a hungry shark. I want to take it back. I would if I could, but I can't. I need to leave. Now, before I say something even more stupid.

I drop my head and walk out of her room.

TWENTY

This dance sucks.

Taylor spent the entire dinner identifying the calorie content of every piece of food on our table. Which is only slightly more boring than the list she recited of physical activities she'd have to perform to burn off said calories. Who would have guessed it would take her an hour and fifteen minutes of Zumba to burn off the calories in the double chocolate layer cake they served for dessert? Not me.

Who cares? *Definitely* not me.

Everyone else is done and gone from the table, and Taylor's still finishing her salad. Maybe if she'd stop calorie-obsessing and eat faster, we could dance off the lettuce and cucumber she's been nibbling on for the last half hour.

She waves her fork in front of me. "Do you know why I chew this cherry tomato twenty times before I swallow it?"

"Because you're so skinny, if you swallowed it whole, you'd look pregnant?"

She giggles and says, "No. But thanks for the compliment."

Be nice, don't roll your eyes, Michaels.

She finishes, "It's because if you chew each bite twenty times, it makes the food more digestible. And by eating slower, you also burn more calories and eat less."

I snatch her plate of forbidden cake and cut off a huge forkful, shoving it in my mouth. "Really?" I say with my mouth full.

"Yep. I read that on the Internet."

I try not to choke as I swallow it down. I lean back and search the dance floor. Laney is slow dancing with Kollin, laughing and talking over his shoulder at some of her friends.

"You want to dance?" I ask Taylor.

"In twenty minutes. It's best to let the digestive enzymes break down the fat molecules before you begin your exercise."

Taylor seemed a lot more interesting last time I saw her. Of course, her mouth was attached to mine and she wasn't talking then.

When I look again, Laney and Kollin separate. Kollin heads toward the refreshment table and Laney walks out the door into the hallway where the restrooms are.

I jump up. "I need to use the bathroom," I tell Taylor. "You stay here and ... digest."

She doesn't even nod. She's too focused on counting her chews. I trot around the tables and into the corridor in time to see Laney enter the bathroom. My brain scrambles to think of a way to explain why I keep impersonating an asshole whenever she's around. I'm staring at my shoes and pacing outside the bathroom when Laney walks out.

"Can't decide which restroom to use?" Her sexy, cherry-colored lips have shrunk to a blood-red dash mark.

Her mouth opens, but words come out of mine first. "You look beautiful, Laney."

Her head tilts. She's running my words through her bullshit detector.

"You really do. I swear." I hate how timid my voice sounds, but I can't seem to locate my testosterone. "I only said that thing before, the thing about the makeup, because … because I didn't want you to get in trouble with your mom." I fake a smile as phony as Kollin.

Her eyes narrow, but she doesn't say anything.

"Listen," I tell her. "That whole thing came out stupid. I'm sorry." I'm rubbing my sweaty palms together so frantically, if I had some hand soap I could lather the whole hallway. "I just wanted to tell you that. I know I joke around easy enough, but I never seem to say the serious stuff right." I look at the ground. "Like how great you look."

I shove my hands in my pockets before I chafe them raw.

When I glance up, Laney's face is relaxed with a full smile again. Her left eyebrow lifts. "God, you're good." She shakes her head and laughs. "No wonder you get all the hot girls. Lines like that make *even me* all tingly." Nodding, she regards me skeptically. "You know, Michaels, if you decide to go to college, you could major in sweet-talking."

Okay. Not the reaction I wanted, but at least she's not mad anymore.

She circles around me to leave and I catch her elbow. "Wait." I don't want to be done talking to her. I don't want her to go back to Kollin, and me to go back to Taylor, and for her and me to spend the rest of the night *not* being together.

"I ... I solved the riddle," I blurt out.

"What?"

"Numbers 35:17. I figured it out."

"You did?" I have her undivided attention now. "What's it mean?"

"I googled it this afternoon and—"

"There you are!" Kollin's voice calls from the end of the hall.

Laney's back is to Kollin, but it's obvious she recognizes his voice. She scrunches her face with annoyance. I know she's disappointed about not being able to talk about the Sevens and it has nothing to do with me, but it gives me a little thrill. We share a private connection that Kollin will never be part of.

She mouths *Later* and walks off to join him.

I watch as he throws an arm around her shoulder, glaring back at me. He whispers something in her ear.

Her response slices through me: "We bumped into each other, that's all. Give me a little credit. It's Talan."

I get why she said it. And the thing is, I've said the same kind of thing about a few girls myself. But her words ... they cut me like a razor.

TWENTY-ONE

I'm waiting for Laney at the island in the kitchen, eating a bowl of cereal, when Marcus strolls in with his tie in his hand and a grin on his face.

"Dude," he says. "Where were you? You and Taylor left so early, you missed the excitement. Or were you two busy making your own excitement?" He wiggles his eyebrows.

"Uh, yeah," I mumble. "We just wanted to get out of there after a while. What'd I miss?"

"The police showed up."

"Boyle found the vodka Vanessa smuggled from her home visit?"

"No. Listen to this." He pulls up a chair next to me and I sigh inside. Marcus is my best friend, but he can stretch a simple story into a two-hour documentary. "Someone dug up a grave in the Rucker Road cemetery. Security called the police, and they came to find Boyle."

"What?" Suddenly I remember the skull that's sitting in my backpack. "Do they know who did it?"

"They think it was a student, or a group of students. Shannon went outside to get some fresh air and overheard the whole thing. One of the cops told Boyle that *remains* were stolen!"

I'm sweating, and I don't know why. I can see the spoon shake in my hand. So does Marcus, apparently.

"I know, right? It's sick," he says.

"Why do they think it was a student? That end of campus has no fence. A townie could have done it."

"Yeah, here's the creepiest part. Someone spray-painted the side of the mausoleum. They wrote *the Sevens are back* in red letters."

My stomach feels like Marcus kicked it with his cleats. "What?"

"I know. Freaky, huh?" He hops up and shoves his chair in. "Gotta go. I'm gonna see if Jake heard."

My hands are numb. Actually, my whole body is numb. I stand up and shake my arms out, pacing back in forth in front of the sink. None of this makes sense. If the Sevens wanted to remain a secret, why would they do that? It had to be Kane and the Pillars. They just wanted it to *look* like the Sevens.

Where the hell is Laney?

I dump my cereal in the sink and take off for my room. I lock the door and dig through my backpack, lifting out the skull fragments. I've got to ditch them somewhere fast.

I spot the floor vent by my bed, lift it out, and drop the bones inside, sliding the cover back in place. Then, back to the kitchen to wash my hands and wait.

Damn it, Shanahan. Where are you? *Please be okay.*

I'm standing at the sink scrubbing my hands for the hundredth time when Laney finally strolls in, humming.

"Best. Dance. Ever," she says.

I bend back to make sure we're alone and say, "It's one in the morning. Did you forget we have a curfew?"

She checks the clock. "It's not even 12:30. And I got an extension because Student Council had to stay late."

"An extended curfew, huh? Oh yeah, that's fair."

Laney slides out of her pumps and tosses them by the door. "What do you mean, *fair*?" She bends her leg up and rubs one of her heels. "I was cleaning up. What do you care, anyhow?"

"I don't." I check the hall to make sure we're alone. "I just figured you'd want to talk about the grave robbing. I'm sort of surprised you couldn't pull yourself away from Kollin for five minutes so we could talk about the Sevens." I slump back against the counter. "Are you committed to this or not, Shanahan?"

"Pull *myself* away? I *did* go looking for you, but you left early. With Taylor. What was I supposed to do? Scour the bushes and alleys? Follow your bread-crumb trail of discarded clothes to track down whatever closet you two were hooking up in?"

"I left early," I snap, "to come home. I told Taylor I was feeling sick. I assumed you'd come home early too, so we could finish our conversation about the clue. It's called sacrifice. It's one of the seven virtues, if you remember."

"Well, if you'd told me that's what you were doing,

maybe I would have come home. It's called communication, if *you* remember... Wait a minute." Her head shakes. "What did you say before? Did you say grave robbing?"

"You didn't hear about it?"

"Hear what?"

"Someone dug up a grave in the old cemetery and stole 'remains.' Then they spray-painted *the Sevens are back* on the side of the mausoleum."

She pauses to take it all in, sliding into a chair. "The Sevens wouldn't do that." Her eyes widen. "But the Pillars would. That's where they got the skull they threatened you with. They must be trying to frame the Sevens... Or you."

"No duh."

"What if they're trying to set you up? You're already on thin ice with Headmaster Boyle. Maybe you should drop out of the Sevens before you get expelled."

"I'm not quitting. We agreed we're a team. Until the end."

"Then we've got to solve these clues faster. We have to figure out how to help the Sevens before something worse happens to you." She hops up and moves a foot in front of me. "What were you trying to tell me earlier?"

"Laney, I figured it out. *Numbers 35:17* is a Bible verse. It says that if a person strikes someone with a stone and kills them, they're a murderer. I combined it with the half clue *Mary always wore a helmet* and figured out what Mr. Singer was trying to say."

"What?"

"Think about it. Mary supposedly died from a head injury during a horse-riding accident. That painting showed all those awards to remind us she was an expert rider. An expert rider who also wore a helmet all the time. My guess is her body was found without it, and Singer had reasons to suspect her injury wasn't an accident. I think Singer was saying that his wife was murdered. If, like the last poem said, we 'memorize all we learn in this game,' I'm guessing the murderer was someone on the Singer Board of Directors."

"Wow." She lifts her eyes to mine. "Talan. Wow!" She tackles me in a hug like I just made the game-winning play. When she pulls back, our eyes lock.

Her hands slide to the top of my shoulders. Her excited smile slowly relaxes into a strange grin and her gaze travels down to my mouth.

My head is swimming from the closeness of her.

There's a look in her eyes. I know this look, I think. Laney leans closer, slowly, then closer. I definitely know this move. Instantly, she freezes.

Her eyes widen and she leans to the right to look behind me. Not a second later, Mom Shanahan appears at my side.

She's staring at Laney's hands on both sides of my neck.

Laney looks from her mother to her hands and back to me. She pats my chest awkwardly. "Th-that's great that you made up with Taylor. I'm happy that everything's better with you two." Her arms drop and she sidesteps me. "Hey, Mom."

Mom's face is starched with suspicion.

"Well, it's been a long day and I'm exhausted." Laney kisses her mother on the cheek. "See you guys tomorrow."

Laney and I duck out opposite doors, leaving her mom standing there with her mouth open like a hungry bird.

TWENTY-TWO

I lie in bed, staring at the ceiling and dissecting the almost-kiss. What the hell is wrong with me? I've hooked up with a hundred girls at this school and I'm worked up over one almost-kiss? I roll over, punching the pillow into a different position.

I've got to be losing it. I'm crushing on Delaney Shanahan? The Proud Prude? The master at annoying me?

I toss and turn all night. By 6:00 a.m., I quit trying to sleep. Might as well not waste all this thinking on a girl. I haul a heaping bowl of cereal to the computer room and start researching the murder of Mary Singer. The articles all say that Mary's body was found without a helmet, although no one seemed to make a big deal out of it. I swallow my last Froot Loop and check my email before logging off. My pulse accelerates when a message pops up:

To: tmichaels56@Singer.edu
From: Number 7

The next clue is *around*
where the last one was found.

Be wise. Utilize
all these lessons you learn,
for *columns* and *riddles* are there to discern.
Just be sure to do right
When it is your turn.

I've got bad news and GOOD NEWS
for your next clue.
Your founder was wise…indeed.
Are you?

Laney is still sleeping, but I'm too excited to wait for her. I jot a note on my napkin and slide it under her door:

CHECK EMAIL. MEET YOU THERE.

I bundle into my coat and bury my head deep inside my hood, blowing warm breath on my hands as I cross campus. The sky is dark and overcast. Naked trees tremble in the wind, while campus is barer than their branches.

When I get to Founders Hall, I head straight into the rotunda. A sleepy-looking custodian eyes me as he empties a garbage can, but no one else is stupid enough to be up this early on a Sunday. I check my watch like I'm meeting someone and mosey around the perimeter until I end up at the photograph of the Board of Directors.

Finally, the custodian pushes his cart through the door, and it slams behind him. I pull out my printout of the email and review the first part:

> The next clue is *around*
> where the last one was found.

I'm standing between the painting of Mary Singer and the photo of the Singer Board of Directors. Okay, Number Seven, or whatever your name is, I'm back where the last clue was found. Is there something "around" this picture you want me to see?

My eyes circle the frames and the wall around the pictures, but nothing stands out. After a couple minutes, I give up and skip down to the next section of the email:

> Be wise. Utilize
> all these lessons you learn,
> for *columns* and *riddles* are there to discern.
> Just be sure to do right
> when it is your turn.

Okay. Think, Talan. The first part is easy—we need to use what we've learned so far from all these tests. But what does *be sure to do right when it is my turn* mean?

So what *have* we learned so far from these tests? My memory rewinds through our challenges—the messages hidden in the pictures... the half-clue poem that appeared when the letters were blacked out... the pediment proverb... the secret in the dedication plaque... all the way back to the first left-right-left poem that led us through the Singer underground.

The instant my brain makes the connection, energy buzzes through my body. I'm bouncing on the balls of my feet, looking at the doorway a few feet down from where I stand.

Be sure to do right, when it is your turn. Like that very first poem, this one is also a play on words; it's directing me to go *right* at that *turn.*

I turn right down the hallway and skim over the last section of the poem.

> I've got bad news and GOOD NEWS
> for your next clue.
> Your founder was wise… indeed.
> Are you?

Tucking the paper in my coat pocket, I scan the walls, floors and ceilings of the hallway, examining everything from the outlets to the fire extinguisher.

And finally … there it is—a framed newspaper article on the construction of Founders Hall. The paper is yellowed with age, but the title is clear as a billboard: *GOOD NEWS FOR SINGER ENTERPRISES MEANS GOOD NEWS FOR SINGER STUDENTS.*

I've got bad news and GOOD NEWS was my next clue. I guess I just found the good news.

I engross myself in the article, reading every letter and word, leaning forward until my nose almost touches the glass.

"Boo!" My heart detonates at the voice in my ear. I swing around, fist clenched and jaw set.

Delaney jumps back, her hands in the air. "I'm unarmed.

Relax." She laughs and steps around me. "So what's up, Watson?"

My heart thunders under my sweatshirt. I cross my arms. "*Watson?* Please. While you were sleeping in with your stuffed dolphin, I was already up researching Mary Singer's obituary and solving the next riddle." I repeat myself from last night. "It's called sacrifice. It's one of the seven virtues, if you remember."

"Yeah, whatever." Laney rubs her hands together. "So I got the email. What'd you figure out?"

I peek out the end of the hallway, turn, and smile at her.

"I figured out that 'do right when it's my turn' meant I was supposed to turn right into this corridor. And the clue about 'bad news and good news' has something to do with this." I point to the news article on the wall behind me. "I'm not sure about the 'bad news' part, but this pretty much nails the 'good news.'"

Laney reads the title over twice and a grin swells across her face. "Nice work."

"You mean 'Nice work, Sherlock,' don't you?"

She rolls her eyes. "You haven't solved this one yet. You said yourself that you still need to figure out what the bad news is."

While she pouts, I lean in close to the glass and skim the article once more, running my finger under the rows of writing as I read them. *And there it is.*

"Found it," I say. "Better luck next time, Watson."

Laney hip-checks me out of the way and studies the picture. "Where? What is it?"

"Laney, 'check the column along with the row.' Just like the earlier clue."

GOOD NEWS FOR SINGER ENTERPRISES MEANS GOOD NEWS FOR SINGER STUDENTS

When William and Mary Singer decided to help underprivileged and at-risk children attain an excellent education in a secure setting, they never imagined the joy they'd receive back.

During an interview, Mr. Singer said, "Mary and I overwhelmingly felt that helping these fine young men and women would ultimately be our greatest achievement in life. What we didn't understand is how much we'd grow to love them."

During the past decade, Singer School has grown to over five times the original enrollment. "My late wife would be amazed at all we've accomplished—her dream was to provide a nurturing and safe environment for as many children as possible. This new phase of construction allows us to do just that."

Years ago, Singer School struggled to house just over 400 students. An increase in funding is being used to construct new homes and classrooms, renovate old buildings, and hire additional staff.

Funding for these projects was generated due to the amazing success of Singer Enterprises worldwide. Mr. Singer credits this exceptional growth to savvy investments and sound managerial strategies laid out by the Singer Board of Directors. "Next year promises to be even better," Singer stated.

Despite his remarkable success, Singer warns that exceptional earnings bring their own share of problems. He said, "There is good and evil in everything. The important thing is to consider the needs of everyone involved and make careful decisions that provide for the best long-term scenario."

One building project in particular has been near and dear to William Singer's heart. Just yesterday, crews started phase two of construction on Founders Hall and Auditorium, which will ultimately include a museum of school history, rotunda, and auditorium.

Expected completion of Founders Hall is fall of next year. "My goal is for this project to provide an everlasting tribute in memory of Mary Singer, my late wife. She loved this school and the children in it. I believe Founders Hall will become an essential part of our school community, providing a sense of pride, identity, purpose, and spirit."

Laney runs her finger down the first letter in each row and sounds out the message. *"What do you do when your family depends on your enemies?"*

Her mouth falls open and she shuffles back a step. One hand rises to her parted lips as the other spreads like a fan across her breastbone. "Oh my God."

I stare at the words in amazement and think back to the

hidden tunnel. "Remember the message the Sevens left on the elevator door? *A prudent question is one half of wisdom* or something? Do you think this is the prudent question they were referring to?"

She glances at me and flashes me a grin. "What I think is that you have a wicked good memory."

The back of my neck grows warm, and it spreads to my ears and cheeks.

I turn back to the article. "But this news story contradicts what we've been told about the Board being murderers and liars," I say. "Singer is quoted saying good things—that they made smart decisions that paid for the growth of the campus and student body, two things that were important to him and his wife."

"They could be brilliant businessmen and still be liars and murderers," Laney says. "I think that's what he means when he says 'his family depends on his enemies.' He's asking what was he supposed to do? Our school and the kids he considered his family depended on the very people he suspected of killing his wife."

"Wouldn't he be so angry that he wouldn't care? I mean, he thinks they killed his wife, who he obviously loved a lot. We're talking about murder here."

"Unless he couldn't prove it," she says. "Or he wasn't sure which of them was behind it. It's not like he could fire an entire Board of Directors, especially one that's that been so successful, based on a hunch or circumstantial evidence like his wife not wearing a helmet. I don't know much about business, but I'd imagine that could ruin a company's reputation and the value of its stock. Which basically means our school would be ruined too, since we're completely funded by Singer Enterprises. I'm guessing Mr. Singer needed to be dang sure he could prove who murdered his wife before he acted on it."

"I can't imagine having to play normal around the scumbags who murdered the woman I loved. But I guess his school, *her* school, *was* on the line. What a shitty position to be put in. But you're right. If there was *obvious* evidence of foul play, the police would have gotten involved. Everyone always assumed Mary Singer died from a riding accident."

Laney's eyes travel from the article to me. "So I wonder how Singer answered his prudent question then? What *do* you do when your family depends on your enemies to survive?"

I smile down at her. "You form a secret society of students to protect them."

The hallway echoes with the sound of the door opening in the rotunda.

Laney whispers, "I guess we're done for now. I'll go out the front door and you wait a few minutes and leave through the back."

I nod and we hightail it in opposite directions.

The minute I step outside, a voice stops me cold. "You there. Michaels. Not so fast."

I'd know that annoying bark anywhere. I spin around and Headmaster Boyle glowers at me. The small boy standing next to him shrinks back a step.

"What are you doing at Founders Hall this time of the morning?" Boyle asks.

I flash him a bright smile to match my halo. "Research for a paper, sir."

"Homework? You? At this hour of the day? And I suppose you want to sell me the marshland on South Rucker Road, too?"

No, but I wouldn't mind drowning you in it. "I don't know what you mean, sir."

"I mean, you're probably looking for trouble. Fortunately for you, I'm about to change all that." Boyle puts his hand on the shoulder of the boy cowering next to him. "This," Boyle says, "is Jack Dominguez."

He's a cute kid, a bit scruffy with huge eyes and a tight-lipped frown. He's wearing oversized cowboy boots and his right hand clings to a Woody doll from that *Toy Story* movie.

"Hey, Jack."

"You live in Canfield House, correct?" Boyle asks me. I nod and he says, "Jack is a new student moving into the Hampton House today. I need you to drop him off for me. I just got a call and his houseparents are handling a discipline emergency. I would do it myself, but I have a meeting in the Executive Building in five minutes."

It's not that I don't like kids. I just don't know any. Don't know what they like or how they think or even if we share the same vocabulary.

"I can't," I tell Boyle. "I have to—"

"No, Mr. Michaels," he interrupts. "The only thing you *have* to do is what I tell you to do. Now take Jack straight to Hampton House. I'll call and let them know to expect you in fifteen minutes. Don't leave him until his houseparents dismiss you. Do I make myself clear?"

"Yes, sir," I say through gritted teeth.

Boyle nudges Jack between the shoulder blades and he takes a couple tentative steps toward me.

"Good luck, Jack," he says before leaving the two of us alone, staring at each other.

"Well, come on then," I tell the kid.

Clutching Woody in one hand, Jack drags his beat-up cowboy suitcase in the other. When he nears me, I notice his lower lip quivering.

"Here, let me get that, buddy." I reach down and grab the luggage. "By the way, I'm Talan."

I give him my hand to shake, but he just stands there, clutching Woody to his chest and staring at my fingers. His sad puppy eyes are welling up.

Damn you, Headmaster Boyle.

The way he tries to blink his tears away makes my shoulders slump. I reach my hand down and gently take hold of his. "Is this okay?" I ask him. "I like to hold hands with my new friends."

He nods, clenching his trembling lips.

"C'mon. Don't do that, kid. You'll be okay." I tug him forward by the hand.

Struggling in his boots, he takes three steps for every one of mine. I walk super slow, watching his eyes survey the streets like he's landed on an alien planet. We make it to the corner and he tucks his chin down. I can't hear a peep, but I know he's crying by the way his tiny shoulders bob up and down.

Awww, geez.

He pulls his arm away and hides his face in his hands. I kneel down and reach for him, unsure what to do next. I pat his back with awkward little taps, feeling useless until he falls weeping into my chest. His skinny arms wrap around my ribs and his shaking body melts onto mine. My arms bundle him while he sobs into my shoulder. Snot and tears soak my hoodie, but I couldn't give a damn. I'd give anything to make him feel better right now.

At this moment, I understand why the Shanahans do what they do. And why William and Mary Singer founded this school. Why Coach Gaspari pumps up even the suckiest players and why my counselor refuses to give up on me. People gotta look out for one another.

I'm clearly hanging with Laney too much.

Jack's breathing settles after a couple minutes, and he lifts his head.

"You feeling better, little man?"

He wipes his runny nose with his sleeve and nods.

"Here, hop up." I turn my back to him. "I'm gonna give you a real Talan Michaels horseyback ride all the way to your new house."

He climbs up and once I have him good, I grab the luggage and gallop all the way down Mill Street to Homestead Drive. When we get to his house, I set the suitcase down and slide him off carefully.

I crouch next to him and point at Hampton House. "This is your new home, Jack."

He looks at it the same way I look at a dark, cramped closet. His hand slips back into mine and holds on for dear life.

"Can I tell you a secret?" I whisper. "Mr. and Mrs. Foster are the nicest, coolest houseparents here. I promise. You're going to have so much fun, so don't be scared. Okay?"

He nods and I walk him to the porch. The door opens and Mrs. Foster steps out. "Hi Talan, thanks for bringing him." She bends down with a huge smile. "Hi Jack. We've been waiting for you. All the kids are so excited to meet you." She holds out her hand for him, but he cowers behind my leg.

He looks up at me and squeezes my fingers even tighter.

I kneel beside him. "It'll be okay. I promised, didn't I? You're gonna like it here." I point across the street. "Now, you see that house with the bright red door?"

Jack leans around me.

"That's where I live. We're brothers now, so if you ask your housemother, you can come over whenever you want and hang with me. Okay?"

He nods.

"Anytime you feel scared or lonely, you get your butt over and ring my bell. Got it?" He giggles at the word *butt*.

Jack finally lets go of my hand and takes Mrs. Foster's. She grabs the suitcase from me, and Jack steps through the doorway with big clunky steps.

"Hey, Jack?" I say. He looks over his shoulder at me. "Your past won't dictate your future." His forehead grows lines like I said it in Chinese. "It means you're gonna be happy here. Just give it a chance and let people help you."

TWENTY-THREE

As I walk in the front door, Dad breezes by with a bucket of tools in his hand. "Talan, your friends are waiting for you in your room."

"Who?" I ask, yanking my hoodie over my head.

As he heads for the garage, he calls back, "Zack Hunter and Cameron Something-or-other."

The hairs on my neck stand up. I turn, and Laney is watching me from the family room. She frowns and lifts her palms in a *what's up* gesture. I shrug, trudge to my room, and slowly open the door.

Zack stretches back on my bed, while Cameron stares at a poster on my wall. When he notices me, Cam says, "I didn't know you liked the Broken Popes. I can get you tickets and an off-campus pass for their April concert if you're interested."

I toss my hoodie on my bed. "What do you want, Cameron?"

"Why don't you close the door so we can talk?"

When I go to shut the door, I notice Laney standing in the hall outside, listening. I keep it open just a crack.

"Mind getting up?" I ask Zack. "That's my only comforter. I'd hate to have to burn it."

His lip snarls and he starts to say something when Cameron waves him to stop. Zack stands up and I notice something. "Nice penny loafers."

"They're Cole Haans," he says, all cocky.

"Well, you should give them back. She might need them for the sock hop."

Zack lunges forward, but Cameron's arm flies up to stop him. "It's a designer, Tal."

I interrupt him. "I know who he is. I was making fun of Zack." I look them both up and down. "New North Face jackets too? Did you rob the Executive Building?"

"They were a gift," Cameron says. "From Mr. Kane."

"Oh. A gift. Is that what you call selling out for money?" I get comfortable on my bed, lying back and bending my arms behind my neck. "Why don't you tell me what you want so I can get back to sleep."

"Mr. Kane has a message: If you can't beat us, join us."

I sit up. "I can beat you? Awesome. Let me grab my bat."

Cameron's dying to let me have it, but he can't. I can see it in his eyes. It's not self-control that's holding him back. It's Stephen Kane. "Let me ask you something," he says. "Have you heard about the damage the Sevens did around campus?"

"The Sevens didn't do that," I snap.

"How would you know?" Zack says.

"I don't. It's just a hunch, but it seems more like something a group of six douchebags might do."

Zack clenches his fist. "You really should be more afraid."

"Afraid of what? You?" I laugh. "You're the ones who should be scared."

"We don't have a thing to worry about."

"Oh, I think you have a few things. Seven, to be exact."

"So there is a Society of Seven," Zack says.

"I have no idea what you're talking about. You keep talking about it, not me."

"If you tell us what you know, we can make your life very easy. You might as well reap the benefits of Mr. Kane's friendship. You'll never be able to stop us."

"If you don't think we can stop you, then why are you here?"

"*We?* So you *are* working with others."

Damn. "I didn't say that."

"You did," Cam says. "Tell us what you know, Michaels. What have you found and who's helping you?"

"Hmm. Well, I found a new friend today. A little kid named Jack. Just moved in across the street."

"No one is going to want to be friends with you when we're done with you."

I need to shut my mouth before I say anything else.

Hopping up, I stare down at Cameron. "You know what the best part of having ADHD is? I'll forget all about you and this stupid conversation the moment something more interesting comes to mind." I stare off at the ceiling. "I wonder if there's any Cocoa Puffs left?"

I walk to the door and open it. My heart skips a couple thumps when I see Laney just outside. She spins around and dashes down the hall. I look back over my shoulder, relieved that they couldn't have seen her from where they're standing.

"Oh, are you two still here?" I tell them. "You know your way out, right?"

I open the door wide and they take the hint. When they pass me, Cameron pauses to whisper, "We can make things very bad for your friends."

"I know," I say through gritted teeth. "That's exactly why we're going to stop you."

His eyes narrow as he hustles out, and I follow them down the hall. They reach the front door just as Josh, Jake and Marcus walk in.

Marcus' stare moves from them to me. When the door slams, he says, "What? Did you feel like slumming it today, Tal?"

I stall because I can't think of a reason I'd be talking with those two. "What do you mean?"

Marcus crosses his arms and gives me a look he usually reserves for offensive linemen. *What the hell?*

"We were supposed to practice drills with Marcus this morning, remember?" Jake explains.

Shoot. That's right. Marcus is gunning for a scholarship and Coach mentioned some colleges were coming out to scout this month. We were gonna practice with him at 7:30.

"Sorry. I had detention."

Jake nods at the door. "What were those two assholes doing here?"

"They … they heard I had weed and came to buy some."

Marcus' head jerks back. "Weed? Where would you get weed?"

"Got me. That's what I told them."

He opens his mouth to say something, but stops when we hear Mom coming around the corner. She eyes them and says, "You boys get those muddy clothes off right now. I won't have you messing up this clean house."

"Yes, ma'am," Josh says.

Mom corrals them toward the showers, leaving me standing there alone.

Behind me, Laney whispers, "This is one weird day."

I turn to see her leaning against the door frame. "You're telling me."

"First, you get up early on a Sunday," she says softly. "Then, we find a secret message in Founders Hall. And now, two Pillars try to bribe you to keep your mouth shut about information you don't have. Not to mention I watched you skipping all the way down Mill Street with a kid on your back."

I throw my shoulders back. "I wasn't skipping. I was galloping. Girls skip. Guys gallop."

"Where do you get these weird gender hang-ups?" she says. "I can gallop if I want. You can even skip if you want."

"But I don't want to. 'Cause I'm a guy. Guys don't skip."

"Forget I said anything." She crosses her arms and comes over. "So what'd you make of Cameron and Zack's little visit?"

"Did you hear all of it?"

She nods, and I squeeze the back of my neck. "I'm afraid I said too much again."

"I don't think you told them anything new. They already suspect someone's resurrecting the Sevens and that you're involved."

"Yeah, but I confirmed there are other Sevens. You heard them. More than ever, we need to be sure we're never seen in public together."

"And we can't be alone together at home because of Mom," she reminds me. "This isn't going to be easy."

———

That night, Dad walks into dinner late. "I just got off the phone with Headmaster Boyle," he announces. "In light of the grave robbing and recent vandalism around campus, he's enforcing a 9:30 curfew for everyone." He pans each of our faces. "If any of you know who was involved in this, I suggest you start talking. In the meantime, say goodbye to your social lives."

There's a chorus of groans. Except for Marcus, who mumbles under his breath, "Damn Sevens."

TWENTY-FOUR

Monday morning, I'm standing at my locker before first bell, so tired that I almost miss the black envelope taped inside the door. I rip it down and slide out a hall pass stapled to a note that says:

In case you didn't notice, there's a lesson there for you.

Marcus appears over my shoulder and says, "What's that about?"

"Nothing." My hands fumble with the note and I almost drop it. "I have an appointment with my counselor today."

"Uh oh. Did Boyle figure out it was you that put the *I HOPE YOU'RE AS HOT WHEN I'M SOBER* bumper sticker on his Prius?"

"No. Not yet anyhow." I'm not sure what to say; I hate lying to my friends. It's not the same as BS-ing a teacher or whatever. I settle for a half-truth. "Ms. Bennett is still hounding me about my college plans. I guess they're in a hurry to get rid of me."

Out of the corner of my eye, I spot Laney strolling down the hall. When she opens her locker, her widening eyes tell me that she found an envelope too.

"What are you looking at?" Marcus says. "Talan?" He checks over his shoulder and then back to me. His eyes get all squinty. "Is there something going on between you and Laney?"

"Shanahan? No." I grab my math book and fake-shudder. "Definitely not."

"Why? She's cute enough." The way his gaze returns to her, roaming all over her body, bugs the shit out of me.

"She's going out with LeDouche. And quit looking at her like that. She's practically your sister."

"She's clearly not my sister. I'm black, if you haven't noticed. She's my housemate." He elbows me and wiggles his eyebrows. "A housemate with great boobs."

I shove him hard without realizing it, and he drops his folder. "What, Tal? Don't tell me you never thought about her like that. You saw her in that dress."

"It's Laney." I glare at him. "Knock it off already. I don't like you talking about her like that."

"Okay, okay. She's your sister, I get it." Marcus bends down to pick up his folder and I lift my eyes and catch Laney watching me. She looks around before sliding her black envelope from behind the book she's holding. I nod that I got one too.

Marcus stands up and I slam my locker shut.

"Think you can stay out of detention long enough to work on drills this week?" he says. "Scouts are coming to the Hershey game and I want be ready."

Ah, man. I keep forgetting I promised Marcus I'd practice with him. He has a lot riding on the next few games if he wants that D2 scholarship.

"Sure. How about tonight? After dinner."

"Sounds good." He slaps me on the back and leaves for class. "Catch you later."

The minute I get to English, I flash the hall pass at Professor Gaytan and she dismisses me. I bundle up in my hoodie. The frozen grass crunches under my feet as I cross the courtyard. Between the cold morning air and anxiety over this next clue, I'm practically sprinting across campus to Founders Hall. The blue pass directs me to room number seven, otherwise known as the Singer Museum of School History.

I tiptoe inside and toss my backpack next to a chair. The vacant room is crowded with tables and a slew of display cases stuffed with school memorabilia and boring historical stuff about Singer Enterprises.

Opposite me is a long wall covered with old photographs, news articles, documents, and artwork. I wander along the bookcases that line the other three walls. The brass plate next to them explains that the books were donated from Mr. Singer's private library. I step back and my eyes follow the shelves all the way to the ceiling. Almost two stories up. No wonder the guy was so smart.

"What a coincidence." I jump at Laney's voice.

She tucks a lock of hair behind one ear, then plops her backpack on the table and unzips it. "So, what'd *your* note say?"

I pull the paper from my pocket. "It says, 'In case you didn't notice, there's a lesson there for you.'" I glance up at her. "Did you get the same one?"

"No. Looks we each got a half-clue again." She hands hers to me, then leans close while I read it:

If you read between the lines, there's a second one, too.

Laney walks around me and starts scoping out the bookcases.

"What are you doing?"

"It's elementary, Watson," she says. "The note says, 'In *case* you didn't notice, there's a message there for you.' It's got to be another riddle. The message must be in a book-*case* or some other kind of case we wouldn't notice, like a display case or trophy case or something."

"Oooh. Well played, you little brainia—" I catch myself before I finish.

Laney's eyebrows scrunch together. "No, you can say it—brainiac. I told you, I don't care what you think. I'm glad I'm smart."

She walks around the room and her lavender scent pulls me behind her like a leash. "What I think," I tell her, "is that I wish I was as smart as you."

Laney spins around and glares at me. "Cut the act, Michaels. I'm so sick of hearing that. You *are* as smart as me.

Just at different things." She says it so casually, I think she might actually mean it.

"Yeah? Like what?"

She taps her fingers on top of a trophy case. "Are you fishing for compliments, Tal?" She slides her hand off the cabinet and crosses her arms. "Okay, I'll say it. Like how you're figuring out these clues faster than me. You've always been able to figure things and people out easily. You just use your learning disability as an excuse to be lazy. That doesn't change the fact that you're smart."

She does mean it.

I take a deep breath and savor the moment. "No one else has ever called me smart before."

"Yeah? Well maybe that's because you make fun of smart people. Or because you act like you'd rather be a player and an idiot jock." She pushes past me. "Listen, I know you better than anyone, and you're as smart as any person I know. Whether you want to admit it or not. And you know I'm not saying that just to flatter you, because I don't even like you most of the time." Her mouth puckers. "You think I want to admit you're better at this Sevens stuff than me?"

It's the shittiest compliment I ever got. And the best. I turn my head so she doesn't see the smile I can't seem to shake.

My eyes catch on some glass behind the door.

Laney's standing on tiptoes, rummaging through a bookcase. I tug on her sleeve. "Hey, hold up. I think I might have found it."

She slides a book back onto the shelf and grunts. "Gosh

dang it!" She follows me with angry, clunky steps to the opposite corner of the room.

"Check it out. There's a display case behind the door. You know, like a 'case we wouldn't notice.'"

She quietly shuts the door and the two of us huddle in front of it. "Huh. It's a collection of stuff about William and Mary Singer," Delaney says.

My eyes travel the line of photos along the back and settle on one of Mary. She looks about seven or eight, smiling atop a horse with her parents standing next to her. Wearing a helmet, of course.

In front are some scattered photographs of Mr. Singer as a boy. In the very center, there's a funny one where he's dressed up as a king in a paper crown and a pillowcase cape. Each of his arms is draped around the shoulder of another dirty-faced kid. His smaller sidekicks are dressed like knights, wearing aluminum foil helmets and holding garbage can lids like shields. One waves a toilet plunger as his sword and the other raises a broom handle. The caption underneath says: *William Singer at nine years old, pictured with his foster-brothers and life-long friends, Caesar Solomon and Carmine Rathbone.*

"You gotta be kidding." I squint at the faces, pointing out the younger one. "It's Professor Solomon."

Laney crouches lower. "Oh my gosh." The corners of her mouth lift as she studies the snapshot. "Solomon looked like a little troublemaker back then. Hey… that other boy is Carmine Rathbone. You know, the guy who was Chairman of the Board before Kane. They must have grown up together."

"Do you think it has anything to do with our clue?" I say.

"I don't think so. This photo doesn't give me any kind of 'message between the lines' unless it's trying to say something about Solomon."

"Yeah, that's not enough to go on. Let's keep looking."

We're squatting shoulder to shoulder on the floor when Laney's gaze hones in on a large photo at her end of the cabinet. In it, William Singer is addressing an auditorium full of Singer graduates decked out in their caps and gowns.

A smile grows on her face as her eyes dart from side to side over a quote that's next to the picture. The moment she looks at me, I know she's figured something out.

She scoots aside so I can read it:

"I want you to know that there's a secret
to being successful—follow your heart. Like a
map, it will lead you where you need to go.
Never get discouraged by life's struggles.
Just focus on the big picture and push aside
your doubts. Let hard work and character be
the framework, and you'll find what you need
to be successful and happy."—William Singer

I don't get it right away, but I don't want to tell Laney that. She thinks I'm smart and I'm not about to prove her wrong. I reread the clue: *In case you didn't notice, there's a message there for you. If you read between the lines, there's a second one, too.*

Laney's grinning at me, and clearly she can't wait. "Talan, *read between the lines*. Just skip every other line—"

"Okay!" I cut her off because I just figured it out myself:

"I want you to know that there's a secret
map, it will lead you where you need to go.
Just focus on the big picture and push aside
the framework, and you'll find what you need."

"So there's a map! A secret map to what?"

Laney straightens up. "I guess the first thing we need to do is find the big picture he's referring to."

I spin around toward the wall that's full of pictures. "That's easy enough." I walk toward a humongous painting hanging in the very center—a collage made by Singer students who were asked to paint what they wanted to be when they grew up. It's a bright, mosaic mess of shapes and images, like someone ripped a painting into pieces and glued it back together all wrong.

"This is definitely the big picture," I tell her. "Pull some chairs over and we'll check it out."

After staring into the canvas a few minutes, I surrender. "I got nothing."

"Me either." She sighs. "If this is supposed to be a map that shows us where we need to go, we're screwed."

I tap my finger on my lip. "Wait a minute. We're supposed to 'push aside the framework.' Maybe the map isn't in the painting, maybe it's behind it. Watch the door and I'll try to take the picture down."

Laney climbs down to stand guard, and I move my chair closer to the painting. I grab onto the frame and try to lift it, but the corners are screwed into the wall. It's not going anywhere.

Next, I push the frame from the right side, and—

Click.

The entire canvas pops forward and slides left on some kind of hinge mechanism.

"You did it!" Laney whisper-yells from the doorway.

From where she's standing, she can't see what's behind the picture—a map with a note stapled to it:

Fourth Test—Justice: The truth will set you free.
Time: This Evening. 7:00 P.M.

    2 get N the tunnel
    U must use the key.
    4 an entrance like this is legendary.
    F U R reading this note.
    U can solve this next clue.
    O. UR founder was YS. NO.
    R U?

I slide the papers out from under the flat clips that hold it there. After gliding the picture back in place, I spread everything out on the table.

Laney locks the door and comes over. We lean over the blueprint, studying the buildings and landmarks.

I run my fingers along the dark double lines that run between three buildings. "I don't remember these roads."

Laney surveys the drawing. "They're not roads. They're tunnels, I think." She points out the larger shapes at the ends. "Look. These are all the newer buildings. The ones Singer would have been constructing in Phase I. The double lines can't be roads. They stretch from building to building and travel right through things like the graveyard and softball fields."

She's right. The lines cross campus in perfectly straight paths that would have to be below ground.

"That son of a gun." Laney grins as her gaze skims the paper. "Singer must have gotten the idea from the steam tunnels in the older buildings. But how did he pull this off without being discovered?"

"William Singer was one of the richest men in America when he died. Money makes things like this a lot easier." My finger navigates one path to a square on the paper labeled *Singer Res.* "What's this?"

Laney leans closer and inspects it. "That must be Mr. Singer's residence. According to the map, this is the northwest corner of campus. His house is the only building that far north."

"You mean Headmaster Boyle's house?"

"Yep. Mr. Singer built a home on campus to live in while he oversaw the construction. When he died, the school decided to use it as the headmaster's residence."

"You mean there's a secret tunnel that leads to Boyle's house? Oh man, this could be great."

Laney points to another tunnel that dead ends in the cemetery. "Where do you think this one goes?"

"You got me. Maybe Singer planned to build something there but didn't live long enough to finish it."

She surveys the bottom corner of the diagram. "Check this out. The last tunnel ends at Winchester House."

"There's a secret tunnel to the Pillars' residence too? Finally, *we* get some perks."

"That's probably where the Sevens lived. On our parent tours, we talked about how Winchester was originally built as a dorm where they tried out coed housing. I bet Singer really built it so the Sevens who lived there could travel to his house and back undetected."

"Okay then. So what's the clue tell us to do for this test?"

Laney reads over the paper. "It translates simple enough," she says. "To get in the tunnel, you must use the key, for an entrance like this is legendary. If you are reading this note, you can solve this next clue. Oh, your founder was wise, indeed. Are you?"

"They've been ending a lot of our clues with that same question."

"Yeah, I noticed that too. But what about the rest of it? We need to find a key to get in the tunnel, but there's no hints where to look."

"Yeah there is, Watson. It's all right there." I smile. "Lane, think about it. How it says: *You must use the key* and the entrance *is legendary.* Get it? Key? Legend? Like for a map? They're talking about a map key, not a real key. The map key must tell us how to get into the tunnel."

She looks me up and down. "If I didn't know how much you hated books, I'd swear you spent your nights reading mystery novels."

You know how it feels when you get a great score on your ACT? Me neither. But I'm betting the way I feel now is pretty close.

We scrunch together and check the map key at the corner of the paper. Voilà. Running across the bottom of the legend, underneath all the symbols and their meanings, is a row of random letters that could easily be mistaken for a serial or file number:

A¢ IR N XMN D NJL N TRS

"Based on the way the clue is worded, I'm guessing we're supposed to read it like the characters are words. Like how *F U R reading this note* translates to *if you are reading this note*," she says.

"Makes sense. So let's see … " I sound out the characters. "A-cent … I-R … and … X-M-N … the N-J-L in T-R-S. Huh?"

"Ascend higher?" she offers.

"Oh, right. So it's *ascend higher and* X-M-N … Ex-em-en. It's *examine!*" I blurt out. "Ascend higher and examine the N-J-L in T-R-S."

"N-J-L in T-R-S." The two of us repeat it over and over out loud.

"T-R-S," Laney says slower. "Tee-r-s. Teee-rs. Tears! You have to ascend higher and examine the en-jail in tears."

"Awesome." I slap her back. "Wait, what's an en-jail?"

Her eyes light up. "Angel! Ascend higher and examine the angel in tears."

"Angel in tears?" I'm lost. "What's that?"

"Where would we find an angel in tears?" She studies the map for a second, then smiles and points at the end of a tunnel. "I got it."

"The cemetery?" I ask.

"Mary Singer's mausoleum. Remember? That huge statue inside with the angel mourning over the casket? It's got to be that. The tunnel ends somewhere in the graveyard, and she's definitely an angel in tears... And remember how they had us return our invitations there? The Sevens must have been inside that statue the whole time." I feel a shiver run down my spine, but this time, it's a cool feeling.

Laney glances at the clock. "We need to get going." She scoops everything up. "Here. You take the map." Folding it neatly, she slides it in my backpack. "We'll meet at the cemetery at 7:00 tonight."

"That won't be easy. Boyle's house is right down the road from there and Security is probably pretty tight after the grave robbing. Maybe we should meet in the woods behind the library at 6:30. We'll cut around to the back of the cemetery so no one sees us from Rucker Road."

"Okay. Six thirty on the path."

We hustle into the hall but freeze when we hear footsteps coming from the rotunda. Headmaster Boyle turns the corner and almost runs us over.

"Ms. Shanahan... Mr. Michaels... It seems as if we

keep bumping into each other. What are you doing at Founders Hall this time of day?"

"Research, sir." Laney digs through her backpack and hands him her hall pass. "We're working on a project for Professor Solomon's class."

Boyle checks her pass and hands it back. He looks me up and down next. "I'd like to see yours, too, Mr. Michaels. We need to be *extra* careful until we discover who's behind the recent acts of vandalism. Wouldn't you agree?"

What a dick. I pull my pass from my pocket and slap it into his open palm. He skims it with his beady eyes, and disappointment washes over his face. "Very well then. Get moving to your next class before you're tardy."

I'm about to comment about him being the reason we'd be late, but Laney gives me a pleading look. I crumple the pass in my fist and push past him.

"Thank you, Headmaster," Laney says.

She catches up to me and we scurry across the atrium. When I hold the door open for her, I turn and see Boyle glaring at us from the opposite side of the rotunda. He's leaning against a column, his arms crossed in front of him. The way his eyes zero in on us gives me a chill, like he's targeting us through the scope on a rifle.

TWENTY-FIVE

After football practice, I drop my gym bag on the floor of my room and trudge straight for the shower. Suicide sprints killed me today.

Back in my room, my legs feel like Jello. I tug on a pair of shorts and collapse on my bed. My body's beat, but my brain won't stop thinking about the tunnel map. I roll over and stretch as far as I can, to reach my backpack without actually having to get up, and tug the map from the back pocket.

I've only been skimming it a few minutes when someone knocks on my door.

"Who is it?" I call, stuffing the paper behind my pillow.

"Laney," she whispers. "Can I come in?"

"Sure."

She hesitates at the doorway, and I know why. We aren't supposed to be in each other's rooms, especially with the door closed. She checks the hall before quietly locking the door.

Then she walks over and points at my bare chest. "Showing off your six-pack?"

"I just got out of the shower."

Before I can get up and grab a T-shirt, Laney climbs next to me. She sits so close that our sides are touching.

She tilts her head and whispers in my ear. "I need to tell you something, and it's not good." She winces and finishes. "There was more vandalism last night. They're assuming it was a few people, because they totally destroyed the football stadium. There was some major damage."

"*What?*"

"They tore up the field and trashed the bleachers. They even broke into the concession stand and threw stuff everywhere. There was Sevens graffiti spray painted all over the place. Things like *F— you Singer School* and *the Sevens are back.*"

My hands twitch from anger and fear. "So that's why we had practice in the fieldhouse today..."

"They're trying to keep it hush-hush until they investigate further, but I was checking the student council mailbox and I overheard them talking. Headmaster Boyle said he'll be overseeing security on campus until they catch whoever is behind this."

When she looks at me, her lips are trembling. "I'm worried, Tal. Why are they doing this? Are they trying to scare you or frame you? I don't know what to do anymore. The Sevens are incredibly important to me, but I don't want anything to happen to you."

"Are you thinking we should tell someone? Maybe your parents?"

"No!" Her voice quivers. "My parents can't know. They'd never let me do this, and then I'd never find out what happened to my real mom. You made a vow not to say anything. I'm okay with you dropping out, but please keep your promise to me." When she looks up at me with her eyes all watery, my gut turns to mush.

I wrap an arm around her shoulder. "I didn't say anything about dropping out. It'll be fine. I'll be careful. I promise." Without thinking, I bundle her close and kiss her forehead.

The second I do it, I'm paralyzed. Laney and I don't have the kind of friendship where we hug or kiss. Hell, we don't even touch when we pass the salt at dinner. My arms tense like wood around her back, and I hold my breath waiting for her reaction. I'm a mannequin trapped in a pose while my brain scrambles to come up with a joke I can crack when she pushes me away.

Only she never does.

She nestles inside my arms instead. It's obvious she's lost in thought about something, but she still seems pretty damn comfortable.

And so am I.

I'm not used to girls touching me. Well, not like this anyway. I'm blown away by how different this feels. Lying here all peaceful, with uptight Delaney Shanahan all soft and cuddly, snuggling me like a body pillow.

I allow myself to exhale. My hand rests on the center of her back, rising and falling with her even, steady breaths. Her body forms to mine, and I catch a whiff of that lavender stuff again. She lies in a daze with her hand resting over the scar on my chest.

"Stay right there," I say, sitting up. "I'm cold. I'm just gonna grab a shirt real quick."

"No." She nudges me back against the pillow, trapping my eyes with hers. "I've seen them before," she whispers. "They don't bother me."

She lowers her head to my chest again and rides her finger over the raised scar that sits over my heart. I reach for her fingers, but she gently nudges my hand aside. "It looks like an S," she says.

"It is. For Superman."

She laughs softly and traces over the scar again. "How did you get this, Talan?"

I stumble over my words. "I...I've told you. On a playground when I was little."

"No," she says quietly, without looking at me. "How did you really get it?"

I'd push her away, but it feels too good, like I've been starving for her touch. Her fingers glide warm and tender over my bare skin. That ticklish "S" is totally screwing with me. My nerve endings are whipped into a frenzy. I try to think of something besides her, but it's too late. My body is painfully aware that I'm lying half-dressed and alone in my bed with Laney, her hands running over my bare chest and her warm curves molded to mine behind a locked door.

Maybe I should try that kiss again, only this time...

"Talan?"

Laney jerks her head up.

"Please tell me it was you that just said my name," I whisper.

Terror colors her cheeks as she slowly shakes her head from side to side.

"Talan? Are you in there with Laney?" It's Mom Shanahan.

Laney jumps up and yanks me off the bed so hard that I land on the floor with a thud.

"Yes, we're in here!" Laney yells a little too enthusiastically. "You can come in, Mom. We're not doing anything."

Mom jiggles the knob, but the door won't open. "Why is this door locked?" she shouts.

"Oh fug!" Laney trips over my backpack in her rush to open it.

She reaches it about the same time I notice that the map and the Sevens' clue are still spread out on my bed. I dive across the mattress, scrambling to bury the papers under my bedspread before Mom sees them.

When her mother walks in, I'm sprawled bare-chested across my bed, sweating profusely and trying to smooth out my tangled sheets and crumpled comforter. Laney stands next to the doorway, gnawing nervously on her thumbnail. Her hair is mussed and her face is redder than a sunburn.

I'm not sure what it looks like we were doing, but from the expression on Mom's face, she isn't giving us the benefit of the doubt anymore.

Ah shit.

TWENTY-SIX

"You two. In my office. Now!"

Mom's voice is calm, but not a relaxed calm. More like the calm-inside-the-eye-of-a-hurricane calm. My neck and back tense as I yank a T-shirt over my head and follow her through the house to her office.

Marcus and Juan are talking in the kitchen when we pass. Marcus takes one look at Mom and his eyebrows skyrocket. He looks sidelong at me and mouths, "What happened?"

Mom turns into her office and points to two chairs, which we sit in like soldiers. The click from her shutting the door sounds like the door of a death-row cell sliding into place.

She says nothing as she paces back and forth in front of us, rubbing her hands together. I know her. She's mentally running through every child psychology seminar she's ever attended to figure out how to handle this. Meanwhile, my brain wrestles to think of an excuse for why we were in my bedroom with the door locked.

"You can stop freaking out," Laney blurts out. She looks her mom straight in the eyes. "I'm not hooking up with Talan."

Mom's shoulders relax some. Thank God one of us has a reputation for honesty.

"Start talking," Mom says.

Laney leans forward in her chair. "I'm telling you the truth. Talan and I are friends, that's all. I'm with Kollin, so lighten up already."

Her mother leans her butt against the desk and studies us. "I know something is going on with you two."

You're right. It's called the Society of Seven.

I shrug my shoulders and play dumb. "What are you talking about? Nothing's going on."

Mom's fingers grip the edge of the desk as she stares us down. "I've noticed you two spending a lot more time together lately. And, well, it's only natural that the two of you might be finding yourselves attracted to each other."

When Laney rolls her eyes, Mom says, "Are you going to tell me I'm imagining this? Every time I turn around, you two are alone together, whispering and touching each other."

"Right." I choke out a laugh. "Now you're definitely imagining things. Laney and I are spending time together because Professor Solomon assigned us to do a group project together. We're hanging more, but it's not romantic. We're just friends."

She gives me her *yeah, right* look.

I look her straight in the eyes and hold up my hand. "I swear to you, there's nothing physical going on between us. If I'm lying, may I never play football again."

She taps her fingers on the desk. "Then why was the door locked?"

"We were talking about some personal things, that's all," Laney insists.

Mom crosses her arms. "What could be so personal that you need that kind of privacy?" She waits for me to answer, but I flounder to come up with an excuse.

Laney blurts out, "You're pretty nosy for someone who thinks it's okay to keep secrets from other people."

Mom flinches, then glances uncomfortably between Laney and me. There's an awkward period of silence where I pretend that I have no idea what they're talking about.

Mom's jaw clenches. "Answer the question."

Laney exhales loudly. "Talan was sharing some things that are stressing him out, okay? If anything, you should be happy about that. You've been telling him since he was little to communicate his feelings. Well, he's finally talking to someone about stuff that's troubling him. Instead of jumping to conclusions, you should be encouraging that."

"What would Talan be so upset about that he needs to talk to you behind a locked door?"

I've pretty much accepted the fact that I'm gonna be grounded until graduation when, all of a sudden, Laney announces, "He's realizing his time at Singer is running out, and he's freaking about it. He's scared because he's gonna be homeless after graduation."

Mom jerks her head toward me like she might be buying it. "You are?"

Shitshitshit. What is Laney thinking? Why couldn't she

tell her I had an STD or a meth addiction or something? Now Mom's going to expect me to talk about my feelings and emotions and crap. I'd rather she thought I impregnated the pompon squad.

"Talan." Mom's voice gets all babyish. "Is this true? Did you tell Laney you're worried about where you're going to be next year?"

"Well, yeah, but—"

Laney talks over me. "Singer expects students to move on once they graduate. But for Talan, this is the only home he's got. He has no idea what he wants to do, but he knows he isn't welcome here come June. It's like he's being abandoned all over again. Only this time it's Singer School that's throwing him out."

My chest tightens. I never said those words aloud, but somehow Laney heard them. They make me feel seven years old and alone and shitty, all over again.

I'm angry and nauseated, but I can't deny anything without getting us in worse trouble.

"I'm sorry, Talan. That *is* a lot to deal with." Mom rubs her forehead. "I should have anticipated this. Your counselor contacted Dad and me because you won't make any decisions regarding college next year." She shakes her head. "I've always said that Singer should handle transitioning differently." As she moves in front of me, my eyes hopscotch around the room to avoid hers.

"I'll discuss this with Dad and we'll sit down and talk about it," she says. "There's nothing to worry about. You're not being abandoned. You're starting a wonderful new phase in your life, that's all. This will always be your home."

I can't look at her.

"Okay, Talan?"

I nod and stand up to leave, but she blocks me before I get anywhere. "Wait. We're not done yet." She gently nudges me back into the chair, then leans back against the desk again, drumming her fingertips on the front edge.

The tone in her voice has shifted from anger to compassion to fear all in the same minute. "I still need to warn you two against spending so much time alone together. Even if it is innocent, I can't help feeling that there's something developing between you two."

Yeah. Unfortunately, it's a secret society.

When Laney rolls her eyes again, Mom reaches out and squeezes her wrist. "You listen to me." She gives Laney a fevered glare. "Singer School made an exception allowing us to houseparent boys with a daughter in the house. That's only because we were already fostering boys when Laney was born, and there weren't any openings in the girl homes. But every year, we sit in our review and we're drilled on what precautions we take to separate you from the boys. The administration takes this stuff very seriously. Issues like teen pregnancy and sexual abuse are serious concerns, particularly for schools like Singer."

"I know that." Laney's voice is quiet and sincere. "We get it."

"Then you also know that the administration would have to remove Talan from our home if they suspected you two were romantically involved. I want you both to think about that for a minute. There aren't any openings right now in any of the senior high homes, which means Talan would have to be referred out to Child Services. That could get complicated."

She looks directly at me. "You're eighteen now. I'm not sure they could even place you in foster care at this point. That means your greatest fear could come true—you'd end up alone and homeless."

My throat tightens. The idea of getting kicked out before graduation leaves a sick sadness in my stomach.

"You don't have anything to worry about." Laney's face is pale. Her voice shakes when she says, "I would never let that happen."

"Good. I'm counting on that," her mother says.

I stand up again and Mom snares me in a huge bear hug. Trapped in her arms, I lean my chin on her shoulder and glare at Laney. She misreads my eyes and gives me the thumbs-up sign.

Mom pulls back and grips my shoulders. "Talan Michaels, you will always be part of this family. Dad and I will make some time this week and we'll have a long talk about your feelings and concerns. We'll work through this together. I don't want you worrying. Okay?"

"Ummm…" I nod. "Sure."

Mom tousles my hair and nudges me out the door. She calls to Laney, "It's your night to help with dinner. You should probably get going on that."

Laney follows her mom out. As she passes me, she whispers, "Remember. The woods. Six-thirty."

TWENTY-SEVEN

After dinner, Laney leaves to "hang with Kollin." I load the last plate in the dishwasher and announce that I'm going to work out.

As I head out to meet her on the path behind the library, my chest and muscles tighten with each step. This time, it has nothing to do with the Sevens. Laney's conversation with Mom replays in my head and I can feel the anger seeping from my pores.

I opened up to Laney in a weak moment, and she blabbed it. This is why I don't let people in. I'm not some helpless headcase, and I'm sure as hell not going to be her latest charity project. I'll be on my own in a year and I'll handle it fine myself.

I swallow back the lump in my throat. Damn it, I will not lose it now. Especially in front of Laney. Why the hell did I ever open my mouth?

When she sees me approach on the path, Laney rises from the log she was sitting on. "I'm nervous," she says. "I don't have a good feeling about tonight."

"Why did you say that?" I blurt out.

"It's just a feeling." Laney turns and starts walking the trail.

"No!" I grab her arm. "To Mom. Why did you say all that stuff about me being homeless and"—the word catches in my throat—"abandoned."

Laney's preoccupied, checking out the landscape for security. I wave my hand in front of her face to get her attention. "The stuff I told you was personal. It's nobody's business but mine. You had no right telling anyone that."

Her head cocks back. "What's the big deal? I was backed into a corner. I couldn't tell her about the Sevens, and it was the only other thing I could think of. I'm sorry."

"I'm sorry too. This is why I never open up to people. They always screw me. Thanks a lot."

Her posture stiffens. "I didn't screw you. I didn't know what else to say, and—"

"Why couldn't you make something up? Shit, Laney. Tell her I got someone pregnant. Tell her I have an eating disorder, or, I don't know, tell her I'm a cutter. Whatever."

She shakes her head. "Are you serious?"

"What were you thinking? Can you at least leave me with my pride? Are you trying to ruin my reputation here?"

Her expression goes from worried to pissed. "Your reputation as what?" She gets in my face. "An idiot? What's your problem anyway? It's okay to say you got someone pregnant, but not that you're scared about your future?"

"Damn it, Shanahan!" I slam my fist on a tree. "Now Mom's going to expect me to rehash everything I'm feeling. She's going to drill me on every worry and thought I have about college and crap."

"What's wrong with that? She's trained to help kids deal with stuff like this. She'll help you feel better."

"Talking doesn't make things better, Laney. You'd know that if your life wasn't so damn perfect. You with your perfect family and your perfect life and your perfect boyfriend."

"*Perfect?*" Laney screams, jutting her jaw at me. "I'm so *sick* of that word! You throw it around like a curse. If you only knew. My family, my boyfriend, my life—none of it's perfect. There's no such thing as perfect. If you look close enough, there's a hole in everything. Of course, you don't get close enough to anything to know that, do you?"

"What's that supposed to mean? I have tons of friends."

"Yeah, but you still keep your distance, don't you? I know more about you than any of them, and that's only because we grew up together. Let people in. Let people help you, Talan."

"Don't you get it?" I ball my hands into fists. "How is letting people get close supposed to make me feel better? Everyone leaves me eventually ... even here. The only family I have is dismembered the moment they hand me my diploma. You and my friends will scatter to colleges and trade schools and lives that don't include me anymore."

"Then come to college too."

"How? They don't give scholarships for C's. And how am I supposed to get loans with no parents to co-sign? After I graduate, there aren't any more dead benefactors to look out for me. To buy my clothes and books and pay for tutors when I get behind."

"Your counselor can hook you up with loans and grants. Maybe get you a job on campus."

"Don't you think I thought of that? I'd have to work full time. College is going to be hard enough for me. How am I supposed to work that much and take classes and figure everything else out on my own? I'm not smart like you."

"Bull. The problem isn't that you're dumb. It's that you're scared."

"No kidding." I'm practically shaking now. "You think I like admitting that, Laney? That I know that this is the best my life is ever going to be? That after Singer, I'll be a nothing again?"

She grabs my elbow. "Listen to yourself. What happened to that cocky guy that mows down linemen on the football field and makes all the girls crush over him?"

"He's graduating. He's going back to the exact shithole he crawled out of. Back to being a lonely, homeless loser that people look down on. You want to know what happens to that guy? He's struggling in a shithole apartment working some lame-ass job delivering pizzas or running the Tilt-A-Whirl. That's *my* future, Laney."

She clutches both my arms and holds me still. "You're wrong. You can do whatever you want. Haven't you learned anything at Singer? How many times did they drill us that we're 'defined by our character and not our circumstances'? You're smart. And good. And strong. You're a fighter and a survivor. That's who you *really* are."

I've never cried in front of another person and I'm not going to start now. I try to pull my arms away, but Laney grips them so tight, I'm trapped.

"You. Were. Made. For. College," she says. "Meeting people and partying and taking classes in things you actually enjoy? *That's* your future. You were meant to do bigger things. That's why the Sevens picked *you*. They could see it, and you know what? It's always been obvious to me too." She releases me and says, "You're the only one doubting it."

I bury my face in my hands and shake my head. "I was hoping... I thought..." I drag my fingers through my hair and mumble, "If only this Sevens thing was real."

"It *is* real."

I swallow to keep my voice from cracking. "I've been thinking about this a lot. That if we did all this and it worked out, maybe the Sevens would reward me. But not with cash. Maybe the Sevens could help with tuition and set me up at college. Then I'd have a shot after all. Maybe I *could* be something more. I mean, the Sevens picked *me*. They chose you, and you're the biggest overachiever I know. The idea of a brotherhood with money and secret connections that had my back if I was loyal to it? If this worked out, I'd finally have a damn chance."

Laney moves closer and squeezes my shoulders. "The Sevens were smart to choose you." She moves her face so I can't avoid her eyes. "If I had to choose one person to go through this with, someone who's sharp and brave and loyal, it'd be a no-brainer. I'd pick *you* in a heartbeat." With a glint in her eye, she adds, "Assuming Channing Tatum wasn't available."

She bats her lashes and I'm lost in those damn eyes for a second. There's a fluttering in my stomach that makes me worry I'm going to start crying or drooling any second. It takes everything I have, but I pull her arms down and lean away. "All right. Enough. Don't get all mushy on me."

I move her hands to her sides, but I can't seem to let go of them. I gawk at her a little too long. "I think our therapy session is about done here, Dr. Shanahan. It's been cathartic, but I've reached my emotional-sharing quotient for one day."

Laney grows a full-face grin. "You realize you just used the words 'cathartic' and 'quotient,' right, Michaels? Those are pretty fancy vocabulary words for someone who insists he isn't smart."

"Yeah, well, don't ask me to spell them."

"C'mon." She grabs my arm and tugs me down the path. "We have a justice test to finish."

TWENTY-EIGHT

The cemetery looks different from this side. The graves are older and smaller, with fewer details to remember people by. It makes me think of the Sevens in a sad way. Does anyone remember them now?

Laney and I walk side by side, surveying the graveyard for security. My eyes lock on something in the distance. There's an enormous winged monument pointing to a grave below it. It's déjà vu and I don't know why. As we approach it, it comes to me—it's the statue that terrified me when I was little. That night that I ran away during the storm, and Laney and Mr. Shanahan brought me home.

I point it out. "I wonder if that might be the angel in tears? We should see if she's crying. We don't want to rule anything out."

Laney circles around the front of the statue. "This one? She's not crying; she's looking at all the headstones. I remember reading about this statue. She's supposed to be contemplating all the lives that are lost too young. You know this is the original tomb for Mary Singer, right? They buried her here first, and then moved her remains once the mausoleum was completed."

"No kidding. No, I didn't know that."

Laney and I slink back to the mausoleum, my eyes on alert all the while.

This time, there are no candles to greet us inside—just a strong odor. Flowers. Seven red roses rise from a vase that's mounted on the wall next to William and Mary's vaults.

Laney glances from the flowers to me. I hear her gulp in the silent room. We immediately gravitate to the marble sculpture in the center. Like I remember, the grieving angel stretches her arms across the top of the stone coffin, resting her tear-streaked face on the lid.

Laney circles the figure. "The entrance to the tunnels is inside here, I know it."

"If the Sevens were waiting inside the statue when we returned our invitations, there must be a trap door here somewhere." I try to budge the casket lid up, but it's a solid piece of carved granite.

She grabs my waist from behind. "Let me get on top of you."

"Excuse me?"

"On your shoulders. The clue specifically said 'Ascend higher and examine the angel in tears.' If you lift me up, I can examine her from above."

"Ooooh. Okay." I fake like I'm disappointed, but her sneer warns me she's not in a joking mood.

I bend forward and Laney uses the sculpture to boost herself up on my shoulders. Unsteady at first, I hoist her carefully and walk to the end of the casket. She peers over the top of my head and studies the angel from high up. She's quiet for a minute, her eyes skimming the form like it's a *Where's Waldo* picture.

"So how long have you dreamed of wrapping your legs around my neck?"

Her sigh makes me snicker.

"All my life," she says. "Only it was my hands … strangling you." She slaps the top of my head. "Quit being a pig, you're distracting me."

She leans forward slightly and loses herself in thought again. "I think I found something," she finally says. "Take a look at the angel's hands."

The angel's chiseled arms extend over the surface of the coffin, her lifelike fingers resting delicately on the lid. It's harder to see from my viewpoint, but it looks like she's pointing at something. On both hands, the thumbs and last three fingers curl slightly under toward her palm, while both index fingers lie straight and stiff.

Laney says what I'm thinking. "The angel is pointing at that corner. Let me down. Quick!"

I help her off, and we rush to check it out. Shoulder to shoulder, we run our fingertips along the elaborate details carved on that end of the coffin. There are two rectangular panels on each side of the casket, each edged with detailed moulding.

Laney's fingers trace the border of one of the rectangles.

"It's hard to tell because it's so dark in here, but I think this could be a seam. Like the lip around a door."

"So how do we open it?"

"The angel is pointing right"—Laney follows both fingers to a point at the end of the casket—"here."

She bends lower and feels underneath the rounded lip of the lid. Her eyes widen. "I feel something. There's a hole here. She reaches her hand deeper, her finger sliding out of view. "There's something inside it. I think it's a—"

Click.

She smiles up at me. "Button."

Her grin spreads to her eyes when she sees the right side panel of the coffin slip inward and to the left, tucking itself behind the other half of the casket.

We poke our heads inside the wide gap. Four feet below is a wooden landing. To the left of that are stairs that drop into darkness. It's incredible, like we're in *Harry Potter* or something.

Laney climbs inside. "I'll go down and see if they left us flashlights again. You wait here."

She can read my mind now, apparently. This stairwell is tight and dark and there's no way I'm gonna do a tunnel in pitch black. Still, I'm worried about her going down the stairs alone. I climb in and watch her from the landing. Just as she reaches the last step, a light flashes on and illuminates the small, cramped space.

Laney stands on the bottom landing, clutching the front of her shirt and staring into a doorway on her left.

"It's a room," she calls up. "There's a light on a motion sensor. Close the secret door and come on down."

From inside the statue, the button Laney pressed is easily visible. I push it and the side panel slides smoothly back in place. The wood steps creak under my weight. The narrow stairwell is solid concrete on both sides. It descends toward another concrete wall, but at the bottom, there's a doorway on my left leading into a small room.

I step into a dungeon-like space, which spans around eight square feet. Its concrete walls are painted a dirty white. A floodlight with a motion sensor is bolted to the ceiling in one corner, but there's nothing else to the space but a dusty slab floor.

The space is warm, considering. There's a weird scent I can't make out, a mustiness mixed with the smell of markers.

Laney runs her hands over one of the walls. Her long hair bounces across her shoulders as she bends and stretches, pressing and pushing the surface. When she reaches to feel higher, her sweater inches up to show the bare skin of her lower back. Low slung jeans hug perfect hips and long legs.

It hits me like a fever—I'm finally alone with that body. When I think of those curves, and her dark eyes, and those plump lips, well, being stuck in this dungeon doesn't sound so bad. Locked out of sight, it's like a private hideaway. Dim lighting. Safe from unwanted interruptions. My ADD brain has some fun with that thought until Laney looks over her shoulder and catches me checking out her rear.

"What are you looking at?"

It's not like I can lie at this point. "I was thinking a private place like this could come in handy sometime." I lift my eyebrows.

"Geez. We're in the middle of a virtue test. Is that all you ever think about?"

"Is this a rhetorical question?" I smile, but she's not having it.

"Honestly!" Her cheeks grow redder by the second. "I'm telling you, Michaels, you better not even think about bringing another girl here."

"*Another* girl?" I swagger toward her. "You mean you only want me to bring *you* here?"

"What *I mean* is you swore a vow of secrecy. Telling someone about this place could ruin everything. I can't believe I have to remind you—"

I stop her before she uses up all the oxygen in this place. "I was kidding. Please. I'd never betray you or the Sevens for a stupid hookup."

Her face relaxes. "Good."

"On the other hand, I don't think it'd break any rules if *you and I* were to come here sometime to ... "

I pause to let her mind fill in the blanks, hoping it's as dirty as mine.

She blinks a few times and then pinches me. Funny thing is, she's smiling when she spins around and starts fondling the wall again.

I peek over her shoulder. "What the heck are you doing, anyhow?"

"I'm trying to figure out where the tunnel is. The poem said the map leads to a tunnel, not a secret room. The entrance has to be here somewhere." Her shadow bounces around the room as she moves past me.

I lean my shoulder against the wall next to her. "You know what these shadows make me think of, Lane? Remember when I first came to live at your house? How you were constantly bugging me to come out of my room and play?"

She nods, her arms searching a little slower now.

"Do you remember that time you built that huge pillow and blanket fort?"

Her fingers freeze, and she stares sideways at me. "You remember that?"

"You stocked it with Oreos and milk to lure me in."

Laney's eyes drop, then lift to mine. "Chocolate milk. Your grandma told us you loved dipping them in chocolate milk. I used it as bait. It was the only way I could get you to leave your room."

The whole scene downloads in my head. "We sat in that tent all night, making shadow animals with the camping lantern hanging in the corner. Just the two of us, playing *Uno* and *Sorry!* and stuffing our faces. It was fun."

Her eyes pinch at the corners. "That's not what you said at the time. You said you were only doing it so I'd shut up."

"I lied." I stare down at my feet, scuffing the front of my shoe on the cement floor. "I did like it," I confess in a quieter voice. "I was just being mean because I was mad at you."

When I look up, her head is tipped to the side. "I know. You were always mad at me. Why was that, anyhow?"

When she stares up at me with her sad brown eyes and lopsided smile, it's hard to remember why. As the words finally sputter from my mouth, I'm stunned by my answer. "Because you'd never let me be unhappy."

Laney chews her lip. "Yeah. I guess I've always been like that." Her eyebrows lift along with one corner of her mouth. "You always said I was an annoying do-gooder."

"I lied about that too." I lean my head against the wall. "At least the 'annoying' part."

She nudges my arm lightly. "Don't look so guilty. It was a long time ago." Her lips curve into a friendly smile. "I'm sure you thought I was a real pain. I couldn't bear to leave you alone for a second back then." She gets lost inside a thousand-mile stare. "I had such a crush on you."

"You did?"

She shakes me off. "You knew I did." She slides her hands into her back pockets and shrugs. "Don't worry, it was a long time ago. I got over you soon enough. I figured out we were never meant to be the moment you kissed Jada Jones."

"I kissed Jada Jones?"

"You don't remember? I had some girls over for my birthday and you boys dared us to play spin the bottle. On your turn, it landed perfectly between Jada and me. I practically hyperventilated when you looked at me, but you leaned right past and kissed Jada instead."

"I don't remember. I swear."

Laney elbows me. "It's probably hard to keep track with all those hookups, huh?" She laughs, but it still feels awkward.

Her hands return to the wall.

"I would have remembered if it was you."

She looks over her shoulder at me. "What?"

"I would have remembered the kiss if it was with you."

"Oh, I know." She feels her way around the last wall. "I

probably wouldn't have, though." Then she throws her hands in the air. "Aaargh. I give up. Where'd they hide the entrance?"

I pull out the map and try to get my bearings for a second. "The tunnel starts at the south wall. Which is actually the wall with the stairs."

We rush to the stairwell and glide our hands over the southern wall. "It's solid concrete," Laney says. "Just like the room."

I walk down to the last step. "Did you ever see that old TV show about the Munsters?" I ask.

"Really, Talan. Can you reign in your ADD for a just a second? I'm trying to think here."

"It's relevant. I promise. I used to watch this old sitcom with my gram called *The Munsters*. It was about this suburban monster family. They had this pet dragon named Spot that would shoot fire out of his nostrils."

"Can we get to the point here? We're dealing with an earlier curfew, don't forget."

"Right. Anyhow, Spot lived under the stairs. The staircase would rise up and reveal his den or whatever."

I can tell the moment it clicks with her. Her eyes widen and she clambers down the stairs. "Grab that end and let's see if it lifts."

It swings up so smoothly, little Jack Dominguez could do it. And underneath? Our hidden tunnel.

But that isn't what starts my heart racing. There's a message taped to the floor:

Can you guess what awaits
(along with your next clue)?
There are five Sevens pledging in all,
counting you.

Now it's time that you meet
the rest of your crew.
Oh your founder was wise, indeed!
Are you?

TWENTY-NINE

There are three other pledges? If this is supposed to be good news, why do my insides feel gutted? Why should I trust other pledges? Maybe it's selfish, but I don't want to share this Sevens thing with anyone else. Or maybe it's Laney I don't want to share.

Laney peeks inside the dark opening and lowers her voice. "I didn't see this coming."

"I thought there might be others in the beginning, remember?" I remind her. "But when we never saw anyone at our tests, I assumed it was just you and me."

She grabs my arm. "This is bad. Why haven't we run into them before?" Her jaw drops. "Maybe it's a trick. What if you were right and this was a joke a whole time? What if people are pranking us and they're waiting inside, all set to humiliate us?"

Before I can answer, Laney starts rambling. "No, it couldn't be. There's too much to this for it to be a joke. Unless"—she runs a hand through her hair—"it's some kind of insane genius that's been putting us through this. And now he's tired of the game and wants to murder us." Her lips tremble. "Or maybe it's one of the surviving Sevens that's come back to kill more innocent people, like he did Mr. Singer."

She shakes her head. "What am I saying? I don't believe that for a minute. They were innocent. It can't be, unless—" She's talking faster than a schizophrenic auctioneer.

"Laney—"

"But who else would be pledging? And why didn't we see them when we solved our clues and—"

Her head's going to explode if she keeps this up. "Laney! Relax. Take a breath."

She rubs her palms together furiously. "Sorry. I'm just shocked. What do *you* think about this?"

I shrug. "There's nothing *to* think about." My voice sounds calm, but my stomach's in knots. "We don't have a choice. We have to go 'in the tunnel' to figure out what's going on."

"You're right." Laney takes a deep breath. "Let's do this."

She climbs into the channel on her hands and knees, and I'm right behind her. We're on all fours now, traveling down a long rectangular chute with a light at the end coming through an opening on the left.

"I'll go first," I whisper. "If it's something bad, I'll scream and you take off through the staircase door."

She nudges me back. "No. I'm the one who wanted to join the Sevens in the first place. You kept warning me that you thought it was sketchy. I'll go first in case something's wrong and you wait here where it's safe."

I wiggle in front of her. "I'm twice your weight and a foot taller. I'm going."

"Oh for Pete's sake." She glances at the opening at the end of the passage and crawls alongside me. "We've been partners through everything else. I guess we might as well see this through together." She shoves me hard. "Unless I beat you to it!" She races away on all fours for the opening.

I regain my balance, dive forward, and grab her legs. "Like hell you will!"

Laney lunges head-first for the opening, but I pull her back. She grabs onto my shirt as I climb over her. We wrestle and twist around, rolling over each other and banging against the walls as we scoot forward, until we both end up falling through the hole together and landing on hard concrete.

"Owwww."

I blink my eyes open, and what I see drives me to shove Laney behind my body. A pair of dark, angry eyes hovers above us.

"*Hijo de puta!*" he says.

I doubt my own eyes until Laney's voice confirms what I'm seeing. "Jose? Jose Aguilar?"

"*You two* are pledging the Sevens?"

I'm about to ask him the same question when another face appears. Emily Dombrose bends over me, rolling her eyes. Why does every woman do that to me?

I push myself up, resting on my elbows, when a third

body comes into focus. *Damn.* I'd recognize that voice and argyle sweater anywhere.

"Laney!" Kollin charges past me and drops to his knees.

Laney sits up and squeals, "Kollin?"

He flings his arms around her. "Why didn't you tell me? I had no idea you were involved in this."

When Laney pulls back, she's wearing a ginormous grin. "Same reason you couldn't tell me. Our vow of secrecy."

Kollin helps her up and pulls her into another hug.

Now I know what a pumpkin feels like when its insides are scraped clean.

I lift myself up. "Think you can you save the reunion for another day? The five of us have a lot to talk about."

I barge between them and look around. We're gathered at the end of a narrow concrete tunnel. The hallway is lit only by a few staggered bulbs dangling from the ceiling. The space is chilly and reeks of something rancid.

Behind me, Kollin tells Laney, "I can't believe it. Where've you been all this time? Did you get clues and puzzles like us? The three of us worked as a team, so I never guessed there were other pledges."

"Laney and I were a team too," I grumble.

Emily crosses her arms. "So the Sevens gave you tests too?" she asks. "Like the message in the dedication plaque, and reading between the lines in the hidden case, and the pediment proverb?"

"Yep." I nod toward the opening we just crawled from. "The secret room and this tunnel are part of our fourth test. For justice."

The five of us gravitate into a circle. "It sounds like we got the same tests, but at different times," Emily says.

"Do you think there are more pledges coming?" Kollin asks. "I mean, there's only five of us, and it's the Society of Seven."

Emily shakes her head. "No, the note under the staircase said there were five pledges in all."

Laney's face brightens with a strange smile. "It makes sense if you think about it," she says. "Two of the original Sevens survived but were never found. Five of us plus two of them makes the Sevens complete."

Jose lingers at the edge of our group, twitching like a cougar in a cage. He cocks his head back, his dark eyes targeting me. "So why did you vandalize the school?"

"That wasn't *us*," Laney says. "It was probably Kane and the Pillars." She glances at me and says, "We think they caught on that the Sevens are onto them, and now they're up to something."

"So you know about Kane and the Pillars?" Kollin says.

"Yeah," Laney says. "We took an underground tunnel from the library and spied on them one night. They were partying in the Executive Building. Kane was plying the Pillars with gifts and booze. He said something about selling the company and needing their support."

"We took the tunnels to spy on them too," Kollin says. "But we didn't see a party. We caught the end of a Board of Directors meeting one afternoon where Cameron Moore stood up and spoke on behalf of the Pillars. He said that, as representatives of the student body, the Pillars gave their full support to whatever proposals Kane suggested regarding the sale of our school. After the board members left, Kane gave each of the Pillars an envelope with cash. From the comments Nick Robinson made, it was *nice bank*."

"It's obvious the Pillars are being bribed," I say. "We think the Sevens are being resurrected to stop whatever they're up to."

Jose shakes his head. "The Sevens were murderers. The two who lived escaped with all that money. Why would they care what happens to the school now?"

"Don't believe that story for a minute," Laney says. "There was *never* any proof of any of that. I've read every article ever written on that night. The police went by circumstantial evidence and what Kane said he heard when he came upon the fire. And it's obvious what a lowlife he is. What *really* happened that night, no one knows."

Laney's eyes ping-pong between the three of them. "We figured out from the clues that Singer suspected someone on the Board of murdering his wife, but he couldn't prove anything. We think he started the original Sevens to protect the school if anything happened to him too."

Jose steps away from the group, kneading his hands as he thinks.

Kollin ignores him and asks Laney, "Do you have any idea who's sending us these messages?"

"Hey! Come here," Jose calls out. He points at something a few feet down on the wall.

There's a message scrawled there:

KN S R NME.
D2R -> @ D † N 2 C Y

As we gather around it, our voices stutter and blend together, eventually sounding out the message simultaneously: "Kane is our enemy. Detour right at the crossing to see why."

"Kane is our enemy." Jose looks blank-faced at Laney. "Just like you said."

"What crossing?" Emily asks.

"Check the map." I pull our copy from my pocket, and Emily plucks a duplicate from her jacket.

Laney huddles next to me. Her finger travels the route we're supposed to take and it ends up right at the headmaster's residence.

Despite the fact that I'm stuck with Colon Le Douche in a rank, claustrophobic dungeon beneath a graveyard, I'm pumped over the best news I've had all year. "They're showing us how to get into Headmaster Boyle's house using a secret tunnel? I was hoping it was true."

My imagination runs wild. I now have access to a tunnel that I can use anytime I want to prank the principal. Too bad I didn't know about this last January when Marcus and I built that giant snow penis on his front lawn. A getaway route could have saved me a month of washing desks.

Kollin holds his hand up. "I don't know about this. Breaking and entering is a little risky, even for you, Michaels. If we get caught or arrested, it'll cost me my scholarships. I need that money for law school. I've worked half my life for that."

"It's too late to back out now," Emily reminds him. "We took a vow." She tugs on the bottom of his sweater. "C'mon, babe. We'll be careful. Our school needs us."

Babe? Did she just call him babe? The furrows between Laney's eyes tell me she caught that too.

Kollin massages his forehead. "You're right. Of course. But we've got to be careful." He shoulders his way between Laney and me and starts down the tunnel. "And we better hurry. We haven't got a lot of time."

The four of us follow him down the dimly lit corridor, panning our heads from side to side like windshield wipers. The limited light casts creepy gray shadows around us. It reminds me of my *Cyber Combat Zone*, except that it's smelly and damp and I'd shoot my teammate Kollin in a heartbeat.

The air reeks of a snakey odor, like the reptile building at the zoo. I search around me for the source, but all I see are the murky walls trapping me in this concrete catacomb.

Claustrophobia sets in and the sensation of being smothered in a dark grave begins to choke me from the inside out. My knees weaken. My neck grows clammy and blood starts to rush into my ears.

Jose and Kollin are leading the way like they're in charge, but I don't care. I need a minute to pull it together. I take the rear alone, until Laney's pace slows to match mine. She takes one look at me and her face softens. She threads her fingers through mine. It's gutsy, considered Le Douche is fifteen feet ahead of us.

When she squeezes my hand, my heartbeat settles some.

The five of us tread silently through the murky channel.

Every now and then, I twist around to check we aren't being followed. I'm no chicken, but I'm also not as naive as these guys. After all, no one knows we're here. They'd never find our bodies. *Do dead bodies smell like snakes?*

After a while, everyone slows down and I drop Laney's hand. I'm glad when she stays close by.

We approach our turn on the right.

"This must be the crossing," Emily says.

We all veer down the dim corridor.

A few more yards and Emily squeezes Kollin's arm in front of me. I glance to see if Laney notices, but she's not next to me. She's stopped at the intersection behind us, staring at the wall on the left. I walk back to see what she's gawking at. There's a faded heart drawn just a few feet down from the crossing. Faint letters inside spell out:

AJ

loves

KB

Laney startles when I reach over her shoulder and touch it. "That must have been spray painted by one of the original Sevens. I doubt anyone else knew about this place."

She doesn't respond, but Kollin does. "What are you two doing back there?"

Jose and Emily trail him to where Laney stands in a trance. They follow her eyes to the graffiti on the wall.

Emily bends closer to read the handwriting. "AJ loves

KB." She straightens up and turns to Kollin. "You think that was written by one of the original Sevens?"

"Must have been," he says. "The only other people who knew about this tunnel were the guys who built it and Singer. Think about that. One of the original Sevens stood in this exact spot almost twenty years ago and wrote that. They were probably heading off to a secret meeting at Mr. Singer's or something."

Delaney still hasn't moved from her original position.

"Lane?"

She doesn't answer me.

"You all right?"

"They were kids like us." Her eyes are on the wall and far away at the same time. "They wrote English papers and dressed up for dances and fell in love." Laney traces the heart with her finger. "Until someone killed them."

Her hand drops like a heavy weight. "Singer School was their shot at something better. All they got is forgotten. Written off as murderers who got what they deserved." Her eyes zero in on the wall. "They weren't, though. They were as innocent as us."

She swallows hard and pushes by us down the dimly lit tunnel, walking five feet ahead with her head down. We pass looks but say nothing. Laney's always been tenderhearted, but I'm not sure why some old graffiti would upset her like this. I want to talk to her, to help her, but Kollin is here. That's his job, but he's talking with Emily instead.

We follow Laney quietly for a few minutes until the tunnel dead ends. Laney and Emily are instantly on top of the wall, running their fingertips across the hard surface, searching for a seam or hidden door. Jose and Kollin inspect the side walls, prodding and pushing each section.

There's no room for me. Watching them, an old fear rises in my gut. *Is this some twisted trap?* I spin around to check again if we were followed. The long corridor behind me is empty, but something glints in the darkness. There's a faint light bleeding through the slats in a ventilation shaft that sits low on the wall to my left.

A moment later, I'm on my knees. "Guys! Over here, I found something."

I tug until I'm able to pry out the metal vent covering. Behind it is a three-by-three opening with a greeting written on the inside wall:

A ¢ ℰ𝑅

"A cent?" Jose says.

"No, *ascend*," Emily says. "Ascend here. It's another one of those letter messages. What's the deal with that anyway?"

"I'm sure there's a reason. There's a reason for everything with the Sevens," Laney says. She sticks her head inside the opening and looks up. "It's another passageway. There are rungs going up the wall."

Emily climbs in first, then Jose and Kollin.

Laney holds back. "Will you be okay?" she whispers.

I nod, and she scoots inside and starts climbing. Looking up, I see the others already at the top, crawling out through a hatch twenty feet above us. I take a deep breath and follow Laney.

When we near the top, Kollin looks down through the opening and holds his finger to his lips. Laney climbs the remaining rungs and takes the hand he's offering. He wraps an arm around her back and leaves me alone to help myself out.

The room we've entered is narrow, maybe six feet wide by twelve feet long. The walls enclosing us are solid red brick, except for a single window to my left, which is the only source of light in here. It sits chest-high and looks out into a formal living room full of antiques and fancy furniture. It's so stuffy and boring and proper, it's got to be Headmaster Boyle's house.

I squeeze between Kollin and Emily to get a better look and my knee bangs into something. There's a large metal box protruding from the bottom of the wall, directly below the window.

"Shhhh." Kollin snarls at me like I just pulled a fire alarm.

I bend down to inspect it. The box stands about three feet tall by three feet wide, and extends off the wall about a foot. It's secured to the floor by a hook on each of its three sides.

Laney whispers in my ear, "Is that a trap door?"

Before I can answer, Jose taps our shoulders. He jabs his finger toward the window, pointing at something in the adjacent room.

It takes me a minute to figure out what he's showing us there—a massive mirror on the wall opposite us.

I glance between the brick wall that's a foot in front of me and the reflection in the mirror hanging across the room. I'm seeing two sides of the same wall, at the same time. It finally sinks in—we aren't looking through a window at all. We're standing behind a one-way mirror that hangs above a humongous marble fireplace.

Voices emerge in the distance, and the five of us scrunch together to spy through the glass. Headmaster Boyle enters the room with Stephen Kane. Boyle putters toward the center of the room while Kane folds his cashmere coat over the back of a sofa.

Kane eyes a decanter on a bar cart nearby. "Mind if I make myself a drink?" We hear his voice clearly through a cold-air return in the wall.

"Help yourself."

Kane fills a tumbler with clear liquor. "Do you want one?"

Boyle sits down in an armchair, propping his elbows on the arms and steepling his fingers. "What I want," he says, "is to know why you called this meeting."

Kane's saccharine smile practically glows from across the room. "We're moving up the date. To December."

Boyle leans forward in his seat. "December? Why so soon?"

"Just playing it safe. One of my Pillars thinks that a student might have gotten wind of what we're doing. That kid who insulted me during the assembly. What was his name?"

"Talan Michaels?"

"Yes. Him. He accused Cameron of being up to something and mentioned something about the Sevens returning. I called the boy into my office, but he played dumb. It might be nothing, but I don't want to take any risks when I have a billion dollar deal in the works."

Boyle laughs. "He's not the sharpest student. I doubt he poses any threat."

My face burns.

Then Boyle adds, "So that's what the Sevens vandalism has been about? We'll catch him soon enough."

"The vandalism," Kane says, "was my idea. If someone is thinking about causing trouble for us, I needed a way to discredit them."

"So you're going to frame Michaels for it?"

"Michaels and whoever else he's involved with. The Pillars told me who his closest friends are—Marcus Johnson and Jake Welch and quite a few girls. We're watching all of them. I doubt they're bright enough to sabotage this deal, but you can never be too safe. Kids with nowhere else to go have nothing to lose."

"Fine," Boyle says. "I have a meeting in twenty minutes. Why don't you just tell me what you want from me."

"The Li Yuong Group has agreed to a ridiculously lucrative deal for Singer Enterprises, providing we eliminate the complications regarding Singer School. They don't want the limitations involved in funneling profits back into a philanthropic boarding school. Only William Singer was foolish enough to think that was a good idea."

"So what does that have to do with me?"

Kane pulls an envelope from the breast pocket of his suit jacket and sets it on the end table next to Headmaster Boyle. "This is a copy of Singer's Deed of Trust—it explains how he left all his assets to the school when he died."

Boyle ignores it. "I have copies of this already. Kane, what's your point?"

Kane sets his drink down and makes himself comfortable on the couch, stretching his long arms across the back of the sofa. "The newer board members already agreed in private to support me in selling the school and company, but my attorney Katherine Jones believes a few of the old-timers will put up a fight. They'd never allow the company to be sold if they thought it'd jeopardize William Singer's vision for his precious school."

Headmaster Boyle chuckles. "Well, doesn't it? The deed was written to ensure the school could continue to help *underprivileged* students."

"The deed also gave the Board the authority to decide what's in the best interest of the company, as long as it protects the school," Kane says. "Singer School will still exist, just in the form a private boarding school. As long as we keep a decent number of scholarship and charity cases, we can still claim Singer as a philanthropic institution. Once we convince the Board that the changes are worthwhile, we're set. We only have one loophole to close."

"What loophole?"

Kane twists a large gold ring on his finger. "As you know, William Singer included a clause in his will that assigned several unnamed students as trust protectors—the infamous *Society of Seven*. If the Sevens ever felt that the Board was making a decision that'd hurt their school, they could present the Trust Protector Document at a board meeting and take over as trustee, essentially firing the Board of Directors."

Boyle checks the time on his watch. "So what's the problem? The Sevens are long gone and the Pillars are in your pocket."

"But the Pillars are only substitutes for the Sevens. Singer specifically mentioned the Society of Seven in his will and the deed. They're the actual trust protectors. The issue is, Singer left the individual Sevens' names out 'for their protection,' stating that the Sevens only needed to present the Trust Protector Document at a board meeting to assert their authority. Consequently, anyone claiming to be a Seven could present that TPD document and complicate this deal."

"I thought that no one knows where the TPD is?"

"They don't, as far as I know. Carmine Rathbone drew up the original document for Singer. Rathbone told police that Singer said he was going to hide the TPD until he finished mentoring the Society of Seven. I've scoured the school and offices myself and found nothing. As long as that TPD remains lost, we're golden. My legal team has worked out everything else."

"So you have no problem kicking out underprivileged and abused kids?" Boyle asks.

"Don't act like you care about these delinquents, Matthew. I happen to know that you hate your job here."

"And how would you know that?"

"Katherine Jones told me."

"So you're working with Katherine," Boyle says. "When did that happen?"

"I hired her as legal counsel when I became Chairman. She worked under Carmine Rathbone and was very familiar with Singer Enterprises. Turns out we have quite a lot in common."

"Your love of money?"

"Not entirely. We both started out with nothing and earned our success. There's nothing wrong with a wealthy lifestyle, Matthew. Give it a try. I heard you're sick of hassling with students and child welfare agencies and having nothing but a pathetic paycheck to show for it. Katherine's the one who suggested we garner your support. You should be grateful to her. Half a million is a pretty generous stipend for someone in your shoes."

Boyle presses his linked fingers to his mouth and considers Kane's words. He tilts his head. "What would you need me to do?"

Kane's eyes brighten. "The Board holds your opinion in high regard. When they ask for your input, I need you to support me wholeheartedly. Make a convincing argument and back it with whatever educational studies or nonsense you can. I don't know . . . argue that it's healthier for underprivileged and at-risk students to be mainstreamed with children of different social classes. Pretend it has something to do with diversity or fitting into society. I don't care what line you use, just sell them on the idea."

Boyle taps his mouth with his hands and thinks. Then his slitted eyes lift to Kane's. "I want six."

"Excuse me?"

"Six hundred thousand dollars. With early retirement and a significant raise when the school goes private."

Kane's mouth snakes into a twisted grin. "I'll see what I can work out. I'll be in touch."

"Don't take too long." Boyle shifts to his trademark scowl. "Or I may decide I want seven."

Kane holds out his scarred hand for Boyle to shake, but Boyle ignores it. He pushes himself up and out of his seat. "I have meeting to get to. I'm sure you can find your way out."

Boyle strolls out of the room without a backward glance. A second later, a door slams in the distance.

Left alone now, Kane parades around the empty room, taking in his surroundings like he just won them in a poker bet. He refills his glass of liquor and walks right up to the one-way mirror.

Everyone freezes. Does he suspect we're here?

Kane ambles along the front of the mantle, lifts a picture of William Singer off one end, and smirks at the photograph. His upper lip curls. "That's what you get for picking the wrong Sevens."

He grabs his coat and glides out of the room, slamming the door behind him.

THIRTY

Jose steps backward, his voice trembling. "What exactly did we just witness?"

Kollin's lips pale into a tight line. "We just watched the devil make a deal for our school. I can't believe frickin' Boyle would sell us out like that."

"He's always been a scumbag," I say.

"To you maybe," he snaps.

"They're turning Singer School into a private school for rich kids?" Jose asks. "That's as far from its purpose as you can get. They can't do that, can they?"

"Apparently. You heard Kane. He's got a team of lawyers making sure everything is legal."

"What about Kane's comment that he's behind the vandalism?" Emily says. "Talan, what exactly did you tell Cameron?"

"I said something after I got the invitation. I had no idea

this was real at the time; I thought the Pillars were pranking me. I told Cameron I knew about the Sevens and that he was screwing the wrong person. That's it, I swear. I didn't know enough to say anything else. I hadn't even returned the invitation yet. You heard Kane—they're just being careful."

"You said enough to put us in danger," Kollin says.

"They don't even suspect you, Kollin! Kane named a couple of my buddies that aren't even involved in this. If the Pillars are watching them, they aren't gonna find anything anyway."

"He's also watching you. You're putting us all at risk."

Laney jumps between us. "Talan had no idea what this was back then." She looks at all of us. "We can't waste time fighting. Our friends, all the younger kids here—they need us."

"Fine," Kollin says. "Well, at least we know why we're here now. The Sevens are being resurrected to find that Trust Protector Document and present it at the December board meeting before Kane sells our school."

"No problem," I snort. "Except for one thing. How the hell are we supposed to do that?"

"We'll figure it out." Laney's wide smile seems out of place. "We just have to work together."

Jose shakes his head. "This whole thing is so . . . I thought the Sevens were just a . . . a . . . secret gang. The invitation talked about granting our desires and getting rewarded. I thought it'd be a gang where we made some money and broke some rules. I didn't think—"

Laney cuts him off. "Man up, Aguilar. Did you expect

to get a Great Reward for partying at a secret clubhouse and learning a secret handshake? You read what the invitation said: 'To whom much is given, much is expected.' This is about our home, Jose." She jabs him hard in the chest. "Your home. My home. The home of two thousand kids—most of whom have no other place to go. This may be the most important thing you ever do in your life. Don't you dare quit now."

Jose answers in a whisper. "I didn't say I was gonna quit." He stands there, red-faced and nodding at Laney, his chin dropped like he was squared with a sucker punch.

Sweet little Delaney Shanahan just brought the ruckus. She's standing there all bossy, with her chest out and her hands on her hips. It's probably a good thing LeDouche opens his annoying mouth right then. His know-it-all tone kills the mood before I start breathing heavy on his girlfriend.

"Delaney's right," he says. "We owe it to Mr. Singer and our friends to see this through. If there's something we can do to save our school, and the Sevens obviously think there is, then we need to figure it out. ASAP."

I hate that I agree with Kollin LeBeau almost as much as I hate that we're working as a team now. I turn my attention back to the one-way mirror and stare off into the abandoned room. I take a step closer and lean in. "They left it."

Laney turns my way. "What'd you say?"

"They left it." I point to the side table next to Boyle's chair. "The copy of the deed. We should take it. Maybe we can use it for evidence or something."

The four of them peer through the window at the envelope forgotten on the table.

"Are you crazy?" Kollin says. "You can't steal that. They'll know someone was in here."

"They'll never miss it. Boyle left first—he'll just think Kane took it with him, if he even remembers it. And Kane left without thinking twice about it. He'll assume Boyle threw it out since he has copies. They'd never miss it."

"The Sevens never said anything about taking anything. This is your idea, not theirs," Kollin says.

"It's a good idea!" Everyone jumps when Laney speaks. "We might need it as evidence someday, or maybe it has some other information that could help. How do we get it? I'll do it."

Kollin scolds her. "Laney, you're not serious."

"I think we can get in through the fireplace," I say. "This metal thing is probably the way into the headmaster's house. Think about it. There's no chimney behind this fireplace, just this weird box below the one-way mirror."

Laney kneels next to the metal structure. "Help me figure this out, Talan." The two of us unlatch the side hooks, pulling and pressing and pushing the cold steel box until—

Squeeeeeek.

The heavy container slides left on rollers hidden underneath. Suddenly, the back half of the fireplace hearth slips to one side, creating an opening into the room. This must be how the Sevens got in to meet with Singer.

Laney crouches low and creeps through, navigating around the logs in the grate. "Careful," I warn her. "Don't get soot on that fancy rug."

"It's decorative. They're fake logs." Still, Laney steps out of her shoes before she tiptoes to the end table. She grabs the envelope and rushes back to the fireplace. Slipping her shoes back on, she bends low and climbs back through the opening. As I help her inside, Emily and Kollin slide the box back in place and re-latch the hinges to secure it.

Laney clutches the envelope tight to her chest. "Ahhhh, my heart is beating like crazy." Her big-ass grin is aimed at me. "Oh, Talan! That was exciting!"

The glimmer in her eye makes me laugh. I know exactly how she feels. That rush you get from doing something impulsive and risky.

Kollin glares at me. He steps forward and pulls Delaney's fingers away from her shirt, sliding the envelope out. "This better have been worth it."

Leave it to LeDouche to ruin a beautiful moment. "Relax, LeBeau."

Kollin opens the envelope. "I interned at an attorney's office last summer. I'll email my mentor and see if I can get some info about Trust Protector clauses. In the meanwhile, I think we should leave the deed in the secret room below the mausoleum. In fact, if the Pillars are on the lookout, we should probably hide everything there—the clues, the maps, everything that could tie us to the Sevens. Kane isn't the only one that's out for us. Headmaster Boyle isn't exactly on our side either."

"I hate to break up the party," Jose interrupts, "but we need to get out of here. It's gotta be close to curfew."

The five of us hurry down the chute, crawling back through the tunnels and out the staircase. My body finally relaxes when we reach the secret room under the mausoleum.

It doesn't last long.

There's a huge, yellowed piece of paper taped to the wall now.

> *"A prudent question is one half of wisdom."*
> *Dwell on this for your last test,*
> *When you're on your own, and all alone,*
> *Beginning your final quest.*
>
> *Knowledge is gained through fact compilation;*
> *But wisdom is born in its simplification.*
> *Columns and half clues to find and combine.*
> *Words that are letters read between the lines.*
> *Use all you've learned, and you'll solve the last clue.*
> *Your founder was wise*
> *In deed,*
> *Are you?*

Behind me, Laney says, "We'll wait for the next clue, then. If something comes up before then and we need to talk, Talan and I use this signal where we tug on our ear."

"Sounds good," Kollin says. "Let's go."

We follow him up the stairs, pausing at the top. He peeks out the slit where we returned out invitations. "It's clear."

He presses the hidden button and we straggle through the door in the marble casket. Laney closes it, and one by one we sneak out of the mausoleum and race home.

When we reach our back door, Laney goes in first. I wait a few minutes and walk in.

Marcus meets me in the kitchen. "Where you been, man?" He's pissed.

"What? At the library."

He walks over, looking me up and down. "Really? Is there a lot of mud at the library? 'Cause your shoes are caked. And why did you tell Dad you were working out? I went to the rec center and the stadium, everywhere, looking for you."

"What are you, my nanny?"

"We had plans, remember? You promised to help me with drills."

"Oh. Man. I'm sorry. I forgot."

"Another lie?"

"What are you talking about?" I brush past him but he grabs my arm.

"You said you left the dance early because you and Taylor wanted to be alone. Taylor says you weren't feeling good and dumped her at her door at nine."

"So what?"

"So she says you've been acting weird, and you know what? I agree. When I went by the stadium looking for you tonight, I saw all the damage there. Coach told me what's going on. They're talking about canceling the rest of the season. Did you know that? It was Stephen Kane's suggestion. He says it'll pressure the students to turn in the perpetrators."

"Can they do that over some vandalism?"

"So you already know about it, huh? That's odd, considering they kept it under wraps all day. Or did you hear about it 'at the library'?"

"Are you accusing me of trashing the stadium?"

"I'm not accusing you of anything. But weird shit is going on and you're acting strange lately. You're gone all the time with these lame excuses. You seriously want me to believe you've been at the library? You haven't turned in a single chem assignment all semester."

"I wouldn't trash the football field. You know me better than that. We've been friends since third grade."

"You're right. That's how I know you're hiding something." Marcus shakes his head and takes a deep breath. "Tal, I know this graduation thing is getting to you. If this is some anger thing, you venting on the school or something, you gotta stop."

I look him square in the eyes. "I had nothing to do with the vandalism. Nothing. I swear on our friendship."

"Then where were you? Why all the sneaking around?"

"Just trust me, okay? I'm not doing anything bad."

"Then why can't you tell me?"

"I just can't. Please, Marc. Give me some credit."

He drops my arm. "Fine. But no more lies. If the games get canceled, I don't get scouted. And that means no scholarship. I'm not the only athlete who was counting on that, either. I don't care if it was my mother—if I find out who ended our season, I'll personally narc them out to Boyle."

THIRTY-ONE

Rumors spread all morning, but the announcement at lunch makes it official: "Due to recent events and widespread vandalism, the Board has canceled all extracurricular activities for the fall season, pending investigation of these incidents." Moans rise up across the crowded room. "In addition, the Board of Directors is offering a $10,000 reward for information leading to the arrest of those involved."

Kane said he could make things hard for my friends. Score one for the bad guy.

So why do I feel so guilty when I'm innocent? I stare at Laney's table and tug my ear when she glances over. She nods toward Kollin, but I shake my head. I really want to talk to her alone. My head is spinning about Marcus and the Sevens and Kane. Laney has a way of slowing the world down.

I scoop my lunch up. "Where you going now?" Marcus asks. There's an edge to his voice.

I'm too flustered to think of an excuse. "I've got a meeting with my counselor. I'll talk to you later." I rush out and head down the hall.

I collapse in a chair in Solomon's room, tapping my fingers to the pounding in my head. The door slowly opens and I finally exhale. But it isn't Laney.

Marcus crosses his arms on his chest. "Meeting with your counselor, huh? Does Ms. Bennett rent space from Solomon now?"

"What are you—"

"No!" Marcus says. "No more bullshit. I want to know what's going on. Why are you blowing your friends off, and where do you keep sneaking off to?"

He's pissed and he isn't gonna let this go. I can't tell him the truth, and my mind is racing too fast to come up with a lie.

"Tell me what the hell is up or I'm going to Boyle. I don't care if you are my best friend. If you have anything to do with this Sevens shit, you're screwing a lot of people. It ain't right. You're headed for trouble, Tal."

I stare at him, emotionless.

"This is your last chance. Tell me who you're sneaking around with."

"Me."

Marcus twists toward the voice in the doorway. His jaw drops lower than mine when Laney repeats herself. "Talan's been sneaking around with me. We're hooking up. I didn't want Kollin to find out."

Marcus glances between us, clearly not convinced. "Laney Shanahan—a cheat? No way. Plus, that doesn't explain the night of the dance. He lied about why he left early. You were there the whole time, Laney. You stayed later than anyone. You guys weren't hooking up that night."

I walk around the desk to buy myself some time to think. "I was . . . jealous. Watching her with Kollin was bugging me, so I told Taylor I didn't feel good so I could go home."

"But why wouldn't you tell me? It's not like I'd tattle to Kollin." Marcus has this hurt look on his face—the kind you see on abused kids who know better than to trust people. "We've never kept a secret from each other before. I asked you a few weeks ago if something was going on with you and Laney. You straight up told me, 'No way.'"

"He wanted to tell you, but we didn't have a choice," Laney says. "We can't risk my parents finding out. Mom already caught us once. Remember when she called us into her office?" Marcus nods. "Mom caught me in Talan's bedroom. We made up an excuse, but now she's really watching us. If they learn Talan and I are in a relationship, they'll remove him from our home. There aren't any openings in any of the senior houses, so Talan would be referred out of Singer. He's eighteen now—too old for foster care placement. He'd be out on the street."

Marcus shakes his head, then shrugs. "I don't know. It doesn't add up. You two sneaking around? You drive each other nuts."

"Oh for Pete's sake." Laney shoves Marcus aside, grabs the collar of my shirt, and pulls me into a knee-buckling kiss. With our lips locked, her hands slowly glide up my chest and around my neck. She kisses so good, I forget to breathe. All I can think about is how great this feels. How soft her hands are running through my hair. How warm her chest is against mine. How sweet her mouth is, and how great she tastes. She must have had strawberries for lunch. It's all better than I imagined.

Oh hell, who am I to waste an opportunity like this? I cup my hands around her bottom and scoop her body closer. Before you know it, I've forgotten Marcus is even there.

"Well, I'll be damned," he says.

Laney pulls away to catch her breath, staring up at me with her face and lips all red.

Marcus shakes his head. "I never thought I'd see the day when Talan Michaels was whipped by a girl. What the hell is going on at this school? Grave robbings. Secret societies trashing campus. And Talan Michaels and Laney Shanahan falling for each other? I'm scared to drink the water." He plods out of the room with a stunned expression.

"Thank you," I tell Laney. "Really. Thank you, thank you, thank you."

She yanks her arms off my neck and backpedals. "I did it for the Sevens."

"Sure you did." I wink.

"What's with the tongue? And did you have to grab my butt?"

"My tongue wasn't rolling around by itself in there." She's cute when she blushes. "And the butt grab? I did it for the Sevens too."

"How noble of you." She punches me hard. "So is that why you called me here?" She peeks out the door to make sure we're alone. "To tell me Marcus was suspicious of you?"

"Right. He accused me of being involved with the Sevens. Some of our tests happened the same nights as the vandalism, and I didn't exactly have good excuses for where I was. Then last night, I promised Marcus we'd practice drills and I forgot. I told him I was at the library, but my shoes were caked with mud from the woods. And, well, I guess you heard the rest of it."

"That was close."

"I hate lying, Laney." The pounding in my head returns. "You heard that they're canceling all fall activities. Thank you, Stephen Kane. He told me he'd make things hard for my friends."

"I know. Everyone here was already pissed at the Sevens for getting our curfew moved earlier. I heard them talking after the announcement today. They're also canceling senior night and the winter awards banquets. I've been looking forward to that since I started high school."

"Marcus and some of the athletes will probably lose their scholarships over this." I collapse in a chair. "I don't know what to do, Lane. It's my fault for opening my big mouth in the first place. Maybe we need to tell an adult."

"You can't," she barks. "We don't know who to trust. I mean it. I don't even want you telling my parents."

"What about Solomon? If he's sending the clues, he needs to know what Kane is up to."

"We don't know for certain it's him. You said it didn't sound like him on that phone call. And how could he navigate the tunnels at his age? Right now, the best thing we can do is finish these tests and find that Trust Protector Document."

THIRTY-TWO

There's a black envelope inside my locker the next morning. Ever since Marcus' interrogation, I'm paranoid people are watching me. I bury the note in my backpack and sneak to the bathroom to read it.

> *Fifth Test—Faith:*
>> *"Faith is taking the first step even when you don't*
>>> *see the whole staircase."—Martin Luther King, Jr.*
>>
>>> *Time: Sunday, 7:00 P.M*
>>> *Location: Even angels harden over the loss*
>>>> *of innocence.*

Laney and Kollin are the only two in Solomon's room when I get there early for class. Kollin moves to stand watch by the door. "Did you get the note?"

I nod.

Kollin pokes his head into the hall again before grabbing the seat next to Delaney. "So Lane and I have been talking about this. We think the location refers to the mausoleum. The test will probably be waiting there for us on Sunday."

"That's what I figured, too. We need to be extra careful," I add. "Now we've got Kane and Boyle and most of the school after the Sevens."

"About that…" Kollin says. "Laney told me about your predicament with Marcus and with her mom's suspicions, and I came up with this great idea."

"I can hardly wait to hear it."

"I think you should fake like you're going out with Emily. It's the perfect alibi for Mrs. Shanahan. Emily's the perfect cover since you'll be together anyway for the rest of these tests. You can tell Marcus you're hanging with Emily so Mrs. Shanahan doesn't get suspicious of you and Laney."

I hate to admit Kollin had a good idea. "Maybe. I don't know."

"Too late," he says. "I already told Emily and she agreed. She wasn't thrilled, but she's willing to do it for the Sevens. You're two happy lovebirds from here on out."

Before I can ask who made him boss, we hear voices in the hall. I slip into my desk in the back row. Kayla and Cameron come roaring in the room, laughing and bragging about the hot tub Kane is having installed at the Winchester House. I'm disgusted that Kane would waste money on something so stupid at the same time I'm wondering how I can sneak over there and use it.

The rest of our class gradually finds its way in, including Emily, who makes a show of saying, "Hello, baby! How's my hottie today?" She plops a loud smack on my lips. I wipe my mouth and notice the entire class staring at us. They're all snickering at me. All except Laney, who's looking a little peeved. And Jose. Who for some reason is looking even more pissed off.

Then I notice the looks passing between the Pillars. I just thought of a reason why Kollin's plan might *not* be a good idea: guilt by association.

———

Days pass, and our canceled after-school activities are gradually substituted with extracurricular bitching and moaning. Not that I blame anyone. I still can't believe I'll never get to play football again.

Almost as sickening is Emily's constant lovefest. Patting my rear in the hallways and showing up at our doorway just 'cause she "needs a little taste" of me. It might make Mom feel better seeing us together, but Emily's fun and games are ticking me off.

It's 6:30 on Sunday night when Chris comes to find me in Dad Shanahan's office. "Emily's here," he snickers. "She says she came to pick you up"—he makes air quotes—"'because you're taking too long and she can't stand to be apart from you anymore.'"

There's a stapler a foot away from me I'd like to nail her with right now. Oh well. At least she gets me out of this never-ending meeting with the Shanahans. Mom follows me out to the foyer, where Emily stands grinning like a troll.

"So where you kids going?" Mom asks.

I was gonna say "rec center" when Emily answers, "The English department is doing poetry readings from a woman's perspective."

My housebrothers are in the adjacent family room, and I swear they all bust out laughing at once.

"Knock it off, boys. It wouldn't hurt you all to get in touch with your feminine side once in a while," Mom says. She's clearly not helping.

I whisk Emily out the door, tugging her to the street by the elbow. "Why do you keep doing that? We're supposed to be a team, remember?"

"Just having fun."

"You're just pissed because I wasn't interested in hooking up that night in the graveyard."

"Trust me, you're not the Seven I want to hook up with."

"What?"

She walks faster. "Nothing."

"No, what'd you say? You're interested in Kollin, aren't you?"

"It's none of your business."

"Has something happened between you two?"

"I don't have to tell you anything."

"Are you and Kollin hooking up?"

"Stop bugging me. You keep your mouth shut or I'll tell your friends you like to wear my underwear. Got it?"

We head for the student center, but veer toward the

woods as soon as we're sure we're alone. "Did you bring all your clues?" she asks.

"Of course." Thankfully, Laney reminded me of our plan to bring all the Sevens papers to stash in the secret room for safekeeping.

Emily and I make it to the mausoleum in five minutes, and the three other Sevens are there waiting. Kollin presses the button and the secret door in the casket slides open.

Laney taps her foot on the floor. "Of all days to be late," she says to me.

"It's your fault," I tell her. "Mom and Dad held me hostage in their office all afternoon with a long, pointless discussion about my 'promising' future. The only way I got them to shut up was by filling out some college apps. What a waste of time."

"You'll thank me one day," Laney says before heading into the stairway. I'm the last, so I clamber inside and push the button to seal us in. The first thing I notice is that the stairs are darker than usual tonight. There's hardly any light seeping out from the secret room.

The muscles in my neck tighten when I turn the corner and see why. The room is illuminated entirely by candlelight. Dozens of lit candles sit in the center, forming the shape of a seven. It's awesome, but also kinda eerie.

The candles have barely burned down, which means whoever lit them was just here. Are they waiting under the stairs or listening to us somewhere?

Emily bends down and picks up a black envelope. She takes a deep breath and slides out a letter. "Here goes test number five," she says, and reads the note aloud:

The success of the Sevens requires unconditional trust between members. Tonight's challenge will test and build that bond, for each pledge must reveal their most intimate secret to the group. No one leaves until all have confessed.

Allow me to go first: Eighteen years ago, six other students and I were chosen as Sevens and given virtue tests almost identical to yours. Upon completion, we were to learn the Great Revelation—the location where William Singer hid the Trust Protector Document.

With one final test to solve, William Singer summoned us to meet at the cemetery chapel. But there was to be no meeting. Two of us arrived late, and the horror that greeted us there would change our lives forever. Our friends and founder had been murdered—victims of the same dark fate that had befallen Mr. Singer's own wife. We feared for our own lives, and, later, for being framed for crimes we did not commit. For two decades we have remained anonymous, ashamed that we failed our vows of courage and sacrifice. That ends now.

The actions of Stephen Kane threaten Singer School. The Society of Seven has been resurrected to solve the mystery of that night and to locate the Trust Protector Document. If we fail, our school and your home will be destroyed forever.

Beware, brethren. There are murderers among us.

Emily slips the letter back in the envelope with shaky hands. She slowly lifts her eyes to the four faces gawking at her.

"Laney was right," Kollin says. "The Sevens were innocent, and they need us." His eyes linger on Jose. "This isn't about a secret gang or a way to get something for ourselves anymore. It's about our families. A lot of people are depending on us."

I'd like to be so noble, but I can't. I keep thinking that we're being watched or listened to. The dark room has me edgy and the candles burning down aren't helping.

Laney speaks up from where she sits at the end of the 7. "All right then, let's get on with it," she says. "This test requires us each to confess our innermost secret. We can do this."

She glances at Kollin and Emily, and they drop their gaze. She lifts her eyebrows at me and I shake her off. When she looks at Jose, he's wearing an expression of panic.

"Oh, for Pete's sake. Fine. I'll go first." Worry lines cover her forehead like skid marks. Her eyes narrow on the candles in front of her, as if the words she needs are written there. "It's a big one." She takes a breath and pans each of our faces. "Remember, we're sworn to secrecy."

The muscles in my face tighten to mirror the seriousness in Laney's.

"Go on, Laney." Kollin squeezes her shoulder. "Maybe they can help."

"Wait a minute." My head jerks around. "You already know what her secret is? She told you?"

"Of course she told me."

My cheeks burn. "You told Kollin but you didn't tell me? I opened up to you about stuff and the whole time, you were keeping secrets from me?"

"This is different. I had my reasons for telling Kollin."

My shoulders slump with a heavy thought. "Are you pregnant?"

"No, I'm not pregnant!" She trades glances with Kollin.

My mind is brainstorming all kinds of scenarios. "Did you two run away and get married or something?"

"No, you idiot. Nothing like that."

"Well, tell us already."

She hesitates. The candles flicker, making it harder to read her expression.

"Go on, Lane," Kollin says.

She stares up at the ceiling and says, "I'm adopted, only my parents kept it a secret."

Oh, that… Relief pours over me. *I knew that.*

My shoulders instantly relax, but Laney's confession seems to bug Emily. "So you're adopted," she says. "A lot of parents have trouble telling their kid that."

"There's more to it." There's a tremor in Laney's voice. "My birth mother was a student here. She was a Seven."

Wait. What?

Emily and Jose lean forward the same time I do. "She was a Seven?" I say.

"When my parents lied about my adoption, I started looking for information. They went shopping one afternoon and I searched their bedroom and attic looking for my birth certificate or adoption paperwork. I uncovered a trunk with all this weird stuff in it, like a black cape and an envelope just like the ones we've been getting, with a letter in it. I started to read it, but my parents came home. I got out of the attic just in time.

"They caught me in their bedroom, but I made some lame excuse. I don't think they believed me, but they let it go. A few days later, they were at Josh's baseball game so I snuck back into the attic. The trunk was gone. They must have moved it to hide it from me."

"You think the trunk belonged to your real mom?" Jose says.

"I know it did. The letter said 'make sure Delaney knows I loved her' and 'keep my baby away from danger.'"

"How do you know she was a Seven?" Emily asks.

"In the letter … it said 'tell my daughter that the Sevens were innocent and worthwhile' or something, even though they were 'destroyed by the lies of evil men'—I remember that phrase. That's all I read before they came home."

"Lane," I say, "maybe Mom and Dad are protecting you from something."

"And maybe they're part of the 'evil men,'" she says. "Remember, the letter said to be sure I knew she loved me, and they certainly didn't do that. They didn't even tell me she existed. Even after I confronted them, they never said anything about her or the Sevens, much less defended their innocence."

"I don't think your parents—"

Laney interrupts me. "Here's another thing. Remember

how I volunteered in the administration office filing new student applications last summer? *Every student* is required to have a birth certificate and health history on file, but I don't. I searched my own file and couldn't find one. The folder checklist was stamped to indicate it was received, but the certificate itself was missing. Someone took it. My parents aren't the only people hiding this."

"Listen to yourself, Laney. Do you really think your parents could do something evil?"

"I wouldn't know, Talan, because they won't talk to me. But it makes sense if they're trying so hard to hide this."

I can't believe what she's saying. "They love you, Laney! They're good people."

"You're the one who said never to trust anyone. Why would my parents lie if there wasn't something bad to hide? I need to know the truth. I'm keeping their secret, at least for now. I don't want to get them in trouble or break up our home, even if they did steal me as a baby. But what if they had something to do with hurting my real mom? I don't know what I'd do if that was true."

She rubs her eyes with her palms. "I need to know what happened. That's what I want for my Great Reward. I want to find my real mother and clear her name for good."

Kollin rubs her shoulder and Jose smiles weakly at her. Emily sits quietly, picking at a hole in her jeans.

"So now you know my innermost secret. Whoever is behind resurrecting the Sevens knows that secret too. There was a message on the white board in the lab room where I found my invitation to join the Sevens. It said: 'You were born to be a 7.' Only the word "be" was crossed out, like they were also telling me: 'You were born to a 7.' They knew about my mom."

My stomach lurches as I realize something. She's already so sad, I hesitate to ask. "What if she died in the fire?"

"No, I did the math. She would have been three months pregnant the March they were murdered. That means she was one of the survivors that never came forward. I think she was scared. She was probably protecting me."

She kneads her hands together. "I need to know what happened to my mother. I need to save my school and clear the Sevens."

After sitting quiet, Emily finally looks up at us. "If anyone understands that, it's me."

THIRTY-THREE

"My turn," Emily says abruptly. She swallows hard.

Then she stretches her legs straight in front of her and rubs the tops of her thighs. In the candlelight, her somber expression makes her look ghostly.

"I got pregnant when I was fourteen," she says. "Danny was eighteen and didn't want it. Or me." Her voice wavers. "I kept the baby, but it was harder than I ever imagined. Money was already tight before Amelia was born. And my neighborhood isn't exactly safe. To be responsible for someone you love in a neighborhood like ours, well, you don't know what that feels like."

"I do," Jose says. "My mom sent me here after my older brother was killed in a drive-by. We've been trying for three years to get my younger brother into Singer. There aren't any openings yet."

"So you get it, then. Sometimes you do what you have

to." Emily's talking faster now, her hands gesturing in some hyperactive sign language. "I couldn't do school *and* work *and* take care of Mellie too. But I couldn't bear to give her up for adoption either. My mom had an idea. She enrolled both of us at Singer. That way, we both got a decent place to live. Mom could work, and I could finish school like a normal teenager and still be with Amelia at the same time. It was the perfect plan until the first time I heard her call her housemother 'Mommy.' I cried for two days."

She buries her face in her hands. Jose scoots close and rubs her back.

After a minute, Emily clears her throat and wipes her face. She twists toward Laney. "You're doing the right thing trying to get your answers. I want my baby to know me more than anything, the same way you're trying to know your mom. That's why *I* joined the Sevens. The invitation promised that the Sevens would grant my greatest desire. I want to be a good mom to Mellie. I want to finish school and go to college. The Sevens are my only chance…"

Emily takes a deep breath. "So that's my secret. The toddler everyone thinks is my sister is really my daughter. I pretend everything's perfect, but my life is one big messed-up lie."

In a flash, I remember something Laney told me. "There's no such thing as perfect," I say. "If you look close enough, there's a hole in everything."

When I look up, Laney's smiling at me. "That's how the light gets in," she says.

THIRTY-FOUR

"You're not the only one living a lie," Kollin announces.

His eyes latch on Delaney's. She gives him a half smile and nods, like she's there for him no matter what.

I want to puke.

A corner of his mouth lifts slightly. "I'm in love."

You've got to be kidding me.

"That's your big secret?" I say. "You and Laney have been going out for over a year. Everyone knows you're the perfect couple. That doesn't count as a secret."

He gets quiet and stares at Laney. She nods so slightly, I might have missed it if I wasn't already glaring at her.

"It's ... not Laney," he says.

I straighten up. "What?"

Laney drops her eyes.

Kollin repeats in a deeper voice, "It's not Laney." He frowns and tilts his head, his eyes never leaving her. "Laney's the best. She's just not my type."

Though I'm not exactly disappointed to hear that, I'm seething that Kollin would hurt Laney like this. I slap my hand on the ground and point at him. "You're hooking up with Emily. I knew it!"

"What?" Emily says.

"What?" Jose says.

"What?" Laney says.

"It's Emily!"

"No, it's not," Emily says.

"No, it's not," repeats Kollin.

"It's not?" I ask.

"No!" Emily says. "I'm into Jose."

"You are?" I say.

"Really?" Jose says, busting into a grin.

When Emily blushes bright red, Jose whispers, "Girl, I'm crazy about you, too."

What the heck is going on?

I turn to Kollin. "Dude, are you kidding me?" I clench my fists to keep from strangling him. "You hurt Laney for a girl who doesn't even like you? What the fuck is wrong with you? You have Laney Shanahan. What the hell else could you want?"

"A guy."

I must not have heard right. "Say again?"

"I'm not interested in Emily or Laney or any girl!" Kollin shakes his head at me. "I'm gay, Talan. Everything with Laney is an act. She's my best friend. That's all."

His face is so smug, so matter-of-fact, I want to … to …

"You son of a—" I lunge across the floor, knocking

over several candles. I cock my arm back but Laney holds it behind me. "When were you going to tell her? Your honeymoon?" I yell.

Kollin scuttles backward. "Laney already knows! She's always known!"

The words spin in my head. I take a moment to process them as my arm falls limp to my side. I turn to Laney. "And that's okay with you? You don't mind? I don't understand."

"Kollin and I were never dating, Talan," she barks at me. "It's always been an act."

"But *why?*"

"We have an arrangement." She looks wilted. "Only upperclassmen with straight A's and full privileges are allowed to leave campus to go on dates. We fake like we're dating so we can go into town."

"Why do you need to go into town?"

"To research the Sevens and my real mom." She drops to the ground next to me and sighs. "It started when I got the mail one day and saw a bill for a storage unit in town. We have tons of space in the garage and the attic, so I put two and two together and figured that that's where they hid the trunk. Kollin agreed to act like we were dating so I could check it out, only I couldn't find the right key to open it. Other times, I've gone to the town library so I can research online without worrying about my parents walking in on me. I've read every article ever written about the murder of William Singer and the investigation of the Sevens. That's how I know so much about this school. And the Sevens."

Jose turns to Kollin. "So why do *you* need to go into town?"

"That's where my boyfriend lives. Nathan and I interned together at the law firm last year. It's the only time I get to see him."

Someone's playing a hell of a joke on me. "No way. You're telling me you're gay?" I put my hand on his leg. When he glances at it, I jerk it away. "Oh. Sorry," I blurt out. "That was totally innocent. I'm not, you know, like that."

Kollin rolls his eyes. "Don't be such a phobe, Michaels. *You're* not my type either."

"Good." I sigh, then I realize how dumb I sound. "I mean. I only meant … " But nothing I say can explain away stupid. "So why don't you just come out? Most kids here wouldn't judge. You're a big deal at this school. No one's going to mess with you."

"Maybe. But they'd treat me different." He looks at my hand. "Like you just did." He moves away from me, and I'm embarrassed. "I'll come out when *I'm* ready. I don't want to be defined by my sexuality. Gay is only one part of who I am. And even more important, when I am ready, I want to tell my father first."

"He doesn't know?" Emily asks.

"I don't see him enough for him to know. He's deployed in Afghanistan. It's not something I can just Skype him about. I love my dad, but he's an old-school marine. I plan on telling him after graduation. If he's mad, well, I'll be on my own in college anyhow. Well, not exactly alone. Nathan is going to U of I too."

Emily leans back, her mouth winding into a smirk. "I knew you and Shanahan were faking it the whole time."

"You did not," Laney says.

"Yeah, I did. It's so obvious."

"It was?" Jose and I say at the same time.

"Well, duh. Did you ever watch them? Kollin is always kissing Laney on the cheek or the forehead. That kind of kiss says, 'You're cute' or 'we're friends.' When you're into someone, you aren't going to kiss them on the cheek." She lifts her eyebrows. "It's Body Language 101: if you're crazy about someone, you kiss them on the mouth with all you've got."

I shake my head at Laney. "So this is for real?" I can't help snicker. "This whole time you were faking you had a boyfriend, and you were really alone? That's so stupid. Why would you settle for that?"

"Shut up, Talan. Not everyone needs to bang everything in sight, like you."

I shake my head some more, as if I can throw off the shock of it. "You were single the whole time and faking it?"

"Shut up already!" She leans forward, her face pinched and red. "You know another reason I did it? I was sick of you teasing me about never having a boyfriend. Like it's any of your business. I'm sure you're happy now, though. Now you can go back to making fun of me like you always did. You just better remember your vow and do it in private. We're sworn to keep each other's secrets."

I try, but I can't stop smiling.

"Shut up, Michaels, or I swear I'll choke you! You... you jerk! I noticed you still haven't shared your secret. Well, it's *your* turn now. Tell us, so *we* can make fun of *you*."

THIRTY-FIVE

I stare at Laney and she groans. Her voice rises. "Tell us your stupid secret so we can get this over with and get out of here already." She glares at me with toxic eyes.

Everything I've heard tonight swirls around inside my brain. Before I can talk myself out of it, I'm crawling toward Laney. I kneel in front of her, but I can't speak.

Laney glowers at me, suspicious eyes scrutinizing my every twitch.

Should I do this?

The words come out shakier than my hands: "My secret comes in two parts." I take a deep breath, but I still feel winded. Maybe because my heart is pounding like crazy. "Part One."

I slowly tug my hoodie and shirt up and pull them off me.

She glances at my chest before her eyes return to mine.

"The scars," I say softly, "weren't from a playground."

In my peripheral vision, Jose winces.

I close my eyes so I can think. My throat tightens until it's hard to swallow. "Anthony was my mother's dealer first," I manage to spit out. "Then her boyfriend."

Blood swooshes in my ears. My mouth and throat are drier than a desert. "He finished his masterpiece in stages, so it wouldn't be as obvious."

Even shirtless, I'm sweating. I take another breath and lift a shaky finger to my chest. "The S came first. He said...he said...I deserved my own Scarlet Letter."

My skull is pounding now. I lean forward and tuck my chin until I can swallow back the boulder in my throat.

I straighten up and slowly twist my bicep to show them the burn mark there. "The T on this arm came next."

I clench and unclench my fists. "There's a U and P on my back that aren't as legible. He did those in one sitting...literally," I whisper. "He sat on my ass and held me there while he wrote on me with a razor blade."

My heart hammers inside my chest, pounding under the S like a rioting prisoner.

"There's an I on this arm"—I inhale sharply—"that's easy to hide." I rotate my right elbow so they can see.

When I bring my hand up to point out the right side of my chest, it's shaking uncontrollably. "He planned on wrapping it around me and finishing on this side. But that day, he changed his mind."

Every muscle in my body tenses to fight off the memory of it.

"He decided he'd carve the final letter on my forehead.

He said it was perfect. S-T-U-P-I and the D on my face. That way, even if I hid everything else with clothes, the D would always be there to remind me that I was dumb."

My head is dizzy and my throat clenches down on every word I speak. "My mother was lucid enough to hide me that day," I choke out. "She told Anthony I ran away and he believed her. I hid in a dark closet, still and stiff for hours, until they finally left to score drugs."

I stare sidelong into the candles to try to refocus. "I tried to get out, but the door was locked. Fortunately... or unfortunately... they got arrested that night. DCFS found me two days later..."

My eyes gravitate to Laney's. "The day I ran away from Singer. The day you and your dad came and found me in the cemetery? I was going home. I was scared he'd hurt her if I didn't let him finish."

Tears track Laney's cheeks. Her teeth burrow into her bottom lip.

I blink and swallow a few times before sitting up.

Breathe deep. Breathe deep.

"Now... Part Two of my secret."

I scoot forward on weak legs toward Laney and softly brush her hair back. She watches me like I'm a magician who's pulling a quarter out of her ear.

I tip my head toward hers. Slowly, slowly, I inch my face nearer and nearer until my mouth just grazes hers.

I wait for a red light. But Laney doesn't balk. She doesn't grimace. She doesn't turn away.

She closes her eyes, leans forward, and presses her lips to mine.

It's soft at first, like a light rain. Then I cup my hand around her neck and kiss her full and hard. When she kisses me back, my brain travels somewhere I've never been. My body warms with an intoxicating buzz until, all of a sudden, Laney freezes.

I jerk back to check her reaction.

She doesn't have one. Her mouth hangs open. Her face is stiff and her forehead is covered with worry lines.

My stomach plunges like a broken elevator.

Kollin's voice echoes behind me. "What ... was that?"

"Weren't you listening to anything I said about body language?" Emily says softly. "When you're crazy about someone, you kiss them full on the mouth. Talan is showing us he's whipped on Laney Shanahan."

Laney looks at Emily and then me, and I don't deny it. She moves her mouth to speak, but nothing results but an expression of terror.

"I know I said I never wanted a girlfriend," I whisper to her. "I didn't want to get close to anyone. But I want to get closer to you." I can't take my eyes off her. "You said it your-self—we make a good team. I think we'd be great together, Delaney. Let's take a chance."

Her face twists like she's in pain. After ten years together, I know what that means. She's torn and she doesn't know what to do. Which can only mean one thing. *She's rejecting me too.*

My arms and legs grow shakier. I scoot backward to the dark wall, wishing it would swallow me.

I'm sweating and my face is burning but I rush to get my shirt and hoodie back on anyway. The silence blares louder than the front row at rock concert. I want to blow the candles out and hide in the darkness.

"Oh my God." Jose's voice rises above the awkward quiet. "What have I done?"

He jumps to his feet. "I screwed up! I'm sorry. We gotta get out of here quick! NOW!"

"What?" Kollin says. "Why?"

Jose's hopping around like there's a fire alarm going off in his head. "I'll explain later. Get up! Everyone! Out! Now!" He reaches for Emily's hand and pulls her up.

"Why? What's wrong?"

"I don't have time to explain. I didn't know. I'll make it right, I promise! Right now we've got to get out of here. Fast!" He yanks my arm so hard it hurts.

"Dude! What are you doing? We still haven't heard *your* secret."

The four of us are on our feet now. Jose talks fast, herding us toward the stairs. "My secret is I betrayed you. All of you. I told Principal Boyle about the Sevens. He might have followed me for all I know. You need to get out of here. Now!"

Emily gasps. "You told?"

"It was a mistake," Jose says. "I told the headmaster way back, when I first got the invitation. I had no idea what the Sevens were about then. Same as Talan. I told Boyle that someone was resurrecting the Society and inviting students to join. I'm sorry. I'll make it right, I swear!"

Jose is bouncing around so frantically, I'm scared he'll kick over some candles and burn someone.

"Boyle was pissed when I told him," he says. "I had

no idea he was involved with Kane. He told me to gather information so he can catch everyone in the act."

Emily sags against the wall. "Jose, why would you do that?"

"I'm sorry. I should have told you sooner. I didn't know what to do—everyone said the Sevens were murderers. I figured they were just another thug gang, same as the one that killed my brother. I figured I could work a deal with the headmaster: if I narced, maybe he'd help get my brother into Singer. He's been on the waitlist for three years and he's getting in trouble back home. So I proposed a deal to Boyle. I told him I'd gather information in exchange for getting Manny in."

Kollin grabs Jose's collar. "What were you thinking?"

"Stop!" I wedge myself between them. "We don't have time for this." I turn to Jose. "What exactly did you tell Boyle?"

"I only told him about the invitation and first note so far. The more we got into this, the more I started having second thoughts. He doesn't know about any of you or the tests, but he's been pressuring me for more info. He's suspicious of me now—I'm sure of it. He may even be following me for all I know. I caught him watching me the other day. You need to get out of here and stay away from me."

He herds everyone up the stairs. "I swear I won't betray you to him. No matter what. I'll say I lied, or I'll make something up. I'll figure it out. Just go before we're caught!"

THIRTY-SIX

We scramble out of the angel statue, then creep through the door and down the steps of the mausoleum.

"We need to meet to talk more about this," Emily whispers.

"Not now!" Jose says, gently pushing her forward.

"No, I think now is the perfect time." The voice comes from the side of the mausoleum. It's deep. And older. And angry.

Headmaster Boyle steps out of the shadows and aims a flashlight at us.

Shit.

"Jose, did you trade teams? I had a feeling you were lying. You know you've betrayed your school."

Oh God. We can't run now. There's nothing we can do.

"You're right. I did!" Jose yells back. "When I lied to you. I made the whole Sevens story up. I tried to trick you to get

Manny into Singer, but I can't go through with this, okay? I lied. I'm responsible for everything. Even the vandalism."

"Interesting," Boyle says. "Because the police are convinced several people were involved."

"No. Just me."

"Right. So you went to all this bother to re-invent a secret society and then changed your mind at the last second?"

"That's right. I couldn't do it. I mean, who would believe Laney Shanahan would be involved in the Society of Seven anyway?"

"I would. She has plenty of motive after being overlooked for the Pillars."

"No. That's not it!" Laney says. She shuts up instantly, biting her lip.

"Well . . ." Boyle walks to the top step and peers down at her. "Why don't you explain it to me then."

Laney glares up at his beady eyes. "There's nothing *to* explain. I got an anonymous note that someone needed my help and to meet them here, so I came."

"Me too," Emily says.

"And me," Kollin adds.

"I sent them," Jose said. "I sent those notes to trick them so you'd catch them."

"Mr. Aguilar, that makes no sense, considering you didn't even know I'd be doing rounds of the cemetery tonight." Headmaster Boyle balls his hand into a fist. "And the fact that you're wasting my time with lies that will be easy to refute later is insulting. But I'll be generous. Once. I'll give you each one chance to confess right now, or I'll have the police here in ten minutes to charge all of you. If you tell me the truth, and what everybody's part was in this little secret society, you'll be personally exonerated. In fact, I think I'll even let those of you who are smart enough to confess share in the reward money the Board offered."

The five of us stand silent.

Laney's eyes fix on the ground. Headmaster Boyle steps in front of her, lifting her chin with his finger. "You're perhaps the biggest disappointment of all, Ms. Shanahan. How could your parents be so blind to this activity going on in their own home? Michaels doesn't surprise me, but you? You're about to lose your scholarships and ruin your family's reputation. How will your parents pay for your court costs when I fire them? Certainly, a momentary lapse of judgment shouldn't cost them their jobs and you your future. Tell me what's really going on, and I'll make you a hero for turning everyone else in."

Laney blinks twice. "I got an anonymous note in my locker saying someone needed my help and to meet them here. So I came."

"How sad." Boyle shakes his head. "A bright future lost with two sentences. LeBeau..." He strolls around Laney to Kollin. "I would have thought you were smarter than this. Considering you'll lose not only your scholarships, but any chance of practicing law as a career when I'm through with you, I think you should reconsider your options. Expulsion versus a commendation for protecting your school, not to mention a considerable reward check that will come in handy for college. The choice should be simple for someone with your ambition."

Kollin glares at him. "I got a note in my locker. It said to meet here at seven. That's all I know."

"You'll regret this," Boyle says icily. "Emily Dombrose!" He points at her. "I'd advise you not to be foolish like the others. Doesn't a generous reward and my personal recommendation for a full scholarship to the school of your choice sound more sensible than an arrest record? Or would you prefer to return with your sister to a life of poverty? Tell me everything and help yourself while you still can."

Emily stares over his shoulder with a hardened glare. "I got a note in my locker telling me to be here at seven. That's all I have to say."

Boyle's red face looks like it's going to explode. He waves a shaky finger at Jose. "Your brother is depending on you. Your mother will be devastated. We had a deal, which I will still honor if you tell—"

Jose gets in his face. "I told you, I lied. I sent the letters to set them up so I could get Manny in. I have nothing else to say until I talk to my lawyer. We're *all* done here."

"Not so fast." Boyle wears the crooked grin of a man who knows he holds all the power. "I still have one card to play."

He crosses his arms and struts over to me. He threatens me with his eyes, unblinking and glued to mine. "You have the most to lose and the most to gain, don't you, Talan? You've always struck me as an opportunist with some street smarts. I want you to consider your choices. In one hour, you'll be sitting in a jail with no one to bail you out. You have no family, and I doubt you'll have any friends left when word gets out what you've done to this school. When I kick you out of Singer, you won't even be eligible for foster care. If and when you're released from jail, you'll be homeless. Personally, I'll enjoy throwing what little you have to the curb. I doubt anyone here will even care that you're gone, considering the trouble you caused your fellow students. *I* certainly won't miss you."

Behind him, Laney's eyes well.

"On the other hand"—Boyle brings me back to attention—"you could be the hero who stopped the guilty parties. Since none of your fellow Sevens were smart enough to accept my offer, that leaves the full $10,000 reward for you. Not to mention I have quite a bit of pull with the Board now. I'm sure I could persuade them to help you in your post-graduation plans."

My stomach twists at the realization that I'm going to be alone and homeless again. For an instant, I consider his offer. My breath catches as I remember Stephen Kane telling me he and I were alike.

"Here's my confession," I say. "I got a letter and showed up tonight to see what it was about." With my history, I'm done at Singer and I know it. Might as well enjoy my *bon voyage*. "And I won't miss you either, you fucker."

Boyle whips his flashlight against a tree.

"So that's it then?" he shouts. His eyes trace an angry trail across each of our faces. "You've all made your final decision?"

Silence.

Boyle storms toward Rucker Road. "Follow me, then!"

We trail him between the tombstones, like lambs to slaughter. Twenty feet in, Boyle freezes near the winged angel statue that marks Mary Singer's original grave. He stares at a dark mass on the ground where the angel points. "What's that?"

Kollin is standing closest to it, five feet away. "You there. LeBeau," Boyle bellows. "Pick it up."

Kollin reaches down and lifts up a long black piece of fabric, leaving more of them in the pile on the ground.

"What is it?" Boyle snaps.

Kollin holds it higher, and it falls in folds. He grabs a corner, turns, and straightens it. "I think it's a cloak." He holds the cape by the collar to show Boyle something. "There's … " He lifts his eyes to the headmaster's. "There's a seven embroidered inside."

Boyle walks over and snatches it from Kollin. He holds it out for us to see, giving us a wide smile.

"I believe," he says in a gentler voice, "there are actually five cloaks. One for each of you."

He tosses me the one in his hand, and I catch it.

What the … ?

Crossing his arms on his chest, he looks at each of us and says, "Congratulations, Sevens. You just passed your sixth test … For sacrifice."

No way.

"I guess I should introduce myself." A grin consumes his face. "I'm Number Seven."

THIRTY-SEVEN

Pigs are flying in a frozen hell somewhere.

Boyle busts out laughing. "Mr. Singer would be proud. I knew I selected the right Sevens!"

"Sir?" Laney says. "Are you saying…" She doesn't finish. She's too smart. Too careful to be tricked into giving anything away.

"I'm saying *I* sent the tests. I gave you the exact same invitation and virtue challenges that William Singer gave me and my friends eighteen years ago."

The five of us exchange glances, but none of us says a word.

"Don't believe me?" He smiles. "Good. You *should* be careful. But I can prove it: the column messages, the pediment proverb, the angel in tears—essentially everything we learned from Mr. Singer, I showed you. There are only two people alive today who'd know those secrets—the two surviving Sevens."

"*You* sent the clues?"

"Yes. I switched the order of a couple of the tests because I wanted you to witness Stephen Kane in my home that night; but you now have every clue the original Sevens had at the time of the murders. In fact, the note that's taped to the wall in the hidden room beneath the mausoleum is the original. That's the last letter Mr. Singer ever gave us, I'm afraid."

"But why are you doing this?" Emily says.

"Well, Ms. Dombrose, you should know that by now. The same Stephen Kane who lied about the original Sevens eighteen years ago is back to destroy Singer School. It's time I kept my vow of courage and finish what Mr. Singer trusted me to do. I'll do whatever it takes to stop Kane, but I need your help."

Jose looks Boyle up and down. "Why would you need us?"

"There needs to be a legitimate Society of Seven if we're going to make a legal claim to take over the Board. And more important, I need your help to find the Trust Protector Document before the next board meeting."

"Do you have any clue where it is?" Jose asks.

Boyle puts his hands in his pockets and looks thoughtful. "Mr. Singer said that the Sevens would know where the TPD was after the last test. The night of the murders, he called us to the chapel to tell us something. We assumed he was gathering us to give us the final clue. We'd been waiting for it for a while by then. Of course, we never got the chance to solve it."

Kollin rubs his chin. "There's something I've never understood—why would the Board want to get rid of Mary?"

"Singer heard that the Board was angry because Mary insisted that company profits be used to expand the school. Their priority was to channel the revenue to investments that would triple the stock value." He glances between us. "Any other questions?"

"What about the money that went missing?" I say.

"We never knew anything about any missing money. Over the past eighteen years, I've searched every part of Singer's residence, the tunnels, and every inch of Founders Hall looking for that TPD. In all that time, I never saw any evidence of any money. My guess is that was a ruse to frame the Sevens. None of the Sevens would have taken it. They were the best of the best."

Blame it on my ADD, but I can't help myself. "Then why'd Mr. Singer choose you?"

"Well Talan, I asked him that same question once." Boyle's laugh surprises me. Then his voice gets quieter. "William had great faith in me. He said that I only needed a chance to overcome the damage of a broken childhood. He told me that he knew I'd rise above it one day to do great things." A corner of his mouth lifts. "It's the same reason I chose you, Talan. You remind me of myself at your age."

Why do people I hate keep telling me that?

Laney steps forward and touches Boyle's sleeve. "We shared *our* secrets. Now I need to ask you about one. Was the other Seven that survived my mother?"

Boyle hesitates, then nods.

"Both your parents were Sevens. Your father and mother were the closest thing I had to a family. The night of the murders, she confided to me about the pregnancy. That's why we were late for the meeting."

His gaze drifts to the burnt-out chapel ruins in the distance. "When we finally arrived, we had no idea what was going on ... we watched through a crack in the mausoleum door. A student was struggling with the chapel doors, but the walls were already burning and caving in. When police and fire trucks pulled up, we took the tunnels back to Winchester House to find the Sevens. We realized later that they'd been murdered, just as William Singer suspected had happened to his wife."

"Why didn't you go to the police?"

"We were scared for our lives," Boyle says. "And for yours, Delaney. Not to mention that the Sevens were being framed for Singer's murder. There was evidence of arson, and later, the claims of stolen money. The student who discovered the chapel burning told police he was jogging down Rucker Road when he heard Mr. Singer shouting for help, screaming that the Sevens were trying to kill him. Based on his statement, investigators theorized that the Sevens murdered Singer for his money, then got trapped in the fire they lit to hide the evidence." Boyle's gaze bounces between us. "That student was Stephen Kane."

Emily gasps.

"I knew it!" Laney squeezes Boyle's wrist. "Is my mother alive? Tell me who she is."

Boyle's eyes soften. "I'm sorry Delaney. It isn't safe to tell you yet. But it will all be revealed soon, I promise. When our work is done, fail or succeed, you'll know everything. I can tell you that she loved you enough to give you a better life with the best people she knew. Everyone at Singer adored the Shanahans. Which brings me to my next subject." Boyle eyes each of us. "You can't tell your parents. Not your parents, not your houseparents, not your best friends. Nobody. There are people to protect. Do you understand? No matter what, you say nothing."

We nod, but it isn't enough for him. "No," he says. "I want you to raise your hand and swear. No matter what, you won't mention anything you know about the Sevens. Not even under questioning. Not even to help another Seven."

One by one, we lift our hands.

"What I wrote in my note to you was true," he says. "There are murderers among us. I lost six people I loved the most in the world, all at once. I won't let that happen to you."

The bell tower bongs nine times and Boyle's cranky headmaster voice returns. "You need to hurry back. I'll hide your cloaks in the secret room. In the meanwhile, think hard on all you've learned, and be careful. Kane and the Pillars are watching everywhere. The less we're seen together, the better."

THIRTY-EIGHT

The forest is darker than the tunnels. Jose, Laney, and Emily walk ahead, jabbering about the insane night we just had.

I'm glad. Because once I started running the events through my own head, I remembered my humiliating confession to Laney. God, how can I even face her now?

I drag behind them.

"I'm impressed," Kollin says. I barely noticed him beside me.

"What?"

"I underestimated you. I don't know if I was in your shoes if I'd have turned down Boyle's offer. I mean, to be arrested, friendless, homeless, and penniless. That took guts." He gives me pity eyes. "It sucks you don't have a family."

"I do have a family—the Sevens, the Shanahans, and Singer School. And I'd never let anyone hurt them. Especially not Laney."

Kollin watches me for a second. "Are you in love with Laney?"

"Love?" I think of my nameless father and the mother who let crackheads babysit me. "How would I know?" I watch Laney walking ahead and random thoughts spill out. "I think about her nonstop, whatever that means. The way she smells. How fun it is to tease her. She makes me insane one minute and insanely horny the next. Is that love?"

I can't believe I'm pouring my guts out to Colon LeDouche.

"Christ, Kollin. You saw what happened. After I kissed her, her face went totally blank. How could I misread her so completely? She obviously only sees me as a friend. Or worse, like a brother. Now I freaked her out and wrecked everything."

"I don't know about that," Kollin says. "I think Laney's always had a thing for you."

All of a sudden, the Sevens, Boyle, even the threat of being murdered gets relocated to the back of my mind. "Really? Why do you say that? Did Laney say something?"

"She talks about you constantly." He looks sideways at me. "Nice things."

"She does?"

"Yeah. Like I'll tell her, 'Someone needs to buy that guy a razor,' and she'll say, 'I think he looks hot.' And I'm always saying, 'I don't know how you can stand that ass-hole,' and she'll get mad and say, 'He's actually a good guy. You just don't know him like I do.'"

"Thanks." I rub my neck. "I think." My chest tightens.

"But if that's true, why did she look like she was gonna hurl when I kissed her?"

"I have no idea what's holding her back. Maybe because you come on to everything with two X chromosomes? I know Laney pretty well. She must have told me a hundred times she'd rather wait for something great than settle for something just to have a guy. I'm sure it's from being brought up with six brothers. She'd rather wait for something real and romantic."

"I'm romantic. Ask any of the girls I've hooked up with."

"The fact that you've hooked up with half the girls at Singer doesn't make you romantic. It makes you risky. Laney doesn't want to be someone a guy just 'hooks up' with."

"But it wouldn't be that way with her."

"Well, how would she know that? It's like being the last one picked in gym class."

"She's not my last choice. She's my first. I never wanted a girlfriend before."

"Maybe you need to prove that to her."

"How? What do I do?"

Kollin chuckles. "Are you asking me to help you?"

"Yeah. I am. Will you?"

"For Laney." Kollin's face gets serious. "But if you hurt her, I'll bury you. I don't care if you're a Seven or not."

I elbow him. "So how does a gay guy know so much about women?"

"How does a guy who's hooked up with a hundred girls know so little?"

"Touché." I look him straight in the eye. "…So you'll help me, Kollin?"

"Of course. We're Sevens," he says. His answer makes me feel bad for all the times I called him a waste of oxygen. "Just call me Cyrano."

"Who?"

"This is going to be harder than explaining quantum physics to a four-year-old."

I kick a rock in my path. "It can't be any harder than finding a document that's been missing for two decades when we don't have a clue where to look."

"That's true." Kollin rubs his forehead as he walks. "If only Singer didn't wait so long to give the Sevens that final test." He shakes his head. "I gotta be honest, I just don't see how we're going to solve this. How does Boyle think we can figure out in a few weeks what he couldn't in almost two decades? What does he expect us to do? Channel William Singer and ask him where he hid it?"

I shrug.

"This school means a lot to me, Talan. I love my dad more than anything, but this is the family that raised me. I can't imagine that Singer School might not be here next year." Kollin's shoulders drop. "Some of my best friends are sophomores and juniors. What's going to happen to them?"

Chris and Mike and Jack Dominguez and a dozen other faces appear in my head. I get a desperate, queasy feeling.

The forest ends ten yards ahead. We say goodbye, and Kollin, Emily, and Jose veer off the path toward their student homes, leaving Laney and me alone.

Might as well face this.

I catch up to Laney and she gets all fidgety. "Maybe we should walk separately," she says.

My stomach sinks. "Okay. But I need to tell you something."

She glances at me with worried eyes.

"I'm going to wait for you, Shanahan. 'Cause I'd rather wait than settle for something that's not you."

God that sounded stupid.

I jog ahead so I don't have to see her reaction.

THIRTY-NINE

I can't believe I'm at school a half hour early.

"Kollin?" I say.

He looks around the door of his locker. "Michaels...what are you doing here already?"

"Couldn't sleep. You?"

"Same." He lifts a hand to the top of his locker and hangs there, a dazed look in his eyes. "We've had a lot to think about. We have a few weeks to find that TPD or our friends are homeless. No pressure, huh?"

"I know. It's mind-blowing." I check the empty hall. "Listen, can I throw an idea at you?"

"Sure." He slams his locker closed and leans back against it.

"I was up all night thinking, and, well, maybe there's more to those tests."

"What do you mean?"

"One thing I figured out early on is that William Singer never did anything without a reason. You know? Everything ties together to show us something else, right?"

Kollin nods.

"Well, I was thinking about a couple things Boyle said. Like how Singer told the Sevens they'd know where the TPD was after the last test. And how the Sevens had been waiting and waiting for that final clue, so they assumed that's why Singer called them together that night at the chapel."

"Go on," he says.

"Well, what if the Sevens already had the last clue, but they just didn't realize it?"

He tips his head back. "What are you saying?"

"The poem Singer left in the hidden room after they finished their sixth test—what if that *was* the last clue? I can't remember all of it, but I'm pretty sure it said something about being on their own and alone for the final 'quest.' A quest is a search to find something valuable, right? It has to be the TPD—what else would it be? Maybe that poem was saying that the final test for wisdom was to use everything they'd learned to find the TPD on their own."

He stares, and I'm not sure if he's thinking I'm crazy or a genius.

"Yeah ... I'd need to reread that clue, but you could be right. Man, you have a good memory." There's actually shock in his eyes. "Laney was right—you are a brainiac."

My insides feel like they're vibrating. "I'll go to the mausoleum tonight and copy the poem word for word. You come over later to hang with Laney and we'll brainstorm together when I get back."

He smacks me on the arm. "If you're right, we might have a shot of finding that TPD after all. That's an amazing catch."

What's amazing is how much more I like this guy than I did twenty-four hours ago.

Then Kollin's face gets all serious. "So, did you get a chance to talk to Delaney last night?"

"No."

"I'll feel her out for you today," he says. "I'll put in a good word for you."

Kollin LeBeau is a nice guy? Marcus had it right—weird stuff *is* going on.

Speaking of Marcus, right then he turns down the end of hallway with Josh and Jake.

"Shoot," I whisper. "Don't let anyone see us all friendly or they'll know something's up." I give Kollin the evil eye and whisper through gritted teeth, "Act like we're fighting."

His face busts out into a wicked grin. That's more like it. He drops the book in his hand and shoves me hard in the shoulders. "You fucking loser, stay away from me!"

Wow. And I thought I was a good actor.

"I'm not afraid of you," he says, shoving me harder.

I regain my footing and lunge at him. The three of them are near us now. I grab Kollin by the neck and slam him hard into his locker, feeling awful when I hear the metal bang. When I stretch my arm back to throw a punch, my prediction is fulfilled. Marcus grabs me and yanks me away.

"Dude!" Marcus says. "What are you thinking? You can't do this here. You'll be expelled."

Josh and Jake wedge themselves between us, their stunned gazes ping-ponging between Kollin and me.

Kollin bends over and picks up his book, pointing the thing at me while nursing his head. "Good thing your friends have better sense than you," he says all cocky. "I'd love to see trash like you get kicked to the curb."

Crack me up, that was Boyle's line from last night.

I take a wild swing from behind Marcus. Pointing at Kollin, I hiss, "Watch your back. I'm not through with you."

I'm thinking we deserve an Oscar when I notice the stares of the other students milling around their lockers now. Cameron Moore and Kayla Kaminski whisper as they glare at me.

When Jake grabs my sleeve to haul me out of there, I shake him off like I'm still pissed. I walk away on my own, all dramatic and pouty, and head toward my English class.

Cameron follows me in the room. "Notice anyone missing this morning?" he says. "Or were you too busy with LeBeau to realize your girlfriend wasn't around?"

It takes a second to figure out he's talking about Emily. "What are you up to, Moore?"

"Nothing. I just noticed her in Headmaster Boyle's office. That's all."

I want to pound the grin off his face.

"I'll let you in on a little secret," he says. "There was an anonymous tip that she was involved with some of the vandalism around school. The police called her into Boyle's office for questioning."

"An anonymous tip, huh? Yeah, that'll hold up in court."

"You never know." One shoulder rises with his eyebrows. "Maybe they'll find some evidence in her locker."

"You dirtbag…"

"Mr. Kane is giving you another chance. Are you ready to turn over what you know, or do we need to step up our game?"

"You think I'm afraid of you? Bring it on."

"You sure about that?" he says. "Marcus already lost his chance at a scholarship and Emily is being cross-examined as we speak by an officer who's good friends with Mr. Kane. One by one, your posse will fall. You're running out of time, Talan. The only reason Kane hasn't ruined you is that he's hoping you're smart enough to give him what he needs before he destroys every last one of your friends."

Heat flushes through my body. The thought of Emily being framed for Cameron trashing our school makes my muscles knot. I think of Marcus not getting a football scholarship and the Shanahans losing their jobs. I think about Headmaster Boyle losing six people who meant so much to him when he was just seventeen. And then I think of two thousand kids wondering where they'll be in a year, just like me.

I grab Cameron's collar. "I have a message for you to deliver to Mr. Kane." I'm squeezing the fabric so tight, Moore gags. "The Sevens *are* back, and Kane and the Pillars are going down. We'll have that TPD in hand for that board meeting, so get ready for an ass kicking."

I slam Cameron to the floor and he scuttles back, blocking his face with his hands before stumbling to his feet and racing out of the room.

As great as it feels to take Cameron down, damn! *What have I said?*

I collapse in my seat, shaky sick, trembling as the rest of the class wanders in. Jose parks himself next to me, leans over, and whispers, "Did you hear what happened to Emily?"

"Yeah, Cameron told me."

"At least Boyle will be there. He'll help her somehow."

After class, Jose pulls me aside. "If you hear anything more about Emily, let me know." We exchange phone numbers just as Marcus turns the corner. His eyes zero in on Jose and me.

"I gotta go. We'll talk later," I say.

Jose jogs off in the opposite direction before Marcus walks up.

"What's up?"

"Hey," Marcus says. He looks past me, his brow furrowed. "What were you and Aguilar talking about?"

"Nothing. Just shooting the shiz."

"Since when have you been friends with Jose Aguilar?"

"We sit next to each other in a couple classes. Why the third degree? Are you spying on me now?"

"I'm not spying, you jerk. You were upset this morning and I came to see if everything was okay. We used to be best friends, remember? I guess you forgot that, now that you're hanging with Cameron Moore and Jose Aguilar."

"I'm not hanging with Moore. I told you he came to the house looking for weed."

"Which you don't do."

"Which is what I told him."

"You say a lot of things, man. You're also stressed and moody all the time. Seriously, beating on LeBeau in the middle of the hallway? What were you thinking?"

"He was bugging me. He's a douchebag."

"He's not the only one."

"What's that supposed to mean?"

"You're the one cheating with his girlfriend." Marcus rubs his face. "I'm sorry. I don't want to judge you and I don't want to fight. You're my best friend. But something's going on with you and you won't tell me what. Are we friends or not?"

"Of course we're friends."

"Then tell me what's wrong."

I want to tell him, but I can't. I took a vow. It's for his sake too. His sister is a freshman. If Singer closes, she'll have no place to go and he'll be freaking out over how to help her. And what if Kane hurts him to get information on the Sevens? I can't risk him being involved with this.

"Everything's fine. You're worried about nothing." I hold out my fist for him to bump but he just stares at it. He bumps my shoulder as he passes me and heads to his next class.

Marcus doesn't talk to me for the rest of the day. In fact, a few of the guys are treating me cold. It's getting to me, but I have bigger problems right now. They do, too. Only they don't know it because they're riding on my shoulders.

FORTY

The quiet at dinner is so strained that even Mom asks if everything's all right. No one says a word to me, even as we clean up afterward.

When my housebrothers leave to play *Cyber Combat Zone*, I sneak out the front door. I need to get to the mausoleum and back in time to talk to Kollin and Laney.

I'm jogging near the end of my street when two figures dodge behind the last house. Dressed in black, with hoodies pulled over their faces, they trail me from a distance across campus. I decide to duck into the library and take the elevator up. After a while, I take the back stairs down and sneak out the rear exit.

It wastes a lot of time, but at least I'm alone when I hit the woods. I race to the mausoleum and slip through the secret door in the statue. Standing on the landing, I realize I have to go down the stairs in the dark. Alone.

My throat tightens.

It's twelve stairs, and then the sensor light goes on. I can do this. But what if it doesn't go on? What if I'm stuck in the dark or trapped down there alone or … *No. I can do this.* It's twelve steps. Twelve.

I push the button to close the door and trap myself inside the black. One, two, three … I count my quick steps to the bottom room and thank God when the light goes on. I practically fall into the room, heaving in a panic attack that I wasn't prepared for. Jittery and lightheaded, I plop down and try to catch my breath.

When my hands finally steady, I pull out my notebook and scribble the poem word for word off the wall. There's something out of place with it, but what? I read the first letters going down, thinking it could be another one of those column messages, but I get nothing.

I go over the poem so much I have it memorized. It says to use what we've learned to solve the last clue, but what do we use it *on*? It's like we're missing a half clue. Unless we already have it and don't realize it. I pull out the map and see if I can apply the clues we learned earlier to come up with something. After a half hour, I'm just frustrated.

I jam the paper in my bag and jog up the stairs. Right in front of the secret door, I hear a voice outside and freeze.

"I don't know, Cam. That was bad." The male voice trembles so much, I can't make it out. "Did you see all the blood? He wasn't moving. What if we killed him?"

I peek out the narrow slit under the angel's fingertips

and see Cameron Moore shake Iman Kabal. "Get a grip. He'll be fine in time. Mr. Kane wanted it to be bad."

"But what if he dies? We were just supposed to back up Kane in some board meetings, not trash the school and beat the crap out of a kid."

Cameron peels off his gloves. "We're in this now, so deal with it."

"I want to go home," Iman says. "I'm gonna be sick."

He's not the only one. What did they do? Who did they beat up?

Cam grabs his arm. "Get it together." He pulls Iman's gloves off him and tosses both pairs aside. "We'll hide everything here, just like Kane said. He'll plant it in Michael's locker with the master key, and no one will ever suspect us."

Michael's locker? As in, Talan Michaels? As in me? Iman's not the only one who wants to throw up now.

Cam peeks out the mausoleum door.

"Let's go," he tells Kabal, and they both take off running.

The sensor light clicks off and my shaky hands have trouble finding the switch to open the door in the dark. When it finally slides over, I fall out of it and land on a bottle of spray paint and a steel rod. They leave red paint on my hands, or at least the can does. The red fluid on the rod might be blood.

This is what they plan on planting in my locker?

Like hell. I throw everything down the stairs and hit the switch to close the hatch.

I run all the way home, stopping only to wipe my hands on some soggy leaves in the woods. There can't be any paint or blood on me in case someone sees me. I linger on the back porch before going in, searching my hands for any red stains.

The kitchen looks empty, so I creep through the back door. The family room is buzzing with voices. I kick off my damp shoes and use the break to scrub my hands and do a final once-over of my coat and clothes.

I try to steady my wobbly legs so I can look for Kollin and Laney. But the closer I get to the family room, the shakier I get. Someone's bawling. *Laney.*

"What's going on?" I ask. I feel flush and lightheaded. I'm sure I'm as pale as a baby's butt.

Laney sits sobbing on the couch, her parents propping her up on both sides. The rest of my housebrothers huddle around her like a barbed-wired fence.

"Oh, Talan," she wails. Her face is a blotchy red-blue color.

"What's the matter?" I count heads, and our family is all present and accounted for. "What happened?"

Dad staggers over and whispers in my ear, "Someone attacked Kollin LeBeau tonight. He's in intensive care with swelling on the brain and significant internal injuries. They induced a coma to relieve some of the intracranial pressure, but it doesn't look good. They're trying to reach his father in Afghanistan."

I lower myself into a chair before my legs give out. "Do they have any idea who did it?"

"No, but a custodian saw two figures dressed in black running away from the scene. And there was a red seven spray-painted on the sidewalk next to Kollin."

My hands squeeze the arms of the chair to keep the room from spinning. Laney is across from me, wrapped in her mom's arms, dazed and still sobbing. When I look higher, three sets of eyes target me like a drone. It's clear who Marcus, Jake, and Juan think is responsible.

"He'll be okay, Laney." My voice shakes. "Don't worry. And they'll catch who did this."

Laney nods but keeps her face buried in her mom's shoulder. I want to help her so bad. To hug her and tell her I'm here for her. But I can't with her parents there. And maybe she wouldn't want me to anyway. I don't know what to do.

So I leave.

Marcus and Jake follow me to my room. "Where were you tonight?"

Even as I say it, I know how stupid it sounds. But I can't come up with anything else when my thoughts are so wrapped around Laney. "Library."

"I was at the library. I didn't see you."

I lift my arm to block my doorway. "It's a big library."

"What happened to Kollin is messed up."

"Yeah, it is," I say.

"Whoever is doing this Sevens stuff needs to be stopped."

"No kidding."

The thought of Kollin lying on a gurney with his head bashed in is making me woozy. Kollin, who was willing to help me with Laney despite me picking on him. Kollin, with his stellar future waiting for him. Kollin, with a father who loves him, who's flying over an ocean hoping his kid will be alive when he lands.

And it's my fault.

It should have been me. No future, no family, no great loss. That should have been me.

"Talan, we're your best friends. We'll stand by you, but you have to let us help you," Marcus says.

Marcus and Jake are the closest thing to brothers I've ever had. But now, all I can think about is that they could be next. Lying in a hospital bed like Kollin, their bodies mangled because Kane suspected they were Sevens too. All because of being friends with me. All because of my big mouth.

"Fuck you," I say to their stunned faces. "We're not friends anymore. Leave me alone and stay the hell away from me."

I slam the door on them. And on the life I used to have.

FORTY-ONE

Laney is gone when I get up the next morning. "She had a pretty bad night," Mom says when I come into the kitchen. "She insisted Dad take her to the hospital to see Kollin this morning."

I walk to school twenty feet behind my housebrothers. It's like being in kindergarten all over again. They won't talk to me. And that's okay, because anyone who has anything to do with me is in danger now.

They aren't the only ones watching me with suspicious eyes. Word of the assault got out to all student homes last night. As I walk to my locker, there's a hallway of stares branding me. Cameron Moore waits for me, leaning against my locker and smiling smugly. There's a "7" drawn in permanent marker on the front.

"It's not too late," he whispers as he walks around me. "Mr. Kane is still willing to make a deal."

At lunch, I sit down at my usual spot and the table goes silent. One by one, beginning with Marcus, the entire group gets up and moves. It's déjà vu. A scene flashes through my head from elementary school, with the same script except everyone was holding their noses.

I stare at Laney's table. The chairs where she and Kollin usually spend lunch are vacant, like no one dared take their place. I get it. I'm scared too. Scared Kollin won't make it and that Laney will never get over losing her best friend. I know how hard that is because I just lost mine... Marcus.

Does she blame me for saying too much to the Pillars? Is that why she couldn't lift her face from her mom's shoulder to look at me? Did she finally figure out I'm trouble and she doesn't want anything to do with me?

I crinkle my lunch bag and my eyes drift away from their empty chairs. The rest of their table glares at me. Actually, the entire lunchroom is glaring at me.

I know I look guilty. I feel guilty. If I hadn't opened my stupid mouth, none of this would have happened. I wonder if any of the angry faces staring me down called me in to the police. I wonder if Marcus has, or will.

Will he tell the police that Laney was cheating on Kollin with me? Will he tell them how I left the dance in a jealous fit over Kollin, or how Kollin and I came to punches a few weeks back in our family room?

One good thing—if Marcus tells on me, the police will report back to Stephen Kane. Then Kane will know Marcus isn't a Seven, and he'll leave him alone.

But then...

My gut twists and my throat clenches until I think I might pass out. *If Marcus tells Officer Lynch that Laney and I were secretly hooking up, and it gets back to Stephen Kane, Kane will assume Laney's a Seven. Who knows what Kane would do to eliminate Laney as a threat?*

It's bad enough that Laney would be ostracized like me, walking the halls as the new villain of Singer School. But she'd also be vulnerable to whatever violence Kane decides to inflict. Terror sears through me and I can't sit still. I shove my chair out and bolt for the door.

Please brain, work for me for once. Think of a way to stop this from happening.

I duck into Solomon's room and dump my lunch bag across a desk, poking at a lot of stuff I have no intention of eating. A few minutes later, Marcus comes in, and I ignore him.

His expression is torn. He's riding a fence of friendship and anger with me. "Did you hear about the board meeting? It's not a rumor, either. The Pillars heard it firsthand from Stephen Kane."

"What are you talking about?"

"The Board is meeting on Friday to vote on selling Singer Enterprises and the school. They're disgusted with all the bad press and everything going down here—the vandalism, violence, and gang activities on campus. They're talking about changing this to a private school. Did you know that?"

I stare at him, blank-faced.

His teeth clench. "Tal, did you hear me? Mr. Kane wants to 'weed out the riffraff' by changing Singer to a private boarding school that only gives scholarships to under-privileged students with 'unblemished' records. They'd only keep students with a 3.4 GPA or higher, perfect records, and proven accomplishments. Do you know what that means?"

Before I can answer, he says, "It means my sister and a lot of our friends are done here because Kane and the Board are pissed at the Sevens." He rubs his forehead, dropping his gaze to the ground.

His hand freezes on his brow as his half-lidded eyes slowly lift to mine. "Please tell me that's not red paint on your shoelace."

I must have missed a spot last night. "You're ridiculous," I say, hiding my foot behind my other leg.

His eyes trap me. "I keep telling myself there's got to be a good reason for you to be acting like this, Tal. But it's getting impossible to believe anything you say." He sighs. "You know, I haven't told anyone about you and Laney yet."

He's such a loyal friend. I'm not sure if that makes what I'm about to do easier or harder.

"What do I care?" I snap at him. "I dumped Shanahan right after we told you about us."

I look him straight in the eyes. He has to believe me. For his sake and Laney's.

"So I couldn't care less if you tell on her. I never cared about her in the first place. You know I've never wanted a relationship with a girl. I just wanted to see if I could seduce perfect Laney Shanahan before I graduated. Go out with a bang…literally." I laugh. "Only the Proud Prude bailed. She said she couldn't hurt Kollin like that, so I dumped her. She even confessed to LeDouche and the loser forgave her. They were 'working it out.' Why do you think she's so heartbroken now that his head's smashed in?"

"You led Laney on just to screw her?" Marcus' eyes burn a hole through me. "Who *are* you? That's our housesister you're talking about."

He shoves me and I fly backward off my chair. I stumble to my feet.

"What?" He pushes my shoulders again. "Was it some sort of gang dare or something?" His face tightens. "I'm going to narc you out so bad."

"Good," I yell. "Go ahead and tell on us. My reputation's already ruined. What do I care? At least I'd have the pleasure of ruining the Proud Prude's too. I'll tell everyone I nailed her and they can hate the both of us. I'd love to humiliate Kollin with that. *If* he ever wakes up. It's the perfect payback for two goody-goodies who annoyed me every day for the past ten years. Even her parents will be crushed."

"You don't care if you hurt the Shanahans?"

"Why should I?" I brush myself off. "They don't care that I'm graduating in six months with nowhere to go. They'll replace me with another body and never think twice about me."

Marcus balls his hands into fists. "What the hell happened to you?" He throws a punch and I duck. I spin around, twisting his arm behind his back and trapping him in a headlock.

"Gentlemen!" Headmaster Boyle sprints through the door. "What's the meaning of this?" He yanks me off Marcus.

"Do you know what kind of pressure the administration is under with everything going on here? Do you really think this kind of behavior is a good idea?"

Neither of us says anything.

"Marcus, get back to lunch. Michaels, you're coming with me." He wrangles the back of my shirt in his fist and shoves me forward. "There are some police detectives who'd like to speak to you in my office."

When Boyle steps around us to scoop everything back inside my backpack, Marcus whispers, "Looks like I don't need to tell on you after all. But if you hurt Laney or the Shanahans, I'm warning you, Kollin won't be the only one with a bashed-in skull." He ends it with a look that could put *me* on life support.

The best friend I ever had wishes I was dead.

I can't think about that. He'll always be the best friend I ever had. That's why I have no choice.

Headmaster Boyle zips the backpack and whips it at my chest so hard I barely catch it. He squeezes my elbow and jerks me forward, towing me through the door and down the hall to his office.

When we're finally out of sight of Marcus, I whisper, "Geez. Can you take it easy? That hurts."

Boyle relaxes his grip. "Consider it payback for all the grief you've given me through the years." He casts a sidelong smirk at me. "Did you know I was accompanying DCFS on inspections the day you set up the sex doll in my car?"

"I might have heard something about it." I turn my grin into a scowl in case someone's watching. "Hey,"

I whisper, "if you've still got that, can I have her back? I think she'd be a lovely addition to Stephen Kane's office."

Next thing I know, Boyle's fighting to make his grin look like a scowl too.

Damn. Maybe we are alike.

With a loose hand on my collar, Boyle steers me down the hall. "I only have a couple minutes to talk to you before the police do," he whispers, "so I'll get to the point. As you probably figured out, Kane is trying to frame you for the attack on Kollin. Apparently some Pillars witnessed a public fight between you two yesterday. It was the opportunity they'd been waiting for to set you up for a serious offense."

"It was a fake fight," I say.

"I don't doubt that, but the police will. In Emily's case yesterday, a student made an anonymous call to the Galesburg Police Department, claiming they heard her brag about the vandalism. I'm assuming that was one of the Pillars too. Kane heard that Emily was your girlfriend, so he assumes she's involved. He wanted her expelled before the board meeting, even managed to plant an empty spray paint can in her locker. I was able to remove it before the police came to interrogate her."

"So Emily's been cleared?"

"The lead officer on the case is an acquaintance of Kane's, so it took a bit of convincing. I gave Emily an alibi for the night the stadium was vandalized. I said she'd been meeting with me—inquiring about employment on campus. They questioned why I'd meet with a student after hours for that, but in the end they couldn't refute it."

"The whole thing infuriated Kane," he finishes. "He's livid I didn't do more to prosecute Emily."

"At least they believed you," I say.

"Unfortunately, it'll be harder to defend you, Talan. The police had several witnesses report that you slammed Kollin's head into a locker and threatened him yesterday. One caller also mentioned seeing you out alone last night. Where were you? Do you have an alibi for 8:00 p.m.?"

"I went to the hidden room under the mausoleum to copy the poem. I think it'll lead us to the TPD."

Boyle freezes in place. "What do you mean?"

"I think that poem might actually be the clue for the last test—the one for wisdom."

Boyle glances around the empty hall, then pulls me into a vacant classroom and shuts the door behind us.

My brain scrambles for a way to explain it. "Singer was an eccentric dude, but his clues were carefully worded and kind of… practical. Most of the tests he gave us built on each other or fit together for the next clue. At first, I assumed he did it that way to protect the secrets and the Sevens in case someone else accidentally stumbled on a clue. Then I started thinking there was probably more to it."

Boyle smiles. "There was always *more to it* when William was involved."

"Exactly. So I started thinking about that last poem he left on the wall in the secret room." I dig out the copy in my backpack and show it to him.

"See how Singer wrote: *When you're on your own, and all alone, beginning your final quest?* Why would he specifically mention that you'd be on your own for your last test? I mean, you were on your own for every test, right?"

Boyle nods.

"So maybe he meant *on your own*, meaning without direction from him."

Boyle's eyes drift while he thinks.

I point to the poem. "And he used the word *quest*. What else would you be searching for?"

Boyle rubs his chin and says, "Mr. Singer told us that we'd know where the TPD was after the final test. We just assumed that meant that he'd tell us after the last challenge. But in retrospect, you may be right. Maybe Singer meant that finding the TPD *was* the last challenge. You know, we all wondered why he took so long giving us that final clue. He'd given us every other test back-to-back."

I run my finger down the paper to the bottom of the poem. "And notice how it says: 'Knowledge is gained through fact compilation; but wisdom is born in its simplification.' Your final test would have been for wisdom. And here it says, 'Use all you've learned, and you'll solve the last clue.' I think Singer was saying your wisdom challenge was to apply the clues you already had to figure out where the TPD was."

Boyle's eyes glaze over as he stares, pondering the poem. "This changes everything," he says. "We assumed Mr. Singer called us together that night to give us the last clue. But maybe he was calling us together for another reason—to check why it was taking us so long to finish the test, or"—his face goes slack as he finishes—"to warn us."

He scratches his thumbnail back and forth across his

bottom lip. "All of our prior tests were labeled with the number and virtue, same as the ones I gave you. I guess we assumed the final test would look like that too."

"So what do you think?"

He stares up at me. "I think I chose well when I picked you." He squeezes my shoulder. "Have you told the others about this?"

"Just Kollin."

Boyle winces at the name. "Kane had no idea that LeBeau was a Seven. If he's willing to assault an innocent kid just to frame you, he's desperate enough to do anything. We need to find that TPD before someone else gets hurt. I'll call Emily down for an appointment and relay your idea to her. She can pass the information on to Laney and Jose. If we all start brainstorming, maybe we can come up with something."

He points toward the doorway. "For now, we have to focus on the detectives waiting to interview you. You're going to need an alibi for last night. Could you say you were with Jose?"

"I already told my housebrothers I was at the library."

"Damn." Boyle sighs. "I guess we'll have to make that work somehow. Just be extra careful from here on out. I'm assuming that they'll try to plant evidence on you too."

"I took it already!" I tell him. "I hid it last night." In the madness of the morning, I'd forgotten all about it. "When I was coming up the steps, I heard Iman and Cameron talking inside the mausoleum. They must have come straight from beating up Kollin. They were leaving the evidence there for Kane, so he could plant it in my locker later. When they left, I tossed all of it down the stairs so they couldn't use it against me."

"Excellent." He exhales loudly. "Now we just have to get through this interrogation." He opens the door and guides me down the hallway again, navigating me by my forearm.

The office is bustling with students and teachers when we walk in. Boyle points to his door and barks, "Get in there. Now!"

He grabs his messages and tells his secretary, "Rhonda, can you call down Emily Dombrose for a meeting?" She nods and Boyle follows me into his office, where two officers are waiting.

A tall, pale detective stands in one corner. His eyes cover me like a CT scan.

Boyle slams the door shut. "This is Talan Michaels," he says. "If you're pressing charges, I'll need to call his guardians so he can retain an attorney."

"Not necessary," the second officer says. He's short and chubby, sort of grandfatherly, with an out-of-place smile. "We're simply gathering information. No need for an attorney yet." My guess is he's the good-cop half of this good-cop/bad-cop team.

"There were a number of tips called in last night and this morning. Too many to ignore." Bad Cop glowers at me. "All of them reported an altercation yesterday between Mr. Michaels and Kollin LeBeau. Is that true, Mr. Michaels?"

"Kollin and I have never gotten along, but I'd never physically hurt him."

"Never? Because every caller mentioned you slamming his head into a locker and threatening him."

"We were pushing each other around. It wasn't a big deal. It's not the same as beating someone with a metal rod."

"How did you know about the metal rod?" Bad Cop says.

Boyle's face cringes behind the officer. Another boner move thanks to my stupid mouth.

"I heard about it this morning. Everyone's talking about this."

"It's funny they knew that fact when it hadn't been released."

"Well, I'm sure the person who did it knew it. He obviously let it slip."

The cop's eyes close in on mine. "That's what I was thinking."

Good Cop intervenes. "Look at me, Talan." His voice goes all soft and understanding. "We have a boy who could die any minute. Maybe the person who did it didn't mean for it to be that bad. Maybe he was pressured by gang members, or it was committed in anger, or accidentally. We have no way of helping that person unless he comes forward and confesses what happened. If he were to share what he knew ... well, we could make things easier for him."

"I don't know what you're talking about. I don't know of any gangs at Singer."

Good cop makes a disappointed-grandpa sigh. "We believe there are students starting a gang based on the legend of the Sevens. The vandalism, the assault—these are all typical gang behaviors."

"I wouldn't know."

"Where were you last night at 8:00?"

"You said you were gathering information," Boyle interrupts. "But it sounds like you're interrogating Mr. Michaels. If that's the case, then I'm obligated to obtain legal counsel for him."

Bad Cop muscles over to Boyle. "We keep trying to interview students here, and you keep interfering. What's the problem, Headmaster?"

"The problem is, I don't want Singer School sued for infringing on Mr. Michael's rights to due process. I'm wondering why you're not worried about that too."

Good Cop changes the subject. "Let's try this another way. Did Mr. LeBeau have any enemies?"

"I wouldn't know. We weren't friends."

"Would someone have reason to dislike him or want him out of the picture?"

"I wouldn't know," I repeat. "We weren't friends."

"But you're friends with his girlfriend, Delaney Shanahan, aren't you?"

I pause to keep my composure. "She's my housesister."

There's a knock on the door that rescues me. "Excuse me for a minute," Boyle says.

He opens the door and his secretary pops her head in. "Sorry to interrupt, but Mr. Kane is calling from his car. He says if you don't pick up immediately, he'll be over in twenty minutes to fire our whole staff."

"Just what I need." Boyle rolls his eyes. "Thank you, Rhonda."

He closes the door and clicks the phone on. "You're on speakerphone, Stephen. We're in the middle of questioning Talan Michaels. Can this wait?"

"No, it can't. I don't like what's happening at my alma mater. Have they arrested that hoodlum yet?"

I clench and unclench my fists.

"They're just questioning him, Stephen."

"Is Officer Lynch there? Paul, are you there?" Kane calls out over the speaker.

"Hi, Stephen," Bad Cop replies. "Yes, we're in the process of investigating last night's assault."

"Did the headmaster inform you about Mr. Michaels' angry outburst that disrupted an entire assembly earlier this year?"

"I hardly think that's relevant," Boyle murmurs.

"Is that you, Matthew?" Kane says. "And here I thought we were on the same page about aggressively prosecuting the students destroying our school." Kane's voice grows more and more irate. "I'm beginning to seriously question your intentions here. Not to mention your ability to maintain the safety and welfare of the students."

"I represent *all* the students, Stephen. There's protocol to consider. The police are perfectly capable of uncovering the truth within the guidelines of the law. I have no intention of interfering in their investigation."

"Matthew, I'm disappointed you haven't been more… helpful in your pursuit of the guilty parties."

"Maybe I don't see the benefit in disregarding due process to indict someone. I'm sure the officers would agree."

"Is that right?" Kane's reply is edgy as a machete. "I see how it is," he says. "Lynch?"

"Right here," Bad Cop says.

"I'd like you to call me with an update when you're done." Boyle clicks the phone off.

Good Cop places his hand on my arm. "Talan, I'm going to ask you once. Did you attack Kollin LeBeau last night?"

"No."

"Did you have any reason to want to hurt him? Gang pressure or rivalry or pent-up anger?"

"No."

The cop sits back in his chair.

Boyle crosses his arms. "I'm no detective, but several things come to mind here. How does a kid like Talan, who can't leave campus, get access to spray paint? Why would a senior who practically *lives* for football want to destroy the stadium mid-season? And if there was gang involvement, wouldn't they be smart enough to have worked out alibis with each other? Maybe these are things you all should be considering."

It takes all I've got to keep my voice calm. "Can I go now?"

"Gentlemen, I'm going to have to ask you to leave," Boyle says to the cops. "I already wasted yesterday morning hassling Emily Dombrose based on nothing but a malicious anonymous tip. I'm already behind on paperwork from that issue, plus I've got meetings with contractors this afternoon to repair the statue and stadium."

Lynch glares at Boyle. "Would you have any problem with us checking his locker?"

Boyle looks at me.

"That's fine," I say. "It's number 1515."

"Okay then." Boyle stands and opens the door for the officers. "Rhonda, can you get the master key and open Talan's locker for the detectives? When they're satisfied, please show them out."

She types a code on a security safe and pulls out a key. The officers follow her into the hall. When they're out of sight, I tug Boyle back into his office and shut the door.

The words rush out of my mouth. "What did you say to your secretary about a master key?"

"I had her get it to open your locker. It's easier than looking up and remembering the combination. That's how I've been leaving you your clues."

"I know how the Pillars planted stuff in Emily's locker yesterday. Last night, I heard Moore tell Kabal that Kane had a master key. They must have stolen it to plant the evidence in Emily and my lockers."

"But there's only one key, and it's locked up."

"Who has the code?"

"Rhonda, me, and a couple teachers who have authority to act in our absence—Caesar Solomon and Julie Bennett."

"Would either of them have any reason to help the Pillars?"

"I doubt it. Ms. Bennett came to me privately and protested the new Pillar choices. And Professor Solomon is disgusted by the way Kane is interfering with our school." He pauses and says in a lowered voice. "Unless Professor Solomon slipped and gave it out in a...weak moment."

"What do you mean?"

"Consider this part of your vow of secrecy," Boyle says. "Professor Solomon is...a bit fond of alcohol. I've let him stay on at Singer because it's never affected his job performance during the day. But Carmine Rathbone once warned me that alcohol causes Caesar to do careless things. Maybe he let the code slip to Stephen Kane or the Pillars when he was under the influence. That's something I'll need to look into. For now, I better change the passcode."

I follow him out to the front desk, where he plays with the keypad on the safe. He opens the safe door just as Rhonda returns. "Did you see our friends out?"

"I did," she answers. "You never saw two more disappointed people when they didn't find anything. Are we going to have to do this for every student they get a tip on?"

"I hope not," Boyle says. "Here, let me put that back." He takes the master key and locks it inside the safe. "Can you write Talan a pass to get back to class?"

She hands me a slip and I go to get my backpack from Boyle's office.

I hear Boyle ask, "Did you call Emily Dombrose down?"

"She should be here any minute," Rhonda says. "What are you meeting for this time?"

Boyle stumbles over his words. "I, mmm...why do you ask?"

"Just wondered." Then she adds in a hushed voice, "Do you think those two are behind the gang violence?"

"No!" He says it so loud, everyone turns. Boyle rubs his neck and says more calmly, "I assure you, there is no gang violence at Singer School."

"No gang violence, huh?" Stephen Kane storms through the door and pounds his fist on the counter.

I duck behind the shelves in the alcove to listen.

"I assure you, there *is* gang violence," Kane rants, "whether you are willing to confront it or not."

Boyle gives him a cool glare. "The police will determine who's behind the crimes and handle them appropriately."

"It sounds like they're trying but you keep interfering."

Boyle lowers his voice. "How dare you come into my office and criticize me in front of my staff. I'm following procedure here. I'm not going to do something that puts this school into legal jeopardy."

"You should be more concerned with your students' safety, Matthew, not to mention the property damage and bad press for this school and our company. I know I am. In fact, I've called an emergency board meeting to discuss it on Thursday."

"What?"

"You heard me. You know that I've had changes in mind for some time. I've decided to bring them up for a board vote."

"But that's too fast," Boyle says.

"This school is in dire straits. I can't believe you're so lackadaisical about the welfare of your students."

"How dare you say that! I think you better leave."

Kane draws his head back like a serpent poised for attack. "I thought you were on my team," he says.

The whole office is watching now, none of them realizing the undertones to what he says.

"It's obvious I can't count on you in my endeavors to improve Singer School," Kane says. "You aren't protecting the well-being or the safety of our students."

"I'm done listening to your drivel, Mr. Kane."

Emily walks in right in the middle of the storm.

"Emily, please come in," Boyle says. She marches past him into his office.

"You have time for this vandal and not for the CEO of Singer Enterprises?"

"That's exactly right," Boyle says, slamming the door in Kane's face.

I've never seen Headmaster Boyle lose it like that. It was awesome. But I can't help thinking he's said too much too. He gave his hand away.

We really are alike.

FORTY-TWO

The rest of the day drags like a dead body. My mind is caught up in one thing—keeping Laney and my friends safe. It's the only thing I care about until 3:18 p.m., when I trudge up the driveway of my house.

"Talan!"

I'm afraid to look. Afraid there's a fist or threat or egg about to be hurled at me.

"Talan!" The voice is younger. And surprisingly friendly.

"Talan!" There's a tug on my hand and I look down and see Jack Dominguez grinning up at me. I didn't recognize his voice, probably because he didn't say a word to me the first time we met. Now he's all breathless and animated. He squeezes my legs and says, "My best friend Talan is here!"

Three little boys his age run up next to him, but he says, "I need to talk to Talan. You go and save me a swing." They pout a second, and he orders them, "Go! I'll come, I promise."

They shuffle off to the park without him, bummed that they lost their ringleader.

I crouch down to his eye level. "How's it going, my man?"

He returns my high five and says, "Greaaat!"

"So you liking it here?" His head bobs with these huge nods. "I told you, didn't I?"

He squeezes my arm with all he's got and nods some more, his face bursting into a smile. I can't help ask, "So what's the best part?"

He signals for me to lean close and whispers something in my ear.

"What?" I laugh. "I couldn't hear you, buddy."

He cups his mouth to my ear. "No one hits me here." He stares up at me with round eyes. Then he shakes his head in case I need convincing. "No one!" he repeats.

He grabs my bicep and kisses the exact spot where my T scar is buried under three layers of clothing. The irony chills me.

For the first time since lunch, thoughts of Laney are replaced by something even more important: I have *three* days to find that TPD.

I *have* to find that TPD.

FORTY-THREE

The next morning, everyone's camped in the kitchen when I slink in before school. For once, they're not gawking at me.

They're staring at Mom Shanahan, who's standing in the phone closet screaming into the receiver as Dad props the door open to listen. Laney catches my eye and lifts her eyebrows.

"It's not true!" Mom yells. "The truth will come out, and then I hope he sues for libel. I've known Matthew Boyle for over twenty years. He's a good, decent man and an excellent headmaster."

Now *I'm* staring. I nudge between Chris and Mike to hear better, but Mom slams the phone down. She ricochets around us in a dash for the family room and switches on a news channel.

"What's going on?"

"Shhh," she says, holding up a finger.

She turns the volume up as the anchorman says, "The headmaster at Singer School was arrested last night on suspicion of sexual relations with a minor, police reported this morning. Matthew Boyle is being held in the Galesburg Jail in lieu of $265,000 bail. Boyle was taken into custody last night in a wooded area near the 500 block of Rucker Road along with an unnamed seventeen-year-old student, according to Galesburg Police Sergeant Paul Lynch."

Mom inhales sharply. "Well, I'm sure there's a reasonable explanation."

The screen switches to Officer Lynch standing beside Stephen Kane outside the police station. Lynch reads from an index card, talking into a mound of microphones shoved in his face. "Police and Child Protective Agencies learned of the relationship yesterday afternoon when two students reported witnessing a romantic encounter between Boyle and a female student. One of the students confronted the girl, who allegedly boasted of sexual relations with the suspect. Investigators staked the property and found the student and Mr. Boyle in the woods at 1:18 in the morning. Both Mr. Boyle and the minor deny the allegations, but have refused to make any further statements. Mr. Boyle is scheduled to be arraigned Friday in Glendale Municipal Court on felony charges of sexual misconduct with a minor."

Officer Lynch steps back and Stephen Kane takes center stage. His name appears underneath the caption *Spokesman for Singer School.* "As a proud alumni of Singer School, the idea that a trusted authority figure would abuse his position to take advantage of a vulnerable child is shocking and disturbing. We commend the students who came forward, as well as Sergeant Lynch and the county's Child Protective Services Agency, who took immediate and appropriate action as soon as the allegations surfaced. Mr. Boyle has been suspended without pay, pending the outcome of this investigation."

I desperately want to talk to Laney, but Marcus is giving me the evil eye. While my housebrothers debate Mom Shanahan over the likelihood of Boyle's innocence, I hightail it to school to find Jose and Emily.

At first, I think Jose must have read my mind. He's leaning against a locker when I turn down the empty hallway. "So you heard?" I ask.

He shakes his head. "Heard what? I'm waiting for Emily. She was supposed to meet me here fifteen minutes ago."

"Dude, Headmaster Boyle was arrested last night for having sex with a minor. It was all over the news this morning."

"What? Who was the student?"

"They're not releasing that."

"No way." Confusion spreads across his face. "Not Boyle. Do you think Kane set him up?"

"Of course! I don't have any proof yet, but it's got to be Kane. He had a huge fight with Boyle in the office yesterday. I heard the whole thing. It's pretty clear he thinks that Boyle is getting in the way of his plans."

"Shhhh," Jose says, eyeing something behind me.

When I turn, Cameron and Zack are strutting our way. Cameron snickers and my fists twitch at the sight. "I had a feeling I'd find you here with some of your *gang*," he says.

"What are you talking about?" I say.

"You and Emily both hanging with Jose all the time? I hardly think that's a coincidence."

I turn my back to him. "Get lost, stalker."

"Why so rude?" he says. "And here I was trying to be nice. I wanted to say how sorry I was to hear about your sweetheart."

I'm lost until Zack says, "God, how embarrassing to find out that your girlfriend's been hooking up with the headmaster."

Jose jerks his head around. "Are you talking about Emily?"

"Kayla and Nick caught them pawing each other." Cameron's smirk makes me want to puke.

"Sure they did," Jose says.

"Pillars never lie," Cameron says. "Emily admitted it to Kayla, too. She even bragged that they were meeting last night in the woods. Fortunately, Kayla told the police so DCFS could catch them before it happened again."

"Son of a—"

I grab Jose before he can strangle Cameron.

"Smart move, Michaels," Cameron whispers. "You can't afford to have another Seven in trouble without the headmaster around to protect you anymore. Now that Mr. Kane is taking over the school, your lucky breaks are over."

"Kane is taking over? Who told you that?"

"Kane told us Pillars to spread the word that he's cleaning house around here. He's moving into the headmaster's residence as we speak."

My head is already exploding when Zack goads me

more. "Damn. If I knew a hottie like Emily Dombrose was desperate enough to hook up with losers like you and Boyle, I would have done her a favor and given her a ride myself. It's too bad she was sent home before I got a turn."

Jose lunges for Zack. I pull him back with everything I've got, but I barely keep them apart. I'd love to watch Zack get crushed, but Cameron's right. It's just Laney, Jose, and me now. We don't need to make it any easier for Kane by getting expelled for fighting.

"No, Jose!" I spin him aside. "We know it's BS. The police will figure out it's a lie. You don't want to get busted over this."

"Good thing you got a friend like Michaels," Zack says. "Or maybe not. A lot of his friends seem to be experiencing bad luck these days."

Cameron moves closer. "You know, Mr. Kane would be happy to help your friends if you'd only provide a certain document. In fact, he'd make it *well* worth your cooperation."

"The only way I'd give him that TPD was if it was covered in anthrax," I say.

"Shame. 'Cause he's running out of patience, and you're running out of time." Cam turns and saunters away, with Zack trailing behind.

Students start trickling to their lockers, staring at us.

Jose whispers, "Meet me at the secret room after school. Make sure you aren't followed." He adds, "I'll tell Laney too."

FORTY-FOUR

That afternoon, I cut around campus the long way just to make sure I'm not trailed on my way to the mausoleum. Jose is already in the hidden room waiting for me.

"Let's take the tunnels and see if we can learn anything by spying at Boyle's house," he says, lifting the staircase.

I hold it still. "Wait... isn't Laney coming?"

"I never had a chance to talk to her." He crawls inside. "She was surrounded all day by people asking about Kollin."

We navigate the tunnels to the headmaster's house in silence. It's broken by the sound of voices as we climb the rungs to the room behind the fireplace. Jose holds a finger to his mouth and I nod. We creep up behind the one-way mirror.

Kane strolls in front of the fireplace, talking to a familiar-looking redhead. She's sitting on the sofa, tapping a pen against a notepad on her lap. There are papers and a laptop spread out next to her.

"But why frame him?" she says. "You agreed we needed his support at the board meeting."

"I did, but Boyle's become more of a nuisance than a help. He's interfered with everything we've set up so far. We can do this without him."

"How do you figure?" the woman says, twisting her pearl necklace in her fingers.

I realize now where I saw her before—she was the woman onstage with Kane at the Pillar assembly.

Kane loosens his silk tie and collapses in a chair opposite her. "With Boyle's arrest and the recent 'crime wave' on campus, it'll be easy. I'll convince the Board that change is necessary to restore the levels of excellence William Singer intended for his school. Even the most stubborn board members will be grateful I intervened; this is clearly a crisis."

"What if the headmaster tells the Board how you bribed him to get his support?"

"Do you really think anyone would trust anything Boyle says at this point?"

"True." The woman nods, then smiles slightly. "So how the hell did you get the headmaster to meet that girl in the woods at 1:00 in the morning?"

Kane leans back in his chair, lacing his fingers behind his head. "Cameron called Boyle and said he needed to confess something about the vandalism but was scared. He asked him to meet him confidentially in the woods after midnight."

"And the girl?"

"Zack forged a note with Talan Michael's signature and left it in her locker, telling her to sneak out to the woods at 1:00 a.m. for Sevens' business. Michaels is notorious for his "night crawling," so she bought it. The Galesburg police were staked out and waiting."

With a glint in this eye, Kane adds, "It worked perfectly. There were records already of Boyle meeting privately with Emily over the past few days. With all that, the police were able to get a warrant."

I want to punch the grin off his face.

"They did all the leg work for us," he finishes. "And the Pillars look like heroes. Brilliant, huh?"

"Quite." She sets the pen and notepad aside, walks over to the bar cart, and pours two drinks.

"And that's also six hundred thousand more for us," Kane says. "Not to mention that getting rid of Matthew allows us to scour this house looking for the TPD ... and the hidden cash."

She hands a glass to Kane. "You really think there's money hidden here?"

"It's possible. When the detectives investigated Singer's murder, they learned there'd been regularly scheduled armored car deliveries from his personal vault to his home for almost a year. But they couldn't find a safe here, or any evidence of large purchases."

She sits back down with her drink, crossing one long leg over the other. "So maybe Singer gave it away. Or like the police suspected, maybe the Sevens stole it."

Kane jiggles the ice in his glass. "The Sevens were never aware of it."

"How would you know that?"

"I overheard a conversation once between Singer and Caesar Solomon. Singer was explaining how he'd selected some students to protect his school in case anything happened to him. He said that down the road, he planned on surprising them with a fortune for their loyalty."

"So why did the police think the Sevens took it?"

"Because I never told them about that. They based their theory on my eyewitness account of the fire—where I said I heard Singer screaming that the Sevens were trying to rob and kill him."

"So you lied?"

"I took some license with the truth, but that's not germane to this conversation. Right now, we need to focus on securing that TPD. The money will be a nice bonus if we find it."

"You're a remarkable man, Stephen." The woman stands up and casually strolls around the room. "Cunning," she says, "and successful at getting what you want. It's too bad Mr. Singer didn't realize what was in front of him. If you'd been chosen as a Seven, things would have turned out differently."

She stops at the far wall to study a portrait of William and Mary.

"That's exactly what I told him. When I found out Singer was forming a secret society, I volunteered my services."

"And he refused?"

"He said he already selected his pledges. He was an ass to me and furious at Solomon." Kane stares at his glass, then chugs down the rest of his drink.

"Why?" she asks. "Because he thought Solomon told you about the Sevens?"

"That, and other things." Kane sets his glass on the table next to him and rubs his forehead. "Needless to say, Singer chose the wrong Sevens. Naive and stupid, every one of them. William Singer was a fool to the end."

The doorbell rings. "Would you mind, Katherine?" Kane says.

She carries her drink to the door and opens it. "You're late."

The six Pillars traipse behind her into the living room. "We got here as soon as we could," Cameron says.

Kane rises to address them. "I want each of you to take a room upstairs and search it for that TPD. Katherine already took apart the downstairs after police left this morning. Look through bookshelves, behind cabinets, anywhere Mr. Singer might have hidden papers. And use these." He tosses them a box and Zack pulls out a pair of latex gloves.

As they each slide on a pair, Kane turns to Cameron. "Were you able to plant the evidence in their lockers?"

"No." With a wicked smile, Cameron adds, "We figured out something even better. Zack overheard the football coaches talking. With the season canceled, they decided to collect the gear and uniforms for next year. They had the custodian empty the football bags from the players' lockers so they could inventory the equipment tonight. All the bags were lying there in a stack. We figured out which were Marcus' and Jake's and stuffed the evidence inside them. That's why we're late, actually."

"Great work!" Kane slaps his hand on Cameron's back. "This couldn't be more perfect. The coaches will stumble on it and call the authorities for us. Excellent plan, Cam!"

Kane continues giving the Pillars directions, but I'm done listening. I take off down the rungs and back through the tunnels.

"Talan!" Jose whisper-yells behind me.

My heart's pumping like a jackhammer, drenching my brain with dizzying thoughts. Back at the mausoleum stairs, I wait long enough for Jose to catch up.

"Those are my best friends," I pant. "I have to get whatever the Pillars planted before the coaches find it."

Jose grabs hold of my arm. "You'll get caught. Maybe we should focus on the TPD. We're running out of time."

"I won't be able to concentrate knowing my friends will be expelled. Kane has hurt enough people on account of me. You stay here and spy, and I'll get back as soon as I can."

I run up the stairs with Jose a step behind me. "I'm coming with. You heard what Boyle said. We need to stick together."

We sneak out of the mausoleum, but motor once we hit the woods. The fieldhouse is a few blocks away. We've got to make it before they close the school for the day.

The rear entrance is still unlocked. Jose peeks through the wired window on the door, straining his neck to one side. "The bags are piled up against the back wall."

"Is anyone in there?"

"No."

I swing the door open, rush to the rancid-smelling pile, and start sorting through the player bags.

"How do we know which are Marcus' and Jake's?"

"They're labeled with the jersey numbers. Marcus is eleven, and Jake is thirty-five, no...thirty-six."

We tear through the bags in search of those numbers and haul them out. Jose weeds through Jake's equipment and pulls out black clothes splattered with red paint stains. I find the same in Marcus' bag, along with an empty can of spray paint. Jose stands up, juggling everything in one arm while he bends to zip the bag closed.

"Freeze right there!" a voice booms.

Busted.

FORTY-FIVE

My holding cell is six by eight feet, with three brick walls, a cage door, and a stainless steel toilet in one corner. I can see Jose in his cell, caddy-corner from me, but we're too far apart to talk privately. Neither of us has spoken since we were arrested four hours ago.

Coach Gaspari told the police that it looked like we were putting clothes and spray paint in some football bags. We say nothing. God knows I've already done enough damage opening my stupid mouth.

Sergeant Lynch unlocks my cell door. "Your bail's been paid. Your attorney is waiting at the front desk."

As I follow him down the hall, Lynch tells Jose, "You're going to be a while. Your houseparents just got ahold of your mother and she's going to need some time to arrange bail."

Jose grimaces at the mention of his mom, and I feel like crap. So much of this is my fault. Why'd I get involved in the first place?

As I step out of the holding area, I see Mr. and Mrs. Shanahan sitting at a desk, being interviewed by a detective. I can read their thoughts from their faces. They're angry and stunned and sick to their stomachs. Something inside me breaks when Mom's eyes well. My days at Singer are over and we both know it.

That's why I had to make a new plan for myself.

That's why I walk straight past them without saying a word.

That's why I didn't use my one phone call on them.

Dad catches my sleeve as I pass by. "Where you going, son?"

But I'm not his son anymore. I knew it'd be over eventually. I need to cut ties while I can still protect them. "I'm eighteen," I say. "I'm a legal adult. I don't have to tell you anything, and I don't need you here."

Mom looks like I slapped her. When Dad grabs my arm, I peel his hand away and plod over to the front desk, where Stephen Kane waits with a stack of papers.

"You won't be sorry," Kane says. "Making a deal with me is the smartest thing you ever did."

I'm sickened by my own words: "Just get me the money and I'll give you that document."

"I told you, Michaels. You and I have a lot in common."

"And leave the Sevens alone," I remind him. "We do this my way, or no TPD. You still don't know who the other Sevens are. You cross me, and I'll let the other Sevens turn that TPD in at the board meeting."

"Just so there's no confusion"—Kane repeats what I told

him on the phone—"you want fifty thousand dollars and a limo to the airport, in exchange for the TPD by 8:00 a.m. tomorrow?"

"And you stop hassling my friends."

Kane's lawyer appears at my side. She looks down her nose at me. "I'm Katherine Jones. I'll be representing you as your attorney. You're to say nothing until we talk privately. Did they read you your rights?"

I nod.

"Stephen, let his houseparents know that he's being released into your custody. I need to sign some papers so we can get out of here."

Kane walks back to the Shanahans, while Katherine takes her paperwork to the clerk.

I look around and see Laney watching me from the waiting room, tugging her ear. I need to get rid of her before Kane sees her. When I'm sure no one's looking, I hurry over toward her and pull her into a doorway, out of sight. "You need to go away. Now! Before Kane sees you."

"What's going on? What happened? The police searched your room and found the skull in your vent." Laney is talking a mile a minute. "They told Mom and Dad you were caught planting evidence in Marcus' and Jake's bags. Marcus was so pissed, he totally narced you out for everything."

"Did Marcus mention anything about you?"

"No, but he's so hurt. He thinks you tried to set him up."

"Everyone leaves me eventually. I'm better off this way."

"Better off what way?"

"It's over. I cut a deal with Kane. I told him I'd get him

the TPD if he agreed to bail me out and give me enough money to leave town."

"What are you saying? What about the Sevens?"

"There's nothing we can do now," I say. "We have no idea where the TPD is and that board meeting is tomorrow morning. It's best to keep quiet. Kane still has no idea about you. You have a bright future and you'll graduate before the school goes to hell next year. They're still going to need houseparents, but if you piss Kane off, he'll be more than happy to fire your mom and dad. Don't blow it all for nothing. I'm taking care of myself. You need to do the same."

Laney's voice trembles. "Where will you go?"

"I'll make a fresh start somewhere. I'll have enough money to take my time and figure things out. That's all I ever really wanted out of this in the first place. The money. Kane will set me up good. In eight months, you'll be in college and I'll be on a beach somewhere and we'll both be happy. That's all that matters."

"No it isn't, and you know it."

"It's over, Laney."

"No!"

"Yes! The Sevens are finished. Kollin's dying, Jose is behind bars, Emily's been sent home, and Headmaster Boyle's career has been destroyed … it's over."

"You said you loved me that night in the mausoleum." Her eyes brim with tears. "How can you just leave?"

I've got to convince her. "'Cause that's what people do, Delaney. They leave." I peek around the corner and see

Katherine scooping up the paperwork. I make sure to stare deep into Laney's eyes. "It's over," I say firmly.

I slip back into the lobby, leaving her standing there alone.

Don't look back. Keep walking. It was going to end eventually.

I join Kane and Katherine at the front desk.

"You'll be spending the night with me," Kane says. "Well, mainly with Katherine. I have an appointment with my banker to withdraw your money. Maybe you could take Katherine to get the TPD while I'm gone."

"No way," I say. "I expect to see the money and a limo waiting with the door open before I hand that to you."

"Fine." He looks me up and down. "But don't try anything. I'll be setting the alarm system in case you're thinking of running. I already added extra security all over campus for the board meeting tomorrow. You couldn't run ten feet without being caught, not with the entire student body and staff turned against you. And if you try, there'll be no one to bail you out next time."

"You keep your end of the deal," I say, "and I'll take care of mine."

FORTY-SIX

Kane's chauffeur drops us off at the headmaster's residence. "Wait here," Kane tells his driver. "I'll be out in a few minutes."

Katherine and I follow him to the room with the fireplace. She tosses her coat and briefcase on the couch, and Kane points to a dial pad on the wall.

"See that?" he tells me. "This burglar alarm is wired for every door and window in this residence. If you even think of escaping, Security will be on you before you can say *prison sentence*. I'm not sure how long I'll be, but Katherine's been kind enough to keep you company in my absence."

There goes my plan to run for the mausoleum.

Kane keys a code into the keypad. "This gives me thirty seconds to leave the house," he explains to Katherine. "Then it sounds an alarm the instant a door or window is opened. Be careful not to accidentally set it off."

He bolts for the door and slams it behind himself.

Katherine crosses her arms and stares me down. "I must say I'm surprised. Stephen was right about you all along." She circles around me, eyeing me with disdain, and I feel like that dirty kindergartner all over again. "You *are* like him. I told him you'd be a problem, but he was convinced you'd look out for yourself in the end."

The words sting like venom. I'm *not* like Kane. We had similar childhoods, but *I am not like him.*

"I need to make some calls," she says. "We have an important meeting in the morning, you know. I trust that you heard what Stephen said. Attempting to escape through a window or door guarantees your return to jail. This time, without our help."

I nod.

"I would stay and babysit you, but there's some kind of rodent infestation in this part of the house." She points to the fireplace. "I think something's got a nest in there. I heard a strange squeaking earlier."

Squeaking from the fireplace? I try to keep a poker face.

"You might be used to living in that kind of squalor with your background," she says, "but it makes me ill just thinking about it."

After Katherine takes her briefcase and heads upstairs, I rush to the fireplace. I push on the interior wall and it moves slightly.

When I hear her talking on the phone, I shove the side-wall hard, shift the fireplace over, and clamber through. Just as quickly, I close it and latch the bottom hinges. I'm out of breath, wheezing from exhilaration and fear.

I have ten hours to find that TPD.

I descend the rungs and run all the way to the secret room beneath the statue.

The light flashes on and Mr. Singer's poem appears like a ghost on the wall. When I step forward, my foot hits something that rolls away, rattling. I jump back. The can of spray paint I tossed down the stairs a few nights ago comes to a stop inches from the pile of papers we stashed here.

I pick up the can, and it reminds me of the heart graffiti in the tunnel. I can still picture Laney tearing up over that. I get it now—it was her parent's initials in that heart. Her dad, who was murdered, and her mom, who she'll never know now. My chest tightens when I think of Laney hurting and alone.

I guess Kollin was right. I do love Delaney Shanahan. If only I could have told her that when I said goodbye. If I don't find that TPD, her last memory of me will be how *I* abandoned *her*.

With a shaky hand, I lift the can and spray-paint a heart on the wall. Inside it, I write:

TM
LOVES
DS

A voice emerges from the stairwell. "Like hell we're done."

My hand flies to my chest and I drop the can. My breath hitches until I see who's standing at the stairs.

"Laney, what are you doing here? ... And did you just *swear?*"

"I came looking for you, Michaels." Laney leans against the doorframe. "I knew you'd never bail on the Sevens. Or me. You're a lot of things, but you never let your friends down. I also know how stubborn you are. You'd never let Kane get away with this."

"How'd you know I'd be here?"

She steps down off the last step. "I didn't. I knew you left with Kane, so I came to spy on him to make sure you were okay."

"So you're the one who unlatched the fireplace door?"

Her head tilts. "No. I just got here. Was it open? Is that how you escaped?"

I nod.

She straightens up. "Oh man, Kane's gonna lose it when he sees you're gone." She rubs her neck. "I'm scared, Talan. We're almost out of time. What if we don't find that TPD?"

"I'll find it. You need to get home. Your parents already hate me. They don't need any more headaches."

She moves closer. "They don't hate you. They didn't buy the whole *Talan is a villain* act either. But they couldn't figure out why you had the skull in your vent and what you were doing putting spray paint in Jake and Marcus' bags. I just wish we could tell them."

"You need to get back."

"Forget it. We're a team. I told them I'd explain everything tomorrow night. I figure we'll have our answer either way by then."

"And they let you go?"

"Well . . . not exactly." She gnaws her thumbnail. "I left them a note."

"You what?"

"I reminded them how they told me I had to trust them when I asked them about my mom. Now *they* have to trust *me*. I wrote that I'd be away overnight and warned them that if they called the police or told anyone I was gone, they'd be putting me in danger."

"So basically, if we make it through this, your father's gonna kill me anyhow?"

She laughs, and I swear I feel a thousand times better than I have all week. She steps toward Mr. Singer's poem taped to the wall. "Emily explained how you figured out that this is our last clue."

"Yeah, but I still haven't been able to solve it. I've read it a thousand times. Something's not right about it, but I can't figure out what."

Laney turns completely around and says, "Well, it was genius, Tal." She pauses, then jumps up and kisses me.

"Wow," I say. "A 'good job' would have been enough."

"No it wouldn't." She cranes her neck to the side and points to the wall behind me. "Nice heart."

I'm mute. I don't want say something that'll wreck the smile on her lips.

She stares straight into my eyes. "It's mutual."

"But that night . . . why didn't you say anything when I confessed how I felt?"

She glides her hands to my shoulders. "I was scared. You

know what Mom said. If she caught us, you'd get sent away. After you finally opened up and told me how afraid you were of that, how could I risk hurting you? I didn't know what to do. I took a vow of sacrifice—how could I risk making you homeless just because I liked you? I thought you understood that. I thought that was why you said you'd wait."

"So you *do* like me?"

"You figured out all those complicated clues and missed something so obvious? I guess that makes me Sherlock after all."

She blushes and gets all quiet. I know she wants me to kiss her but I'm suddenly tweaking with nerves. I've done this a hundred times, but they all just seem like practice for this one girl.

While I'm overthinking it, she grabs my collar and pulls me down for a kiss. Our noses bump. We turn our heads the same way and they bump again.

She rubs my cheek with her thumb. "Nothing's easy for us, is it?"

"No, but you know what they taught us," I whisper. "If at first you don't succeed, try, try again."

She laughs, and we slide right into this amazing kiss. My arms bundle her close and she tightens her hug around my neck. I'm caught up in all of it, until Laney eventually pulls back so we can catch our breath.

"Wow," she says.

I lean my forehead against hers. "I guarantee I won't forget *that* kiss."

She hugs me and whispers in my ear, "Maybe we better focus on the clue."

I nod, but I'm not ready to let go. I rest my chin on her shoulder.

She says softly, "Talan? What happens to us if we don't find that TPD? What's going to happen to you?"

I stare over her shoulder at the poem that's been stuck in my brain lately like an annoying song I can't shake. Laney plants a kiss on my neck. The poem goes fuzzy in my brain.

I refocus, but Laney kisses me again, just below my ear.

"Well, call me Sherlock," I say.

"What?" she mumbles, kissing me a third time.

"Call me Sherlock," I say slower.

It figures that when I finally hook up with Delaney Shanahan, I have to stop in the middle of it. I muster enough strength to nudge her back and look her in the eyes. "I figured it out, Delaney. I know what's different in the poem."

My smile is too much to contain; it courses through me. I nod to the clue behind her. "It's the question."

She drops her arms and spins around. Her gaze hopscotches over the paper:

"A prudent question is one half of wisdom."
Dwell on this for your last test,
When you're on your own, and all alone,
Beginning your final quest.

Knowledge is gained through fact compilation;

But wisdom is born in its simplification.

Columns and half clues to find and combine.

Words that are letters read between the lines.

Use all you've learned, and you'll solve the last clue.

Your founder was wise

In deed,

Are you?

She shrugs. "You mean 'A prudent question is one half of wisdom?'"

"No. The question."

"What question?"

I walk around her and point to the last two lines. "The question at the end. We've seen it in so many of the clues, we sort of ignore it now. The part where Singer wrote *Your founder was wise in deed, are you?* Look how he spelled it. It's *in deed.* Two words. Not *indeed,* like all the other times. That's our clue. Singer was saying there's wisdom *in* the Deed of Trust."

Laney stares at the poem. "Huh... *Your founder was wise in deed, are you?*" There's a gleam in her eyes. "Wait a minute."

Her back stiffens and her eyes rise to the top of the poem. "Talan, *that's* the prudent question Mr. Singer was talking about all along! That's why he repeated it so many times. *Your founder was wise in deed, are you?* is the question that's 'one half of wisdom.' The Deed of Trust is a half clue. Which can only mean that—"

"We apply the clues we've learned to the deed to find the TPD."

Laney points to the poem on the wall. "Singer even told us which clues to use," she says. "Columns and half clues, words that are messages, and reading between the lines."

I drop to my knees and rummage through the papers on the floor, pulling out the deed we stole from Boyle's house the night of the justice test. "I told LeBeau we'd need this."

The mention of his name extinguishes the grin from Laney's face.

"They're bringing him out of his coma in the morning." Her eyes glisten. "I don't know if you heard that. By tomorrow afternoon, we'll know if he's going to be okay."

Guilt burns like poison in my gut. "Maybe you should be home tomorrow morning, waiting for word with your parents."

"No." Her head swings slow from side to side. "This is where Kollin would want me to be."

"We need to find that TPD then. It'd the best get-well present we could give him." I stand and flatten the deed against the wall next to Mr. Singer's poem. "Let's apply those clues to the deed and see what we get."

She stands next to me and reviews the poem. "*Columns and half-clues* taught us to read the first letter going down for a message. *Words that are letters read between the lines* must mean we take every *other* letter going down, and then read them like words, like we did with the map key."

Running her finger down the first page of the deed,

Laney reads every other letter out loud. "D T P D S N D M T 2 M."

I repeat it slower and sound out the obvious words: "The TPD is in the empty two M... Two M... Two M?"

"The empty tomb!" Laney screams, "The TPD is in the empty tomb!" She's jumping up and down like she just found the thing.

It almost kills me to say, "We're in the empty tomb, Lane. We all searched this whole place when we were looking for the tunnel entrance. Boyle said he searched too. I think someone would have found it by now if it was here. We're right back where we started."

Just the same, we go up the stairs and probe every inch of the interior of the casket all over again. After that, we inspect every section of the walls and stairs and examine every corner of the secret room beneath it. It's been hours, and we've got nothing but the growing fear that time is running out.

Every second that passes reminds me that by this time tomorrow, I'll be homeless again. Or jailed. Or worse, if Kane finds me.

Laney falls back against the wall and slides down to the floor, landing on the pile of velvet cloaks.

I huddle next to her and wrap an arm around her slumped shoulders. "Maybe if it we sit quiet for a while and think," I say. But really, I just want to hold her as much as I can before I have to leave Singer forever.

I shudder at the thought, and Laney pulls up a loose cloak and wraps it around my shoulders. It takes me back to that time when we were little—the night I ran away in the storm, when she wrapped her coat around me.

After so many stressful days and sleepless nights, I'm crashing physically and mentally. My head falls back to the wall and my eyes flutter closed. I space out for a moment, and my mind returns to that stormy night in the cemetery.

My voice is trapped in my throat. My feet won't move. A burst of lightning close behind me sends me flying forward into the swampy soil. The air is still crackling when I push myself up on shaky arms and see the most terrifying sight of all. An enormous winged statue towers above me, pointing at a grave. Is she saying it's for me?

My eyes flash open and I hop up so fast, I knock Laney over. "We aren't going to find the TPD here!" I'm doing a touchdown dance while Laney stares up at me with worried, drowsy eyes. I fall to my knees in front of her and cup her face in my hands. "We aren't going to find it here because *this* isn't the empty tomb. *This* is the empty statue."

She squints her eyes like I need therapy.

"Oh, my little Watson," I tell her. "Don't you get it? The TPD is in the empty tomb. The *original* grave where Mary was buried, before her body was moved here." I say it slow so it sinks in fast: "William Singer hid the TPD in Mary's *original* grave!"

Now Laney's doing her own version of a touchdown celebration. I grab her by the hand and pull her to the stairs. "Let's go. Now!"

"Wait," she says. "We have to be careful. Kane probably has people looking everywhere for you. Maybe I should go by myself."

"No way. We're a team."

She tosses me a cape. "Then put this on. It'll give us some cover. Maybe it'll bring a little luck too."

"Oh yeah, 'cause it worked so well for the last group of Sevens."

"Shut up, Michaels. Just do it. We've got to hurry."

She slides into her cape, pulling the hood over her head. I copy her and we tiptoe up the stairs. Everything's pitch black and silent beyond the peephole. We sneak out of the statue and crack open the mausoleum door.

"It's clear," she whispers.

We creep through the trees toward the winged angel statue that marks Mary Singer's original grave, scanning the cemetery for Security. We're alone. For now.

The angel stands atop a square pedestal with one arm outstretched and the other pressed against her heart. Laney reaches the monument and frisks the stone like airport security.

"No, Laney." I'm on some kind of roll, because I know this one too. "The poem said 'if you use all you've learned, you can solve this last clue.' Think about it. We found the secret door in the mausoleum by following where the angel's hands were pointing. If we 'use what we learned,' then we do the same thing here. Follow the angel's fingers to where she's pointing."

"You are *so* freaking smart." Her words pump me like a pre-game pep talk.

Laney kneels in front of the statue and follows an imaginary line from the statue's pointer finger to a section of the base below it. Digging her nails into the dirt, she feels along the side of the marble.

Her eyes widen inside her velvet hood, and I know she's found something. She stretches and wiggles and grunts until finally…*click.*

The interior section of the pedestal drops down instantly.

I reach my hand inside and it's packed with cold, heavy, rectangular bars. I can't tell what they are in the dark. I lift one out and hand it to Laney. "What is this? There's a ton of them in here."

She studies it under the light of the quarter moon. "I think it's…oh my God, it's gold!" She hands it back to me quick, like she's afraid to touch it.

I roll it around in my hands while it sinks in. There must be millions of dollars of gold here. More money than I could ever spend. With just a few of these, I'd be set next year. I'd be set forever. I bet Laney would even let me take one or two.

But I don't ask. Because it's not important anymore.

"I just realized something," I tell her. "You know the legend about how Mr. Singer would come to the cemetery every night and visit Mary's grave?"

She nods.

I store the bar back inside. "He was probably bringing these, little by little, to hide. The cemetery was probably off limits back then, too. No one would have known."

I reach my hand deeper and knock over a large, square object. I shimmy it out and show Laney. "It's a security box."

"You open it," she says, cuddling up to my side. "I'm too nervous."

I tug the lid up and there it is—the TPD. Or, as the document is titled, *Addendum to the Singer School Deed of Trust: Assignment of Trust Protectors.* I unfold it in all its confusing glory. I was never a fan of reading, but it reads like legal hieroglyphics.

Laney's eyes jump from the document to me. Her grin peeks out from beneath her hood. "We did it," she whispers.

"We haven't done anything unless we can present this at the board meeting at 8:00 a.m."

A light flashes in the distance. "Talan, there's a car coming!" Laney whispers.

She faceplants on her stomach, and I drop down next to her. We lay low in our cloaks as Security slowly drives down Rucker Road. After they pass, Laney pokes at the button to close the pedestal door. We stand just as headlights reappear, forcing us to dash for the mausoleum. I'm squeezing the security box so tight that it's digging into my ribs, even through the cloak.

We rush inside the mausoleum and jab the button on the side of the granite casket. The door takes forever to open. We slide in and shut it just as voices appear.

Looking out the slit, I see two security guards enter and search the room with flashlights. "I could have sworn I saw someone run in here."

A second voice replies, "Let's check the woods."

They leave, and we tiptoe down the stairs to the secret room. We collapse on the cold floor, breathless and shaking.

"Kane probably has Security searching everywhere for you," Laney says. "How are we going to get to that meeting? By tomorrow, he'll have the Executive Building in lockdown. The Pillars and police will be posted all over campus."

"Not to mention all the students that would love to turn me in for a $10,000 reward."

"Wait." Laney jolts upright. "I have an idea. If we can get into the library, we can take the utility tunnel to the Executive Building. We can probably pry the vent open in that back room. It's big enough to climb through."

"We still have to get to the library from here," I remind her. "And it doesn't open until 8:00. How do we cross campus in broad daylight? Everyone is after me."

"Unless…"

I lean forward. "Unless what?"

"There's one tunnel we haven't taken yet. The one to Winchester House. That's fairly close to the rear of the library. Maybe we could make a run for it from there."

"Winchester House? Get serious. The Pillars want us gone more than anyone. Are we supposed to pop out of their fireplace, grab a Pop-Tart for breakfast, and head off to the board meeting together?"

"Do you have a better idea?" she says.

I huff, "Guess not" and grab the TPD from the security box. I stand and shove it into my back pocket. "Get the map. It's time to visit Winchester House."

Minutes later, we're cruising down the corridor. We turn

left at the very end and take that passage until it dead ends too.

Laney rubs her hands across the cement surface. "Now where's *this* entrance hidden?" When she rolls her eyes, they do a double take at the ceiling. "Maybe it's that."

She nods up at a fluorescent light fixture directly overhead. "It's recessed into the ceiling, so it has to be cut into the concrete. Which means there's probably an opening behind it."

"Here." I bend down. "Get on my shoulders and check it out."

I take my cloak off and help her up. With a little maneuvering, she climbs on and I lift her to the light fixture.

"It's hot," she says. She covers her hand with her cape and pushes the light up. It lifts easily, and she slides it over to one side, then pokes her head into the opening.

"There's an attic ladder!" she squeals. Her hands stretch inside and roll out something metal. "Scoot back," she directs me. She carefully draws out the ladder, unfolding it to the ground.

I help her down and follow her up the ladder through the hole in the ceiling. It leads to a narrow space, similar to the one behind Mr. Singer's fireplace. There's another one-way mirror, which looks out into the family room of the Winchester House. But this time, there's no fireplace—the mirror spans an eight-by-ten section of one wall. The glass is divided into horizontal rectangles.

We angle our heads to see through separate panes, but our view is blocked by books and knick-knacks that sit in front of the glass. With a little maneuvering, I can make out Zack Hunter stretched on a sofa watching television.

Laney cups her hand to my ear and whispers, "We're standing behind shelves. This must be a built-in bookcase with mirrors along the back."

I step back and locate a seam in the center of the mirrors that's the size of a door. The left side is hinged and the right is latched tight. "This must be how they got in and out of Winchester House," I whisper. "It's the old hidden-door-in-a-bookcase. Very *Scooby Doo*."

"Don't get too excited, Shaggy." She points at Zack on the couch. "We still have to figure out how to get out without being caught by the Pillars."

Just then, Kane barges through the front door, dragging a wobbly Professor Solomon by the arm.

"You stupid little man!" Kane twists Solomon's arm behind his back and screams at him. "You were going to expose me with a letter?"

"I'm done living this lie." Solomon's words are slurred and raspy.

Zack jumps off the sofa a second before Kane shoves the professor on it.

"What are you doing here?" Kane barks at him.

"I live here, sir."

"You're supposed to be scouring the campus for Talan Michaels."

"I d-did," Zack stutters. "He isn't anywhere. I also spread the word that you doubled the reward money. Now that everyone thinks he tried to frame his friends, there isn't a person on campus who wouldn't turn him in the second they saw him."

"Help me." Solomon grabs Zack's sleeve. "Call … police."

"Get to bed!" Kane orders Zack. "Now! I need you up early to stand guard for Michaels and his gang, just in case."

"But what about Professor Solomon?"

"Keep your mouth shut and get to your room. You've seen nothing!"

"You murdered them," Solomon mumbles at Kane.

"NOW!" Kane screams at Zack, who takes off for the stairs.

"Murderer," Solomon whimpers from the couch.

Kane paces in front of him. "Look who's talking. This whole mess is your fault. You should never have made a pass at her."

"I was drunk," Solomon moans.

"You killed her. You're no better than me, Uncle."

"No. I threw the stone to stop her horse. She was rushing to tell William. She wouldn't even stop to put her helmet on," Solomon whimpers. "I never thought it'd buck her off."

"But it did. You killed her. And then you convinced William it was someone on the Board so he wouldn't suspect you. You're as guilty as I am."

Solomon is pitiful, blubbering and grabbing at Kane's shirt. "I confessed. William would have forgiven me. Eventually. He would have if you hadn't killed him."

Kane wrings Solomon's wrist and he flinches in pain. "No, he would have turned you in, you fool. We both would have been kicked out of here. *You'd* have gone to jail. I did you a favor."

"You did it for yourself. You wanted his money. And you were mad because you weren't good enough for the Sevens."

Kane paces in front of the bookcase. "Well look at me now. I made out better than any of them."

"Because you killed them."

"That was an accident too. I only planned on killing Singer."

"Those children," Solomon wails. "They tried to save him. You locked them in a burning building." The old man's sobs turn to gasps and he clutches his chest. "I'm done... being blackmailed."

He stumbles to his feet, but Kane shoves him hard. Solomon hits his head against the arm of the sofa and falls motionless against the cushions.

Laney inhales sharply and I cover her mouth with my hand. Cameron and Iman straggle through the door and freeze when they see the professor passed out.

"Never mind him. Did you find Michaels?" Kane yells.

Iman's voice shakes. "There's no sign of him anywhere. No one's seen him since this afternoon."

Kane pulls an envelope from his pocket and shoves it at Cameron. "Hide this letter until I can destroy it."

Cameron slides the envelope into a book that sits on the shelf in front of Laney. She takes a step back, even though we know they can't see us.

"You." Kane points a finger at Iman. "Keep an eye on the professor until I can figure out what to do."

"He doesn't look well, sir," Iman says.

"He needs his medicine."

"What if he dies?"

"All the better," Kane snaps. "We can dump him on campus and it'll look like he passed away from natural causes."

Iman's jaw drops.

"What should *I* do, sir?" Cameron interrupts.

"Get some sleep. I want you up early to search campus for Michaels one last time before the board meeting. I told the police that Michaels threatened to kill Katherine, so we've got extra officers patrolling the grounds, too." He slithers to the door. "I've texted you all instructions for the morning. Do your part and we'll be set for the meeting."

Kane leaves, and Iman collapses into a chair opposite Professor Solomon. "I just want this to be over, Cam. Everything's so screwed up. What if the professor wakes up? Am I going to have to kill him? This was supposed to be about bullshitting at some board meetings, not kidnapping and murder."

He buries his face in his hands.

"Stop being a pussy," Cam says. "We're in too deep to back out now. If this doesn't play out like Kane wants, our lives are over." He plods to the stairs. "Just get some rest. You and I have to check the woods in the morning."

Iman sits trance-like in his chair, keeping vigil over Solomon and preventing us from sneaking out.

With her mouth gaping, Laney waves me to the back corner of our little space.

"Did you hear all that?" She squeezes the back of her neck. "Did Professor Solomon kill Mary Singer?"

"I think he did … accidentally. And Kane just basically admitted to killing William and the Sevens."

"But why did Solomon say he confessed to William? That doesn't make any sense. Why would Singer start the Sevens if he knew it was Solomon that killed Mary?"

"He must have confessed right before Singer was murdered. Maybe that's why Mr. Singer called the meeting at the chapel. To tell the Sevens it wasn't the Board after all."

Her eyes scrunch. "Did you hear Kane call Solomon '*Uncle*'?"

I nod. "You know, when Kane first called me into his office to offer me a deal, he mentioned he had an uncle that dumped him at Singer. It must have been Solomon."

"It sounds like Kane was blackmailing him and Solomon had finally had enough. He was clearly going to turn Kane in with that letter Kane had. We need to get it as evidence, Laney. And we need to get Solomon some help."

"How are we going to do that with Iman standing sentinel?"

"We have to wait for a lucky break. The minute Iman dozes or goes to the john or whatever, we'll go in there. You grab the letter and I'll dial 911 and leave the phone off the hook. Then we bolt for the front door. We'll hide behind the library, and when it opens at 8:00, we'll race to the elevator and take the tunnels to that board meeting."

The fear in her eyes infects me too. "What if we don't make it in time? The meeting starts at 8:00."

She's right, but I can't bear to have Laney Shanahan, eternal optimist, giving up so soon. "We'll make it." I flash her my dimples. "You know me. I'm always late."

FORTY-SEVEN

It's been hours, and Iman hasn't budged. If anything, he's more alert and intense. Leaning forward in his chair, his hands rigid on the armrests, he studies the professor as if he's counting every shallow breath. The stress twisting his face probably matches mine.

Laney and I have alternated taking short naps, but we're just as exhausted. I nudge her arm and she wakes slowly. She glances around, realizes where she is, and straightens up.

"Anything new?" she whispers.

"Zack and Samantha left over an hour ago. They said they're checking out the school and then standing watch at the south end of campus. Cameron checked the woods, but he's already back. He told Iman the police were still searching for me. Campus security is on high alert too. Especially around the Executive Building.

"And the other Pillars?"

"Nick left a few minutes after Zack to patrol Rucker Road,

and Kayla is staking out our house. I'm starting to freak a little, Lane. The board meeting is in a half an hour and Cameron and Iman are still home. How are we going to get out of here, much less to the library elevators, without being spotted?"

A moment later, we have our answer.

"You ready to go?" Cameron breezes into the room and startles Iman.

"Should we really leave Professor Solomon? What if he needs us?"

"We're better off if he dies. It'll save us the work later." Cameron pulls up Iman and tugs him by the elbow. "C'mon already. We still need to check the rec center."

The front door shuts and Laney reaches for the latch on the back of the bookcase. "Are they really gone?"

"Yeah. You ready?" The two of us unhook the door and push. The door creaks open and some knickknacks fall out. Laney grabs them while I close it behind us.

"Get Solomon's letter," I remind her.

She pulls it from the book on the shelf, and I grab a phone on the side table and dial 911. When the dispatcher answers, I whisper, "Send an ambulance," and leave the phone off the hook so they can trace the call.

We race outside, but we've only made it halfway through the yard when I hear, "It's Michaels! Get them!"

Two figures appear in the distance. Cameron and Iman must have only been a few houses down. We take off running, but Laney still has her stupid cape on and it's flapping in the wind and slowing her down. Cam gets close enough to grip the flying fabric from behind and pull her down. I turn to help, but Iman is closing in on me.

"No, Tal! Run!" she screams.

Even as I speed up, I sense Iman catching me. His thin runner's frame gives him the advantage, but I'm doing better than I thought I would. Then I hear a rippling noise, and turn to see the TPD lying on the grass behind me. I spin around and snatch the document just as Iman dives on top of me.

We roll around a minute until I hear him say something. "Punch me," he hisses. "Cam can't see me with your back to him. "

He stops fighting me and I pin his arms. Breathless, I sputter, "What?"

"Punch me and I'll fake like you knocked me out."

I'm dazed, looking down at two worried eyes.

"Michaels, you idiot!" he says through gritted teeth. "They'll kill you if they catch you. Fake-punch me already and get your ass out of here."

I'm floored when it sinks in. My adrenaline is bursting and I punch him harder than I mean to. Blood spurts from his nose.

He lays there groaning as I stagger to my feet and take off running. Laney is wrestling Cam in the distance. They're tangled in the cape and she's kicking like crazy. It makes me sick that I can't help her.

I reach the back of the library and duck behind some bushes by the door. When I'm sure no one's around, I wiggle the handle. *Unlocked.*

My body throbs with excitement. Only... that must mean it's already after eight.

I whip the door open and take off for the elevators. As

I stand there stabbing the button, a voice calls from behind me. "You there! No running in the library!"

When the door opens, I dash inside. Twitching fingers hit the *close* button a million times as I struggle to remember the first test in my head.

Close with two. Seven times the LL. Seven times the HELP.

I poke the "2" button and then start on the Lower Level button. One-two-three-four...

My eyes flick up and catch a security guard watching me from a nearby bookshelf. His eyes widen when he recognizes me.

"Stop!" he yells, circling the shelves.

The doors close in slow motion as the guard charges for the elevator.

I jab the LL button again. *What number am I on?* Five—six—seven times. Right before the doors snap shut, the guard dives for the elevator button.

Panic rolls through me as I bang on the HELP button. One-two-three-four-five-six-seven times.

The elevator lurches. My legs are shaking so bad, I stumble back and hit my head on the wall. The light reads that I'm bound for floor 2, but the elevator's dropping. It rattles and bangs and stops hard.

I sigh in relief, lifting myself on unsteady feet as the lights dim and the back panel finally glides open.

I was up the whole night planning what we needed to do, but the scene I now face never once occurred to me. I'm staring into the same pitch-black, claustrophobic, suffocating sewer-hole-from-hell. Only this time, there's no Laney.

And no flashlights.

FORTY-EIGHT

I can't do it.

I can't feel my legs, much less make them move from the security of the lit elevator. I'm six years old all over again. Trapped in a dark closet that reeks from my own urine. Terrified of dying alone in the dark with no one to help me.

My brain screams at me to hurry but my body betrays me. I'm paralyzed in place. The adrenaline that surges through my veins has no outlet. It backs up like a clogged pipe and clamps down hard in my chest. My heart pounds out of control, making me lightheaded.

The room in front of me blurs slightly. The crumbling walls and dirty concrete floor are swallowed in fuzzy shadows. My stomach clenches to fight the wooziness.

The back elevator panel starts to close and I block it with a shaking hand. I take a deep breath and look into the terrifying abyss.

I can do this. I repeat it like a mantra. *I can do this.*

I'm not six anymore. I'm not weak. I'm not helpless. And I'm not stupid.

My past will *not* dictate my future.

I step off the elevator and race down the tunnel to get every last second of light before the elevator closes. My arms are stretched to touch the walls as I run. I need to feel for the intersecting passages so I don't miss any turns. One wrong move and I could be lost in this underground tomb for an eternity.

I concentrate on the poem and getting to that board meeting, instead of on the vulnerable feeling of charging into complete darkness with my arms wide open.

When darkness fills you up with fright,
Tread straight, straight, straight into the night.

I'm running at a good pace, despite the fact my arms ache from being held up. I'm dizzy in the darkness, but my fingertips tell me that I've now passed three passages—straight, straight, straight like the poem commands. My body is weak from stress and lack of sleep. The musty, rank smell tempts me to stop and throw up, but I don't have time. I'm only halfway there.

Then it's the next verse.

Left, right, left—the soldier's pace—

When the wall suddenly disappears on my left, I turn sharp down the opening before re-centering myself in the blind corridor. I shake my arms out for a second and then return them to skim the walls as I jog ahead.

Please be okay, Laney.

It tortures me to think about what Cameron could do to her. But I had no choice. I have to finish this.

After an eternity, the bumpy bricks end once more and I know that's my cue to turn right. I let my throbbing arms drop for a just a minute, and then they're up again, searching for my last left turn. The tunnel seems endless, even though it's only been minutes. I press my palm to the wall and stagger on. When I hit the next gap, I veer left down the tunnel.

What time is it now? I block the thought from my head. I can't think about the fact that, after all this, I might still be too late. I bury the fear and recite the words from the remainder of the poem, over and over again:

> *Until it leads right to a place*
> *Where everything you thought you knew,*
> *Will turn around. And you will, too.*
> *Left to sort what's wrong from right,*
> *And why you're going to have to fight,*
> *to take what's left*
> *and make it right.*

I turn right down the last passage and see the light ahead. This time, when I lift myself out of the gopher hole and into the utility closet in the Executive Building, I'm greeted by the sound of adult voices blending together. The good news is the board meeting is being held right in the adjacent room.

The bad news is everyone's celebrating the sale of Singer Enterprises.

FORTY-NINE

The knot in my chest squeezes like a heart attack. I climb the ladder, hiding in the shadows and watching the proceedings through the slats in the vent.

A Donald Trump look-a-like is patting Stephen Kane on the back. "I think we all agree that this is the best thing for Singer School and our shareholders. I speak for everyone when I say that I had no idea the school was in this type of decline. I shudder every time I hear a news report these days. It's definitely time for a change, and your plan will benefit the students as much as the shareholders."

Defeated, I collapse against the wall. The serious faces gathered around the long table agree with every word Kane mutters. Maybe I never stood a chance anyhow. Me, with my bumbling words and clumsy brain. A troublemaker with a crappy past and no future.

"So shall we put it to an official vote?" Kane says with a grin.

What's this? My body stiffens as twelve blue suits nod in agreement.

"Let's go ahead and make it legal then."

They haven't voted?

Kane toddles to his place at the head of the table. He smiles down at Katherine, who's seated to his right, tapping her pen with nervous excitement. "All those in favor of selling Singer Enterprises to the Li Yuong Group . . ."

"Stop!" I scream with all the breath in my lungs. "Stop immediately!"

Startled heads turn in search of the bodiless voice. I bang against the vent, desperate to knock it out and show myself. All eyes move to the vibrating slats, where I'm kicking the other side of the metal grate with all my strength. The covering flies out and clangs as it lands on the polished wood table. The board members jump back like it's a bomb.

"What's the meaning of this?" Kane bellows.

I swing a leg through the narrow opening to slide out the hole, but it's tight around me. I grunt and wiggle myself through. My body flops hard against the wall, and I dangle from the opening. Sharp edges slice the insides of my knuckles, forcing me to let go. I crash to the floor in a thud.

Kane recognizes me and rushes to the door. "Security! Get Security in here now!" he screams down the hall. "Someone call the police immediately!"

My ankle twists and pain shoots through my leg. "Owwww!"

As I struggle to get up, I see the petrified expression on the faces of the board members.

Kane points at me. "That's the gang leader that's been

destroying our school. He's dangerous! SECURITY!" he screams again. The board members rise to their feet.

"No! He's lying. I'd never hurt anyone. Kane's been lying about everything! Please. Just listen to me." I hold my arms up to show them I'm unarmed. "I'm just a kid. A student here. I'm here to represent William Singer's wishes concerning this school. Look, I have the Trust Protector Document."

I reach in my pocket and notice the Trump-double duck down, like I'm going for a gun.

"Please … look!" I hold it high. "This is the authentic TPD from William Singer. It gives me authority to stop these proceedings."

The board members are stunned, their eyes hopscotching from Kane to me, absorbing all of it.

"Please. Someone," I beg. "Just read it. As bearer of this document, I have authority to intervene." I hold it out, but no one takes it.

Two security guards rush in and I limp to the opposite corner of the room.

"Restrain him," Kane says. "Hold him until the police arrive."

"No! I'm a member of the Society of Seven and I have a right to stop this vote." I glance at the puzzled faces surrounding the table. "Stephen Kane is out to destroy everything William Singer worked for. I can prove it. You owe it to Mr. Singer and the students here to hear me out. I also have proof that Stephen Kane was involved in the murder of William Singer and the Sevens when he was a student here. Look—"

I reach for the envelope with Solomon's confession before I remember that Laney has it.

"Now I've heard everything," Kane bellows. "Do you think anyone would take the word of a juvenile delinquent like you? How dare you make such ludicrous accusations!" He turns to the security guards, "Don't just stand there! Do your jobs, for God sakes!"

The board members glance at each other, looking for answers. They shrug and blink and purse their lips, but no one helps me. The guards circle opposite ends of the table, cornering me.

Words, don't fail me.

"Please," I beg. "Two thousand kids depend on this decision. You can arrest me afterward if you think I'm lying about this. But I'm not. I possess the genuine TPD that gives me the authority to legally stop this vote. I swear, I'm only trying to do the right thing for the kids at Singer School."

One of the security guards grabs my elbow and yanks me toward the door, but an older board member rises from his seat and blocks us. "As the longest-serving member on this board, I'd like to hear what this boy went to such great effort to say."

"Oh for heaven's sake," Kane barks.

"No, Stephen," a gray-haired woman says, cutting him off. "Let the boy speak his peace."

"This is nonsense," Kane insists.

I shake off the guard and thrust the papers at the older board member. "I swear to you that this is the original Trust Protector Document referred to in William Singer's will and Deed of Trust. The one that assigns the bearer the right to oversee the trust."

Kane parades around the table, mocking me. "So this criminal, who the police have been searching for all night, just happens to possess the legendary TPD after it's been missing for eighteen years? I've never heard anything so ridiculous."

"I'll explain everything later, I swear," I promise the table of pinched faces. "For now, I'm asserting my right as a representative of the Society of Seven to stop this vote."

The older board member unfolds the document and skims the first page.

"What a scam." Kane comes from behind him and snatches the TPD from his hands. "Our legal counsel will confirm that this delinquent is presenting a fraudulent document."

"And that legal counsel would be me." Katherine charges over, wearing a vicious smirk. Kane hands her the paper with a glimmer in his eye. The room is silent as Katherine's eyes scan the document, line by line.

Blood rushes to my face. I'm done. I have no shot of arguing against someone professional and educated, someone who's actually fluent in these legal hieroglyphics.

In a minute, I'll be hauled out of here in handcuffs, with no one to bail me out this time. I'm trapped in the back of the room and can't even run for it. The door is blocked by a third security guard and the vent is too high for me to reach without a pole vault and a track coach who'd teach me how to use it.

Katherine's slitted eyes finish the last line and slowly lift. Her gaze remains on me as she comes over to where I'm standing.

"I vouch, as legal counsel for Singer Enterprises, as well as on my reputation as a renowned attorney with a Harvard degree, that this document is absolutely"—she smiles over her shoulder at Stephen Kane—"genuine."

Kane's jaw drops first; then the rest of us do an impression of him.

"Katherine, how can you say that?"

"I can say that because I'm certain that this document is binding and authentic." She slowly turns and faces him. "You know that I was a partner at Carmine Rathbone's law firm, right, Stephen? The Trust Protector Document he drew up for William Singer was an unusual one, and this is almost verbatim what he described to me. That's Rathbone's signature and notary stamp. I'm also confident that this is Mr. Singer's signature."

Eleven heads swivel to follow her around the table, toward Kane. "I'd recognize his writing anywhere," she says. "You see…I happen to be one of William Singer's original Society of Seven." She stops a foot in front of Kane, her laser glare searing him with hate. "One that you didn't manage to kill eighteen years ago."

He steps back. His lips part, but the words are stuck in his twisted brain.

Katherine holds the TPD above her head. "As legal counsel for Singer Enterprises, I confirm that this is the original Trust Protector Document prepared and notarized by Carmine Rathbone and signed by William Singer. Consequently, this document gives Talan Michaels, myself, and five other members of the Society of Seven the authority to stop these proceedings. In fact, since we deem it in the best interest of the trust, we retain the right to name ourselves as temporary trustees, effective immediately."

Kane stumbles over his words. "What are you saying, Katherine?"

"I'm saying you're fired, Stephen. Let me introduce you to your replacement. Have you met Talan Michaels?"

Just then, Sergeant Lynch and another officer burst into the room, guns drawn.

"Officers, it's about time," Kane says.

"That's right," Katherine says. "Arrest Stephen Kane."

Lynch looks dumbfounded. "What? Why?!"

"Fraud, malicious mischief, damage to private property, contributing to the delinquency of minors, and aggravated assault on Kollin LeBeau, to begin with. I volunteer to be the first witness to testify against him."

"Add six counts of murder to that!" a voice shouts. Laney's head appears in the vent. She swings a leg and arm out of the opening and totters on the ledge. "Michaels! A little help, please?"

I try to ease her down, but we both end up on our asses.

She hops up and brushes herself off. "I have a statement from Professor Caesar Solomon." She struggles to get the letter out from under her tangled cloak. "Oh, shiitake!" she says in frustration.

"Did she say 'shiitake'?" the Trump-twin whispers. "Mushrooms?"

"She did." I smile as I struggle to stand on my throbbing ankle.

Laney finally wiggles the envelope free from her pocket. "Professor Caesar Solomon has confessed to the accidental death of Mary Singer and to being an accessory to the murder of William Singer and five students almost twenty years ago. In this signed letter, he names Stephen Kane as the murderer of those six victims."

"And we're to believe another delinquent gang member?"

"Gang member?" Laney charges toward Kane, tripping on her cape like a Hogwarts reject. Then, as usual, she surprises me. She hops up, straightens her cloak, and goes badass on him.

Shoving her finger in his chest, she says, "Who are you calling delinquent? I'm the student body president, founder of the Philanthropic Club, and likely future valedictorian of my class. Not to mention my mom and dad have been respected houseparents here for over twenty years. Don't you dare call me a delinquent, you...you murderer! I'm a Seven." She goes chin to chin with him. "We're the best of the best, and you frickin' know it."

"I've had quite enough. This meeting is over," Kane says. He marches toward the door, but he's stopped by several board members.

"You're not done with anything," one says.

Kane tries to push past them, but Lynch grabs him by the arm. When Kane throws a desperate punch at the sergeant, the other officers converge, forcing him to the ground and restraining him with handcuffs.

I finally let myself breathe and collapse into an empty seat.

The Trump-double stares dumbfounded at Kane on the floor and murmurs, "Holy shiitake."

FIFTY

I'm sitting in an interview room just off the main hall of the police station. The clock reads 7:04 p.m. Which means I've been in the same gray plastic chair since I gave my first statement almost nine hours ago.

I'm so exhausted, I can barely lift my throbbing head off the cinder-block wall behind me. My arms ache from holding them up in the tunnels. The insides of my hands are sliced and bruised from climbing out the wall vent, and my ankle kills from the fall afterward.

I don't know if I have a single friend left at Singer. I'm not even sure the Shanahans will take me back. The only thing I am certain of is that Dad Shanahan is gonna kick my ass for putting Delaney in danger.

Other than that, I feel pretty damn good.

Laney sits in another windowed conference room across the hall, talking with Katherine and her parents. I've watched her yell, cry, frown, and shake her head for almost two hours.

But now, something new. She stands and hugs Katherine. After a minute, she hugs her parents even tighter. She slowly turns toward the door and catches me watching her.

I tug my ear, and she laughs.

Katherine opens the door. Her eyes are puffy and red-ringed, but she's smiling too. She tells Laney's parents, "Let's finish the paperwork so we can get the kids out of here."

Katherine's acting as our attorney now. The Shanahans follow her to the front desk, and Laney trudges into my room and crashes in the chair next to mine. She rubs her eyes and rests her head on my shoulder.

"You all right?"

"Yeah," she says. "We still have a ton of talking to do, but I think it'll be okay."

"Katherine seems nice," I say. "Not to mention incredibly smart. In the last ten hours, she's managed to get all my charges dropped, Kane and the Pillars have been arrested, and Jose and Emily will both be back by tonight."

Laney lifts her head. "And Headmaster Boyle?"

"Free and clear. He left with the detectives a few hours ago to gather evidence at the cemetery." I nod toward Katherine. "Your birth mom is quite the overachiever. Sound familiar?"

Laney smiles. She slips her arm through mine and leans her head on my shoulder again.

"So I've gotta ask you," I say. "How did you get away from Cameron?"

"I kicked him in the crotch." She snickers. "Reeeeally hard."

I kiss the top of her head. This time, it feels totally right.

"Have I mentioned how much badass girls turn me on? Although what you did sort of terrifies me too."

Voices emerge outside our doorway. Good Cop walks past, followed by Iman Kabal. Iman stops when he sees us.

"At least it's over," he says.

"Thanks, man," I tell him. "What you did took guts."

"Look who's talking."

Good Cop tugs Iman away, but another face replaces his in the doorway. Headmaster Boyle.

Laney smirks and says, "Hello, Uncle."

"What did you call him?"

"Katherine and Headmaster Boyle are brother and sister," she says, like I've missed a homework assignment. "Turns out he's my uncle."

Boyle sidles in with our jackets. "Get up. Someone wants to talk to you." Smiling, he tosses our coats to us, and we follow him out.

———

Twenty minutes later, we're entering the critical care unit of the Galesburg Memorial Hospital. Boyle stops outside a door. "I need to prepare you before you go in. Kollin looks pretty awful. His prognosis is positive, but he's been through hell."

We nod and Boyle opens the door for us.

Laney and I teeter in, edging between monitors and machines toward Kollin's bedside. Emily and Jose stand on the opposite side of his bed, holding hands.

Laney looks down at Kollin's battered, swollen face and swallows hard. Between the pillows and pads, Kollin's eyes blink open.

"Le Douche," I say, "you losing weight or something? You look better than usual." I lean over the railing so he can see me easier. "So how you doing, buddy?"

"Worse now that you're here," he mumbles. He takes a moment to catch his breath, and then says softly, "I heard we did it." He tries to raise his fisted hand for me to bump, but before I can meet it with mine, his arm drops weakly to the mattress.

I reach down and squeeze his fingers instead. "Yeah...we did it."

His eyes drift to my hand holding his. A corner of his mouth lifts. "Quit hitting on me, Michaels," he murmurs. "I already told you, you aren't my type."

We laugh, but Kollin grimaces in pain.

Boyle moves to the foot of his bed. "Kollin needs his rest, so I'll make this quick. There's a few things I need to share and we'll go."

He looks at all of us. "First, I'm proud of you. I had no idea it would get this dangerous, or I wouldn't have involved you." His gaze lingers on me. "I just knew in my gut that you had what it took to be Sevens.

"And, second." Boyle crosses his arms. "The officers just finished inventorying Mary Singer's original gravesite. One investigator estimated that there's tens of millions in gold." He rests his hands on the metal footboard and leans forward. "As Sevens, as well as interim trustees, you'll have a say in what to do with that money."

Emily speaks up. "I think we should expand Singer and get some kids off that waiting list...beginning with Jose's brother."

"And cover Kollin's medical bills," Jose says.

A breathy Kollin adds, "And help Emily."

"Right," Delaney finishes for him. "So she can go to college and make a better life for herself and her daughter."

We all nod.

"Well, how about for you two?" Boyle focuses on Laney and me. "Do you have a greatest desire we should consider?"

"I'm good," I say. "I think Mr. Singer would want his Sevens' money spent in service to others. You know, with him being all into that virtues crap and stuff."

Laney leans away from me. "Talan Michaels," she says, "who knew that all this time, deep down, you were a brainiac do-gooder?" Before I can argue, she raises her hand. "I did."

Headmaster Boyle straightens up and moves toward the door. "That's very noble of you all. But technically, Katherine and I are also trustees, and we've decided that all five of you will be receiving generous scholarships as well as money for expenses." He turns as he opens the door. "Because *we* knew William Singer better than anyone. And we're quite certain that's exactly how he'd want his Sevens' money spent." Boyle slaps my back before walking out.

For the first time ever, I imagine what college would be like. Where should I go? What the heck do I want to be?

Laney pulls me aside and flashes me a tired grin. She snuggles into me, and I wrap my arm around her. Her hand travels to my chest, stopping directly over the scar on my heart. She slowly lifts her eyes to mine and says, "All this time, you were wrong, Michaels... the S was for Sevens."

I kiss her smile with my own and whisper in her ear, "Don't you mean Sherlock?"

Acknowledgments

First, to my sons Tyler and Austin (aka Wild Thing 1 and Wild Thing 2): you are the loves of my life. Thank you for your outrageous escapades and crazy antics, which provided me with material for this book (and a million more). Now *KNOCK IT OFF FOR GOD'S SAKE, YOU'RE KILLING ME.*

Thanks to my cyber-sister and writing ally, the phenomenally talented Genevieve Wilson. Please never show anyone my crappy first stories, and I won't show them your snarky emails.

Thanks to my agent, Katherine Boyle, who taught me like a mentor and treated me like a friend.

Thanks to the top-notch team at Flux: Editor Extraordinaire Brian Farrey-Latz, Sandy Whoisamazing Sullivan, and Mallory "You're not bothering me" Hayes.

Thanks to talented critique partners who helped with various chapters of the Sevens: Karla Gomez, Helene Dunbar, Dawn Alexander, and Alexandra O'Connor.

What would I be without my young YA readers? Especially the amazingly funny and cool Jenny Manzo, who's read every cruddy story I ever wrote and swore it was wonderful. Thanks also to Dom Guzaldo, Mallory Hayes Stoffregen, Julia Theisen, and my sweet goddaughter Jillian Manzo (you rock).

Thanks to legal eagle Tony Schrank, for sharing his time and expertise to help me work out my (deed of) trust issues.

Thank you to Frank Manzo, a walking Wikipedia of useful facts, for sharing your vast knowledge of everything from philanthropic boarding schools funded by corporate entities to board room etiquette. (And he makes the best beer, too.)

Thanks to Heather Foy, for making me laugh though the humiliation also known as my author headshot.

Special thanks to Scott Ahrens, Director of Residential Living at Mooseheart School and Child City, who generously shared facts and stories about the school he is clearly devoted to. Your passion for the kids at Mooseheart inspired the setting and characters for The Sevens. We owe a debt to you and all educators and administrators who dedicate themselves to lifting our kids up.

And lastly, I'd like to thank my friends and family who helped me overcome the difficult year when the *Sevens* was being pitched and published. I'd never have made it into the lifeboat without you. Much love to my handholders: DJ and Scott Susta, Jodi and Joe Stelmachowski, Frank and Margo Manzo, Mark and Marylou Manzo, Dawn and Jim Schrank, Danette and Mike Moffatt, Carol and John Kirk, Kristy DeSanti, Cindy Prost, Leanna Wahlen, Pam (and Mike) Van Treeck, Helen Zagoren, Mark Claypool (for your website input and generous heart), Laurie Christensen, the Karger clan, Lorene (and Brian) Coffey, and the Dominguez Family. You'll never know how much your kindness meant to me. Which is why I'm telling you in my acknowledgements now…

And finally, thanks to (insert your name here if I missed you. I'm so sorry. You know my memory is crap. I promise to add you on the reprint).

© Heather Foy Photography

About the Author

Lynn Lindquist lives in a suburb of Chicago with two overly social sons and a mutt named Slugger, who wisely hides under the bed most days. The hordes of teenagers that regularly frequent her house (think Panama City Beach during Spring Break) provide fodder for her young adult novels and growing anxiety disorder. Ever since her sons broke the Guinness Record for Largest-Rager-Thrown-While-a-Parent-Was-Out-for-the-Night, she prefers spending her free time at home entertaining friends, cooking, reading, and writing. Thankfully, her favorite things in life are her sons, words, and kids, so she wouldn't have it any other way.